THE PRICE OF FIRE
THE ALCHEMIST'S AGENT NO. 3

E. M. BURNHAM

To my family, who encourage me, and my friends, who enable me

CONTENTS

Chapter 1   1
Chapter 2   9
Chapter 3   30
Chapter 4   58
Chapter 5   76
Chapter 6   90
Chapter 7   125
Chapter 8   150
Chapter 9   176
Chapter 10   191
Chapter 11   199
Chapter 12   221
Chapter 13   240
Chapter 14   253
Chapter 15   271

The Language of Merrilia   311
Author's Note   313
Also by E. M. Burnham   315
About the Author   317

＊ I ＊

Ibram ignored the explosion. The loud clap of thunder and the whoosh of displaced air was no more exciting than the bangs and whistles folk grew accustomed to hearing living so close to the living mountain; it barely rattled the tiled roof of The Blinded Seer. He merely tapped the fallen rafter dust off his bread roll while the potgirl ran about the draughtshop, slinging weighted linen squares over the wide-mouthed pitchers of ale on the customers' tables. Ibram shook his head and sighed. His wedge of cheese was now liberally sprinkled with the remains of a thousand years' neglect of housekeeping.

"Shouldn't you be seeing to that, Agent?" one of the merchants on the farther side of the draughtshop called out to him. "Thought you folk stood in for the village militia around here."

Ibram lifted his head at the low murmurs of agreement from the merchant's fellow travelers. The merchant wore the billowy red trousers and soft laced over-robe of a man from one of the Vissilian provinces further east. He'd traveled a long way to be wrong. Still, as a representative for the Sect of Seven Fires, Ibram needed to be polite.

He mustered up a smile. "Never you worry," he called out. "It's nothing but a little light alchemical entertainment." The merchant did not look convinced; he hunched his thin shoulders and glanced up at the wooden beams which supported the tiled roof. Ibram tried once more. "It will be a story to keep you company on the road west, to be—"

A roiling, bellowing cacophony bloomed at Ibram's left; the explosion slammed wide the wooden latticed window shutters, and shook the walls. Ibram threw himself to the ground, body shuddering as the very air itself tore at his back as if gripping him by the back of his clothes. He hit the rush-covered floor flat, and knocked his chin to the side as he wrapped both arms about his head. His teeth clacked together, his mouth flooded with the taste of hot copper. He heard the men and women about him shouting, some in alarm and some in anger, the creak of overturned furniture and the sharp shriek of roof tiles smashing to ground outside.

Yilka's *megrims*. Ibram groaned through a hacking cough as his lungs shuddered against his ribs; he rocked himself to his hands and knees. The air was thick with dust that clogged his throat and nostrils. He spit and frowned at the sight of blood mixing with the rushes on the floor. The potgirl's mouth opened in a silent scream as she scrambled back under the counter. He poked inside his mouth with his tongue and winced; he'd bitten his lower lip. His ears felt stuffed with wool, the sounds of shock and people running as dim as if he were standing atop a tall cliff. He squinted as he coughed and spat again. A clanging bell pierced the air, and then three more.

That blast had been close by, or else so large they'd lost the living mountain and every alchemist who lived upon it. Ibram's neck was loose as a jelly as he wobbled to his feet, and stumbled into a run out of the door of the draughtshop. Panicked folk ran past him on the street.

The air was yellow with smoke, rather than grey. The center of the blaze seemed to be down the street. Ibram retched at the taste of smoke and dust in the back of throat, and tucked his face into his elbow to breathe through his gambeson. He cast his eyes skyward; he saw the green tree-covered mountains high above Lityen; the ridge looked untouched. The folk screaming as they ran past must have been evacuating from the scene, rather than simply panicking.

Flares shot out into the air, high and bright enough to be seen in midday—two red and one green. The Preceptory of Yseult had seen the trouble; they were on the march. Ibram fell more than stepped off the walkway into the street, and ran smack into a woman with two buckets yoked on her shoulders, pushing past a family clutching their children in their arms. She shouted—or at least he thought she did—her mouth moved. The bells clanged steadily, louder than anything, and his ears refused to hear any less volume.

"Fire!" Ibram yelled, and the woman nodded quickly.

"Fire!" he thought she shouted back, and then rushed past him.

Ibram staggered, regained his balance, and took off after her. An Attendant in green and grey with her gar in hand stood in the middle of the street. She slammed the butt of the gar into the ground and swept her right arm to the left, pushing most of the fleeing crowd to the side. It didn't so much contain the chaos as compress it, but the woman with the yoked buckets ran past to join the line of volunteers heading into the smoke. Ibram ran past the bucket line. The sky darkened from yellow to slate grey as they drew near the corner of the street.

Ibram saw the bucket brigade stretch off to the stone and clay fountain that provided that part of Pillared Circle with its fresh water. His stinging eyes widened. Harsh, caustic smoke filled his nose; he sneezed. The short row of connected honeycomb buildings stood ablaze before him; sparks shot out from their shared chimney, but behind that, shot orange and gold flames high above even the stone chimney. The bakery-mill tower was all afire, flames outlined every beam of wood. A muffled man's voice—almost like Ibram were underwater—floated past his hearing. He looked to the side; Amota Berac stood by a group of villagers, tall and wide as a Jolek's pine tree, directing them into a partially collapsed building. Ibram shook his head and pulled his ears until finally something popped or cleared itself, and the sounds of a great many folk panicking reached his ears in full voice.

"Amota Berac!" he yelled above the din as he made his way towards him. He choked in the smoke, and then cleared his throat. "Berac! *Uncle!*"

Amota Berac turned his head, and frowned until he caught sight of

Ibram. He nodded sharply and then pointed towards the right of the blaze. "Grab some of these quivering feneks, and evacuate The High Climber!" he bellowed in his deep voice. "I've got The Sun Eagle in hand!"

Black smoke belched up to the sky as part of the High Climber's roof lost its fight with the flames. Ibram wrapped his arm about his face again, and nodded. A line of folk stood gawping nearest an intact plinth, hunched together with dire faces as they watched the evening courtyards' collapse.

"Either you're for the water line, or you come with me!" Ibram yelled.

The closest man startled as if woken from a daze. He looked about himself, and then staggered off the walkway in the direction of fountain. A pack of four men and women joined Ibram's side. He nodded, and gestured to the second exit off Pillared Circle.

"There's folk in those courtyards!" he yelled, and charged forward. They followed.

The row of small evening courtyards was closed for the daytime, bless Yilka the Green's third and most beautiful face, but flames ate at their conjoined roofs. He dodged past the ever-growing tendrils of the bucket line to the front of The High Climber. He pressed the back of his hand to the right side door of the evening courtyard, and then the left; both panels were hot.

"I don't see anyone!" one of the women with Ibram shouted. She stood with her hands shading her eyes by the window on the left side of the door, which showed no flames nor belched smoke.

"That's nothing," her companion said. "That's for the door guards! It only looks out."

Ibram backed up a few steps. His chest shuddered with the force of his coughing; his lungs ached this close to the smoke. He could hear the hissing crackle of flames above the noise of the other rescuers, and felt sparks spit down from above, singing his forehead. The thick wooden doors were shut, but the hinges said they opened outward. The strap hinges on either side were in good shape, and they barred both with a thick plank while closed for the day. The place would be cinders before they battered their way through. Ibram shook his head, and wiped sweat from his face.

"Pry open—" he coughed. "Pry open the window!"

The roof of The High Climber was about to join its neighbors. Around them the fire roared, a sooty echoing bellow that rattled Ibram's brains in his skull as its heat singed the flesh of his skin and hands. He drew his sica, and jammed its sturdy curved blade between the wooden lattice frame and the wall. One of the women jammed her own dagger on the opposite side and began to wrench the wood free.

The ground rumbled beneath his feet and refused to settle. Ibram widened his stance for balance. Behind him, drums began to beat. He braced himself with one foot against the wall, and risked a glance behind him. Attendants from the Preceptory of Yseult rushed up the street in three lines, all in green and grey, with bandages wrapped around their mouths. If there had been air in Ibram's lungs for a sigh of relief, he would have done so in a heartbeat.

"The Water's Breath!" one of his little helpers shouted. "They've brought the voice of the river to us!"

Ibram nodded, briefly transfixed. It wasn't often even in Lityen that folk saw alchemy perform its lavish achievements, but the Water's Breath certainly qualified. The double front lines of Attendants carried the broad tapered ceramic barrels braced on their own wooden gars. The back formation, three deep, beat the drums that sent the low rumbling noise up through those same barrels and brought the fire low. As they approached, the flames shrunk back dying under the thud-thumping bass thunder, transmuting the very air into something the fire feared most—as if tons of water were pouring out instead of rings of air. The pressure from the devices made Ibram's ears pop. The heads of the bucket lines surged forward with ragged yells, swinging actual water from the fountain to cover the embers and flames the Water's Breath could not yet suppress.

A brace of Attendants launched themselves high in the air and rolled into a landing nearest the burning evening courtyards. One of them, dark-skinned, taller than a mountain and twice as wide, and who carried a gar that must have been seven feet tall in his left hand, waved at Ibram. Ibram gasped a laugh and shook his head.

"Ahksell!" he called out. "There's a door I need knocked down, if you've a moment!"

Ahksell rushed forward, and lunged with his gar. He yelled as he stamped the ground with his leading foot, and thrust the wooden staff forward. The double doors bubbled inwards as if facing an invisible battering ram, but held. Ibram waved his group of helpers away from the display of force.

Ahksell drew back his gar with a swift jerk, and the doors followed, bowing out; the hinges whined and broke with a shattering crack. Wood splinters flew through the air; Ibram ducked, throwing his arms over his head. The Water's Breath rumbled up from the earth, shaking Ibram's bones from his feet up as it suppressed the fires. He heard answering booms around him as the other Attendants ploughed inside the neighboring structures. The heavy wooden doors thudded to the ground. Ibram bounced out of his crouch and ran forward; an invisible hand yanked him back just as two servants stumbled out of the smoke-filled doorway and collapsed to the ground.

❧

It was the work of hours to put out the flames, even with the Water's Breath in full use, and every hand either throwing a bucket or dragging a body away from the wreckage. The bakery-mill had been the worst of it, of course, but its demise had spelled disaster for its neighbors. When its tower had blown, the alchemists had been forced to collapse the rest of the building on top of it to try and keep the flames from spreading.

Ibram watched the crowds of folk picking through the smoking wreckage from his position by the fountain. The Attendants from Yseult had set down the Water's Breath and left himself and a few other younger agents to guard it, as if anyone with sense would touch an alchemist's property after that little display. Now, several of them— those not brought low from the alchemists' continuous drumming— were engaged in raising large sections of burnt wood and shifting piles of cracked stone to search for survivors. The healers had erected a tent for the wounded, and Ibram could see Doctor Berot yelling at a group of young villagers carrying empty buckets.

Ibram sat down on the edge of the fountain, and coughed. He hacked and spat on the ground, and tugged on the back of his hair. His throat rasped from all the smoke still in the air. He breathed carefully, but wound up with his head between his knees, regardless, as he hacked something acrid free from his throat.

"Ib-la," Amota Berac said, and Ibram lifted his head. "Do Ama na'nu eeteight huskvith, Di monen."

"Ker Ama..." he coughed. "I'll ring a bell to Yilka the Green and break an egg for Catha the Grey," Ibram answered in Vissilian, too tired to remember his Merrilian like a good boy. "Ama can't complain I'm reckless if I'm thanking a goddess or two, to be sure."

His uncle stood before him, just as layered in soot, with scraggled bits of wood in his dark beard. He raised both hands and gripped Ibram's jaw, turning his head this way and that. Ibram twitched his head free, and coughed.

"Feeling better?" Amota Berac rasped, and cleared his throat. He beat little bits of charred wood from his arms and the front of his gambeson, rubbing his torch-shaped bronze brooch clean. "We all of us had a healthy swallow of smoke."

Ibram shrugged and rocked to his feet with a groan. "I've a mind to dunk myself in the nearest stream, if that's what you mean." He ran both hands through his hair, and then tucked it behind his ears. "Have they found the fire suppression tiles?" Ibram gestured to the folk walking amongst the ruins. "How could they fail like this?"

The garden provinces saved space by building close together, in honeycomb buildings that often shared more than one wall. Fire was an ever-present danger, and one only a fool disregarded. The Sect of Seven Fires did a brisk business in enchanted tiles such as usually festooned every building, little mosaics that worked to keep fire away from places it should not enter.

"A flour mill is a dangerous place, no matter what size of business they do." Amota Berac shook his head. He smoothed Ibram's hair back from his face. "I'm sending you back with the Water's Breath," he said. "Ladyship will want her report."

Ibram snorted and coughed again. "What is there to say?"

"She'll wish to know how the Water's Breath performed. We were lucky the fire began when it did, else the streets would have been packed," Amota Berac said with a terrible gentleness to his tone. "There's nothing more to be done here."

"How did that get here?" Ibram asked, and jerked his thumb at the ceramic barrel of the Water's Breath. "I thought they kept that up the living mountain near the practice fields."

"We jumped," Ahksell said behind him, and Ibram whirled around with a frown. Amota Berac released him just before Ibram might have done his neck a disservice.

"Jumped down a mountain?" he asked. "Not even you are that hard on your knees."

Ahksell shrugged, and untied the bandage from the lower half of his face. He stuffed it under his belt, and leaned on his gar. "As you say," he agreed. "Are you going back up to speak with Mentor Hobon?"

Ibram opened his mouth, but Amota Berac beat him to it. "He is, young Solari," he said, and put his hands on his hips. "A bath and a meal as well, if you should remember in what directions the kitchens lie."

"I'll come with you then," Ahksell said. "Tolly and the rest of the drummers need to return the devices anyway. I am not so tired, so I can help carry."

Ibram sighed. "As you say."

$\begin{array}{ccc} \text{❧} & 2 & \text{❧} \end{array}$

Time paused for nothing. Even in the aftermath of a horrible accident, the demands of a bustling village like Lityen and its neighbors ever clamored to be met. Ibram leaned his shoulders against the shelves behind Lady Azadiya's desk, and stared above the petitioners' heads to the well-appointed room beyond. Across the room beneath one of Lady Azadiya's hanging glowbulbs, Amota Berac picked up a stack of bound books lying against one of the thick wall tapestries and began replacing the tomes on Ladyship's shelves, already bulging with scrolls and artifacts lined the curving walls of her office. Amota Evren, stuck at his recording duties near the window, coughed to hide his laughter.

Master Karpin was a little Lordship Ibram dearly wished he might otherwise ignore—someone's second or sixth child—stumped past Ibram's line of sight, hands waving in the air as he circled around the point of his petition to Lady Azadiya. Ibram hooked his thumbs behind his wide leather belt, and watched through ever-slumping eyelids as the man once again listed all the reasons he disputed his neighbor's refusal to pay a stud fee for a pregnant mare.

"Tansy is a strong breeder, Mentor Hobon," Master Karpin

protested with his arms fully outstretched as if he cradled the beast even now.

Ibram shifted his attention to the bubbling liquid inside its glass bulb which hung from the ceiling, throwing a rainbow reflection against the wooden flooring. His back and shoulders ached. Disasters and public works went hand in glove, to be sure, but that meant that for several days now Ibram had been hard at work since the fire at Pillared Circle had been brought to heel. Lityen had its local workers, of course, but agents of the Sect of Seven Fires were often volunteered to aid in disaster relief. Especially the ones like him, attached to the Preceptory of Yseult, since no great noble house held responsibility over their corner of Vanima province.

Amota Berac finished replacing the books, and coughed in Ibram's direction. Ibram sighed, and refocused.

"Surely the inherent value," Master Karpin continued, "in having my horse's blood in *her* stock makes it all the more reason to pay me the worth of the beast's, er, time."

"You let that horse into my paddock," Mistress Inswinger retorted.

"The lock on Tansy's stall broke!" Karpin protested. "I've already released my groom from my service."

"I wanted none of your stallion, regardless," Mistress Inswinger said. "My mare was to be worked, not bred, for a few years more yet."

Ibram rolled his eyes, and didn't care who saw it. The report on the fire had yet to be made, because these dolts refused to vacate their time in favor of more important matters. To be sure, animal husbandry was a fine and time honored tradition, but what divine curse made its practice rely on such folk as these two?

It seemed unfair that in the midst of the actual business of repair and recovery, Lady Azadiya still had to hold open her daily schedule for local complaints and various troublemakers. In her official capacity as Mentor Arbitrator and Lady Make-Peace, every fourth day out of seven, Ladyship and the Attendants in her division acted as a clearing house for the bulk of their provincial problems, sending this merchant up to see the Medicinal Corps under the Second Mentor, or directing a stary-eyed noble daughter up to visit the Third Mentor for shay and no little sympathetic gossip. The meetings which had no other solution were held in her office, generally in the company of no less than two of her agents, and were—in Ibram's considered opinion—less a plea for help, than an extended airing of petty grievances.

He wrinkled his nose. He was perfectly placed at Lady Azadiya's right to see the side of her face. Her sharp chin never wobbled with laughter, nor did her high olive-skinned cheekbones show any sign of a blush. As ever, her dark eyes turned up at the corners like someone had told her a good joke, but she listened to the petitioners with every evidence of seriousness.

Only the twitching at the corner of her mouth betrayed how much Ladyship dearly wanted to laugh. The silver enamel and garnet raven comb holding her hair back from her face twinkled at him. Instead she cast her eyes to the wooden ceiling, which was actually the floor of her private quarters, a loft section that could only be reached by her own mastery of physical alchemy. She sighed and looked back at the two petitioners, and tossed a folded triangle of paper up and down, catching it by its point on the tip of her forefinger, before sending it leaping through the air again.

Master Karpin and Mistress Inswinger did not seem to know how to respond to Ladyship's display. Amota Berac stroked his long black beard and collapsed into the chair, piled high with richly woven blankets for comfort, next to Amota Evren. The wood creaked beneath his weight; he made a show of brushing the arms of his green gambeson and the knees of his grey wrapped trousers. The petitioners frowned heavily in his direction until Ibram coughed to bring back their attention.

"*Let*," Karpin said, with a half-hearted snort. "He jumped your broken fencing!"

"I didn't employ you for the service, you louse, nor asked your opinion on my fencing," Inswinger said. She adjusted her flat cap with its long connecting veil draped under her chin, and crossed her arms beneath her chest.

Ibram tsked, and braved the glares both combatants sent his way. He turned his head, which unfortunately brought his nose closer to his clothing. His knee-length green twill gambeson still smelled faintly smoke, though he'd dutifully hung it from his bedroom window for two nights to rid the quilted fabric of the smell. Lady Azadiya coughed.

"And this fencing, what was it made of?" she asked.

"It was a dead hedge, Mentor," Mistress Inswinger said. "We'd taken a portion out to make a gate open into the lane between our land, but left boards up, which *his* beast ignored just as Karpin failed to keep his own fencing well-maintained!"

While the horse folk quibbled, Ibram ran back over the details he'd accumulated for his own report to Ladyship in the archives of his mind. Amota Evren had been drilling him in memory retention by way of making Ibram form his memories in an illusion of a house cluttered with markers intended to bring forth the relevant information. So far, Ibram could just about picture his bedroom with any kind of regularity, and was working on filling the shelf by his bed. Perhaps he would make this report on the calamity in Lityen into a table lamp burning a too-long wick.

Ibram cleared his throat, and crossed his arms over the row of flat wooden buttons sewn diagonally across his chest, opposite the leather strap with his torch-shaped brooch of office. As the argument wavered on, he idly drew his thumb down his sole button shield, a gewgaw that was supposed to light up to signal rescuers should he be in trouble. He yawned. Since the bakery-mill had taken out the buildings nearest it, he'd been tasked with the rest of the agents to guard the ruins and the surviving apothecary, where the Medical Corps had set up for the wounded, from looters. Ibram had barely been laid out in his own bed before he had had to make his way up the living mountain again.

Lady Azadiya's head twitched slightly. She tossed the triangle of paper high in the air, and pinched her thumb and forefinger together. Ibram winced at the corresponding tug on his ear lobe, and stood away from his slouching on the bookshelf. He drew his hand down the woven strip of tilted, interlocking t-shapes in blackwork along the front of his gambeson, pretending to be smoothing out a stubborn wrinkle. Ladyship caught the triangle of paper as it fell, and sent it high again.

Ibram twisted his stiff neck to the side; the sound cracked in the room like dry sticks. He froze beneath the sudden, horrified attention of the rest of the folk in the room, even Lady Azadiya turned to stare. Amota Evren dropped his stylus onto his traveler's writing desk, and then fumbled it back up again with a shudder. Ibram cleared his throat and shrugged.

"Yes," Lady Azadiya said slowly, as she turned back around. The paper triangle floated to the floor. "This has been an entirely too-detailed interview, I fear to say."

Master Karpin immediately protested. "Mentor Hobon!"

"I'll hear no more of this," Ladyship said. "If Mistress Inswinger's fence is to become a gate, let her complete its construction. She will no doubt have much work on her hands feeding additional beasts, no matter their pedigree. Master Karpin has been negligent with his own stock, and must allow that not locking up a stallion when he knows of a mare in season does not count in his favor." She held up her hand as Master Karpin attempted to protest again. "Should the foal be born without complication, go to the Wheelhouse in Delbrite and offer it up to The Wheelmaker. Master Karpin will pay for the cost of transport in token of his feckless behavior, while Mistress Inswinger will not profit from the additional fine stock. I'm sure The Wheelmaker's overseers have some job they might need doing that requires a horse."

"And if something goes wrong and I lose both foal and mare?" Mistress Inswinger demanded.

Lady Azadiya sat back in her chair. "Am I a doctor to know how to handle your animals, Mistress?" she asked. She leaned to the left, and her heavy dark braid fell from her shoulder. "Evren, have you finished writing?"

"I have," he said, and stood up from the desk with a length of paper in both hands.

"What if I sold the foal to you, Lady Azadiya," Mistress Inswinger offered. "Outside your capacity as Fourth Mentor, but in token of my respect for your family."

"Add that to the missive, Evren," Lady Azadiya said, and did not dignify the bribe with a response. Mistress Inswinger's face slowly turned puce as Ladyship continued, "So it has been duly recorded and will be archived until such time as the circuit judge from the Courts Civil deigns to show their face in Vanima province within the next twelve-day. You may choose to inform whoever that may be of any new developments at such time of their arrival." She raised her right hand palm up and curtly flicked her first two fingers inward. "Ibram, make your bow."

Ibram breathed a not so subtle sigh of relief, and marched to the open doorway. Ladyship never conducted business in a closed room if she could help it. Instead, she relied on the formation of six silencing tiles embedded above her door lintel to keep her conversations private.

He gestured across the threshold, and held his arm outstretched while the grumbling petitioners left the office. He bowed shortly to their backs, hands folded on his stomach, and came back up immediately. Ibram revolved his neck on his shoulders as he turned back to face the room, and shrugged tightness from his shoulders.

"I don't suppose you *are* in the market for a new horse?" Amota Berac asked. He raised himself with a groan from his chair. "My Ina just bought a few Tolti ponies off a train headed for the east."

Lady Azadiya rested on elbow on her desk and drew a small stack of paperwork closer for her own perusal. Her clan bracelet fell down her wrist, the iridescent trimstone and pale bone beads clacked together. She pursed her lips in thought.

"Never in life," she said. "The sect has sufficient rounceys for any trip I might undertake, and if I have need of a destrier again, I shall seek my own clan's beasts from the Red Coast. A horse raised by the sand never loses its footing."

Ibram hid his yawn in his right shoulder. The only destrier Ibram was aware of Lady Azadiya owning was the old black warhorse, well-past its campaigning days. It spent its days eating like a prince in the small paddock outside Ladyship's tower. He'd never yet seen her ride the beast.

Amota Evren raised his thin eyebrows at Ladyship's declaration, but said nothing. He was a quiet one, Evren, a distant relation of Ibram's Amota Tono, both of whom were from somewhere in the north of Vissilia. They had worked in Lady Azadiya's division of the preceptory long enough that they bore the title of uncle with good nature. He wasn't a blood relation, but that made no matter according to Merrilian standards, even if he was merely a co-worker to everyone else. Still, they were both in the way of being a gray area of employ-ment, so to speak. Nobles were allowed a household, but never alchemists. Lady Azadiya being both meant dealing with a certain degree of latitude in hiring. As of yet, Ibram had never seen the man or woman with gall enough to say Lady Azadiya should draw her agents from the common store.

Amota Berac snorted, and cracked his knuckles. "It's past midday," he noted in his deep, booming voice. "Will they all be about questions of breeding stock?"

Lady Azadiya shuddered. "Knock thrice on that window glass for luck," she commanded. "My *kingdom* for an interesting petition—I think it must have been broken pots and ill-matched neighbors all day."

"It *was* a staggering amount of wasted olive oil, Ladyship," Evren said; he spoke quickly as always, like his breath might run out before his words did. "And it cost the caravan its wealthiest member."

Lady Azadiya rolled her eyes, and stood up from her high-backed seat. She tugged the wrinkles out of her sleeves and the folds of her clothes. She sighed as her arms dropped back to her sides, and paced the length of the room to the nearest window.

"The Attendants seem to be diverting a fair few, to be sure," she said, staring down into her garden, which was routinely converted into a secondary way station on especially busy days. "Make note to open a few extra barrels of ale for them, would you, Evren? A good day's work deserves reward."

"And they can't go down to Pillared Circle for entertainment now," Ibram reminded her.

"Indeed so," Ladyship said. "Has Doctor Berot returned with his latest review of the wounded?"

"He's been keeping his patients in the apothecary away from the 'injurious emanations' of the destruction. Should I fetch him?" Amota Berac asked. He sighed, and shook his head heavily. "Naja shin na'lun, Avaena, per Di ploune agoreuo mid bai alligantai."

Lady Azadiya looked at Berac sharply. "Bai alligantai shin agoreuo?" she repeated. "Di shin..."

Ladyship and the agents from the west who worked in her division

—which was most of them—had a tendency to lapse into the western tongue with each other. Ibram's Merrilian was more informally based; it made more elaborate conversations difficult to follow. He slowly repeated their talk back to himself, which sadly meant he lost the thread three stitches back. His ama had taught him the language—he was a Westerner himself, after all, on his mother's side—but not too many folk spoke Merrilian in the Grand Empire of Vissilia outside of the old borders of Merrilia. He could only practice so much when most of his conversation revolved around breakfast and his younger sister breaking his toys after she took them while he slept.

"There are two local fire alliances not speaking to each other, instead of only the one on Pillared Circle?" he asked, and Amota Berac frowned in his direction. "And neither will they speak to Amota Berac? Won't that impede both sides' attempts to get their money for repairs?"

"Ve leusian bo Ibram...amang bo Evren." Lady Azadiya turned back around. "My apologies to you both," she said in Vissilian. "Yes, Ib-la, you caught the thrust of the conversation completely. Folk are often the most difficult to manage when they are at their most stressed."

She looked in Amota Berac's direction. "Wait until Berot comes back," she said. "We've more than enough work in that regard."

"Ibram, have you read Berac's notes?" Amota Evren asked.

Ibram nodded, and clasped his left wrist behind his back. "I know the lay of the land," he said. "The fire in the bakery-mill directed itself across the alley and then burned outward."

Ladyship stretched her arms briefly behind her back and then brought her arms forward and twisted her wrists. Because it was the fourth day of the working week, she had dressed for comfort in thin robes of deep green satin which closed in a wide vee at her shoulders, with one side pinned down to display her yellow linen shift and its embroidered protective symbols in blue thread, that closed in a diagonal line of embroidered satin buttons low at her waist. The light from the window shone on the delicate looped gold chain closed by an enameled bar hung at her neck with an emerald pendant at its center. Her hair was kept back from her face by that raven comb and braided as well. Ibram couldn't see how any part of Ladyship's attire made sitting for hours in conference more comfortable, but since it wasn't his job to attend to such matters, he made no mention of it.

"I wonder why they aren't eager to get the business done with," Ladyship said, and Ibram refocused. "If none of them are speaking to each other, we will have to review the damages recorded by our agents alone."

"Oh, they are speaking to themselves more than enough to make up for it," Amota Berac said. "The problem being that none of them can agree on anything except that it is a terrible accident, terrible."

He shook his head gravely, and Ladyship raised her eyebrows. "Do you think it is *not* a terrible accident?" she asked.

"No indication of any tampering has arisen so far, to be sure," Berac said. "But in their rush not to point fingers at each other, they delay the work of actually assigning a cost to their repairs. They none of them wish to pay out a faunt more than they have to, of course."

Ibram snorted. "What else could it be, but the bakery-mill?" he asked. "The only reason for any of those fire alliances was to protect the surrounding businesses should a fire break out from all that loose flour."

"It does seem the natural source," Lady Azadiya said. "All those floating clouds of dry particles... But I dislike irregularity."

"Regardless of the reason for their hesitance, the fire alliances reports are bound to be irregular even if we do receive them," Amota Evren said. "You know how those petty nobles scream at the loss of revenue. Their factotums are no better, Ladyship."

"Your caution refreshes me," she replied.

"I am not cautious without cause!" he protested. "I remember the last time we had an event in the village—"

"Oh, now you can't judge by that!" Ibram broke in. "Who would believe anyone would try to import a rachtbear so some prince in Bastilat could keep it as a pet?"

"Anyone who has ever met a prince," Lady Azadiya said. "Astonishingly irresponsible folk, princes. I knew one whose life's ambition was to own a breeding pair of animals from every province in Vissilia."

"All twenty?" Ibram asked.

"And a Greater Uplands Wyvern from the Stubai Islands," she said. "The smell alone..."

She sat back down at her desk, and then picked up a wooden slat scroll which lay open there. It was only partially inscribed. She had been disrupted from a seven-day's long meditation on the interchange of all things material into their properties' immaterial, which was her study of manipulation. The little portable furnace on her desk had run day and night while she recorded her experiments. The entire tower smelt vaguely of the burning wood of the slatted scroll she inscribed, and the gelatinous ink the alchemists favored which locked their processes onto the scroll. Alchemical recipes and treatises tended to burn mere paper as soon as they were written down, and at best, the words slid off vellum entirely.

Evren obligingly remembered to rap his knuckles on the glass, a trademark of Catha the Grey, Lady Azadiya's divine patroness. Ibram chuckled, and mimed tapping a bell when Ladyship glared in his direction. Yilka the Green wouldn't be found wanting on his account.

"Do you want the most recent update on the report on the Pillared Circle fire now, Ladyship?" Amota Berac asked. "Or shall I send Ibram for Dihya and a late meal?"

"I have less patience for fools than I do my cook, to be sure," she said. "Ibram, go and find Dihya." She leaned back in her chair and waved her right hand. "Speak on, Berac."

"Yes, Ladysh—" Ibram cut off at a resounding knock on the threshold of the door. He twisted to face the knocker, and viewed Ahksell Solari, filling the doorway as only a man as tall and broad as a door himself could.

"Mentor?" Ahksell's muffled voice called out. "I've a petitioner you should hear."

Ibram squinted at Ahksell from across the threshold, he was ever so slightly out of focus. The silencing tiles created some kind of pressure system, as had been explained to him many times, which could only be felt and not seen by the untrained eye. To Ibram, it felt rather like walking through a heavy curtain. Ahksell said he saw a golden shimmering wall of light when he concentrated; Ibram supposed that meant he could mark a victory down for his own unaugmented perception.

"Ladyship, the fires cannot wait another day," Berac said. "The fire alliances in Pillared Circle and Builders Row are compiling their repair reports even now."

He gestured at Ahksell. Ahksell frowned, glanced behind himself, and shook his head at someone behind him. Ibram craned his neck, but couldn't see who it was.

"If we have nothing to present," Berac continued, "to First Mentor E'garcid for her own audience with the Lord Preceptor, then *his* session with Lady Sebbina's council of ministers will devolve into—"

"We shall be accused of play-acting our role as caretakers of the lands within the imperial boundary?" Lady Azadiya finished for him. "I am strangely aware of the commissioner's ongoing interests in that regard, Berac. Let Ahksell inside, Ibram."

Ibram extended his left arm to the door and half-bowed. Ahksell nodded, and paused to say something, presumably, to the petitioner standing behind him.

"Yilka the Green turns her third face in Ahksell's direction once more, Ladyship," Ibram said.

"Ten faunts says She only looks at you for work after this," Evren said behind him. "I touched glass, after all."

Ladyship grinned, and reached up to adjust her hair comb. "So we shall see," she said. "Ev-la, back to your desk."

She gestured at the doorway. Ibram stepped back so that Ahksell might approach. Amota Berac bowed his head and sighed ruefully at his boots; he was a man of straight lines and one thing only after another. Ladyship's sometimes haphazard conduct often made his day a little dimmer.

The great height and breadth of Attendant Ahksell Solari soon entered the room, ducking his close-shaven head as he did so. Behind him, a small man with curled shoulders scuttled into the room. The man bowed with both hands on his stomach towards Lady Azadiya, who raised him up with a lazy curl of the fingers on her right hand, and then he stood there, quite obviously shifting his weight from one foot to another.

"Mentor Hobon, may I make you known to this petitioner?" Ahksell asked.

Lady Azadiya inclined her head. "You may."

"Master Shokan Dughlat, be known to Lady Azadiya Hobon, Fourth Mentor of the Preceptory of Yseult, alchemist of the Sect of Seven Fires," Ahksell said.

Master Dughlat bowed again, just as deeply, and was raised up one more time, just as quickly. Lady Azadiya leaned on the arm of her chair, and waited politely to hear the petition. Master Dughlat cleared his throat.

"Go on," Ahksell prompted in what Ibram was sure he believed was a quiet tone of voice.

The man jumped, and cleared his throat again. Ibram moved back towards Lady Azadiya's desk to get a better look at him. The man had a wide chin and stubbornly rounded jowls. His eyes were sunk deep into his face and his nose had been broken, badly, in his youth. Ibram squinted a moment, and then drew his head back.

"I know you," Ibram said. "You ran out of the doors when Attendant Solari broke the locks at The High Climber."

The man startled, and then cleared his throat again. "Yes, young master," he said. "I work there as a cleaner—I mean, I will again, once it's rebuilt."

"This is the evening courtyard that caught fire after the bakery-mill exploded?" Lady Azadiya asked.

"Yes, Mentor," Ahksell said, and then gestured to the little man beside him. "That's why Master Dughlat came to see me—you, I mean."

"I was just about to report on the reconstruction efforts," Berac interjected.

Lady Azadiya nodded. "I believe we might hold off a little longer," she said. "Well, what brings you to me, Master Dughlat?"

"The fire, I saw the flames myself and—Excuse—," the man said abruptly, and then coughed into his sleeve. His voice still rasped; he must have taken half the fire's smoke into his lungs.

Ladyship nodded encouragingly at him. She rubbed her thumb

against her signet ring of a mongoose, the symbol of the preceptory. Ahksell had the same one stitched on a patch on his collar.

"Water, Master Dughlat?" Ibram asked.

Dughlat shook his head. "I thank you, no. I'm well enough."

Ibram took a moment to make note of the man, though he had no idea what item Amota Evren might wish him to fashion Dughlat's particulars into. A sculpture, perhaps, for later storage in Ibram's memory vault of past cases. Master Dughlat had made an attempt to clean his face and hands before appearing before her, but his clothes were clearly shoddy replacements for the tunic and trousers he'd been wearing in the fire, made of a rough brown wool with a simple braided belt to hold his purse at his side. His greying hair was short on the sides and longer on the top, a man from further south, though his skin was far lighter than Ahksell's dark tones. He lapped everyone in the room besides Lady Azadiya in years, with deep creases at the corners of his eyes and around his mouth.

"I'm here on account of the fire, Mentor Hobon," he said, displaying a marvelous talent of the obvious. His head bobbed in a quick nod. "Though I don't—Well, I am not certain it's important, only that I can't think of anyone else there would be to tell."

Ibram cocked his head to the side. He glanced up at Ahksell, who caught his gaze and shrugged with his eyebrows. Lady Azadiya folded her hands in her lap.

"Information important enough to share is good enough for me," she said. "Have you brought your employer with you?"

Dughlat shook his head quickly. "No," he said. "He doesn't know I am even here. I work for Master Rennab, Soren Rennab. He and his husband, Albin Finar, are in charge. They think I'm with Neilos piling up what little furniture there is left. Master Rennab is busy with the local fire alliance—too busy for this if it should come to nothing—but I thought, well, it's more of a problem for an alchemist, what I saw, isn't it? And it being the fourth day of seven, I knew even if I wouldn't be granted permission to speak with you—then at least I could tell *someone* and lift the weight from my shoulders."

He stopped talking, leaving all his listeners caught on the bank of that stream of words. From his seat towards the back of the room,

Amota Evren's stylus scurried to catch up over the paper. Ibram stepped forward and scratched the back of his neck. Dughlat's head twitched in his direction; his eyes showed a little too widely in his face.

"Problems for alchemists are our specialty, Master Dughlat," Ibram said. "I don't suppose you saw anyone with a lit pipe in the vicinity of the bakery-mill?"

He knew immediately he'd made a mistake, and if he hadn't, then the strong tug on his right earlobe would have brought his head above water. Simply because the bakery-mill was the obvious culprit, didn't mean he needed to go about shouting in folk's ears. He had lead with the question; Lady Azadiya required more care amongst her agents. Master Dughlat frowned in his direction, and Ibram arranged his face in a more pleasing expression.

"I did not," Dughlat said. He bit his lips together, and took a step towards the door. "Perhaps it's nothing, really."

"But I am intrigued now," Lady Azadiya said. "What troubles you, Master Dughlat?"

Dughlat inhaled slowly and raised his chin. The old man even uncurled his shoulders for a moment, before deflating again. "I saw green fire," he said with an air of someone determined to be believed. "Blue green. Green as the stones in your necklace, Mentor."

"What?" Lady Azadiya asked sharply, and touched her hand to the emerald pendant around her neck.

"Perhaps begin where you began with me, Shokan," Ahksell said quickly. "You were wiping chairs in the back?"

"Yes, I was. We have a little workshop in the back of the building— just near the door to the alley—and had just finished repairing the legs on some of the older ones. We'd moved out into the main room to look over the rest of the furniture, when we heard the first bang."

"And you thought nothing of it?" Ibram asked.

"It was close by, but not so near as to be alarming." Dughlat lifted his palms to the air and shrugged. "If a man is unnerved by explosions in Lityen, he has no business living here."

Ibram's mouth crooked up at the corners. Across her cluttered desk, Lady Azadiya nodded. "And the second bang?" she asked.

"Neilos—that's who was with me—smelled smoke first," Dughlat said, "and then the whole of the world rocked. Mentor, it was as if the building was bending out of the way of the blast itself! We were knocked clean over and I..." He paused and held his hand to the back of his head, "I hit my head against the side of the stage in the middle. When I woke, the entire place was alight, full of smoke."

"And this Neilos could not help you?" Ladyship asked.

Dughlat swallowed and shook his head. "I'm about a head taller and much heavier. I'm lucky I came to on my own."

"This is when you saw the green flame?" Ibram asked. "Before you reached the barred doors."

"Yes, Master, ah—"

"Ucalegon," Ibram said, and Master Dughlat bowed to him shortly. "I wonder why your friend did not try to escape and seek aid."

"Neither of them could see in all the smoke, " Ahksell answered for Master Dughlat. "They wanted to leave, but got confused."

Ibram winced. A man could get in worse trouble than not letting a witness speak for themselves, to be sure, but Ladyship disliked the forming of bad habits. Ibram had already stepped on the witness's testimony once. Ladyship tsked; Ahksell cleared his throat.

"Or, that is what was relayed to me," Ahksell mumbled, and cleared his throat again.

From his wince, Ladyship had most definitely given Ahksell's earlobe a swift tug, even though Ibram couldn't see her hands. Master Dughlat did not register—or pretended not to see—the exchange, and stood there wringing his hands. He chewed his lower lip, and looked up at Lady Azadiya anxiously.

"I saw it as we crawled to the door," Dughlat said. "I was behind Neilos—so that neither of us could lose the other—and I happened to catch my tunic on the back of a chair. When I paused to untangle myself, I chanced to look backwards and—and the flames were green, truly green, like they appear on Nikephoros' Night."

Amota Berac scoffed loudly, and drew his hand down the length of his bushy black beard. "The fire hit a bag of chalcan vitriol, then," he said. "No doubt your masters wished to keep pests from your larder."

"Any place of business on or near Pillared Circle would most likely have its share as well," Ibram said. "They'd make a powerful temptation for weevils and mold."

"But my employers did not have such a bag," Master Dughlat exclaimed. "There was nothing kept along that wall but things necessary for cleaning and repairing the furniture."

Ibram pursed his lips. "What do you use for that, then?" he asked.

Dughlat blinked. "Oil for the finish," he said, "and pegs as needed, of course. Master Rennab long ago removed the kitchen for additional space for chairs. He has everything brought from the caffa instead. It's naught but small food, nuts and wine...bread and brenzamal at the most."

Master Dughlat flinched at the silence that followed his proclamation, but held firm. It was a mark in his favor, to be sure. Not many badoshai would go straight from a fire into the furnace by telling an alchemist a perfectly ordinary municipal disaster might be decidedly abnormal after all.

"To claim a fire has an alchemical touch to it is no little charge, Master Dughlat," Ibram said.

Folk had a habit of saying alchemists knew no law but the Laws of Reality, which they routinely upended anyway. They based it, of course, on the history of all the little kingdoms and former empires swallowed up in the Vissilians' centuries-long war to separate the art of alchemy from the business of ruling. But in point of fact, it was a truth only repeated outside the imperial boundary. To be sure, anyone lodged within the sphere of the Sect of Seven Fire's influence understood that alchemists stood for a great deal more imperial interference than, say, a Great House of Vissilia might—should one ever manage to so offend Her Gracious Majesty Soliya IV.

"I can only say what I saw, Master Ucalegon," Dughlat said.

"Indeed so," Ahksell said.

Ibram's heartbeat turned over in his chest. An accident in a bakery-mill was one thing, but a fire deliberately begun? Very few people might profit from that. Chalcan vitriol by itself, strictly speaking, wasn't an alchemical invention, but it was a key ingredient in several recipes that Ibram officially had no legal knowledge of.

"For how long were the flames green?" Lady Azadiya asked.

"I don't understand, Mentor," Dughlat said.

"You turn and the fire is glowing green," she said. "A strong green or pale? Was it only briefly this color? Did it fade, or continue? What space did this green fire cover?"

Master Dughlat breathed in and then out. "I...a strong green, Mentor Hobon. It lasted all the time I was looking at it, never fading, until I turned to follow Neilos. Say...less than a minute, but more than a second?"

Ahksell shifted his weight from his left to right foot and back; he didn't like that answer any more than Ibram did. Ibram schooled his face into a vision of polite listening, and crossed his arms over his chest.

"And its size?" Ladyship continued.

Dughlat thought for a moment. "I would say—well, the length of the wall that I could see—the middle of the wall was certainly that color, so it stands to reason the root of the blaze was the bottom of the floor."

Lady Azadiya's chin raised; she blinked up at the ceiling and made no reply. Ibram waited for her unfocused eyes to find them all again. Ladyship always needed time to walk within her own mind before asking anyone to join her on the field of logic.

"Berac, the tally of destruction?" she asked finally.

Amota Berac clasped his hands behind his back, and cleared his throat. "The bakery-mill and the stables connected, the evening court-yards that stood behind it—those being The High Climber and The Isconian's Hand—and the cookshops at the second exit off Pillared Circle are all cinders and ruin. The apothecary and the draughtshops that stand a little further back were only damaged, mostly from falling debris. Oh, and The Sun Eagle has lost its front railings."

Lady Azadiya nodded. "And the people?"

"It was a lucky time of day," Ibram said with a swift glance at his uncle. "Four dead, two in the evening courtyard next to Master Dugh-lat's work, and then the final two we think were attached to the bakery-mill."

"You think?" Ladyship asked.

"The body of the miller was found in the street," Amota Berac said, and sighed. "Tari Ozol was his name. The First Finder saw someone who might have crawled up to the ladder attached to the roof to try and quell the fire across their shared alley. When we were able to search, the woman was found underneath a collapsed wall; we believe she was leading the grind donkeys to safety. I'll have to return for a proper identification, but I should think there is little actual doubt. Either Master Ozol or his wife Desta would have come forward by now, if they were alive. Their son was out of the village. I've sent a man for him."

And if the son ran from Amota Berac's messenger, then that told the world a story right there. Ibram nodded to himself, but kept silent. No need for all the possibilities to be laid out in front of Master Dughlat.

"Poor folk," Dughlat muttered and drew a circle over his heart with his thumb. "May their papers be in order at the High Table."

Dughlat followed The Wheelmaker, then, who made up the other half of the High Table of Judgement at The Crossroads with The Speaker. They tended to be practical folk, like Katka and Father. That might make life easier in the long run.

Lady Azadiya tapped her thumb against her signet ring. "Are the Ozols' earthly particulars in order?"

Ibram stepped forward. "Their First Finders have all been duly recorded and statements made. We've only to await the circuit judge, and with ten more burned, and of those only a few severely. Some—" he indicated Master Dughlat, "—did suffer from smoke inhalation, but are otherwise all right. If the fire had happened at night, we might be telling a much sadder story."

She tapped her fingers on her desk, and narrowed her dark eyes in thought. Her head turned; Master Dughlat stood straight beneath her gaze. He lowered his hands to his sides.

"Have you come only to tell me what you know?" she asked. "Or do you have a request as well?"

Master Dughlat swallowed. It was every subject of Vissilia's right to petition for aid from whoever administered their village, of course, but Ibram thought the better of the man for actually taking a moment to think about Ladyship's question before answering. After all, to bring something to Lady Azadiya's attention was one thing, but to call her to action was quite another, and usually left up to folk who ran businesses, rather than served them. Ibram tugged his hair at the nape of his neck. In point of fact, Master Dughlat's employer should have accompanied him. Why skip the man at all? The fire had destroyed his building, and no amount of meetings with the local fire alliance could be so important if Dughlat was truly upset at what he claimed to see.

"When the fires collapsed the roof of my work, we had no aid from the Cohort of Vigilance as I don't believe any of Her Gracious Majesty's buildings or goods were damaged in the fire, Mentor Hobon," Dughlat said, in a slow meandering tone that drew out his smoke-damaged voice. He waited for Lady Azadiya's nod before continuing. "And our local fire alliance is only neighbors aiding each other in common danger. It was you all coming down off the living mountain that halted the flames, and saved my life.

I believe I saw green fire burning along the wall—and I did hit my head—maybe I saw nothing. But if that is the situation at hand, then I am afraid for what might happen next."

"Do you believe your employer set the fire?" Ibram asked.

"No!" Dughlat's mouth dropped open in affront; he took a step backwards from Ibram. "Master Rennab would have no need to burn his home down—nor would it be a crime if he did! He owns the building entire, you know."

That was unusual. Most folk who owned businesses rented the land, or had an 'investor' providing funds somewhere in the property contract. Traditionally, that was how a fair few noble younger siblings made their living in quieter parts of the provinces, away from the heirs and spares of the main family branches.

"Four people are dead," Ibram said.

"I can only say what I saw," Dughlat said. "I have no reason to suspect Master Rennab, nor Master Finar, nor anyone else at The High Climber."

Ibram noticed he made no mention of the bakery-mill, for which Dughlat could not be blamed. It was the obvious choice in such a disaster. The covered bodies recovered from the blaze were carried past in his memory again. Ibram controlled the shiver down his back and paid more attention to his surroundings.

The man spread his work-worn hands. "I merely ask that if the fire was not a natural mistake, then who caused it?"

Lady Azadiya considered Master Dughlat for a moment, and then rapped her knuckle on her desk. "A very good question," she said. "Evren, do you have all that?"

Ibram jumped, and twisted to glance behind himself. He'd absolutely forgotten the man. Amota Evren looked up at him and waved his stylus in the air. "Yes, Ladyship," he said.

"Very well," Lady Azadiya said. "First Mentor E'garcid will have to be informed. Evren, send for a runner."

"Ladyship," Amota Evren said, and exited.

"Master Dughlat!" Master Dughlat jumped at the calling of his name, and Ladyship looked upon him with interest. "I declare your question worthy of investigation."

She paused then, and looked between the men arrayed before her. After all, a fire was a tragedy, but green fire was a puzzle. There was little Lady Azadiya enjoyed more than something which held her attention. Ibram couldn't say he didn't understand her point.

"You appear tired," she continued. "Ahksell shall see you provided with a cooling drink and perhaps a small Braemar's Tonic downstairs. Does wonders for the breath, small difficulty with taste and smell immediately following imbibing."

"Mentor," Ahksell said, and bent his head. He waited while Master Dughlat made his bow, and then led him outside into the hallway.

Ibram clapped his hands together. "Amota Berac—"

"I can look into the matter immediately, Ladyship," Amota Berac said.

She shook her head. "No," she said. "There is more than enough work to go around these days. I'll not separate you from a task already in progress, and I need you to coordinate with Sarrha once the fire alliances have their statements prepared. I grant this work to Ibram."

"Yes, Ladyship!" Ibram exclaimed. Finally, something more interesting than tallying destroyed serviceware. He took a step forward.

Amota Berac frowned deeply, and Ibram cleared his throat. "Uh, I mean, to me?"

"Ahksell, as well," she said. Ibram cut his eyes in the direction Ahksell had walked off, and grinned. "I think it best. You have, together, insights which pair well with our work. Besides, this way Berac can continue to negotiate with the fire alliances and provide support, if necessary."

Amota Berac nodded. His shoulders relaxed. He seemed a little relieved, in fact.

"Ibram, take Master Dughlat back down to the village," she said. "If there is an arsonist hanging about, it's best to know before the next blaze."

Ibram nodded. He moved towards the doorway, and then paused. "Am I solely to resolve the issue of the green fire, or help prove which building was at fault?" he asked.

Lady Azadiya was already returning to her treatise. She looked up from pouring a dollop of water from a small glass flask over the top of the bowl of hardened ink suspended above the oil lamp in her portable furnace. Without looking, her half-finished wooden slat scroll undulated across her desk and settled in front of her.

"Master Dughlat only requested we look into the former," she said, "but the latter will no doubt be revealed in due course of your investigations. It would be an agreeable outcome, to be sure. Take some of the burden of corroboration from your uncle's shoulders."

"And my report, Ladyship?" Amota Berac asked.

"By all means, continue," she said.

Amota Berac cleared his throat, and settled back on his heels; his beard quivered when he stuck his chin out, the picture of a man preparing to give a long account of himself. Lady Azadiya flicked the spark wheel set into the frame of her portable furnace; a single spark jumped from the flint to the blackened wick, a cheery orange flame arose. She began swirling her razor-sharp stylus into the softening ink. Ibram rushed out the door.

❦ 3 ❦

There were days Ibram's stomach withstood relay travel, and times when his mind knew full well that he was safe as possible in the aerial gondola, but nothing could convince his body. He spent the time down the living mountain going over what little he remembered of the laws governing arson and its consequences. Best to treat Dughlat's suspicions as truth and disprove them later, than risk being seen as some badosh puppet trying to cover up a crime simply because it might embarrass his employers. After all, he hadn't been ordered to do that, yet.

Besides, it might turn out to be nothing. Setting a fire wasn't an imperial offence unless it destroyed imperial property, thus the disaster at Pillared Circle was strictly a local matter. If the fire had truly been green and had been set by someone's cold-blooded invention, then the most obvious suspect was someone within the sect. Alchemists liked fire, and most especially when it glowed unnaturally. Ibram was always chasing down older Learners and even some Attendants who preferred to create their own fireworks.

Yet, the sect would not profit from such an act. By common Vissilian law, property owners were allowed to do whatever they willed with their own property. Of course, with the size of the calamity that ensued, a deliberate arsonist faced several charges of murder and not a few fines for the destruction of neighboring properties. Captain Talsconis of Her Gracious Majesty's Cohort of Peace might take an interest then, even if only to send a few warders when Ladyship discovered the culprit. Ibram frowned. Perhaps it would be that woman who headed up the Cohort of Vigilance, if it was a fire-related crime.

Master Dughlat politely ignored Ibram's discomfort leftover from the aerial gondola. Ahksell supplied the candied ginger from an inner pocket of his cloak without comment while they were in company with a stranger. Now, Attendant Solari of the Preceptory of Yseult led them all from where the final station of the living mountain's relay system fed into the road of compacted earth down the side of the ever bustling traffic on the paved thoroughfare that made use of the sect's perpetual wheels to take the trade caravans into the west of the empire, and thence to the Orlindan colonies and the Stubai Islands by way of the Red Coast. It had been a simpler life when he'd been nothing but Lady Azadiya's magpie, sending all those shiny bits of information back to the preceptory for her perusal.

Ibram crunched his piece of ginger. He maneuvered himself to Ahksell's right, a step behind his shoulder as was proper, on the opposite side from where Master Dughlat walked. Since they were on official business, Ahksell carried his gar in his right hand. The walking stick was too tall, and thick as another man's wrist, but he carried it like it was nothing, the ease of long practice.

"They seem in a bit more of a hurry than usual," Ibram said, and nodded at a passing wagon when Ahksell looked over.

Ahksell obligingly made sure his gar hit the ground in front of them as they walked, rather than tangling Ibram's feet. It was a pleasant day, the sky was the pale grey-blue that warned of a soft rain rather than a deluge, and the air smelled of Jolek's pine. He eyed the caravans traveling past their little group, and waved at the merchant he'd met in the draughtshop, just as the explosions began.

The man ignored him. Ibram sniffed. That merchant had nothing to complain about, after all. He was astride a nice little bay cob on his way to profit and adventure. Ibram was about to rifle through hurt feelings and ankle-deep soot.

"It's the fire, I should think," Ahksell said, and pulled the little chain clipped to his cloak brooches further away from his neck. "Bad luck comes in tides, after all. If I had a great deal of goods to transport I would get myself out of town as well."

Ibram grunted, but nodded. He kicked a stone further down the road, and glanced sideways. "And what does your employer think, Master Dughlat?" he asked.

Dughlat blew out his breath, and shook his head. "Master Rennab is a Kilk, young master," he said. "They don't believe in luck, only progress and stagnation."

That didn't absolve him of possibly burning his business down, even if that better explained why it wasn't Master Rennab up the living mountain asking for Lady Azadiya's aid. The Kilk folk had a complicated relationship to alchemy, even inside the imperial boundary. They didn't like the way it manipulated things they believed ought to have been left well enough alone, but they couldn't deny alchemy made life easier. An evening courtyard might want clean water to drink, after all, and what better way than a purification tablet (imperial patent pending) dropped into each copper barrel rather than wasting time with all that distillation?

Ibram supposed it came down to stubbornness. Folk who only had a pantheon of two divinities to fall back on surely would have more on their mind, religiously speaking, and didn't enjoy the disruption. Kind of his servant to circumvent his religious requirements in such a neat fashion; Ibram made note of it. Loyal and clever servants might suddenly forget key facts if their employers appeared guilty.

"To be ruined in a fire is very imbalanced then," Ibram said. "I was getting myself a good meal and a cup of something strong when I heard the blasts. Where was he when it began?"

"I don't know exactly," Dughlat said. "He and his husband were inspecting their other business near the Imperial compound."

"What business is that?" Ahksell asked.

"A caffa," Dughlat said.

A good source of income, especially if they were near enough the social-climbing bureaucrats who inhabited the imperial commissioner's compound. Caffa was an expensive treat, after all. Ibram considered the road again, and the pale stone guardhouse they were fast approaching. Its main gate was guarded—if he could really call it so—by a pair of villagers, women in plain kirtles held above their sturdy boots by heavy metal clips. Their job in a normal village would have been to protect Lityen from banditry coming out of the thick forest that crowded the base of the living mountain. As it was, their true duties lay in counting how many caravans exited the village, and closing the high wooden gates at night. Ibram raised his hand to one of the women as they all three passed beneath the gate and into Lityen.

"I haven't been to The High Climber in quite some time," Ibram said, and poked Ahksell in the side. "Have you, Attendant Solari?"

"Me?" Ahksell jumped slightly. "Oh, never, I don't think. Is it—I mean, *was* it...nice?"

"Good music," Ibram said. "They tended to put on comedies when a traveling play came through. Left the dreary stuff for the other courtyards."

"The best music," Master Dughlat said, and lifted his chin slightly. "Players from all over the empire! Recitations, poets, even drummers from the West. Last seven-day, we even featured a wind harp player from Kandrilat itself."

"A wind harp!" Ahksell exclaimed. He twisted quickly to look behind himself. "I never knew that. Ibram, did you know?"

Ibram shrugged. "I'm not one for ethereal moaning, Attendant."

Ahksell rolled his eyes, and turned back around. "How did you fit one inside the common room, Master Dughlat?"

Dughlat laughed, and then coughed into his sleeve. "Took both doors off and rolled the entire contraption in through Pillared Circle. Master Rennab said it was the best advertisement for the courtyard he could have imagined!"

"A real wind harp," Ahksell said, and shook his head. He looked a little dreamily up ahead at the approaching village. "I wish I could have heard that—they're so rare these days after the..." He trailed off, and a look of discomfort soured his smile.

Fire was on everyone's minds, after all; it was only natural. Ibram took a breath and cleared his throat. "Kandrilat has been rebuilding since the disaster," he pointed out. "You might hear one yet, Attendant, once their artisans start producing instruments again."

Ahksell glanced over; he didn't smile, but his shrug restored good humor to the lines of his face. Ibram looked across him towards Master Dughlat. "Do none of the other workers live on the premises?" he asked.

"Master Rennab and the family have their rooms in the upper floor," Dughlat said, "but they were none of them at home. As for the maid, she's usually out in the markets or readying dishes in the kitchen."

"I thought there was no kitchen at The High Climber?" Ibram asked.

Master Dughlat paused, and then shook his head. "Your pardon," he said. "I should say, there is no kitchen for the courtyard's patrons. The family lives above, and has a small portable kitchen for their personal use."

"But no one was using it on the day of the fire," Ibram said.

Dughlat shrugged. "It's a market day. The maid had gone with Master Finar to the Scribes' Bureau."

"Master Finar is Master Rennab's husband?" Ahksell asked.

"Yes."

"Is this the usual market day?" Ibram asked.

Dughlat nodded. "They stagger working between their two businesses."

"Are there any others on the premises?" Ibram asked.

Dughlat shook his head. "Just a pair of traveling players, in exchange for their reciting, you understand."

"Are they still about the place?"

Dughlat shook his head. "They left on the next caravan," he said. "Travelers never stay in one place if there's no coin to be had."

So it had been Dughlat and his friend Neilos alone at the time of the fire, which could mean nothing, truly. Ibram considered the sky for a moment, long enough for a fellow pedestrian to tread on his foot and send him skipping into Ahksell's side. Ahksell righted him without pausing, and Ibram rolled his eyes. No one ever dared step on Ahksell's toes, after all.

"But you think it deliberate, Master Dughlat?" Ibram asked. He chose his words carefully, mindful of the public arena. Folk cleared space for alchemists in their midst, but that attention came with eyes and ears that picked up all sorts of gossip.

"If it is not," Dughlat replied, and nodded politely to a woman passing by. "Then it is best to know now."

"Would your friend Neilos agree?"

"I think so," Dughlat said, with a touch of reserve. "We spoke about the fire. We agreed to wait and speak to Master Rennab first, but I had a change of heart, and went up the living mountain without him."

The morning crowds were so sparse that the next street past the sundries warehouse behind Masons Square was clear enough that the three of them could walk abreast. A man on a ladder with a bucket over one arm was carefully setting freshly enchanted fire suppression tiles into fresh mortar, both glimmering with icy blue indicolite dust. He wasn't being very careful, the strength of those tiles were greatly lessened by the least scratch. Ibram blinked. There was a thought.

"Do you know what part of the building caught fire first?" he asked.

Green fire didn't just happen, nor was it natural to find it at the back of an evening courtyard. It had to have had a cause. Ibram had paid attention in his classes at the Bedris school when it had suited him, and the types of fire that could be nurtured through alchemy was always a popular lesson. If someone had deliberately devised the fire, then they would have had to get their hands on—at the very least—chalcan vitriol from the east. It was a common import along the major trade routes, able to kill off pests and prevent moldering in the wetter regions of the empire. Some folk even thought it made a fine tonic for upset stomach.

Dughlat's head jerked back. "Caught first?" he asked.

Ibram held fond memories of helping to work the bellows in Father's foundry growing up. He was well aware that fires might crawl wherever they wished if not carefully monitored. "Yes, do you remember seeing the direction the fire flowed out of?" he asked.

"No, I do not. I...surely, it must have been the side nearest the bakery-mill?" Dughlat asked.

Ibram nodded. "Indeed so," he said. "Is that where the building had most of its fire suppression system?"

He steered them down a little alleyway filled on either side with window stalls. It would be better to approach the site of the disaster through a side entrance, rather than one of the main entrances to Pillared Circle, just to avoid prying eyes. There were always folk with nothing better to do than gape at destruction. Ladyship had deployed many of her agents to keep looters out, and Captain Talsconis had even graced them with a patrol of his warders, but that didn't mean a keen eye couldn't spot Ibram investigating a probable crime. And suspicion of a crime involving fire would go very badly for whatever possible suspects the malice of public opinion created.

"I don't know about that," Dughlat said. "I only repair the chairs and sweep the floors."

Ibram glanced Ahksell's way, and kept walking. A woman popped her head out of a window as they passed through, holding out a half-laden tray of flatbreads folded neatly around chunks of glass apple and soft yellow cheese. A little cup full of eating prongs sat half-full on her window sill. Ibram shook his head, and she ducked out of sight with a scowl. Folk who lived so far inside the village most often worked out of their home. If they were lucky enough to have space for a window rather than all sides sharing a wall with their neighbor, then they might do a little business selling a hungry passer-by a bowl of soup or a bag of snacks. Ibram had followed Ahksell and Katka down a million such alleys, nibbling a stuffed roll while they had spent all their faunts buying stickums to set alight or braided grass toys to play with until they disintegrated. Over each window was affixed a fire suppression tile—though some glimmered more brightly than others.

He frowned. Fire was the terror of every civilized community, as quick to spread as pestilence and as deadly as a siege in winter. The High Climber should have had a healthy mosaic of enchanted tiles— moreso even since they were neighbors with the bakery-mill. At the turn of the street, he led the group down past the little row of imperial buildings designated for worship of the Vissilian deities who did not have other accommodation within their corner of Vanima province. Ibram ducked his head as he passed by; each well-timbered, freshly painted honey-comb building—which shared an enormous inner garden courtyard for its assorted clergy—was guarded by a warden, and quite a few had crowds of folk streaming in and out their doors. No doubt those clergy were all praying for safety from fire. Ibram sniffed, and rubbed the back of his head. Well, if they prayed hard enough— and all about the same thing—it might generate enough energy to reach the heavens.

☙❧

The High Climber was even more of a shambles than it had been in Ibram's memory. Bereft of smoke and flame, he could tell that while the front of the building had largely survived, the back half of the tiled roof had collapsed. He seriously doubted that much inside was left to sift through. Ibram frowned up at the soot scrawled up the evening courtyard's walls, and looked at Ahksell from the corner of his eye.

"Do you think it will hold long enough for us to find anything?" Ibram murmured.

Ahksell took a deep breath. "Well, Master Dughlat," he said, rather than responding to an incredibly fair question on Ibram's part, "why don't you show us the inside?"

Dughlat swallowed heavily, but bowed shortly, and stepped over the broken remains of the doors. He led the way inside, and Ahksell followed him. Ibram paused a moment to make note of the wooden lattice frame hanging by one corner from the door guard's window. He touched the wall of the building, the wood was cool to the touch. He squinted up at the large writhing snake painted above the entrance. The fire had caused the red and yellow pigment to bubble and flake away.

"What is it you say, Ladyship?" he muttered to himself. "See what cannot be seen."

He frowned. It was all well and good for Lady Azadiya; the Preceptory of Yseult sought the refinement and perfection of the physical body, the better to perceive the shape of reality. Ladyship could see the anima of a body itself—probably even the soul—and so too could Ahksell. Ibram, on the other foot, had to make do and mend with his own purely unremarkable eyes. He stepped back again, and made a careful study of the remaining front of the building. Apart from the painted snake, there were two empty brackets for torches, presumably placed and lit in the evening. The rest of the front was unremarkable, even the gargoyles that drained water from the roof were simply crude serpents. No extra expense spared there and... Ibram could see small green enameled tiles built into the siding in a long row just above the doors, but they didn't resemble any enchanted tiles he'd ever seen. For all he knew they might be purely for decoration. Common enough to have such little things adorning a wall or six, with some little alchemical cantrip attached to make the neighbors talk amongst themselves. He craned his neck to check beneath what was left of the overhanging tile roof. In point of fact, he saw no fire suppression tiles at all, not even broken ones.

It could simply be that Master Rennab saved money by placing his tiles inside, rather than out, and prayed his neighbors bought outside tiles he could profit from as well. Ibram brushed ashes from his hand, and looked behind himself. A group of younger sect agents milled about twenty or so feet from the most damaged buildings, while the warders had taken up position near the businesses that had suffered the effects of the fire but were not destroyed. A small cadre of villagers with buckets stood at the ready by the municipal fountain, just in case the charcoal timbers still contained a hidden ember.

The crowd of onlookers had thinned slightly; the day was moving on after all, and only youngsters didn't have enough work to keep busy. He thought he saw three young mistresses from the Vo Kaln family in the back, easily distinguished by their light hair and tendency for matching outfits. Some folk said it in house colors and others followed the Southern fashion and proclaimed their allegiance in patches. The line of Warder Claes' back was taut with exasperation as she headed in their direction. A tall man with dark hair stood near the little group of mistresses and maids in the back of the crowd, probably another family servant, surveying the damage with narrowed eyes.

Ibram turned back around, and frowned at the broken bits of doors on the ground. Ahksell had torn them straight off their hinges, probably to avoid hurting anyone inside. It was impressive; Ibram would have to be more careful the next time he asked for a hand up.

Well, there wasn't much for it. Ibram sighed as he drew his sica. The door threshold was over his head, but not enough to make the job impossible. If he couldn't recognize the tiles above the door, then someone up the living mountain no doubt could tell him about them. He went up on to his toes, and jabbed the point of his knife up above the doorway and beneath the nearest little green tile. The fire had turned the mortar into a crumbly mess. He wiggled his knifepoint up and under the tile; it popped off the wall in a puff of dust. Ibram fell back, sneezing, and belatedly closed his eyes. He sputtered, and felt the tile bounce off his chest. He sheathed his sica, and bent down to swipe the damnable thing up.

"Hey! You! Stop that at once!" a man shouted behind him. "What are you doing to my building?"

Maybe Amita Sarrha was wrong; Ibram did spend too much time lost in thought. Ibram spun around, and saw a man of medium height, well-dressed in long blue robes in the southern style, running down the stairs of the shay shop across from the fountain in the middle of Pillared Circle. His fine brown hair was cut short and kept in place by a thin band around his head in such a way that it covered his ears. Kilks kept their ears hidden for some reason. Ibram had never asked why; it seemed rude.

He stepped carefully away from the doorway, but remained in front of it. Ahksell was inside with Master Dughlat after all, and it would be better if he had the opportunity to observe the site of the green fire unobstructed by The High Climber's owner. Ibram resigned himself to making pointed, but subtle conversation.

A few of the other sect agents glanced over at the noise, and then to Ibram. He waved them off, and they went back to ignoring him. Ibram wiped his face with his sleeve once more for good measure, and slipped the loose tile up his sleeve into his hidden leather wallet. He usually stuck a silver picaio up there for emergencies, but it was useful for other things, too.

The man stalked up to him, and Ibram bowed shortly. "Am I making myself known to Master Rennab or Master Finar?" he asked.

The man blinked, caught off-guard. "...I am Master Rennab," he said finally.

"Ibram Ucalegon," Ibram announced with a polite smile. "Agent of the Sect of Seven Fires."

"What is a sect agent doing defacing my building?" Rennab demanded. He waved his hands in the air. "I've already lost the back half, must you demolish the front?"

"My apologies," Ibram said. "I was merely testing the strength of the grout. My family is commissioning the installation of new suppression tiles above my father's workshop, and I wished to see if the craftsman knew his trade."

"Your family?" Rennab paused in thought. "Ucalegon...Kalmar married a Ucalegon, didn't he? The one they apprenticed little Inzhu to...makes jewelry?"

"The very same," Ibram said.

Master Rennab frowned, which was no doubt a formidable expression in normal times. Now, he stood like a man who'd simply outlasted his own energy and knew to recline was to never get back up again. His clothes were streaked in soot at the bottom hem; he'd been walking through his ruin. The connection to Ibram's father seemed to put him a little at his ease. It was no wonder Master Rennab knew one of Father's apprentices—or more likely, her parents; not many of the Kilk folk lived within the imperial boundary, though a fair few made their fortunes outside of it.

"I did," Rennab snapped. He flung his arm out towards his building. "It was perfectly safe under the awning! And don't go taking other people's tiles! Might be useful still."

"Oh, I only touched the grout," Ibram said. He pointed. "Look, it's all gone crumbly, must have been aging in the weather. I'd say it popped off with little help from the blaze, to be sure."

Master Rennab peered above his own doorway, and then shook his head in disgust. He stared around the ground as if the paving stones would raise up the missing tile all by themselves. Ibram let his left arm hang loosely at his side, the better not to draw attention to it.

"Then what did you pick up as I approached?" Rennab asked.

Ibram shook his head. "I just brushed some dirt off my boots," he said. "Ruins the waterproofing, you know, if you let the leather get too dirty. What are your tiles supposed to do? Never seen ones like that before."

Rennab frowned, but exhaustion kept his attention in nicely portioned chunks. "They provide extra light," he said. "Or, at least, they're supposed to."

"Like glowbulbs," Ibram said, even though the entire empire knew adhesive ruined the luminescent sand somehow.

"So my husband assured me," Rennab said, and shook his head. "He bought them from his brother to balance his books with his employer."

Ibram made a noise of agreement. "Recently?"

If that were fact, Ahksell would be able to tell when he showed him the tile. If Master Finar was merely a kind man cajoled by his brother into buying pretty tiles, then all to the good. If Finar had accidentally purchased something more sinister...well, Ibram'd let them both know when he returned the tile. Ibram was only borrowing, after all.

"No," came the curt answer from Master Rennab, who then studied Ibram for a moment. "Surplus stock from an older journey."

"Would you say the grout crumbled for your fire suppression tiles as well, then?" Ibram asked, and he casually let his eyes drift to the extant parts of The High Climber's front entrance.

"I placed those myself with brother-in-law's help," Master Rennab said. His voice bobbed awkwardly; he coughed and then cleared his throat. "They were quite ugly, so I had them placed in the alley directly opposite the bakery-mill. He follows the merchant caravans up through Delbrite and makes a stop for us around this time."

"Kind of him," Ibram said. "How many rows?"

"Two," Rennab said, "just as the inspectors suggest."

Ibram nodded. "Is your brother-in-law around to help you in your time of struggle?"

"No," Master Rennab said shortly. Perhaps they didn't get along. "He came last year, before the big rains."

"A pity, to be sure," Ibram said. "Where did he get his tiles, do you think? The sect makes a fair few kinds, it seems odd to import them."

Master Rennab shrugged, and couldn't stop the yawn which yanked his mouth open wide; he hid his lower face behind his palm. The man did look tired. He'd probably been salvaging what he could from his wreck since daybreak.

"He gave me a fair price for the labor," Rennab said, "and picked up new tiles from the Preceptory of Afsoun on his way out of Lityen. Think he might have a seller's contract with your people—or his company, rather."

Ibram considered the thought, and nodded politely. Old tiles again, perhaps? Unloaded on an unwary family member? Perhaps they didn't get along.

"Since you had a question for me, I have one in recompense," Rennab said.

"A very balanced approach," Ibram said.

"Indeed so. What are you doing in front of my evening courtyard?" Rennab asked. "And don't say it's merely to test my grout. A curiosity I will grant you, but no further courtesy."

Ibram shrugged. "I'm assigned to Mentor Hobon of the Preceptory of Yseult. I go where I am told, and then I see what happens."

"Lady Azadiya?" Rennab seemed taken aback, and then frowned. "I didn't send for her, nor would I ask."

As though the owner of an evening courtyard could send for Ladyship and not draw back a stump where his crooked finger had been. Ibram nodded briskly.

"No fear on that score, Master Rennab," Ibram said. "I'm down here to gain a bit more information about the fire and the repairs necessary, that's most of it."

"Our local fire alliance is already making a study," Rennab said, "and will be ready to present our findings—"

"Ibram, what could possibly be taking you so long out here?" Ahksell's voice broke Master Rennab's building diatribe in half, and left the man gaping as Ahksell emerged from the ruined entrance. Ibram could understand the impulse. Ahksell towered over most folk, but in enclosed spaces and dressed in full uniform, he became especially inescapable.

Ibram leaned back on his heels and crossed his arms over his chest. "Merely speaking with the esteemed proprietor."

Rennab bowed stiffly, but correctly, and was waved back up again. Ahksell's sympathetic face birthed a corresponding wrinkle between Rennab's eyebrows. People simply didn't know how to react in the face of that great bulwark of sincerity; Ibram shook his head, and glanced behind Ahksell into the evening courtyard. Master Dughlat must not have wanted to come outside and greet his employer. Ahksell's gar struck Ibram's left foot lightly, and Ibram moved out of the way. Ahksell held his gar out diagonally so as not to damage the remaining roof, to be sure, but he was always careless of other people's ankles.

"Master Rennab," Ahksell said. "May I pass Mentor Hobon's condolences on the loss of your evening courtyard to you and your family? And mine as well. Even witnessing the fire myself, I had no idea of the size of the destruction! And your family apartments, too. The loss must be keenly felt."

"I...yes," Rennab said. "Thank you, Attendant..."

He trailed off and a soft screen of panic drew over his eyes. Ibram coughed lightly. "May I make Master Rennab known to you, Attendant?"

"Oh, my apologies," Ahksell said. "I rush in where the Runner fears to tread sometimes."

"No, no, it's fine. It's no matter at all," Master Rennab said, and wiped both of his hands down either side of his robe.

"Be known to Attendant Ahksell Solari, Master Rennab," Ibram said.

"I've just been inside with your dayworker," Ahksell said. "The damage is terrible. Was anything able to be recovered?"

"A few personal items," Rennab said, "were locked up in a preservation box, so that the damage was very minimal."

"Really?" Ibram asked. "What all was saved?"

Rennab's lips pressed together; he readjusted the band over his forehead. "My marriage contract, the deeds for our properties... licenses and such."

"That's good," Ahksell said. "That the important documents were untouched."

"I wouldn't say untouched, Attendant," Rennab said, "the fire did breach our apartments, but the damage to the preservation box was minor by comparison. The documents can still be read, even if they are singed, but all I own is what I have on my back now."

Unfortunately, it was a mark—a small mark, but present nonetheless—in The High Climber's favor. In Ibram's recollection, very few malicious criminals allowed their own important belongings to be destroyed. That he and his family had neither clothes nor belongings left was a good sign, but it would have been better for Rennab's guilt or innocence if he'd only had the copies of deeds and letters of permission placed in the Bureau of Records to rely upon.

Rennab spread his arms out in a helpless gesture, and Ahksell sighed and shook his head. "It's truly awful," he said. "Where are you staying? Surely, some relatives might take you in?"

"My husband's business has a small back room," Master Rennab said. "We are sleeping there while the maid moves into the kitchen."

"Good, good," Ahksell said. "I am very glad to hear that."

"Are you here to lead Mentor Hobon's information hunt?" Rennab asked. "Your agent here told me she wants her own reporting."

Ahksell paused; his eyes widened slightly. Ibram nodded, and took a step further back from the pair. He looked up and down Pillared Circle. A large group of prosperous looking folk were flooding out from The Raised Foot on the opposite side, some still locked in conversation, while others appeared deeply immersed in their own thoughts.

"Now, would a responsible subject of the empire such as Lady Azadiya shirk her duties?" Ibram said, still watching what must have been the rest of the local fire alliance dispersing. Interesting that Master Rennab had left early. "Especially in her official capacity as Fourth Mentor. The affairs of Lityen fall under her purview, don't you agree, Attendant Solari?"

"I would, Master Ucalegon," Ahksell said.

Master Rennab turned red-faced. "I never said they did not! It would be a terrible imbalance of power for the sect to neglect its dependent villages."

"It would be indeed," Ahksell said. "Which is why we are here to help. By combining both our findings, we will be able to present the Imperial Commissioner with a clear and unbiased picture of the tragedy as it stands, and rebuild quickly."

"Yes, the damage was extensive," Rennab said, as his body slowly untensed.

"And four people perished," Ibram said. "Did you know them, Master Rennab?"

Master Rennab swallowed heavily, and undid all that good work of relaxing his muscles by clenching his fists. "I knew the Ozols—the baker and his wife, of course. We were neighbors. Their son used to run errands around here. It's terrible, simply terrible."

An interesting fact. Ibram hoped young Master Ozol made a swift journey back home. He had a few questions forming in the back of his mind already.

"What about the other two unfortunates?" Ibram asked. "I'm not certain...players, weren't they?"

"They worked in the evening courtyard next door," Master Rennab said. "Dancers, I believe."

"A sad end," Ibram sighed.

"Yes," Rennab said. "I wanted them for myself, of course, but Dubidat got to them before we could come to terms."

"What sort of dancers were they?" Ahksell asked.

"Candle dancers from the principality of Tekdana," Rennab said. He opened his mouth, paused, and then shook his head. "I fear we will find they caused the fire. The Isconian's Hand was completely destroyed, you know. Dubidat is so overwrought she hasn't been able to make a full accounting of the damage to the fire alliance council."

Ibram tilted his head. The Isconian's Hand, and not the bakery-mill. It was an interesting diversion.

"Tekdana is sixty-six days away by carrack, and then an overland journey of several months," Ibram said. "Surely they had time to practice."

Rennab smiled tightly. "Never the less."

"I think we might stop in to the next building now," Ibram said. He turned and inclined himself in Ahksell's direction. "If the Attendant has no objections?"

"Hmm? Oh!" Ahksell knocked the end of his gar into the cobblestones. "No, not at all. The Isconian's Hand?"

"The very same," Ibram said, and straightened his back.

"I'll wish you luck with your fact gathering, then," Master Rennab said. "Good day, Attendant Solari."

He bowed shortly, and just as quickly disappeared past the remains of his own front door. Ibram tugged on his hair at the nape of his neck and let the man go. There wasn't anything really behind the door anymore, but Ibram appreciated the symbolism of Rennab's exit.

Ahksell sidled away from the ruined entrance. "What's the point—"

Ibram held his finger diagonally across his mouth, and Ahksell ceased speaking. He raised his eyebrows instead, and shook his head, lifting his arms. His gar knocked into the soffit; a roof tile crashed to the ground and shattered.

Ibram rolled his eyes, and jerked his head towards the center of the circle. They stepped out from under the porch together. Ibram saw motion from the corner of his eye; the noise had drawn the attention of the onlookers and Ahksell's uniform of green gambeson and grey trousers had done the rest. The little Vo Kaln girls had fled the area, but the dark-haired man Ibram had thought was with them remained.

"How many small noble houses might own one of these evening courtyards, do you know?" Ibram asked, absently trailing his gaze along the straggling crowd. The younger agents were pushing an excited looking boy of thirteen or so back from a stacked pile of charred wooden beams. His mother looked incredibly unhappy.

"Most of them, I should think," Ahksell said, once they were further away from The High Climber.

"Dughlat said Master Rennab owns his outright," Ibram mused, "but there is nothing to say The Isconian's Hand is not behind on its rent."

"But why would a landlord be so foolish? There's a lot of money in an evening courtyard, isn't there?" Ahksell asked.

"More than in a bakery-mill," Ibram said. "Let's take a peek inside The Isconian's Hand, the fire alliance looks like they're nominating someone to come and question our intentions."

"I'm sure we'll do the decent thing," Ahksell said.

Ibram chuckled. "Look at you, three cups of shay this morning?"

They turned to the building on the left, the smaller evening court-yard closest to the second exit off of Pillared Circle. This one shared a wall with The High Climber and, like that establishment, did not share a wall with the bakery-mill behind it.

"And a bowl of quash you might drown in," Ahksell said. "All that focus and exchange eats up a lot of energy."

"I hope Master Dughlat expressed his appreciation for your hard work," Ibram said.

"He did," Ahksell said, as they walked through the open doors of the building next door. "Not that it was necessary."

Ibram shrugged. "I'd say it was, but it's only my thought that if you save someone's life they should say thank you, to be sure." Ahksell poked him in the back; Ibram jumped and turned around. He reached behind himself and rubbed the sore spot. "Hey now!"

"You might have saved them just as quickly as I had," Ahksell said. "You'd almost got the window frame off by the time I'd got there."

"Of course I would have," Ibram said. "Neither of us are foolish enough to shame the sect and fail, are we?"

Ahksell laughed quietly and shook his head. Ibram grinned, and then sighed as he looked about himself. What was left of the place— the shared wall, the front of the evening courtyard and parts of the floor—smelled rank with smoke, the wood liberally doused in resinous charred soot. The crumpled remains of the tables and chairs lay in disarray, and the second story was collapsed. The entire place was open to the air, completely visible from the blast area of the bakery-mill. Ibram nudged aside half of one of the thick mudbricks which had previously formed the bakery-mill's foundations. When it had blown, the force of the explosion must have crushed anything in its path.

"I've never seen anything like this," Ahksell said quietly. He wrapped both hands around his gar, and leaned upon the wooden staff as he gazed up to the visible grey sky above.

"No, nor I," Ibram said as he surveyed the wreckage. "Saw a barn fire once."

"Really?" Ahksell asked. "When?"

"Storm out on the Salt Plateau," Ibram said. He began nudging debris aside with his right foot, looking for anything which might catch his eye. A body could learn a lot from rubble. "You can imagine how dry it gets. It was a waystation, really, one of those abandoned huts that the Runner's marshals set up for travelers. Only this one was an old barn, big enough for our caravan. Lightning storm took it right out. I've never seen anything like it."

"You weren't inside it?" Ahksell exclaimed.

"Just about to go in," Ibram said, and carefully kicked a broken table leg out of his way. He was slowly making his way to the wall they shared with The High Climber.

Ahksell followed him. "You never told me that."

Ibram shrugged. He'd often dreamed of it, that flash of light so fast it was a lingering afterimage before Ibram recognized what he'd seen, the shuddering thunder that followed it, and then the roof catching fire as if it were the softest feathered tinder. The hushed panicked stillness before the caravan burst into frenzied action. The fisherfolk must have felt the same dismayed shock when the Mad King Honon had sent his alchemists to desiccate Subi Lake and turn them all into salt farmers instead.

"We came out all right," Ibram said, "to be sure. There wasn't much need to dwell."

He pointed to the wall, which ended rather more shortly than connected walls in Lityen typically did. Ahksell stepped up beside him, and leaned his gar on it. The beams wavered, but held.

"Sturdier than I thought," Ibram muttered. He pointed to his ear, and then to the wall again, and then back to his ear.

Ahksell blinked at him, and then realization rushed in. He nodded quickly. "I believe they could hear us," he said quietly, "but if we're quiet it shouldn't matter."

"Why can't you...make their ears forget us, or something?" Ibram asked, and kept his voice low. At his feet, the floor was littered with debris, but nothing looked like something that might start a fire.

There were no wire frames left over from a used stickum, nor any kind of papers to hold the fuel in place. Though, to be sure, paper would have burnt up all together; Ibram couldn't exactly rule it out.

"That is not in the least how ears function, much less alchemy," Ahksell sniffed. "Besides, you remember last winter? During the Feast of Frangi and the winter trials when Tolya cracked her button shield and it brought forth that thing from the local abyss?"

"I'd never broken down a door with an ax before," Ibram said. "Instructional *and* amusing."

There were little hooks screwed into the wall, but he had no idea what their placement meant. He ran his hands along the wooden wall, it was still damp from the water bucket line. He bent his head forward and to the side, but he couldn't hear anyone moving in the next building.

"What I mean is," Ahksell said, "the more simple something looks to do, the more complicated it will turn out to be. So it is with hearing."

"So what did Dughlat show you?" Ibram asked, returning to the matter at hand. "Was it this wall?"

Ahksell ran his hand over the top of his head. "No, actually, the wall where he saw the green flames was completely destroyed."

Ibram blew out his breath in a rush, and crossed his arms over his chest. "Of course it would be."

"Even though I know you believe he might have been lying," Ahksell said.

"Do *you* think he was lying?"

"I don't," Ahksell said. "What does he get if he declares an alchemist is out to get Master Rennab?"

"Notoriety?"

"How so?"

"He proffers information, we might find nothing, and…" Ibram shrugged. "Perhaps he lives his life dining out on the night he saw a drunk alchemist set fire to his own robes and call forth a calamity, and we did nothing about it?"

"That is deeply suspicious and unworthy of you," Ahksell said. "Master Dughlat was right to tell us what he saw!"

Ibram shrugged again. "I never said he wasn't," he said. "I am merely puzzling my way through."

Ahksell tsked and looked away, and then returned his attention to Ibram by staring at him from the corner of his eye. "Worst thought?"

"When I have any new ones, I shall let you know."

Ahksell picked up his gar again, and sighed. "Come on, I will show you the place."

Ibram nodded, and together they walked down to what had been the back of the evening courtyard. Ahksell's gar made hollow thocking noises against the floor as he went forwards. Ibram looked to his left, where the round stage in the middle of the room still stood a step up from the main floor, too charred to walk upon. The two candle dancers would have been housed on the second level, not near the owner's room, of course, but perhaps towards the back above the kitchen. The Isconian's Hand should have had one, but there had been cookshops along the opposite side of this evening courtyard. Perhaps they hadn't wanted to take the risk and brought the food in from the outside.

"Did you think there was a kitchen?" he asked. "If Mistress Dubidat lived there, there must be something, to be sure."

"I don't know," Ahksell said. "I've never been here before."

"Something to look into," Ibram said, and then quickly looked over to the far side of the room before glancing towards Ahksell. "I don't suppose you'd bestir yourself to dowse the flooring with that inverted pendant of yours."

Ahksell sighed, already reaching into his belt pouch. "It's my *introrse* pendant, and I am not looking for water."

"No, but something that might start a fire would help."

Ahksell slid the copper ring over his middle finger and let the arrowhead pendant dangle on its length of twisted wires. He took a deep breath and closed his eyes to center himself. Ibram took the opportunity to walk to the far end of the room, where the walls looked as if a demon had been called up from the local Abyss and sunk its snaggled jaws around the architecture as a fiber-heavy snack. There was a little path carved out of the ruins around him when Amota Berac's work party had made their way inside, and discovered the bodies of the two candle dancers lying together on the floor.

"I don't suppose you would tell me if your friends up high on the living mountain were working on anything green and explosive?" Ibram asked. "Maybe something...very portable?"

Lots of Attendants used their free time to explore the delights of Lityen's evening courtyards. If someone, perhaps out of Afsoun, had lost a pet project and was now too embarrassed to lay out a reward for its return... Well, they'd take it to Lady Azadiya and see what might be done.

Ahksell frowned. "You know very well I couldn't tell you if they had," he said. "No one would tell me anything; it's a completely different field of study!"

"But it is your secondary specialty," Ibram pointed out.

Ibram wagged his head from left to right and shrugged one shoulder. Ahksell sighed. Ibram raised his eyebrows.

"Might gossip fall as rain does," Ibram quoted. "And grow there the seed of discontent—"

"Ugh, no poetry—no poetry, Ibram, you promised!"

Ibram obligingly shut his mouth. Ahksell rolled his eyes.

"No," Ahksell said finally. "When last I visited Afsoun for classes, there was nothing in the atmosphere to suggest a panic, nor did anyone mention they had lost something."

"Thank you," Ibram said. "That is very helpful."

Ahksell huffed and returned to his introrse pendant. Ibram looked down at the upturned table where the two candle dancers had taken refuge when the smoke had gotten too thick. He sniffed the air, but cautiously, and checked behind him to make sure Ahksell remained preoccupied. No need for everyone to have to search this section, to be sure. He crouched down, adjusting his sica to one side, and ran his hand along the floorboards. What had been picked up for burial once the building was cool enough to enter had left its traces, but Ibram was used to that. Little beads of charred silk turned to gritty black powder under his fingers; he shuddered. Whatever those two had worshipped in Tekdana, he hoped They'd taken hold of their souls quickly. Death by fire was unkind.

"Did you meet the famous Neilos?" Ibram called over his shoulder.

"What?" Ahksell asked distractedly. "Oh, no, I didn't."

"Not sorting the leftover furniture then."

Ibram frowned down at the floor, and cleaned his hands off on his trouser legs. When they'd first spoken during the clean-up, Amota Berac hadn't said anything about candles or torches, and most evening courtyards in this part of Lityen didn't have the money for glowbulbs. The fire had burned hot enough and long enough that any wax candle or rush would have been totally eaten by the flames. Ibram looked up to the cloudy sky. He'd been on crowd control then, keeping folk out of the way of the bucket lines and the alchemists' fire-suppressing noise maker.

If as Master Rennab had suggested, the candle dancers had been at fault through negligence, then by all rights the fire would have begun on stage. Ibram tsked and stood up; he put his hands on his shoulders and stretched out his back. Admittedly—and he could admit this to himself—Ibram knew less about fire than he did about evening courtyards. Yet, if the bodies of the two dancers had been found here, then why would the fire spread left towards The High Climber and not the cookshops built up along to the right? He turned around on his heels, and then leaned forward on the balls of his feet.

Ibram had woken up in the alcoves of enough evening courtyards to know their players—traveling or in-house—always practiced where they were to perform. He walked to the middle stage and crouched down again. There they were, fire suppression tiles all in a row. He reached out with his right hand and brushed soot from the nearest tile. It tingled beneath his fingertips, mostly dormant from hard use. If this was their strength after such a conflagration, no wonder the stage had survived.

"I can't find anything," Ahksell announced. "The fire suppression tiles here are mostly intact, but absolutely expended. And they don't seem to have been tampered with."

Ibram raised his head and then stood up. "What about an over-turned lantern?" he asked. "Smashed oil pot?"

Ahksell snapped his pendant back up into his palm, and shook his head. "Nothing out of the ordinary," he said. "About those candle dancers, you don't think..."

"I think these evening courtyards share a wall and a professional rivalry, that's what I think," Ibram said. "You could have a dozen candle dancers and it wouldn't create a flame like that." He pointed at the stage. "And if it were a practice gone wrong, then they would have been on stage where the fire suppression tiles are laid, not out amongst the customers."

Ahksell nodded slowly. "They would have had to be dead beforehand, anyway. Wouldn't they? Otherwise, why wouldn't they have doused the flames themselves, or run out and raised the hue and cry?"

"And, if they were on stage, then why leave the protection of the tiles?" Ibram asked.

Ahksell looked down to his feet; he shook his head. "The same thing Shokan and Neilos were doing, I would suppose. Trying to escape."

"And getting overwhelmed by the smoke." Ibram sighed, and rubbed the back of his neck. "I'll make sure to ask Doctor Berot if the fire killed them both, never fear."

"Come on," Ahksell said on a great inhalation of breath. "We should be looking all over."

They reached the back of the building, and stood staring across the little alleyway where the bakery-mill had once stood apart from its neighbors. By imperial law and sect enforcement, the alleys surrounding bakery-mills were to be kept clear at all times. The windows required for venting larger bakery-mills would have sent airborne flour directly into the alleys and, hopefully, away from the fires of the other buildings.

Ibram had visited most of the bakery-mills in Lityen, running errands for Ama and Kholdo as a child. Typically, they placed their tiles inside along the walls of the mill portion of the building. The evening courtyards would have placed theirs on the outside, to repel flames, while the bakery-mill's tiles worked to contain any fire therein. The thick stone partitions of the building should again have protected the front ovens from the dangers of fire in the back. Their owners were given better than average prices for fire suppression tiles, and inspections were performed regularly. The results of a bakery-mill with all its loose flour in the air set alight by careless folk were, well, the results were plain to see now.

"Here is what I don't understand," Ahksell said quietly as he stared out ahead of them. "If this fire was begun as a calculated act, as green fire might suggest, then how did it spread and why did it not spread as green fire? Or, rather, why did it only appear in that one corner. A powder of chalcan vitriol would explode through the air, just as the flour did. And why start a blaze with something that recognizable?"

Ibram shook his head. "That might have to do with the timing," he said. "If...say the arsonist chose the time of day for when most folk wouldn't be present?"

"I can see fire suppression tiles beyond this wreckage," Ahksell said instead of answering. "Or what's left of them. It must have been a doubled row."

"Yes, but are those enough for two buildings? Three, if you count the bakery-mill?"

It was still the mostly likely culprit. He'd be incredibly surprised if the surviving owner didn't wind up bankrupting himself paying both fire alliances for their repairs, either by contract or in the Courts Civil. Not to mention the murder charges. Ibram whistled low as he surveyed the cracked and burnt mudbrick foundation, the top layer utterly exploded, and the absolute destruction of the bakery-mill itself. He could see all the way back through to the next street. It looked as though those buildings had been sufficiently protected, though a few of the carpenters were already surveying the damages.

Ibram frowned. A small crowd of boys were picking their way through destruction, tossing charred wood into buckets. As he watched, he realized one of them was vaguely familiar. He focused on the boy's face. Pudgy cheeks, pointy chin, mop of unruly black hair... That was an apprentice from the stall Ama liked to frequent down Bubble Alley, one of the ones that made scented soaps.

"Do you think they were tampered with?" Ahksell asked, and Ibram shook his head, attention reclaimed. "The tiles, I mean."

"It would be easy to do," Ibram said, "even by accident."

The alley was choked by debris so thickly stacked it came to Ibram's knees. He cleared this throat, and then looked left and then right. He picked up a sturdy looking hunk of wood; it was lighter for its half-burning, but still serviceable, and tossed it in the scavengers' general direction.

"Away from there!" he yelled, and the boys hooted and scattered. "I'll have to get another agent to look over this end of the disaster."

"The warders were here when the work crews removed the Ozols' bodies," Ahksell said. "Master Comoros told me."

"I'll let Amota Berac know about this too," Ibram said. "There might yet be something recoverable for the Ozols' son."

He frowned at the mess. The only way forward was often through, but if there was a spot with space enough for Ibram to so much as place his littlest toe on the ground safely, he couldn't see it. They'd never find anything in this mess.

"You might be able to break their interior resonance with a scratch," Ahksell mused, "but the sheer amount of them required for a bakery-mill would seem to bely any attempt. I mean, they'd notice if some stranger took a ladder into their back alley, would they not?"

"We could only hope," Ibram said. Though, he'd done a fair bit of snooping simply by pretending to be allowed into places where he surely had not asked permission to enter. Folk ignored a confident walk where they might challenge a stranger creeping into a dark corner.

Ahksell leaned out, gesturing to his right, and Ibram followed suit. The back wall of The High Climber was missing, it seemed like parts of it had mixed with the bakery-mill to fill the alley. The entire place was a shell, the upper floor having crashed down to earth by the far left side. He saw neither Master Dughlat nor Master Rennab. They might have left to report additional loss of property to the fire alliance.

Across the way, Ibram observed the damage done to Builders Row, on the other side of Pillared Circle. There, at least, it appeared that the fire suppression tiles had done their duty. The buildings to either side of the destroyed bakery-mill were heavily impacted but intact. Past the plot of land where the bakery-mill had stood, Ibram noted the work groups already in place to repair the damaged roofs and porches of the surrounding buildings. If he squinted he could see Amota Tono speaking with a man in rough workman's clothes, who waved his hand at the sky, and then used his entire body to mime a large explosion. He'd mention the boys scavenging to him.

A fire with two explosions to mark its inception. Ibram pursed his lips in thought. He suspected the bakery-mill, still, but no one but Dughlat had spoken of a different colored fire. If one could have been seen from the opposite side of the bakery-mill, looking inwards from Builders Row, then they would have been visited by another petitioner. At the very least, gossip would have spread like... Ibram grimaced.

"Like wildfire," he muttered, and shook his head. "Ladyship, your advice wins out once more."

"Sorry?" Ahksell chimed in.

"I am attacking my certainties from the other end," Ibram announced as he straightened up. "If the fire was deliberate—and green fire says it is—then Rennab stands to receive less, does he not?"

"Only true if Master Rennab started the fire," Ahksell said. "There is no evidence yet to suggest he did so."

"Yes, but if he had and it was discovered. He wouldn't profit," Ibram said. "It is not an offense to set fire to your own property, but if it started in his house and damaged the others, any money he might expect from his insurance would not equal the amount he would owe. There's no profit in this fire for him."

"It stands to reason," Ahksell said. "It's about protecting the community from disasters physical and economical, after all, not rewarding a crime. But he might not have counted on the fire growing out of control so quickly."

"And if that is true...then it's another reason why he might not wish Lady Azadiya to inquire further into the fire."

"But he didn't know about Mentor's interest until now, nor the green fire," Ahksell said. "Master Dughlat didn't tell him."

"When did he say that?" Ibram asked.

Dughlat might have had nothing to do with it, in point of fact. The other servant—Neilos—might know more. Ibram sniffed the air and wrinkled his nose.

"Well, that's as may be, but regardless, if the fire began there—" Ahksell pointed right, "—then how did it—" He pointed left, "—jump to the bakery-mill before anyone saw the smoke?"

Ibram shrugged. "I think it's time we peeked into the other buildings affected by this fire. See if they have all their tiles and mark the level of destruction."

"And after that?" Ahksell asked.

"Settle it up the living mountain," Ibram suggested. "First steps should be to know the names of the folk we're dealing with."

❧   4   ❧

The problem of time, according to the alchemists, was that it was finite. Of course, when Ibram spoke to the priests, all they wanted to natter on about was how the heavens or the Plane Divine or whatever folk named it rendered time meaningless through the intrinsic nature of belief. Ibram had no opinion on the subject himself. Only that it seemed obvious to him that, when he had nothing pressing in his working day, time seemed to stretch like honey, and when he was on a mission, time appeared to desert him entirely.

Regardless of Ibram's feelings, it took the rest of the day and well into the night to nail down the framework of the situation as it lay between the fire alliances of Pillared Circle and Builders Row. Given Dughlat's testimony, it was easy to account for the whereabouts of he and Neilos, after all. Verifying where Masters Rennab and Finar, and their maid, had been loitering during the fire had taken more time, but eventually the Scribes' Bureau gave up its secrets and the market supplied them with two separate witnesses for each suspect. The High Climber, it seemed, teemed with friendly folk delighted to stand around and gossip over the dry goods.

Everyone who lived and worked in Pillared Circle knew who worked where, of course, but most folk had been all hands to the municipal fountain, tossing water buckets or breaking down doors. The denizens who had a moment to spare had naturally focused on protecting their own buildings, and not collecting a roll call for Ibram to peruse at his leisure. Sadly, Ibram could not speak to the two fire alliances until they freed Amota Berac from their bureaucratic clutches. To add insult to injury, once they'd finally reached the Bureau of Records, the doors were firmly shut to visitors due to an unforeseen bureaucratic audit.

By the time the paths were lit atop the living mountain, and the lamplighters were patrolling the streets of Lityen, they had discovered a fair many folk had been in the dry market up Preserved Corner and those who hadn't would need to be spoken with one by frustrating one. At the last, Ibram bade Ahksell a more or less polite farewell, and went off home. Katka's examination for her artisan rank as a jeweler was coming up, which meant the whole house was awash in plans and overly excited apprentices; Ibram was declared unhelpful and allowed to collapse into his bed without protest.

The next morning, Amota Berac was again deep in a lengthy discussion with a representative from Builders Row. He could not be bothered for a list of names, but Ibram wasn't without resources. He had dropped half his breakfast bun at the altar Kholdo kept for the household's small gods on his way out the door.

He met Ahksell by the municipal fountain nearest Book Row. Ahksell loitered outside a binder's shop, watching the woman's apprentices lay out thick skeins of recently dyed silk thread. The apprentices were sitting outside and sewing papers or little wooden slats together, according to their rank, and acting as living advertisements for their employer's skill. Ahksell had always had a fascination for the craft.

Ibram came up from behind Ahksell and managed to reach his shoulder without once making Ahksell notice. "Fair morning, wouldn't you think?" he asked.

Ahksell jumped and twisted around. "Son of—oh, it's you."

Ibram grinned. "It is."

"Well, you're late," Ahksell said, and cleared his throat.

"Me?" Ibram pointed at his own chest. "But I have been right here for an hour or more. Didn't you notice?"

Ahksell rolled his eyes, and Ibram laughed. "Are you ready to give the Bureau of Records another try?" Ibram asked.

"As I will ever be," Ahksell said. "What if they're still closed?"

Ibram shrugged. "We arrived too late yesterday," he said as they began to walk in the direction of the imperial compound. "But I have a lady in my mind who might be able to help."

"A friend of your mother's?" Ahksell asked.

Ibram lifted his chin and did not deign to answer. Ahksell laughed, and Ibram slowed his pace so that he now walked a step behind him. Etiquette was etiquette after all. In Lityen, it paid to know who was who and what their interests entailed; Ibram had learned quite early that the folk who worked in the imperial compound thrived in an atmosphere of influence and opportunity. A congenial visit to the Bureau of Records was accomplished by having Ahksell wait outside the tented shay shop near the entrance, while within Ibram cajoled Mistress Izon of the Office of Indemnity—a lady who was most assuredly only an acquaintance of his mother—into providing him with a neat list of names of all the participants of the fire alliance in Pillared Circle as well as the one on Builders Row.

It took some amount of conversation, since no self-respecting government official would allow Ibram, a mere mortal, to take a duly stamped imperial record from its home. In the end, he was allowed to sneak via a side entrance and make a copy of the relevant facts in return for a small donation of time and effort at a future date of Mistress Izon's determining. He also set to memory and paper a few salient points from Pillared Circle's fire alliance contract, before Mistress Izon prodded him out the door at the auditor's approach. An agent's lot was sometimes not an easy one, but Ibram bore it with good cheer.

"It would be so much easier if the Bureau of Vigilance handled these matters," he complained as he collected Ahksell from the bindery into which he'd wandered.

"You hate the mere fact of the warders' involvement in the province, but would gladly give up this fire to Her Gracious Majesty's brigade?" Ahksell laughed. "I don't believe you."

"I never hate anything," Ibram declared.

"Patrolling."

"A grave offence to my feet, but a boon to cobblers."

"Messenger duty."

"Patently untrue!" Ibram declared. "I have never lost a single missive."

"Stable clean up."

"Unfair," Ibram said. "There is no one in the world who enjoys shoveling dung."

Ahksell snickered, like they were children again, and Ibram took the liberty of the crowd to prod him in the side. Ahksell jumped with a shout; Ibram kept walking.

They arrived back up the living mountain in good time, mostly on account of the rain which opened up just as they disembarked from the aerial gondola at the relay station outside the Preceptory of Yseult. Ibram had forgotten his cloak, and Ahksell refused to share, so they ran down the hard-packed earth roads to the preceptory's gates, and then hurried under awning after awning until they reached the end of the compound's main courtyards and had to resign themselves to becoming increasingly damp on the way from the training fields to Lady Azadiya's tower.

"Why is it," Ibram said, as he pushed on the stone door entrance, "that the Fourth Mentor of a preceptory as large as Yseult must live so close to the guard wall? And if she must do so, why can't there be outbuildings with sturdy terraces along the way?"

"If you would remember your cloak, you would not have such concerns," Ahksell said.

Ibram frowned, and pushed on the door again. "It rains all the time," he said. "It would only make sense to build a little something on the training field to escape the downpour."

"Yes," Ahksell said, "it rains all the time."

"You're focusing on the wrong aspect of my argument."

The door refused to budge, usually the tower's main entrance was open whenever folk were awake, and there was always someone working inside. If it wasn't Dihya the housekeeper and her staff, it was Amita Sarrha and the other agents, not to mention the Attendants and Learners crowding the place with their experiments and classes. Ibram touched the lodestone built into the tower, and stood back a few paces.

He put his hands on his hips, and looked up the great expanse of stone. Lady Azadiya's tower was perhaps the finest example of Western architecture a Vissilian might find outside of what had used to be the kingdom of Merrilia. This meant, naturally, that next to the elegant spires and sweeps of Vissilian buildings, the tower seemed a squatty addition to the tiered fortress of the Preceptory of Yseult. Not even the profusion of Spiny Orange bushes that ringed its outsides could make the place seem anything other than a shock.

"What could they be doing?" Ahksell asked.

Ibram shrugged. A long, low bell tone rang out from behind the stone doors. Ahksell drew back the hood of his cloak, and leaned on his gar. The doors opened soon enough, and Dihya, looking not a little frazzled, poked her head out.

"Come in," she said, "come in quickly!"

She stepped back, holding the stone door open in one hand, and Ibram quickly entered, followed by Ahksell. Dihya shut the door just as quickly, and tucked her riot of curls back from her face with both hands.

"What's wrong?" Ahksell asked.

Dihya shook her head. "Nothing, Attendant," she said, with a quick bow. "But Mentor Hobon has requested that we keep all the doors and windows shut until she gives the order. Something about drafts."

"Drafts?" Ibram repeated.

"Yes, for her experiment," Dihya said. "She's taken up the common room for the light, she says, and now we can't move from one room to the next without her say-so."

Ahksell looked above her head into the sunken common room beyond, and nodded slowly. "I can see why."

Ibram leaned back and followed his line of sight. "Oh, Wheelmaker's *spokes*," he muttered. "Thank you, Dihya."

"Less of the blasphemy, Ibram," Dihya reprimanded. "And you may thank me by helping her to finish whatever she's up to. I've linen to inspect and three maids with mending that needs doing stuck in a Learners' exhibition class on the third floor."

"We can only do our best," Ibram said and ambled cautiously out of the entryway and down the short steps to the common room. A Stinging Euphorbia reached its leaves in his direction, but Ahksell—now uncloaked and gar-less—swept it from their path.

In the center of the common room, surrounded by pushed back low couches filled with rapt Attendants, stood a long table set with wide metal chalices each ablaze in different colored fire from red to orange to yellow and then blue to indigo to violet. Ibram felt the heat from the second he stepped foot in the common room; the damp ends of his hair curled dry immediately. Amota Berac waved from his position with the other agents by the burbling fountain; he carried a bucket of sand in one hand as did several others. Ibram waved back. He looked up to the tiled roof above, treated with some alchemical secret that turned them translucent but only in one direction; the higher landings above were ringed with agents and servants, some of whom were clutching tiny Learners in their arms for a better view.

"Now then," Lady Azadiya called out from behind the wall of flame. "What have you learned?"

"A crowd will develop whenever there is something awful to be stared at," Ibram said. He frowned into the nearest flaming chalice. The red flame flickered as he spoke; he took a small step backwards.

"A good lesson, if a little obvious, to be sure," she said as she came around the side of the table. She brushed her hands off; one of her sleeves was burnt to the elbow, but the olive skin beneath was unharmed. "What else do you have for me?"

"Mentor, what are you doing?" Ahksell asked, and leaned over to observe the violet-flamed chalice.

"Don't look at that one too long," Lady Azadiya said, "it burns the hottest."

Ahksell leaned back immediately. Ibram coughed and hooked his thumbs through his belt. His gambeson was uncomfortably damp, but proximity to the chalices was warming him up nicely.

"Are you trying to determine at what temperature fire burns green?" Ibram asked.

Ladyship smiled. An Attendant snickered to Ibram's left. Ahksell frowned in that direction and the laughter ceased.

"An excellent thought, Ibram," she said, and returned to stand by her fiery table. "But in point of fact, green fire is a consequence of physical matter transmutation and not of temperature."

"Chalcan vitriol," Ibram said, and lifted his chin. "It's an ingredient in the Orilindan candles some times."

"Indeed so," she said, and held out her left hand while pinching her right hand's fingers together and pulling upward as if holding a string. A small amount of light grey powder with a spoon stuck in it floated up from the table and over her outstretched palm. "It also grows on damp faunts, oddly enough."

"Hold your breath, everyone!" she called out, and the Attendants closest to her also covered their eyes.

Ladyship took a heaping spoonful of powder and flung it across the table, the flames of all six chalices hissed and spat green flames. As the powder reached each differently colored fire, it flared briefly before settling down into their original colors. She quickly repeated the act to the same effect. Ibram leaned forward, unable to quite look away from the dancing multi-colored flames. It seemed almost that the red and orange fires took the longest to return to their usual color. Lady Azadiya added another spoonful of powder to the red fire and pursed her lips in thought.

"Now," Lady Azadiya began, "I might stand here all day throwing powder onto the flames to turn them green—"

"Yes, please!" one of the older Learners shouted from above. Laughter rippled out from the room as Ladyship looked upwards. The Learner hid her red face in Amita Sarrha's shoulder.

"But it would do me little good," Ladyship said, "for the fire would always burn the powder's effect away and return to its natural state. Ibram, what color were the flames when you observed the blaze?"

Ibram sucked in a quick breath and thought back. He'd put that memory in the shelf Amota Evren had constructed for him, had he not? In a candlestick.

"Orange and red, for the most part," he said, and nodded when Ahksell nodded as well. "A bit of yellow, perhaps, but nothing else."

Lady Azadiya nodded. "Sarrha," she called out. "The reports from the team operating The Water's Breath?"

"On your desk, Ladyship," Amita Sarrha called down.

Lady Azadiya took a smaller spoonful and poured it over the chalice of orange colored fire. Obligingly, its flames turned green and remained so for longer than the right hand side of the table had.

Amota Berac cleared his throat and drew his hand down the length of his black beard. "What does this tell us, Ladyship?" he asked.

She shrugged. "It narrows the path," she said. "I prefer a walking trail to a desert, don't you?"

"I certainly do, Mentor," Ahksell commented.

"Have you something interesting to report?" she asked.

"We bring news, certainly," Ibram said. He stared into the burning chalices. The scent of alcohol stung his nose. Ladyship must have poured spirits in as fuel.

Lady Azadiya set the powdered chalcan vitriol into a bowl on the corner of the table, and brushed her hands over the red flame, a rime of spring green briefly outlined the fire. She glanced over her shoulder. Ibram saw Attendant Zorion, lately of the Preceptory of Afsoun, sitting on the end of one of the couches, a pile of metal lids on the little table at his feet.

"Cover the chalices, and then come up to my office, Zorion," she said, and then looked towards the fountain. "Once you are sure the fires are out, you can open the doors again."

Amota Berac bowed, and grasped his bucket of sand in front of him. Lady Azadiya adjusted her remaining sleeve, and moved across the floor in a rustle of skirts. The sounds of the crowd dispersing rattled down on all sides from above them. Ahksell shook his head, and Ibram tapped his first two fingers on his arm.

"Zorion's still here?" he asked. "I thought Mentor Tikari took him back."

Ahksell shook his head. "She said he was gaining a valuable education and sent his entire infusion array down from the shared lab in Afsoun."

Ibram blinked. "Did she really?"

Remaining in Yseult was more correctly the decision of its four mentors, but refusing the Fourth Mentor of Afsoun was poor inter-sect relations, even if Lady Azadiya was technically her equal. Afsoun was the second highest preceptory in the Sect of Seven Fires, literally and by reputation. It ranked beneath only the Preceptory of Mariae, due in part because it was the most traditionally alchemical; they constructed and invented paraphernalia, and provided the sect with a great deal of its wealth.

"It doesn't seem to bother Mentor," Ahksell said. "He's been spending most of his time with Doctor Berot and the Medicinal Corps. anyway. Come on, she's already on the second floor."

"Well, if he blinds anyone else at least we know what to do now," Ibram said as they made their way past the Attendants rising from the couches.

Zorion placed a lid over the first two burning chalices, starving the fires of air, and then frowned at the blue flames. He picked a small dish up from the table, which Ibram had not noticed before. Some of the Learners surely knew what it was, because Zorion suddenly found himself the sole focus of their close attention. Zorion tossed the contents of the dish into the fire, and they cheered. The fire began to writhe, curling in on itself like the arms of a sea creature; the bowl rocked. Ibram swallowed and grabbed Ahksell's arm. Things began to twist and curl within the flames; the air tasted acrid on the back of Ibram's tongue.

"*Attendant Hilbert Zorion*," Amita Sarrha yelled from above.

Zorion clapped another metal cover over the squirming fire, and the Learners made noises of disappointment. Ibram took the stairs two at a time with Ahksell beside him. A few of the servants had already gathered by the fountain, no doubt already planning to return the common room to its previous configuration. The tower was fast regaining its air of controlled chaos, doors opening and closing as folk went about their business.

When they reached Ladyship's office on the third level, they entered through the open door. Ibram shivered as the heavy feeling of parting a curtain fell around him; Ladyship's silencing tiles were quite strong. He bowed in her direction and then cleared the way for Ahksell to do the same.

"Ladyship, what was that display in aid of?" Ibram asked.

"Dughlat compared the color of the fire to my emerald necklace," she said. "He said he believed it lasted for some span of time."

"Helpful," Ibram muttered.

"Now," Ladyship continued, "give or take my concerns for a wounded man's accuracy... I wished to see how much chalcan vitriol might it take to burn at that color for at least a minute."

"Why?" Ahksell asked.

"Because he did not see green fire during the explosion," Lady Azadiya said. "And if he did not see it, then the fire began before he noticed it because..." She left the rest of the sentence hanging, and raised both eyebrows.

Ahksell frowned in thought, and then cocked his head to the side. "If the fire turned green immediately upon touching the powdered vitriol," he said, and paused. He took a breath, and glanced about the room. "Then the flames could have been of a normal hue to begin with, and then touched something that changed their color which is what Dughlat beheld when he turned around. Or! That the first explosion that Dughlat ignored was a misfire, and the second a delayed reaction... It rained the night before, did it not, Mentor? Perhaps something—a detonation cord or the bag in which it was carried—grew damp."

She smiled upon him. Ahksell ducked his head, and rubbed the back of his neck, grinning down at his boots.

"So it is possible the fire was entirely without alchemical involvement," Ibram said. "But not likely."

"Oh, it was always possible," Lady Azadiya said, and looked over from contemplating her suspended glass ball of liquid. She frowned and tapped it; the viscous fluid inside was grey and quite low. "But we further learned that the temperature of the fire in the evening courtyards was no more than what was natural. Which would not be enough to overwhelm the bakery-mill's fire suppression tiles."

She crossed from the glass ball to one of the bookshelves specially fitted to the curving wall of her tower, and pulled down a book bound in leather with frayed corners. She returned to the side of her desk, drawing her left hand along one of the tapestries hung over the stone walls for warmth.

"Is there a crime here, Ladyship?" Ibram asked. "Should we inform the warders and make a public pronouncement?"

"There is a crime, to be sure," she said. "I am beginning to see its frame, but I still require a better understanding of its function. For instance, there were definitely two explosions."

"Yes," Ibram said. "I remember them. I was eating in the draught-shop not far away."

"So it was loud enough, but not hot enough," Ladyship said. "The two explosions might have been no more than what was needed, rather than accidental at all."

"Ladyship, everything I know of fire is from my father's foundry," Ibram said.

She hummed in thought. "Yes, a sad lack in your education," she said, "but that's Bedris for you. I sometimes think Nieminen is right, and we should simply take over the education of you agents ourselves."

Ibram blinked hard, and felt his eyes widen. He glanced at Ahksell, who shrugged and shook his head in response. Ibram coughed. Lady Azadiya caught his meaning immediately, and snorted in amused exasperation.

"Nonsense, Ib-la, look at how well your mother did with you."

Ama had been an excellent teacher, it was true. Working for an alchemical sect required a variety of skills not necessary for the average arm-for-hire, but his apprenticeship had still been decidedly hole-and-corner, rather than legally recognized as Katka's was. Even his parent's marriage contract had vaguely referred to his mother's first child "following in his mother's family trade" rather than explaining where and with whom she worked. It had made life a bit awkward after he'd left the free school the Preceptory of Bedris ran for common folk. Ibram should know; he now had a crop of cousins—blood-related or otherwise—learning their parents' trade in the sect whom he was officially unaware of.

"I thought the second explosion was the bakery-mill?" Ahksell asked.

"I believe it was," Lady Azadiya said. She sighed. "Just like in Kandrilat."

"Kandrilat?" Ahksell repeated. "Mentor, you can't mean the disaster?"

Lady Azadiya nodded. "It began in a bakery-mill, just as here," she said. "Only it was in a poorer quarter, and the flames quickly grew out of control." She frowned down at the polished top of her wooden desk, and then looked up again, sharply. "What have you learned?" she asked.

"Not much, Mentor," Ahksell said, though his brow wrinkled. "The wall where Master Dughlat saw the green flames was completely destroyed. If not by the fire itself, then most certainly when the bakery-mill exploded."

"It reminds me very much of the stories that came out of Kandrilat, after the great fire was extinguished," Ibram said. "Master Rennab didn't lay fire suppression tiles at the front on the outside of his evening courtyard."

He reached into his wrist wallet, and pinched out the tile he'd pried from inside above the door. He held it up to catch the light. "He has these instead. Claims they add extra light."

"Ibram," Ahksell said, and frowned.

"Cangsa, I'm only *borrowing* it for little while," Ibram said.

He held out the tile in the palm of his hand; the clay square lifted up as if plucked, and flung itself into Ladyship's grasp. She also raised it up to the light, and turned it back and front. Her eyes narrowed.

"There is a slight clustering of aetheric flakes," she said. "Ahksell, can you see the array of light?"

"It's a little...pink?" he said as if unsure. "I can't really be certain of the enchantment...if there is a enchantment attached at all."

She tossed the tile in Ahksell's direction; he grabbed it mid-air, and then stared into the bowl of his palm, frowning. "It was damaged in the fire," he suggested.

"By the heat, not the fire," Ibram said, and Ahksell turned his head to stare at him, eyebrows raised. "What?"

"Nothing," Ahksell protested.

"I am paid to observe," Ibram said. "And I *observed* that the front of the building survived, but I was able to pry that tile out of the wall without much trouble. The grout had dried out completely, and whatever it was made of didn't help the tiles much at all. It stands to reason that a tile exposed to the elements—even protected by a porch roof—would be broken further down by the heat of a fire as big as that."

"What did Master Rennab say it did again?" Lady Azadiya asked.

"Claimed it was an additional light source," Ibram said. "But I haven't yet heard they'd managed to adhere luminescent sand to a tile yet."

"Trust in me," Ahksell said, "if anyone had managed to do that without negating the sand's properties, I would not have been able to keep silent."

Lady Azadiya chuckled. "Nor would any of us," she said.

"So it does not give off light, then?" Ibram asked. "What does it do?"

He touched the little button shield Ahksell had given him. Ahksell called it the Helping Hand; it was supposed to act as an aid to rescue somehow. It gave off a beam of light strong enough to blind a man if he looked at it too closely, but only for a certain period of time. Ahksell caught the gesture and shook his head.

"Oh, that's a different matter altogether," he said. "It's metal, first of all, and nothing so breakable—"

"Porous, Ahk-la," Ladyship interjected. "Clay's fragility is secondary to its porous nature when aligning the anima of matter to its cousin."

Ibram cleared his throat and looked attentive. He had had just enough schooling in the Bedris school to know they were on the edge of technical discussions about which he cared little and needed to know only unofficially.

"But the porosity of glass is what allows the radiance of my Helping Hand to be contained," Ahksell said.

"Barely contained," Ibram muttered.

Ahksell glanced over quickly. "What?"

"So these tiles have *captured* light?" Ibram repeated.

"Not at all," Lady Azadiya said. "The principle behind your button shield is that the act of causing visible light is transmuted into a memory of its equivalent partner."

"Oh," Ibram said.

"Which is why the memory eventually fades, and I need to reignite the spark in the center of the shield underneath the sea glass," Ahksell said.

"Which is not the same as capturing light itself," Ibram said. "I see, of course. Who's trying to do that?"

"It's a bit like the panacea, to be sure," Lady Azadiya said. She frowned and brushed at a long brown scar down her intact sleeve. "Every hundred years or so, some damned fool idealist decides to make their fortune by trapping light in a box. Leaks out the moment you break the loop."

Ibram frowned and scratched the hinge of his jaw. "I thought that was impossible."

"Who does not enjoy a good spar with impossibility?" Ladyship asked. Her Merrilian accent flowed like a stream, much faster when she was amused. "No, it's one of the many youthful follies these young Attendants fall into, and then look back on with admiring embarrassment in their older years. Sadly, this tile is not one of them, merely a common garden peddler's snare. Any light it might create is simply a transference of anima while it's worked upon."

Ahksell held it up to the glowbulb hanging high above him. "It's still pink, but there's a colorless section, like a band of..."

"The tile is green," Ibram pointed out.

"Yes, but I'm not speaking of its outward appearance," Ahksell said. He angled the tile closer to Ibram, and pointed. "I mean this layer here. It's cut so thin I'm not surprised the glaze behind it comes through, and then here it's got an aura of the faintest pinkish emanation..."

"Inset with flakes of red serpentine, no doubt," Lady Azadiya said. "Utterly pointless, but they're popular in the north and east, I believe, particularly among the smaller noble houses."

"If there's an emanation, then it must be good for something," Ibram said.

"And why should one follow the other?" Lady Azadiya asked. She crossed her arms, and leaned her hip against her desk. "All things have some resonance with reality, Ib-la, else they would not exist."

"Then the color of the emanation means nothing?"

"The color is a property of its being," Ladyship said. "It finds use as a tool of identification if nothing else."

"And if it did something, than the emanation would be stronger," Ahksell said. "Especially if it had been working while yoked to a similar tile. How many were there?"

"A fair few," Ibram said. "Twelve, I would say. What are they supposed to do, if you recognize the useless things?"

"They promote serenity and fair feelings," Ladyship said. "And heal the soul."

Ahksell looked at the tile more closely. "All from a few slices of red serpentine." He sighed. "If only that were true."

"Why is it false?" Ibram asked. "Alchemy can prolong the effects of whatever it interacts with, can it not?"

"Reality is the focus," Lady Azadiya said. "We discover its effect and then guide its expression. Even if it did work by itself alone, that little amount of stone would require a person amplifying its properties directly the entire time. Through touch."

"So Rennab is...attempting to settle his customers' minds when they enter The High Climber?" Ibram suggested.

"Is that considered promoting balance or imbalance to a Kilk?" Ahksell asked. "I thought they didn't allow such things as this."

"So far as I have studied, they are allowed to tip the scales so much as they might wish," Lady Azadiya said. "Only it must be to redress an already present imbalance, not cause it deliberately."

"Is that why his building had no fire suppression tiles on its face?" Ibram asked. "His neighbors had so many protections in place, he felt honor-bound to forgo them?"

"There were none that I could see in the wreckage inside," Ahksell agreed. "But when I pressed Master Dughlat while you were outside, he admitted that he had seen such tiles present in the common room and when he would go outside to dispose of the night's refuse."

"It's possible he might have had them, but not in a sufficient quantity, then," Ibram said. "He bought the ones in the alley off his brother-in-law."

"Not the sect?" Ladyship asked.

Ibram shook his head. "Not even with the discounted price."

Ladyship moved behind her desk to the shelves packed with alchemical equipment. She picked up a delicate looking alembic and set it down on top of a stack of papers. "Anything of interest about Master Rennab?"

Ibram tilted his chin up and cast his mind back. "Brown hair, medium height," he said. "Stocky, but not unpleasant to behold. Hair covered his ears properly with a band around the forehead. Believed his husband's claims that that tile provided light; Master Finar took the tiles off his brother—a traveling salesman—in exchange of payment. Angry about the fire, but not undeservedly so, *and* he repeated the name of his neighboring competition twice in our hearing."

"Twice?" Lady Azadiya leaned forward with one hand on her desk. "He wanted you to remember the name."

Ibram cleared his throat and took his scroll of loose paper from his belt wallet. "He did so, to be sure," he said, and waved the bit of paper at Lady Azadiya until she nodded. "This is a list of all the members of the Pillared Circle fire alliance, and a few of the more relevant codicils. There are six members: Soren Rennab, Philendra Dubidat—they own the adjoining evening courtyards—Harken Bine, Carme Salaz, and Otso Sembe are the cookshops by the second exit onto Pillared Circle, and Nescata Corri, the apothecary who got burned running in to rescue her apprentices."

"The bakery-mill was not part of the alliance?" Lady Azadiya asked.

"No, Ladyship. According to the language of the document, it formed because of the already existing fire alliance on the opposite side of the street. I haven't spoken with them, as of yet."

"The terms?"

"Each member of the alliance is required to aid the others in the event of fire, and to supply each other with appropriate funds from a general pool of coin paid into every year in the case of a conflagration. Now—" Ibram squinted down at the paper, "—because of the bakery-mill, each signatory is required to shore up their fellows' defenses with 'every available aid to fire prevention' which Soren Rennab did not do, so far as we know."

"Because as a Kilk he cannot tip the scales of fate to promote either a too beneficial or a too harmful outcome," Lady Azadiya said. She tapped her signet ring, and then shook her head. "I find that answer unsatisfactory."

"Surely not, Ladyship," Ibram agreed. "It's too strict. Does he serve green meat because fate determined it rot?" He turned to Ahksell. "He doesn't, does he? I have eaten there."

"No one is that zealous," Ahksell assured him. "I'm sure of it."

"Kilks believe in an all-encompassing balance, of sorts," Lady Azadiya said, and tugged lightly on the end of her long braid. "Twin deities, one for progression and one for...stagnation, really, and the only way to appease them is to maintain equal worth in Their estimation. It's an unlikely motive."

"It might simply be that he's cheap," Ahksell said.

"Now that, I call very likely," Ibram declared, "but, either way, it's also a reason why he might not come to us about a green colored fire. If the fire began in his building and he did not have the proper protections in place, according to the rules of the alliance he is required to provide the bulk of the funding to rebuild."

"But Master Rennab doesn't know about what Dughlat and Neilos saw," Ahksell said.

"So we think," Ibram said. "It could be that Dughlat told him first, didn't get the reply he wished for, and then came to us. Or that Neilos told him."

"Yes, Neilos," Lady Azadiya said. "What about him?"

"We have yet to encounter him, Mentor," Ahksell said. "Actually, is Erno Neilos a man?"

Ibram paused. "Sounds like a man's name," he said finally.

"Could be a family name," Ahksell said. "One winter, I met a woman named Berac."

Ibram scoffed. "You did not."

"On the Runner's sandals, I swear it!" Ahksell grinned. "She was a fisherwoman, named for her father."

Ibram paused, and then opened his mouth. Then, he closed it. Ahksell's forehead slowly wrinkled.

"Lady Azadiya—" Ibram began.

A heavy hand knocked on Lady Azadiya's door. Ibram turned to look and beheld Attendant Zorion standing in the doorway. Zorion knocked again.

"Find this Neilos," Lady Azadiya said, and sat down at her desk. She raised her hand to Zorion and waved him inside. "Speak to him or her and find out what this person knows. It will be easier to corroborate Dughlat's claims."

"And if Neilos cannot?" Ahksell asked. "By his own admission, Master Dughlat only saw the green fire because his tunic was caught and he stopped to untangle it."

"Mentor," Zorion said as he entered, and then clasped his hands together. "Some of the Learners are requesting a practical demonstration of the Water's Breath. Do you think Attendant Hidara might loan it out?"

Lady Azadiya considered the thought for a moment. "An interesting thought," she said, and then turned her attention to Ibram. "Speak to the neighbors. Perhaps someone in the Builders Row fire alliance saw something, or does not know yet what they witnessed. After all, Pillared Circle is not the only area of Lityen affected. It's possible someone else saw an opportunity, and exploited it."

"In Builders Row?" Ahksell asked.

"Yes," Lady Azadiya said. "They hold their money in the Runner's temple, am I correct?"

"Them, the Pillared Circle alliance, and half of Lityen," Ibram said.

She nodded. "The bakery-mill has been lost, what do the remaining members receive in this event?"

Ibram grabbed Ahksell's arm, and tugged him back a step. "Consider us on the march, Ladyship," he said.

Lady Azadiya nodded. Ibram placed his list on the end of her desk; he'd already memorized its contents. There was much to do, and they had to be doing all of it. His stomach grumbled at him, just loud enough to be felt more than heard. He twitched his head in the direction of the doorway, and Ahksell nodded. They walked out together, while Zorion stepped into the space before her desk.

❧ 5 ❧

A small gathering had congregated by the fountain in Pillared Circle. Ibram spied Amota Berac holding court with a large map unfolded in both hands, while beside him Master Rennab and two others pointed fingers. Ibram took note of the one with a burgundy patch on her chest; that was a representative from the Vo Kaln family. Perhaps these folk were also members of the fire alliance on Builders Row, but that was a question for a different moment. Ibram hunched his shoulders and crowded Ahksell to the other side of the circle to avoid being drawn in. They entered the remains of The High Climber to find a short portly man sitting at a wooden table in a circle of cleared wreckage.

Ibram's foot snapped a stick of wood now more charcoal than chair; at the sound, the man looked up from his scroll of papers. He blinked at them in surprise, and set down his stylus. Ahksell walked down the path that had been cleared to the table, and Ibram followed.

"Good day," Ibram said, as he quickly stepped in front of Ahksell. "Do I have the honor of addressing Master Finar?"

"You do," the man said, and stood up from the table.

"Wonderful," Ibram said, and turned to one side. "Attendant, may I make you known to Master Finar, also owner of this evening courtyard?"

"You may," Ahksell said, with a barely suppressed sigh. Ibram ignored it with the ease of long practice. Etiquette and protocol had its uses, no matter the cost in time spent.

"Master—" Ibram broke off and smiled. "Terribly sorry, but your first name?"

The man spread his hands. He had light brown hair which covered his ears, but wore it loose as they did in the north. His eyes were a cloudy green, but not unfriendly.

"Albin," Master Finar supplied.

"Master Albin Finar," Ibram said. "Be known to Attendant Ahksell Solari of the Preceptory of Yseult."

Master Finar bowed to Ahksell, who performed his part in the social fabric nicely, and then clasped his hands over his belly. Finar's blue tunic and brown wrapped trousers were creased, and ink stains bloomed at the wrist of his left sleeve. A dirty handkerchief lay near what Ibram now saw to be a ledger, covered in soot.

"It must be a horrible time for your family," Ahksell said. "You have my sincere condolences."

Ibram twitched, but remained silent. At least no one could say he had not tried.

"Thank you," Master Finar said. He sighed deeply. "It is altogether awful, isn't it? Almost everything we own, except for that preservation box, which survived only by the Grace of Vieno. If we didn't have my caffa, we wouldn't even have a place to lay our heads!"

"Your caffa?" Ibram asked.

Master Finar nodded. "I own a small establishment in the Street of Ledgers," he said. "It's nowhere near the size of this place, but it will keep a roof over our heads and food in our stomachs while Soren decides what he wants to do with this place."

"Decides what to do?" Ibram tilted his head. "I hadn't heard he was considering not rebuilding the evening courtyard."

Master Finar sighed. "It all depends on how this meeting between your Fourth Mentor Hobon and the two fire alliances works out. Honestly, Soren's heart hasn't been in this enterprise for some time.

We're on different schedules, you know. He, up all night, and myself, working during the daylight hours."

"There is...work enough in your caffa?" Ibram asked.

"Oh, most definitely," Master Finar said. "I owned the caffa when we married, you see, while Soren owned The High Climber, and together we grew both businesses. The truth of the matter is, however, that my shop does more than enough business for it to require the two of us to run it, now that we provide luxuries for many of the folk who work in the Bureau of Currency." He yawned. "Excuse me, we have been up through the night. No, we have been talking about selling the building for well-nigh half the year now. Philendra's landlord has offered us a good price, or she had, before the fire."

Ibram nodded. "That would be Philendra Dubidat of The Isconian's Hand?" he asked. "The courtyard next door?"

Finar nodded. "Yes."

"Who owns that lease?" Ibram asked.

"It's one of the Vo Kalns," Finar said. "I don't remember the personal name, you see. There are so many of them."

Ibram glanced at Ahksell, who raised his eyebrows in return. Had Rennab truly wished to sell? Or had he agreed to sell, but didn't wish his neighbor and competitor to actually profit? If Rennab were truly the arsonist, it was an enticing motive.

"But enough of me talking. How may I help you, Attendant?" Master Finar asked. "My husband is speaking now with another agent from the sect about the property lines in the neighborhood. I am only here to total the loss of our stores and furniture."

He turned and spread his open palm in the direction of the table. Ibram nodded.

"It's our duty to speak with everyone involved in the accident," Ibram said, and clasped his hands behind his back. He made a show of surveying the destruction. "After all, the sect must make our assessments just as you make your own. I spoke to Master Rennab just a little while ago, actually. Have you heard from your brother lately?"

Master Finar seemed surprised. "My brother?" he echoed. "Why— oh, the fire suppression tiles. Achard installed them, you know. It was very helpful."

Ibram nodded. "Yes, that's the one. I was wondering if you knew where he had gotten them?"

"Oh!" Master Finar thought for a moment. "I'm sorry, it's not coming to me... I expect he gets the contracts through his outfit—he apprenticed with them. Kenda Trading?"

He paused with his eyebrows upraised, but Ibram shook his head. "My apologies," he said. "A worthy trading enclave to be sure, but I have no knowledge of it."

"Oh, that's just as well," Finar said. "They've been around for a number of years, but then he does a great deal of business along the southern roads up from Hyperni province before he travels up through Vanima. There's a little alchemical sect down there...ah..."

"The Sect of The Iron Hand," Ahksell supplied with a small note of defeat in his voice.

Ibram raised his eyebrows, but Ahksell quickly shook his head. Master Finar either did not catch the exchange, or politely ignored it, and merely smiled. "That's the one! In Hyperni province, near Ammoni. Though he tells me Lityen is far nicer."

He paused, and Ibram nodded encouragingly. "I'm fond of this village, myself," he said.

Finar chuckled politely. He rubbed his hands together. "He sells their goods along his travels. When he gets up to our bend in the river, he always unloads what little he has left in the travelers' inns and draughtshops, and then purchases from the sect here before making his way up north to Vulprenna."

"He doesn't go into the west?" Ibram asked.

"He doesn't have the same connections there," Finar shook his head. "And he likes the lowlands a little too much to brave the mountains."

"You must follow his career very carefully," Ibram said.

"He's my older brother, you see," Finar said. "I thought for a while I might follow in his footsteps, but then our parents moved here and set up the caffa... Well, you know how it is. We're the only family we have left. It's better to keep in touch."

Ahksell tugged lightly on the collar of his gambeson. He cleared his throat, and coughed to one side behind his sleeve. He took in the disaster surrounding the incongruous desk, and then refocused.

"Is that a list of what has been recovered?"

Master Finar returned to his table, and laid his hand on the open ledger. "It is not," he said, "but only because that list is the length of a page. These papers—" he ruffled the stack with his thumb, "—document how much we have lost."

"It's a heavy duty," Ahksell said. "I am sorry for it."

"Thank you."

"I'm afraid we assumed you and your husband would be quite busy," Ahksell said. "We were hoping to speak with the two dayworkers who were rescued from the fire, Shokan Dughlat and…"

"Erno Neilos," Finar said. "They were here this morning, but I sent them away once we'd been able to clear a space and begin a tally. There simply wasn't any work to do."

"They don't live on the premises, do they?" Ibram asked.

"No," Finar said. "Shokan lives by the Crofter's Guildhouse, and then Neilos has a bed at a tenant inn in Cobbler's Square."

"Would you mind describing this Neilos?" Ibram asked.

Master Finar seemed a bit bemused. "Not at all," he said. "Quite short and thin. Erno has yellow hair, just turning grey at the temples, and blue eyes. No beard to speak of, but he's got the wisp of a mustache and a mark on his chin just here." He lay the tip of his finger upright in the middle of his own chin. "A fishing accident when he was a boy, the hook caught him right there."

"Thank you for your help, Master Finar," Ahksell said.

"Of course."

They each made their bows, and Ibram rose first. He turned to follow Ahksell up and out of The High Climber, but then paused. As Ama said, you had to time your questions carefully, just enough interest to show you were willing, but not enough to show your intent. He faced Master Finar with a smile, and arranged himself to look the picture of a man who'd just remembered something, and thought he might as well mention it.

"Master Finar?" he asked, and the man looked up. "Is there any chance you might speak to your brother soon?"

Master Finar had returned to his seat at Ahksell's leave-taking, and leaned back in his chair now. "Not so soon," he answered after a moment's thought. "Achard is—oh, he should be near Kilgren's Marsh by this point in his route. There's no way to Lityen but through that area, and that can take days depending on the weather."

Ibram sighed and shrugged. "It's a shame," he said. "I was hoping to hear tales from outside the imperial boundary. It's been some time since I was given my freedom, to be sure, and I find I miss it."

Master Finar laughed. "He usually stops at the village of Bromi, and leaves a message to his home office with the Scribes' Bureau."

"Oh?" Ibram asked. "What is his company again?"

"Kenda Trading," Master Finar said. "If you'd like, I can send a message and tell him a potential customer would love a word, next time he's in town?"

"I would appreciate that greatly, Master Finar," Ibram smiled and bowed shortly. "I thank you."

Ahksell coughed behind him, and Ibram made a little show of obeying, just to keep the tone of ease elevated. Once outside, Ahksell poked him in the shoulder; Ibram staggered but regained his footing. He laughed, and Ahksell shook his head. A small group of children staggered past, carrying buckets of wood ash.

"What was that in aid of?" Ahksell asked.

"A merchant must keep records that an inspector might not," Ibram said. "And Bromi is too far by horse, but not too far to send a letter. Friendly requests for information always yield positive results."

"How do you know he can read?" Ahksell asked.

"Most traders connected with a trading firm have some literacy," Ibram said. "And Master Finar just told me they write letters back and forth. Besides, anyone who sells alchemical goods must keep track of them. Horrible things do tend to happen to folk who let those sorts of items wander unsupervised."

Ahksell nodded, and they turned down the street. Ibram made sure to keep pace just a step behind Ahksell's right shoulder. Neither Dughlat nor Neilos lived too far away from Pillared Circle, but Ibram still used the traveling time to his advantage. A child with a bucket stepped out of the way, and recalled another group to his mind. There were a lot of young folk about the scene. The Vo Kalns had been present in the crowd, he recalled, gawking at the smoking remains of their investments, no doubt.

Ibram narrowed his eyes as he and Ahksell wove their way through the crowds up from the second exit off Pillared Circle. The cookshops by The Isconian's Hand had been erased from their foundations. The portable grills had been decimated, the ropes the bread seller had strung up in the exposed rafters of their awning were burnt away completely, and all that was left was the clay wall of the stew merchant. Even that had been cracked down the middle to show the inner shelf where the small charcoal burners would have licked at the three iron cauldrons inset above in happier times.

Without the bakery-mill, the natural conclusion would have been that the cramped stalls were where the fires began. Master Rennab, however, had been far more eager to accuse his neighboring rival, and Master Dughlat had stated he had seen green fire along the back wall of The High Climber. In Amota Berac's report, all seemed to agree that the fire had spread from the bakery-mill outward, but what inside that building could cause a spurt of green fire from that far away? It was a question to contemplate, but Ibram set it aside for the moment. There was a quicker mystery to unravel, after all.

"What got you in such a muddle back there?" Ibram asked.

Ahksell's head jerked up from his pondering of his own footsteps. "Huh? What do you mean?"

"You reacted when Master Finar told us about his brother's connection to another alchemical sect," Ibram said. He grinned, and jostled Ahksell with his elbow. "Professional jealousy?"

Ahksell laughed, and shook his head. "Nothing like it! It was only Master Finar's explanation. That was his trouble, you see."

"His trouble?" Ibram asked.

Ahksell coughed; he looked a little like a man who'd just discovered dirt on his boots in clean company. "I don't like to speak out of turn, but you heard Master Finar. His brother—or his brother's company— have agreements with the Sect of the Iron Hand," he said. "You've never heard of them?"

"Well, naturally."

"They're small," Ahksell said, and thwapped Ibram on the shoulder. "And not very good at their occupation, poor things."

Ibram waited for a bend in the street where they were mostly unobserved, and socked Ahksell right back. Ahksell grinned. Ibram made free to stretch his arms over his head. They had composed themselves by the time they reached the more populated streets again.

"How have they survived if they aren't very good at alchemy?" Ibram asked.

"They really only concern themselves with..." Ahksell frowned and lowered his voice. "You know the cold charms they make in the north? And the lenses they make near the Freezing Sands?"

Ibram nodded.

"The recipes and processes are all kept very secret, of course—"

"Oh, of course," Ibram muttered.

Ahksell ignored him. "—but there's always someone who wants to try and figure out how the thing itself gets done."

Ibram nodded seriously, as if half the Preceptory of Afsoun wasn't dedicated to uncovering the mysteries of other sects' triumphs and profiting off them immediately. A smart alchemist could do worse than obtaining imperial warrants by imitating his forebears' discoveries. Ahksell continued to ignore him.

"Well, *someone's* youngest child—from a noble house—believed himself a true alchemist," Ahksell said, "and convinced his father to buy him an imperial charter *and* the land to experiment on for so-called commissions."

"Probably so he wouldn't muddle into the affairs of the estate," Ibram said.

"Anyway," Ahksell said. "It's only a little factory of vanities, and there's always some kind of problem with their results, but they do enough business that Hilbert Zorion tells me Afsoun's representatives have been competing with their goods up here. Now I know why."

"A wonder they haven't blown themselves up yet," Ibram said.

Ahksell was too good to agree out loud, but Ibram sensed it anyway. It meant no glad tidings for Master Rennab, to be sure. If it could be found out for certain that The High Climber's substandard equipment enabled all the following mess, then it went a far way to understanding why Rennab wanted blame placed on the dancers at The Isconian's Hand instead.

The fire had been immense and, most importantly, it had caught quickly. The buildings involved had been mostly wooden, after all, and a tile could only do so much. Ibram frowned. Amota Berac had probably already seen the preliminary report from the Builders Row fire alliance; he should ask to read it once they went back up the living mountain.

"What constitutes arson anyway?" he asked himself. "What truly sets it apart?"

"Malice," Ahksell answered.

Ibram jumped. "What?"

"You're speaking to yourself again," Ahksell said, and glanced over his shoulder.

"I enjoy lively conversation," Ibram said.

Ahksell laughed. "Well, then."

"It isn't simply malice, though," Ibram said. "It's what... Do you remember the trial they conducted in Kandrilat after the disaster?"

"How could I forget?" Ahksell asked. "The Cohort of Vigilance were in an utter uproar, even here. There was talk of them being put to use to protect non-imperial buildings!"

"Which came to nothing, of course."

Ahksell nodded. "I thought it very smart when the Empress decried that a plaque describing the Court of Chancery's verdict and subsequent punishment was placed in every city, town, and village in the empire. I'm surprised the warders didn't nail one to every passing caravan as well."

"They wouldn't have been half so upset if they had actually caught the arsonist," Ibram said.

Ahksell shook his head. "I don't know," he said. "Half the city was destroyed, after all, Ibram. The inhabitants permanently displaced. It was a tragedy."

"Could have been an accident."

"Could have been," Ahksell agreed.

"On a scale such as that, even for a single crime the punishment becomes unthinkable."

Ahksell nodded. "And then add in rioting, murder, and destruction of imperial property."

"Treason is a terrible crime," Ibram said.

"And so is the punishment," Ahksell said.

"Lucky for all of us the Cohort of Vigilance did not need to involve themselves in this instance then," Ibram said. "But the fact remains Rennab would still have to live here. Who could risk so much on the basis of his neighbors' precautions?" Ibram snapped his fingers. "Badoshai!"

"Only fools," Ahksell agreed. "Or someone very clever."

They turned the corner and then made their way upstream from the traveling wet market that had settled in Stony Road for the month. A clump of folk stood by the makeshift table of a shay-seller, talking loudly about the bakery-mill and its dangerous lack of responsibility. Ladyship's standing policy was that all gossip should be paid attention to, but only reported when one story began to gain strength. Ibram put a tally mark down on the wall of his memory construct; the Ozols and their bakery-mill continued to falter in village opinion.

The sky was turning dark, and Ibram shrugged his shoulders to inch his high collar a little higher. He was almost tempted to do up the button at his neck. It made his neck itch, but the inch of added warmth might be nice. Spring nearest the mountains was always unfairly colder than the sun so high in the sky promised.

"I wonder why Ladyship brought Kandrilat to mind," Ibram said.

"I thought of it, too," Ahksell said, and shuddered. "We were lucky the fire was not worse. If Builders Row had been less strict about their covenants of safety, we would be in much more trouble."

Ibram hummed in agreement. They walked further down the narrowing web of streets that connected the main imperial paved roads through Lityen. Here, they were forced up from the muddy paths onto the wooden walkways. Ahksell hunched his shoulders, and gamely ducked the hanging baskets and painted signs. Ibram grinned down at his boots and continued with his head unbowed. One advantage of his height, to be sure.

He scrubbed his hand through the damp strands of his brown hair, and frowned. If he did not keep it dry, it would begin to curl. He shook his fingers free, and let his arm drop to his side.

Builders Row's fire alliance had been strict in their covenants—unsurprising, considering the bakery-mill. Ibram would have assumed that Pillared Circle's fire alliance would have been just the same, but clearly evidence suggested otherwise if Master Rennab could get away with accepting just any old fire suppression tiles. He tucked his hair behind his ears.

"We need to see about finding Master Neilos before it truly starts to rain," Ahksell said.

"We don't know what Neilos knows," Ibram said. "On the first foot, he could know nothing."

"It's tricky," Ahksell admitted.

"On the second, however, your new friend Shokan Dughlat talked a great deal, but neglected to point out a few crucial facts about the second witness."

Ahksell held up one finger. "He did say that they had spoken before he went up the living mountain, and that they had agreed that Master Dughlat should be the one to come and see Mentor."

"So either all Neilos knows is that his friend saw green fire after hitting his head in an explosion," Ibram said, "or he knew of the green fire and didn't feel strongly about the affair either way."

"Oh, we don't know that," Ahksell said. "He wanted to wait and speak with his employer."

"So Dughlat did say," Ibram agreed. "Our path is clear." He ducked around a young mistress prodding two giggling children down the walkway. "We find this Neilos, we question this Neilos, and then we shake Master Dughlat until all the answers we want fall out."

"Surely, there will be no need for that kind of thing," Ahksell said.

Ibram shrugged. "An agent must be prepared for anything."

Two turns by the municipal fountains bracketing Rag Alley and the Street of Bones by the Hall of Tranquility had the both of them spilling out onto Cobblers Circle. The circle was an older section of the village, lying alongside the road that bordered Old Lityen. As areas of Lityen went, it could have done with a more thorough wash, but it was busy enough with folk plying their trades. The earthy funk of fresh leather hung about the air, unsurprisingly considering how close they were to the tanners' pits up the hill.

Ibram resolved to breathe through his mouth as he and Ahksell stepped down from the walkway and onto the cobblestoned square. The rain was misting down from the light grey clouds. No doubt they'd be slowly drenched before they realized it. A short interrogation of the surrounding shops led them to one of the single-room inns crammed between the shoemakers and their dependent trades.

The lady who ran the inn was only lately returned from her trip to the market with bread and beef for that night's dinner. She was short of time and temper, but Ibram managed to win her over with a magical combination of pleasant courtesy, his sect brooch, and Ahksell's earnest face. Erno Neilos lived on the floor above the small common room with the smoky fire, in a separate room that faced the shared open-air kitchen garden. The building was fairly quiet, most folk being at their labors.

"Strange Rennab doesn't require his workers to live onsite," Ibram murmured as they ascended the creaky stairs.

The light in the stairwell came from one dusty, but well-positioned series of mirrors, angled to reflect the light from a single encased oil torch which hung at the top from a cobweb heavy chain. Ibram sniffed cautiously. The air was still, but surprisingly clear of the smell of the streets or of cooking food. The stairs themselves looked well-swept.

"If he didn't provide space for overnight guests, perhaps he didn't think to require it," Ahksell said from behind him. "And Master Finar did say he was thinking of selling. The new owners might not have kept the workers on."

"Here we are," Ibram said, and stepped out onto the floor. He moved down to the end of the hallway quickly, while Ahksell followed behind. An open window, shutters angled outward, beamed pale light and dripped a small pool of rain water onto the wooden floorboards immediately ahead of him. Ibram heard no movement behind the two closed doors nearest the stairwell, and the door immediately across from Erno Neilos' room was firmly shut.

"I think we should be—"

Something flashed at the threshold of Neilos' door. Ibram halted, and then held up his right hand. Ahksell stopped talking. His footsteps creaked quietly on the flooring, and then Ibram sensed him leaning forward.

The breeze rippled across Ibram's forehead; the something flashed again. A small mirror? Some kind of little piece of tin? The door wavered on its hinges.

"Door's open," Ibram whispered.

"What?" Ahksell said, equally quietly.

Ibram glanced over his shoulder quickly. "His *door* is *open*."

Ahksell's eyes widened. He leaned up, head twisting over Ibram's shoulder, and then slowly nodded and relaxed his position. Ibram nodded back. His hand dropped to the hilt of his sica; he drew it slowly.

Ahksell didn't have his gar. With no real evidence of a crime, his involvement could not be said to be official; that was what Ibram was for. Ahksell flexed his hands at his sides, and then twisted open a pouch at his side. A small wireframed bird lay in his palm. He held it loosely, but Ibram saw the way Ahksell's fingers twitched and the little bird fluttered in response.

"What are you going to do with that?" Ibram demanded, trying to keep his voice down.

Ahksell grinned. Ibram rolled his eyes. "Suppose I shall find out."

As quietly as possible, they approached Erno Neilos' open door. Ibram squinted at the little flash of light as it came again. He frowned. A bangle? A little stamped metal something or other hung by a braided chain that disappeared into the room.

"It's a votive chain," Ahksell said. "Look, there's little feet at the end. It's to hold a candle for the Runner."

Ibram tilted his head. "What do you mean?"

"Someone shut the door too hard," Ahksell said. "Look how long it is. The wall shook and the chain caught in the door."

"And the feet blocked it," Ibram said. He hefted his sica. "So they might not have realized?"

Ahksell chuckled. "Master Neilos might not even be *home*."

Ibram paused, and looked behind himself. Ahksell wiggled his eyebrows at him, grinned, and put his strange little stickum bird back in his pouch. Ibram cleared his throat, and sheathed his weapon.

"It's still strange," he muttered.

"Oh, absolutely," Ahksell said, and nodded. "Always best to be cautious."

"This is also my thinking," Ibram said.

"Better to look absurd than to be caught unprepared."

They were alone in the hallway; Ibram punched Ahksell in the shoulder. Ahksell rubbed the spot as if wounded, deigned to rock backwards in response, and laughed. Ibram turned back around to face the doorway.

"I promise I won't tell anyone," Ahksell said. "If we have missed Master Neilos, then I am certain we shall find him at his work."

"Indeed, indeed so," Ibram said. "Riant, Ahk-la, to be sure."

Ahksell laughed, and then covered his mouth, and attempted to appear serious. He cleared his throat, and shrugged. Ibram walked the last few steps to the room. He pushed open the door, allowing the braided votive chain to swing back inside the room, and stepped inside. There was still information to be had even in an empty room.

Ibram turned around, holding the door open for Ahksell. Ahksell paused upon the threshold; his eyes widened. Ibram followed the line of Ahksell's sight; he dropped the door and put his hands on his hips. The body of a blond man, not very tall but quite thin, with a scarred chin lay twisted on the bare wooden floor of the small room. One hand gripped his straw mattress in the death, while the other clutched at the wire twisted around his wrenched neck.

❧ 6 ❧

Ibram clenched and unclenched his hands at his sides. His heart turned over and thudded into a march inside his chest. He dashed out, pushing Ahksell unresisting to the side and returned to the hall-way. He leaned out the open window into the tiny kitchen garden and saw nothing but waving lines of laundry, slowly soaking in the rain. An older woman stepped out from the building across the way, carrying a basket. She grabbed down the nearest shift from the laundry line.

"You there!" he hollered. "Lady with a basket!"

The woman fell back a step in shock and clutched her basket to her chest. Ibram waved his left arm high in the air. He whistled sharply, and saw her worn face turn ruddy in outrage.

"What cause do you have to go scaring honest folk?" she bellowed up at him. "You barbarian! Swallow your tongue until you've taught it some manners!"

Ibram dropped his arm to the windowsill for balance. "When did you lay out this laundry? Are you only now taking it in from the rain?" he yelled.

"I'll take you in from the rain if you're not careful!"

"May I be known to you, Mistress?" he asked with a sigh. He was the agent in place, now that a crime had been committed. It was his duty to write the report that Ladyship would send to Captain Talsconis, which would no doubt be added to the tome about to land upon the desk of the imperial commissioner.

"Andreseni," the old woman said. "Larrha Andreseni."

Ahksell's footstep creaked across the floorboard behind him; Ibram threw back his left hand to stay his appearance at the window. No good would come of her seeing an alchemist over Ibram's shoulder. It was the wrong hour of the day for there to be many folk about—Yilka the Green had turned her face from him on that point—but no need to spread bad gossip before Ibram laid out a more interesting tale. He knocked the heel of his right palm against the windowsill.

"I am Ibram Ucalegon," he called out, still eying the building opposite for a hint of movement or light behind one of the shutters opposite Erno Neilos' room. "Agent for the Fourth Mentor of the Preceptory of Yseult." And there was the expected paling of her cheek as his occupation, if not his name sunk in. Folk in Lityen were better educated than most outside the imperial boundary; they could read writing when it was spelled out for them.

Ibram leaned out of the window more fully. "How long have you been inside your house?"

The woman's face smoothed into a blank surprise; she blinked up at him, and then looked behind herself, before returning to peer at Ibram as if he were a madman. "These forty years past," she finally said.

Ibram refused to admit defeat. "Have you seen anyone pass this window today?" he asked. "Not a neighbor, but anyone unfamiliar? And don't say myself, Mistress. I count us as well acquainted by now."

She frowned heavily, but something in his face either convinced her of the purity of Ibram's interest, or the laundry basket was becoming too heavy. She hefted it high in both her arms. Slowly, she walked forward down the muddy garden path towards the center wooden pillar which held up the laundry lines. She pulled a few more shifts down while she thought, and stuffed them into her basket.

"No one today that I saw," she said in a careful voice. "Not that I was looking, you understand. Someone has to do the laundry around here. I've work of my own to do, young master, and no apprentice to help me."

Ibram took stock of the buildings which formed the shared courtyard, a dozen shuttered windows surrounded the area. The rain was
only just beginning to strengthen in force. He clicked his teeth
together and then shook his head. There was a body behind him, and
he was growing ever more soaked the longer he stood there.

"I thank you for your time, Mistress Andreseni. What is not
present may be as important as what exists."

She snorted loudly as he stepped back from the window. "Now I
know he's from up the living mountain," floated up to him on the
wind. Ibram put his back to the window, and shook his head.

Ahksell stared at him from the hallway. Ibram walked past and
returned to the room. He wrinkled his nose. Erno Neilos remained on
the floor, quite irrevocably dead. Ibram swallowed, and reached back
without looking to grab Ahksell and tug him fully into the room. The
door swung shut behind him, and then rebounded off Ahksell's back.
Ahksell made a sort of strangled noise, but ignored him in favor of
staring down at the body lying almost at their feet.

"Well, the question of malice has been decided," Ibram said. He
narrowed his eyes. The wire around Neilos' neck was long and finely
made, with two short, fat wooden handles at either end, like a cheese
cutter. An odd, but effective murder weapon. There was quite a puddle
of blood underneath the body.

"I'm the First Finder," Ahksell said in a tone of pure surprise, and
cleared his throat. His face turned ashen.

Ibram nodded slowly. His eyes flicked from the open window with
water pooling on the floor to the opposite side of the low framed bed.

Ahksell breathed in slowly and then swallowed hard enough that
Ibram could hear the click in his throat. He cleared his throat again,
and then shook off Ibram's grip. "I'm the First Finder," he said. "You
have to record my testimony."

Ibram's head snapped up and around. "Yes," he said. "All right, I
will... Statements later. Your introrse pendant, get it out. We need to
know how he died."

"I feel as if we can comfortably guess," Ahksell said, and pointed at
the body.

"Yes," Ibram shook his head. "No, I mean, that could have been how he was attacked, but look at the room." He pointed to the open window and then the four open shelves lining the opposite wall. "There's nothing disturbed on those shelves; they're neat as a garden row."

"Until the one by the bed," Ahksell said. He sounded more sure of himself.

"It's an exception," Ibram agreed. "Ladyship would hate us to over-look it."

"I'll check there first," Ahksell said and finally moved away towards the opposite side of the low wooden bed frame.

Ibram crouched down next to the body, and held his breath. A small breeze from the open window stroked aside the hair on the back of Ibram's neck. Erno Neilos' eyes stared up at him. There was such an unnerving emptiness to a body in death, once the soul had migrated and the anima began to return to the plane of reality. Ibram concealed his shudder, and bent down to take a closer look at the mess of Neilos' neck. The wire had cut deeply on the side, and then the handles left to dangle. Ibram checked the floor about the body's head, enough blood had been spilled on the floor that there was no doubt Neilos had been killed here.

He glanced up. Ahksell paused in fitting the loop of braided copper wire over his middle finger, and bit the corner of his bottom lip. "We should have the lady downstairs notify the temple of the Runner," Ahksell said. He sighed. "Is it known whether he lived by himself?"

"That's why I want you to wave that pendant of yours about," Ibram said. "And check if those clothes might belong to anyone else."

"Good point," Ahksell said, and turned away. He extended his pendant, the trimstone arrowhead at the end of the copper wire pointed forward like a hound pulling its leash.

Ibram's skin prickled beneath his clothes as the sensation of a great unseen hand pressed down on the top of his head and shoulders. He put his own very real hands underneath the body's left side and rolled it over. There was no more blood than he might have expected to find, apart from what had dripped from Neilos' neck in death where the wire had broken the skin. He frowned. No boot print, either, except for a little crust of mud, which could have been picked up anywhere.

He looked again at Neilos' neck. The cheese cutter had done its job, but why use it at all? Unless the killer had arrived without a dagger or sword to set Master Neilos' mind at ease. Unless Ibram was supposed to believe Neilos had done himself in via the most uncomfortable method possible, or that folk just wandered around with cheese cutters in their belts for protection. It also could be that the murder might have been a quick decision spun from opportunity, and not a planned event.

"Is there any food about?" he asked.

"How can you be hungry now?" Ahksell asked.

"I'm not," Ibram said, "Look about you, is there any food?"

"No, there isn't."

Ibram carefully rolled the body back to the floor, and felt the corpse's cheek and tried to move his arm. The limb felt normal in his grip, no sign of bloating. Erno Neilos' body was cold, but it was a wet day and the weather played tricks on corpses, in Ibram's experience. Ibram bit his lip, and touched Neilos' cheek again. The skin retained some suppleness, but the blood beneath had already dried enough to change color. He leaned back, still crouched, on his heels. He crossed his arms over his knees, and took in the room before him.

It was a neat place, almost scrupulously clean. The floor was swept, probably by the small bundle of tied twigs leaning in the corner. An upended washbasin and pitcher lay on the floor by the window, near a ball of much loved soap which lay in a thin crack between the floorboards and a rag of coarsely woven fabric.

They must have fallen in the scuffle. Neilos had died kicking—he'd succeeded in knocking the frame of his bed sideways. Yet his killer had clearly still held the upper hand—definitely stronger—and bore him to the ground to finish the job. The attacker would have gotten blood on their clothes, but he'd have to find the assailant first before Ibram could go poking about in their laundry. Ibram sighed through his nose, and glanced once more at the body, and then to the room around it.

Erno Neilos had had a good job, that much was plain. His room was small, but it looked out upon the open air and the kitchen garden. He had a frame for a half-burnt rush by his narrow bed, and an oil lamp hung from a prettily braided rope nailed to the ceiling. He had a lovely brown wool cloak on a peg and Ibram spied a thick, folded winter blanket on the nearest shelf. He had extra stockings, and the straw in his mattress seemed plump. The blue blanket was edged in red thread. He lived fairly well for a dayworker at an evening courtyard. Perhaps he was frugal.

Ibram put down one knee and bent to look more closely at the floor. There were marks on the wood, like Neilos' boot heels had struck against the grain as they scraped for purchase. He glanced at the pool of water beneath the window; there was a tinge of mud to it. The killer's own footwear, perhaps, and they must have been lucky to not get blood the soles. Lucky, or experienced.

"Lavin blossoms," Ahksell murmured.

"What?" Ibram asked, distracted. He pulled the mattress out of Neilos' grip with some difficulty and raised it back onto the bed frame.

"He put lavin blossoms behind his winter cloak and second shirt," Ahksell said. He pulled a little bundle of dried flowers out from the shelf, the tiny purple flowers bobbed at the end of the thin dry stems.

"Careful about insects, was he?" Ibram asked.

Ahksell slipped the tie off the flowers. He breathed in the lavin blossoms' scent, and then floated two stems across the room for Ibram. Ibram set the flowers beneath his nose, and inhaled the sweet, lightly soapy scent. It went some way to covering the body's odor. He tucked the lavin blossoms in between the top buttons of his gambeson, and returned to searching.

"Yes, but there is something..." Ahksell trailed off, and extended his pendant once more.

Ibram bent to look beneath the bed. He ran his right palm carefully over the wooden planks. Tingling like a roll of pins and needles began building up the sides of his head. A dull thrum of manipulated reality built in his joints and the bend of his spine. His hands spasmed; he flexed them. He slid his palm along the floorboards and felt nothing but the silk of disturbed dust. He wriggled upright, and examined his hand.

"Nothing," he muttered, and wiped his hand on his opposite sleeve.

"Look again, "Ahksell said.

Ibram glanced up, and saw Ahksell's pendant standing out from his palm, the arrowhead vibrating towards the head of Neilos' bed.

"You do it," he said. "I've something obstructing my way."

Ahksell's head twitched in his direction. His dark eyes looked through Ibram, fixed on a point only he could see. Whatever emanation or sign Ahksell saw there seemed to bemuse him. He frowned, blinked once, and then sneezed.

"Thank you," Ahksell said. "But you don't need to worry, I'm fine."

Ibram moved back from the corpse on his knees and sat back on his heels. "I'm not worried."

"I've seen dead bodies before."

Ibram considered Ahksell while the man was distracted by the strings of reality. His color was better, but his mouth was pressed very thin. In his free hand, he kept the lavin blossoms at the ready.

"I am well aware," Ibram said. He pointed. "What's under the poor dead man's bed?"

"What?" Ahksell asked, and then snapped his pendant back into his palm. "Oh right, yes, one moment..."

He knelt down, tucking the blossoms away, and began rummaging on the floor near the head of low wooden frame that kept the straw mattress off the ground. Ibram frowned at Ahksell's back, and tugged his flyway hair behind his ears.

"I am the agent here," he said. "I am only trying to set the scene in my mind, before I must report on it to Lady Azadiya."

Ahksell sighed greatly. "And since I am here, I should do the same," he said. "And Second Mentor Stadat has that course, you know. On recognizing the properties of anima in several states and—"

"And 'murdered corpse' is one of them?"

"Of course not," Ahksell said. "I am only saying you might let me look over the body as well."

"Do you have a Hessele's Cage?" Ibram asked.

Ahksell patted his belt. "Well, no," he said, and frowned down at Ibram and the body. "It's an unsettling moment. I've never been a First Finder before. There's such a responsibility to it, after all." He sat up suddenly and put his arm on the straw mattress. "I'll have to go up before the judge on the next circuit court, won't I?"

"Yes," Ibram said. "You will."

"I've never been to a court before," Ahksell said, and swallowed. "At least, not that I can remember."

"It's a memorable event, I'm certain you haven't suddenly lost your senses."

"I just have to read out my statement. They won't require any more than that?"

Ibram nodded. "I'll take it down exactly, and you won't even need to memorize it."

"Yes, but I'm good at that," Ahksell chuckled weakly.

Ibram shrugged one shoulder, and then tugged the hair on the nape of his neck. "Did you find whatever you thought was under there?"

"Right!" Ahksell dived back under the bed. A scraping sound erupted as the frame moved back three inches. He reappeared, clutching something small in his great hand. "There."

Ahksell tossed it across the straw mattress. Ibram caught it; a bag no bigger than his palm and closed tightly by a green leather cord. He weighed it in his palm, and heard a distinct clink.

"Heavy little thing," Ibram said. He unwound the cord and poured the bag's contents out on to the mattress. Ten gleaming silver picaio coins lay on the disturbed blanket. Ibram's eyebrows rose high of their own accord.

"Well now," Ibram said. "Perhaps Master Neilos wasn't very frugal at all."

"It does seem a little heavy for a dayworker's savings," Ahksell said.

Ibram levered himself to his feet, and scooped the coins back into their pouch. He frowned down at the body as he retied the pouch. They would have to send someone up the living mountain to take the body to the medicinal corps for a proper examination. If Neilos was dedicated to The Runner, another agent would have to inform the temple. Ibram winced. And no doubt an unlucky soul would be tasked to deliver word to Captain Talsconis of Her Gracious Majesty's Cohort of Peace and tell him they would need a space found in Soliya IV's cells for a murderer.

"Amota Berac!" Ibram called out as he ran across the square. "Amota Berac!"

Berac turned at his name, already frowning enough to bristle his long beard, and watched Ibram's approach. So did the small group of agents and regular villagers which surrounded him. Ibram panted as he came to a halt, and placed his hands on his hips; he inhaled through his mouth and shook his head. He counted Soren Rennab amongst the number now facing him, but although he recognized the cookshop owners from previous nights' hunger pains, he couldn't remember who was who. By their clothes, the others were laborers from Builders Row.

"I'm glad to have found you, to be sure," Ibram said.

"What's got you all excited then, young master?" an older woman inquired with an amused laugh.

Now, this one stood out from the rest, both in terms of the richness of her clothing and the fact that the other folk around her gave Mistress Mysterious a generous amount of space about her person. She was a greying beauty, dressed in a red belted apron gown and white shift with a lace cap holding her hair back, a fashion that had fallen by the wayside before the days of Soliya IV's father had run out. Large egg-shaped brooches held her dress together, faceted with glittering stones—gems or glass, Ibram couldn't say. The Vo Kaln's sigil of a dipper bird with fish in its great beak was picked out in gold thread on her breast. What was the Lityen twig of the family tree again...third children? Cousins of better folk? Some kind of landholder, anyway.

Ibram bowed politely, nonetheless. "It's of no matter, Ladyship," he said, and the woman tittered. "Only I do need to speak with my uncle a short moment. Might I borrow him?"

The folk gathered behind Amota Berac shuffled a bit at the request. Perhaps Ibram had left it a little strong. Berac sighed, and closed the ledger he held in his left hand.

"If it is so important, Ibram," he said. "Then we shall have to hear it. Come with me, now."

He passed the ledger to Esti, who had been edging towards the far reaches of the crowd, and pointed back behind Ibram towards the municipal fountain at the opposite end of Pillared Circle. Ibram bowed again, and followed him over to the spot indicated.

"What are you doing running up to me as if there was another fire on your heels?" Amota Berac hissed under his breath. "You know very well that running causes nothing but panic."

"Yes, but I have to—"

"And where is Ahksell?" Amota Berac asked. He lifted his head and glared about as if Ibram had lost him in a card game, or something. "Did you two find spin-lace in one of those back-alley eating-houses again?"

"That was a month previous!"

"You were sick as tarmap in the desert for a seven-day."

"And the seller has moved on to savories, anyway," Ibram said, and made a special effort to keep his voice down. Esti was clearly having difficulties getting the other folk to listen to him. They were one and all focused on the scene Amota Berac was making. Ibram put his back to the crowd. "Ahksell is right where I left him."

"Which is?"

Ibram paused. A man stood beneath an awning of the little shayshop, near the first exit off Pillared Circle. He had long dark hair and a soft face, and Ibram could have sworn he'd been watching Amota Berac. There was something too casual in the way he leaned against the post and crossed his arms. Ibram frowned, and then shook his head at Amota Berac's cough.

"I want it said that this is not our fault," Ibram said.

"To be sure," Amota Berac said. "You've lost him, haven't you."

"Never in life!" Ibram protested. "He's waiting for the medicinal corps to send down their agents to retrieve the murder victim we found."

"*Ibram.*"

Ibram raised both hands. "Ahksell said he needed to look over the room once more, and since I had need to speak with you, it seemed better to split up than wait."

Amota Berac drew in a very long and deep breath, and then pinched the bridge of his nose. "I will finish this assignment," he said. "These quarrelsome folk will cease following me about, and then Ladyship will allow me back up the living mountain, and I shall never descend again."

"Your wife might—"

"Never again!"

"Never again, to be sure," Ibram said and nodded quickly. "Are they truly so awful?"

"Most of them are beholden to that Mistress Vo Kaln, who owned their buildings and land, and so feel they cannot argue with her," Amota Berac said. "So instead, they argue with me. Folk with nothing in their pockets but ashes and crumbs will haggle forever, if it's the only way to get their livelihoods back."

Ibram glanced out of the corner of his eye towards the ruins, still being carted off to clear the area. A fair number of the folk in the work crews seemed to know each other; they worked in concert, pulling out the charred timber and piling it up for removal with a minimum of discussion. Pillared Circle was so far inside Lityen, that the regular trade and traffic surrounding them made the work slow going. Lucky for Ibram's mission, but not for anyone else.

"Can't blame them," he said.

"No, neither can I," Amota Berac sighed, like a bear denied fish in the river on account of flooding. "Well, what's this about a murder victim? And what did you want to know, Ib-la?"

"Only how many members of each fire alliance have been orbiting you," Ibram said. "And for how long, to be sure."

Amota Berac nodded slowly. His lower lip pushed out in thought. "I've been operating out of The Sun Eagle," he said, and pointed in the direction of the draughtshop. Ibram leaned backwards to see around the top of the fountain, and saw The Sun Eagle's painted sign lying propped against the remains of its front porch. "Trying to keep them separated, but talking. Rennab's been available for most of it. His husband has not been involved, but stopped by on his way to open their caffa."

"He was cataloging in the wreckage when last I saw him," Ibram said. He flexed his fingers. The body hadn't been too badly gone when they'd found it. The odds on him dying at night were lower, in Ibram's opinion. It didn't seem likely that Master Finar had woken up early, ran all the way across the village to murder Neilos, and then had calmly given Ahksell directions to his corpse.

"What about Mistress Dubidat and her husband?" he asked.

Amota Berac shook his head. "The husband has been present for all meetings. Early, in fact, which unfortunately doesn't help his wife any."

"She hasn't attended?" Ibram asked.

"She, like the cookshop owners, has a landlady—that Ederetta Vo Kaln, you just spoke to." Berac dipped his chin back in the direction of the grey-haired lady in the lace cap. "They've been dancing attendance on her since she appeared this morning. Before that, it was merely her land-agent."

Ibram made a face; Amota Berac tapped the center of his forehead, and Ibram stumbled back. "Hey now," he protested.

"A still river keeps its fish," Amota Berac said. "Stifle whatever unpleasant thought you just had."

Ibram shrugged. "I am merely interested in the sudden appearance of Mistress Vo Kaln," he said.

Amota Berac tsked, and Ibram framed his own face with both hands. "I am as still as a rock," he said.

"Well enough," Amota Berac said, and clapped him on the shoulder. "Do you see those boys behind me?"

He didn't turn around, but Ibram looked over his Berac's shoulders, and spied the group in question. The boys and girls were all in a milling clump, bumping their buckets or bags and getting distracted by the adults attempting to move around them. They wore rough tunics and hose, though some of the younger children still sported dresses. Ibram was careful not to nod.

"I do," he said, and kept his face pleasant.

"They're from the surrounding farms, and the soapmakers' guild," Amota Berac said.

"What, all of them?"

Amota Berac crossed his arms over his barrel-like chest, and nodded. He smiled as if Ibram had told a good joke, but his tone was low and serious. He spoke only so loud as to permit Ibram to hear him, and none else.

"The building owner," he said, and Ibram took note he was careful not to mention Mistress Vo Kaln by name, "has allowed them access to the ruins she owns, to gather up what ash or cinders might be useful."

"She has?" Ibram asked. "You allowed it?"

Amota Berac frowned. "How could I not?" he asked. "She owns the buildings—or what's left of them. I am merely conducting matters between the fire alliances."

Ibram shifted his weight left to right foot and back again. He bounced on his toes. "They could disturb something I need," he hissed, and then looked about himself quickly. "I need to grab Esti, where did he go this time?"

He started to push past, and Amota Berac stopped him with a hand on his chest. "I've already told him to keep an eye on the little ones, which he will return to doing when we're done here. And we've let it be known that there's a faunt in it for any child that finds something interesting. I've no doubt we'll be hip deep in nails and lantern chains in no time."

Ibram settled on his heels, and shook his head. "Why did she do it?" he asked.

Amota Berac shrugged. "Because she can," he said. "It's her building, if not her dwelling, and she has to recoup the loss somehow."

Ibram felt his lips turn downward, and controlled his expression, even though both a body and a busybody in one day were no partners in calm. He took in a slow breath and let it out.

"Do you know how much she stands to gain from this?"

Amota Berac waggled his hand in the air. "It's difficult to say," he said. "She's not a member of the fire alliance, because none of these buildings are her dwelling. But she has insured the buildings against fire as an owner of the land..." He slashed his hand through the air. "Complications! Contracts! I am no good with these matters. She's the owner, she'll retain control of the land no matter what is upon it, and it's up to her to decide to rebuild or retrench."

Amota Berac waited a moment, watching his face, and then patted him on the chest.

"You and young Ahksell are all right, though?" he asked. "No jitters or dark thoughts? Murdered bodies are bad for the soul."

Ibram smiled. Kivan the Red, Amota Berac's dedicated god,

believed in dying gloriously in battle, or even better, in bed. Anything else, He tended to view as a personal affront to health and safety.

"We are both of us well enough," Ibram said. "I should go and collect him."

"Never let an alchemist at loose ends out on their lonesome," Amota Berac agreed.

Nasty business taken care of, once he had collected Ahksell from the steps of the tenant inn and its landlady's clutches, there was little for them to do but continue forward as they had begun at the beginning of the day. There was no scrying bowl of water waiting in Lady Azadiya's tower for them to divine truth out of, and a fifth murder meant Ibram needed time to consider all the new facets of their investigation. Besides, bodies made him hungry, and Ahksell looked as if he could do with a meal to settle his stomach.

Fortunately, The Sun Eagle had lost its front porch but neither its owner nor her business sense. They'd been protected from the bakery-mill's explosion in large measure by the evening courtyards' absorption of the blast. The draughtshop was doing a brisk business supplying the influx of folk assessing the damage to Pillared Circle with all the food and drink hungry laborers could spare.

Upon entering, Ibram noted that most of the members of the local fire alliances were seated at opposing trestle tables, but Mistress Vo Kaln and Amota Berac himself were absent. The Pillared Circle group occupied the table nearest the cauldron of boiling bunch stew and the Builders Row folk took up space by the wall, well away from the door. The atmosphere was strained, and smelled overly of onion and cask-fish, but by the looks of the potboys blocking the line of sight between the two groups, the proprietors had it well in hand.

It wouldn't do for an Attendant to be seen providing moral aid or physical comfort to either party until the work of the sect agents was done. Ibram herded Ahksell to the other side of the draught-shop before the man could make any impolitic condolences. He stuck his Attendant at the end of a trestle table nearest the open window, and then headed off to the bar alone. The owner was busy but soft-hearted, and once Ibram ran down his list of emphatic yet vague statements about how much alchemists needed to eat to maintain their equilibrium, she was happy to provide them with food. Ibram came staggering back to their table with the rewards of strategy.

"Bread trenchers, crock of brenzamal, fenek *with* vegetables, and even a salad," Ibram said as he laid out the feast between them. An older serving boy carrying an enormous tray in both hands plunked down a pitcher and two small wooden cups in front of Ahksell. "And a cider each for both of us."

The boy swayed off back to the bar. Ibram sat down on the attached wooden bench of the trestle table. Ahksell leaned over the platter of fenek, cut and stewed in Boim wine and covered in roasted vegetables, and rubbed his hand over his mouth.

"I can't say I'm hungry," he said. "We just saw a dead body, after all."

"Death merely reminds us the body must be fed as well as the soul," Ibram said. "Thus, we must not only eat, but acknowledge that we deserve this meal."

"I still think we should have followed the body up the living mountain," Ahksell said.

"And it does you credit," Ibram said. "However, again, I will remind you that we still have several people to speak with before presenting ourselves to Lady Azadiya. It's best to have some context with our corpse."

"And you're hungry."

"And I am hungry," Ibram said. "And so are you, even if you don't notice yet. Eat, here."

He nudged the bigger trencher—the one with the whiter, softer crumb—in front of Ahksell and shifted the large serving spoon in his direction. Ahksell glanced around quickly, and stuck his thumb in the gravy surrounding the fenek. He licked the pad of his thumb clean.

Ibram gasped. "Attendant, your manners."

Ahksell raised his hand to his shoulder and flicked his middle finger in Ibram's direction. "How did you get all this?" he asked. "It's well past time for the midday meal."

Ibram shrugged. "They told me more folk ordered the bunch stew."

Ahksell nodded. He stared down at the food with a pinched mouth. Ibram sighed. He reached out and grabbed a fork from the communal cup in the middle of the trestle table, and then scooped out a dripping piece of meat onto the center of Ahksell's trencher. Then, he smeared the brenzamal on top of the meat. Ahksell's nose twitched.

"Eat," Ibram said, as he dropped the fork by Ahksell's hand.

Ibram could smell the peppery herbs and sharp vinegar mixed into the green cheese from across the table. It was all very typical of spring meals in the garden provinces, when there was a chance of fat summer feasts upon the horizon. Ibram grabbed his own fork and scooped himself out a portion of salad, raw, not pickled, though the crumbled boiled duck egg was all right. He licked his lips and took a long drink of cider, unspiced but tart.

"Oh, that's nice," he muttered. "I needed that."

Ahksell poked up a roasted salsify with a tangle of sawge stuck on top of it. "We could have eaten up the living mountain," he said.

"Better to think on the ground," Ibram said. He pinched meat from the platter with his first three fingers and placed it on top of the salad, ignoring Ahksell's quirked eyebrows. "Look upon the land and draw forth our conclusions."

Ahksell laughed quietly. Ibram grinned and licked gravy off his fingers. He rolled the meat up in salad, picked up the bundle, and then bit off one end. A woman across the room saw Ibram dipping the remaining half into the fenek's gravy and looked away, shuddering. He rolled his eyes, while he pulled his eating knife out of his belt, and laid it on the table for the next time he touched a bite of food in public. He picked up his fork and stabbed the dripping roll-up onto the double tines, and then slid the whole thing into his mouth. He chewed and swallowed. Ahksell delicately separated the meat from the fenek's thigh bone with his own serviceware.

"The problem, as I see it, has layers," Ibram said, and sliced a morsel out his own remaining portion of fenek.

"A murder now," Ahksell said, and nodded.

"Murder always," Ibram said, "strictly speaking. Those four in the fire are doubtless feeling a bit raw about it, stuck on the what-sit on the way to Oblivion."

Ahksell grimaced. "On the Caravan of Plenty, taking the Second Road to the Crossroads," he said. "Really, how do you know nothing about this? It's your own father's religion!"

Ibram brought his shoulder up, and then let if fall. "I had other lessons," he said. "I promise to read a pamphlet later. Right now, I suspect we must focus on the murderer in our midst, and let his victims enjoy The Runner's hospitality."

"True enough," Ahksell said. "And you are correct, though Master Neilos' death feels a bit more immediate."

Ibram chewed his food, and spoke as he dug another morsel free with his fork. "We'll have to find Dughlat and see how close he and his co-worker used to be."

"I saw him standing with Master Comoros outside," Ahksell said.

Ibram perked up from the piled meat on his fork and glanced over the table to the far window. "Amota Berac is still here? I thought he had left for the next round of talks."

Ahksell hmmed in agreement. He stuck his eating knife into the breast of the fenek and dug the potatoes out from underneath. Ibram surveyed the crock of brenzamal, grabbed up a few shards of root parsley from the salad, and dunked his handful into the spread. He ate the results and sighed; they were still tender and herby.

"Any further thoughts on why someone might burn down a dwelling?" Ibram asked around a mouthful of food.

"Illegally?" Ahksell said with a frown. "Setting your own home alight makes very little sense to me, no matter how much money is involved."

"You'll claim the insurance, to be sure," Ibram agreed, "but you'll still have to rebuild the house."

"But they have two businesses," Ahksell said, "and perhaps they prefer the caffa."

Ibram dropped his remaining pieces of root parsley onto his trencher, where it was swamped with gravy, and forked the dripping crumb free of the crust. "A thought," he said. "Arson is only a crime when it damages *someone else's* dwelling. Can The Isconian's Hand be said to be a dwelling?"

"No," Ahksell said. "Not that I am aware."

"But The High Climber is," Ibram said. "Rennab and his family live —*lived*—on the second level."

Ahksell ducked his entire body forward; his eyes widened. Ibram sighed inwardly. Alchemy was not a subtle art, and did not produce delicate folk. At some point, Ibram would have to ask Ama to talk to Ahksell about the fine art of polite conversation on dangerous topics.

"So you think it possible that Master Rennab intended to only burn down his property?" Ahksell asked. "And the faulty tiles led to it spreading out of control?" He raised his first finger. "Perhaps Master Neilos knew of the plan."

"The thought occurred. Neither Dughlat nor Rennab took the opportunity to lay blame on the bakery-mill, which would have made more sense. It strikes me as important that he pointed to his competitor instead, and moreover that he chose to blame those foreign candle dancers," Ibram shrugged. The bench he sat upon creaked as he settled himself more comfortably. "But the most that Lady Azadiya might do is send her report to Captain Talsconis with her strong recommendation that the Empress' justice fall upon Rennab's head and shoulders like a stack of bricks."

Ahksell sat back in his chair. "You've been in noble lands," he said with a weary look in the set of his eyes, "Is it easier outside the imperial boundary?"

Ibram shook his head. "Not especially," he said. "Nobles get to have their own dungeons of course, and the judgement thereof, but truthfully... Same territorial restrictions, different estate of the realm."

Ahksell sighed, and stared at his food. Ibram followed suit, with one eye on his own meal and the other on their fellow customers. Tempers didn't seem to be running high as of yet—most folk were probably too exhausted from the rebuilding efforts—but the edge in the atmosphere bothered him. It spoke to Ibram of patience fraying at the seams, and folk justifiably worried about their place in the world. Life was good in Lityen, but that didn't mean bad things never happened.

Ahksell sipped his cider, and then pointed at Ibram. "Master Rennab knew his neighbors used our own sect's tiles."

Ibram nodded. "Perhaps his trust in his neighbor's precautions was misplaced."

"But even if he burned it down for the money he would receive from his own insurance on the items within the building," Ahksell said, "surely, the fire alliance would pay him nothing. He broke the terms of their contract by not doing all that he could to prevent a fire. And the contents of the place...were they not also insured? It seems a large risk so deep within the village; how could he believe that the other buildings wouldn't be harmed?"

Ibram shrugged. He drank his cider, while Ahksell downed his. He put his cup down, and grabbed for the pitcher just as Ahksell's great square hand reached for it. An Attendant did not fill cups for their agents in public, even if Ahksell had a tendency to forget it. Ibram poured out fair measures for each of them, and set the pitcher down.

"On the first foot," he said, "if Master Rennab is not the arsonist, there is a handy crop of suspects to consider. Perhaps in revenge for that previous thought of yours."

Ahksell nodded while he chewed. He picked up his cider and drank, so Ibram felt free to continue.

"He has bad tiles, puts his neighbors in danger...maybe his neighbor, uh, this Philendra Dubidat decided to show him why they were so needed. And!" Ibram snapped his fingers. "If the Vo Kalns wanted to buy up another evening courtyard, perhaps she even worried that The High Climber would soon be a competitor against which she could not act."

He pushed the salad plate towards Ahksell so he would eat the onions first. Ahksell piled said onions on his trencher, and then meat on top of that. Ibram debated the need for a trencher when he could simply upend his bread in the platter and sop up the drippings. He poked the unbroken crust with his fork.

"It might be a reason to light a fire," Ahksell said, "but to kill a dayworker? Would that not bring too much attention?"

"And there too we run into the problem of reason," Ibram said. "Crime is such work."

Ibram resisted the urge to defy all the rules of etiquette his Ama had crammed patiently into his head alongside several stanzas of Vissilian law. He merely sopped gravy to his bread by means of dipping the fenek meat back into the platter a second and third time. He topped the mess with the salad herbs, for his health.

"What starts a fire?" he asked.

"Usually more fire," Ahksell said.

Ibram refused his first impulse to throw gravy at him. "That is true," he said slowly and clearly. "But what begins it? You're the alchemist, what makes fire from nothing?"

"Oh, a philosophical question," Ahksell said. He cracked his knuckles and thought for a moment, idly chewing his lower lip. "It's a process," he said. "A reaction of objects in reality to a change in, well, a kind of hierarchy of being."

Ibram raised his eyebrows, and then went back to eating.

Ahksell shook his head. "No need for that look," he said. "It's difficult to explain. See, fire is a product of that exchange that.... It's daylight, yes?"

Ibram glanced out the window. "Indeed so."

"Well, we have light," Ahksell said, "and heat, but neither of us can be said to be on fire, yes?"

"I am forced to agree."

"Well, then you see," Ahksell said.

"I can see it's well that you never went to Bedris instead of Yseult," Ibram said. "The Learners would never live up to their title."

Ahksell rolled his eyes. He leaned over the table on his elbows and held his hands out, palms up, over the fenek platter. "There is the anima, the inherent energy of all living things which affects the ability to interact with reality." He wiggled his left hand. "And there is the effect of all living things on our plane of existence." He lifted his right hand, and then interlaced all ten fingers. "Fire is just another way for the anima to express itself, this time by interacting with the ingredients of life. Light, heat, energy generated from its surroundings. If I put one of our glass lenses down in the sun it would grow hot. If I aimed that heat at the wood of this table, it would catch fire. That's the trick."

"But then why powdered vitriol?" Ibram asked. "If it adds nothing to the process?"

"It's common," Ahksell said. "It's flammable...why else?"

Ibram's mouth twisted to one side. "A green fire in a village of alchemists?" he asked. "What better place to lay blame than at the foot of the living mountain? And do we know powdered vitriol was used?"

"What else could it be?" Ahksell's eyebrows flicked upwards in thought. "I think it the most likely addition."

Ibram nodded as he ate. "A bright green flame... But again, by what method would the arsonist have used it?" he asked. "It nags at me."

Ahksell scooped cheese up from its wooden pot. "It boggles me," he admitted. "Four—five people dead. Surely that means there might soon be a sixth?"

Ibram stole a quick glance about the room; they were seen, but not heard by the customers dotting the other trestle tables. Most of them were bunched up closer to the counter and its tempting line of ale jugs. The two fire alliances were debating amongst themselves. A man with long dark hair was seated closest, but was eating his bunch stew with a studious dedication. Every so often, he deposited a fish bone from his mouth to the little bowl by his elbow; he had a clean white bandage wrapped around his left hand, but his fingers seemed nimble enough. He was tall even sitting down as he was, with a soft face, the sort that appeared young well past the age when a body should betray its wear. It was the same man who'd been standing under the shayshop's awning before. A potboy ran past a little too closely, and forced the man to lean quickly out of the way. He smiled at the apology tossed over the potboy's shoulder, and resettled himself, smoothing his long hair back down his front.

Ibram sucked his teeth. No law against hanging about a public square, nor eating a bite when hungry. Yet, the man seemed a bit familiar in the set of his shoulders, even if Ibram could not place him. He made note of the man's features, just in case, and returned to his own meal. If he and Ahksell kept their voices to a polite level and didn't look too suspicious, no one would pay any mind. They might turn the whys and wherefores over between them like playing cards for as long as either he or Ahksell wished, pretending they aided in divinations. Then again, he was an agent of the Sect of Seven Fires with only a lone young Attendant to curb the bad habits and aggressive tendencies inherent in every arm-for-hire.

Ibram leaned forward with his elbows on the table, spied a smattering of gravy on the back of his knuckle, and licked his skin clean. "Your permission to leave the table, Attendant," he said.

Ahksell's eyes widened. "Ibram, what are you doing?"

Ibram grinned and leaned back on the bench. "I wish to bring back knowledge so that you, my captain, might divine the truth."

Ahksell's face scrunched into distrust. "Stay where you are," he said.

Ibram rose, and took a strengthening drink of his cider. "I won't be but a moment." He wiped his mouth on his sleeve. "Save me some cheese!"

"*Ibram!*" Ahksell hissed.

He polished his sect brooch with his sleeve as he walked off past the other tables of customers, lingering over the seven struts that held up the fiery bit at the top. A passing serving boy swerved to Ibram's left, tottering beneath a wide tray of pitchers and wooden cups. Ibram grabbed his shoulder, and stepped out of the path of an upended pitcher, blessedly near empty. The potboy glared at him distractedly.

"Orders at the bar, Master," he muttered, and Ibram waited patiently for his rather too widely spaced eyes to focus. The boy cleared his throat. "Uh, Master Agent."

"Good day to you, young master," Ibram said, and smiled. "Tell me truly, how long have that motley crowd been under your roof?"

The soft-faced man's head jerked slightly in Ibram's direction; he was listening. Perhaps a dayworker for one of the ruined businesses? Ibram pointed his chin towards the two tables of potential killers. The back of his neck tingled. He was aware of the other man, but the other man didn't know it. It could be nothing, but Ibram was paid a good wage to find needles in haystacks, and you didn't do that by ignoring when Yilka the Green rang a bell in your ear.

The serving boy shrugged free of Ibram's grip and turned in place. He frowned in the general direction Ibram had indicated.

"Couldn't say, Master Agent," he said. "It's been all hands to the plow since midday."

The stranger rose in the corner of Ibram's vision, and walked away from his table, leaving his stew bowls and cup. Ibram glanced at the tables of potential suspects, and did not look behind him to see if the stranger was truly leaving. Two picaio to the player whose dice rolled twins; he might run after but never again have all the fire alliance in one place.

Ibram sighed, and removed a folded bit paper from one of the leather purses on his belt. The serving boy's eyes lit with a cunning thought. Ibram held the packet up with two fingers.

"Do you ever suffer from ailments of the stomach?" he asked. "I should imagine it's a constant world of temptation with a cook as good as your employer."

"You're right about that," the serving boy said. "But what's that? I can get a tonic at the apothecary any old day."

"Oh, but this is a special brew," Ibram said. "Concocted solely for agents of the sect. One taste and—swear to all three faces of Yilka the Green—you'll feel as if you could fly."

He waved the packet again. It was true, of course. Kholdo, his parents' housekeeper, always had a packet of ground ginger to hand. Ibram tended to keep the stuff on him for a shay, if his stomach rebelled at the climb to work.

The serving boy's mouth twisted briefly in thought. He was a sturdy lad, and looked smart enough. His white shirt was clean and his yellow tunic was tied neatly. But he was also young, and the young were —in Ibram's twenty-eight years of experience—stomachs with legs, liable to run into problems on feast days.

The boy nodded, and Ibram slapped the packet onto his tray. "They've been here since the morning meal," he said. "Ate half the quash cauldron between the two tables, and then settled in with shay and small beer for the rest of the day. Most of them, anyways. The apothecary left and returned for lunch, and the lady who runs the Isconian's Hand ate little and disappeared before the bunch stew finished cooking."

"Good lad," Ibram said. "On your way."

The serving boy disappeared into the back of the room. Ibram continued onwards. Brisk though the business was in the draughtshop, the noise level audibly decreased when Ibram approached the members of the Pillared Circle's fire alliance. A tense woman with a stiff jaw and straw blonde hair in a severe bun stuck through with black hair sticks crossed her arms over her chest and glared. The bun suited her, even if the glare did not. Ibram tapped the two men sitting with their backs to him, and bowed shortly.

"Excuse me," he said and slung his left leg in the small open space between the two men. They both startled and leaned in opposite directions. "Ah thank you, Lordships, very kind." Ibram leaned further over the table, and sat down. "Yes, my thanks again, only a little more to your right? There's a mouflon, all right then."

"We have been assigned aid from the Sect, young master," the man on Ibram's left said, as he eyed Ibram's torch brooch.

"Just so, to be sure." Ibram sat down at the trestle table and beamed at his new company. "I fear I have neglected my introductions," he announced.

"Have you?" the stern woman across from him scoffed.

"Indeed so, Ladyship," he said. It was always good business to start tall in titling a stranger you had just met. That way if you were wrong, they were flattered, but if you were right, no one could pretend to be offended. "Ibram Ucalegon, Agent of the Sect of Seven Fires."

"Agent of the Preceptory of Yseult, more precisely," the man next to the stern woman sneered. He had a good mouth for sneering, handsome with authority, but a pair of weak brown eyes spoiled the effect. "It's all Westerners up there."

Not strictly true. The preceptory—like the sect itself—welcomed folk from every corner of the empire, though the fine distinction between an agent and an alchemist might be lost to one whose mind was on other matters. Sadly, it was outside Ibram's current bailiwick to reeducate the uninformed.

"To be sure, I am assigned to that august center of knowledge," Ibram said. "I am happy to hear my occupation has preceded me."

"Why?" The man on his right asked.

"Because if I am so known to all of you, then you shall soon be known to me," Ibram said. He tilted his head. "And thence the Attendant eating his meal at my former table. Shall we start on my left?"

A very obvious percentage of the table looked up and over Ibram's head to the enormous physical specimen of Attendant behind him. He waited while they thought through the implied implications, and poked the bowl of caskfish bones they had picked clean from their bunch stew closer to the scattered empty shells of their hardboiled duck eggs. The man to Ibram's left—a rawboned fellow with a thatch of thick red hair bursting from his head—sighed deeply.

"Harken Bine," he said.

The woman across the way nodded sharply. "Carme Salaz."

The angry man next to her clicked his teeth together twice, but answered. "Otso Sembe."

So the three cookshops which had been totally destroyed were now accounted for. Ibram aimed his smile to his right, towards the silent, pale woman sitting next to Otso Sembe.

"Nescata Corri," she said softly, and touched the wide bandage peeking out from the neckline of her loose rose-colored robe. Her light shift beneath could not hide the angry marring of her skin. The right side of her face was puffy and bright red, as if she had suffered a bad sunburn. Her hair was concealed by a blue wrap, but ragged strands stuck out at her temples. Doubtless, the bandage covered the worst of her burns.

Ibram winced in sympathy. "My hope for your recovery gains strength, Mistress," he said. "I thought you would be in Doctor Berot's infirmary for quite some time."

"Burns are not to be laughed at," the man seated next to Ibram said.

"And who might you be?" Ibram asked.

The man jumped a trifle, and turned to his left. He inclined his head and shoulders. "Bernat Guilhem, at your service, Master Ucalegon."

"A member of the fire alliance from Builders Row," a woman spoke behind Ibram. He twisted to his right, and there stood a short plump woman with blue eyes and short red hair, most probably hailing from deep within the middle provinces. She bowed shortly. "I am Philendra

Dubidat," she said sourly, and then sat on Bernat Guilhem's opposing side. "This is my husband."

Guilhem slid his left arm across the table to touch her hand. They smiled at each other; he, overtly fond, and she, like a cat deciding whether to scratch or purr. Ibram made a polite noise.

"Is that so?" he asked. "Which building is yours then, Master Guilhem?"

Guilhem withdrew his hand with a final pat, and then pressed both hands to the tabletop. "I have the pleasure of renting the workshop across from what used to be the bakery-mill," he said. "I'm a member of the carpentry guild."

Ibram nodded. "A joiner?" he asked.

He shook his head. "Nothing so fine," Guilhem said. "It's true I do make furniture, but only the most basic sort. My stock in trade is mostly utensils, really." He shrugged. "Plates and spoons, and the like."

"I'm sure your wife found that an inestimable aid for her own business, to be sure," Ibram said.

Philendra Dubidat rubbed one of the oval hammered brooches which held the straps of her apron closed over her bleached shift. That was how they dressed nearest the Salt Plateau, to the north and east of the garden provinces. She'd traveled a long way to get to Lityen. She busied herself making a plate from the remains of the meal before her, and did not bother to join the conversation. Ibram decided to be more engaging. After all, one of them might have murdered a man.

"Are you at this table representing your wife's interests while she is away?" Ibram asked.

Guilhem opened his mouth, only to shut it again when his wife snorted. "He is not," she answered for him. "We have kept our businesses separate throughout the course of our marriage."

"And how long has that been?"

"Since we were fifteen," Guilhem answered with a smile. "We were born on the same day, you see."

Ibram nodded. "Auspicious."

"For what?" Mistress Salaz asked.

"Never forgetting your own birthday," Mistress Dubidat said with a tired snap. She breathed out through her nose and poked at the bowl in front of her. Her husband picked a large hard-boiled duck egg from the table and handed it to her. The set of her shoulders deflated.

"I was there, you see, helping with the fire. A terrible thing, but you must pitch in in times of trouble," Ibram said, and smiled at her. "I know you were absent, bless the Heavens. How did you hear of it?"

"I was across the way," Mistress Corri said, before she could answer. A strong scent of symphis salve wafted across the table when she moved her bandaged arm. "I thought I'd get myself and my apprentices buns for breakfast, and then—" she swallowed heavily and cut herself off with a quick headshake.

"Heard the explosion," Master Bine said. "Thought it was one of those Attendants again, showing off in the draughtshops near the common land, but when the signals erupted from the living mountain, I knew something was astir."

"Then it was only a matter of following the crowd," Mistress Salaz said. She shook her head angrily. "Our luck ran out."

"All the fires we managed—food cooked and ready for decades and never even a lick of danger near the Ozols' place," Sembe said. "All the care taken...and it comes to this."

"How go the negotiations?" Ibram asked. "I am sorry to lose the pleasure of your leek stew, Mistress Salaz, it went so well with Master Bine's infusions and Master Sembe's pickles and eggs."

"All by design," Master Bine muttered. "All carefully planned and now ruined."

"What was destroyed might be rebuilt," Mistress Salaz said curtly. "Though I don't know where."

"What about you, Master Sembe?" Ibram asked. "You were with Master Guilhem. What did you see?"

"A great noise, and then an even greater panic," Master Sembe said. "The place went up like an Orilindan candle."

"Oh?" Ibram asked. "Green and red and purple? That sort of thing."

Every stickum peddler and vermin remover within the imperial boundary would know how to obtain powder of chalcan vitriol, after all. It wouldn't be hard to purchase some and then reap the reward while spiting the landlord. Ibram kept his demeanor pleasant and his ears open, but his eye ticked, nonetheless.

Master Sembe frowned. "No need to play the fool, Master Ucalegon," he said. "I only meant to say the bakery-mill went up fast, and took my livelihood with it."

"Gutted us like caskfish," Master Bine said. "All that work gone, and precious little chance we'll have to bring it back again."

Ibram leaned back. "You won't rebuild?"

"We four all rented our buildings from the Vo Kaln family," Mistress Dubidat said.

"But not Mistress Corri?" Ibram asked.

"I inherited my home as I did my trade," she said. "The apothecary has been here since—oh, my great-grandfather's time!"

"I'd hoped to say the same, some day," Mistress Dubidat and drank her shay as if it were poison. "The Vo Kalns have been diffident in their concern for our welfare."

"Oh now, Philie," Guilhem said. "It's still too soon to worry for that, surely."

"So says you," Otso Sembe snorted. "You've a business to return to, and a bed when you get there. The both of you do! It is Carme, Harken, and myself who have nothing but the Sect's charity to fall back upon."

"You three slept in your stalls, then?" Ibram asked.

He let his eyes narrow in thought. Cookshops were small affairs, and in his memory those three were no different. Taller than most cookshops, perhaps, maybe enough so that their owners would work below and sleep above. The cookshops had been positioned to face the second exit off Pillared Circle; their backs to the now destroyed evening courtyard owned by the Vo Kalns. And if Mistress Dubidat lived above her husband's workshop, then The Isconian's Hand was the only building damaged by the fire to be legally considered merely a building, and not a dwelling at all.

Amota Berac had mentioned something, but as always, Ibram had not been paying close attention. There had to be a copy of the law back in Amota Evren's archives; Ibram had a vague memory of something important about dwellings and fire. The Code of Enyabi the

Younger was barely readable in the dead of winter, much less the joy of summer; Ibram had been forced to memorize large swathes of it as a child.

"They had been built as additions to support the crowds in Pillared Circle, usually leaving the evening courtyards," Mistress Salaz confirmed. "We all lived above and worked below."

"Then luck was with all three of you to be away from your stations," Ibram said. He mimed ringing a bell, and the table was briefly graced with a wave of confused faces. "Not much in the way of business during the day?"

"I am the only one reliably open for business in daylight," Mistress Corri said, and touched her bandage again. "As I understand it, the others see greater profit in serving the night's crowds."

"Got all the folk coming out of The High Climber and The Isconian's Hand after their performances," Master Sembe said. "And the workers off Builders Row."

"So where were you?" Ibram asked. "If not at home."

Mistress Salaz's head twitched; her chin rose. "I was at the market," she said. "Gathering supplies for that night's meal."

"As was I," Master Sembe said, but stumbled on his dismount when he glanced at Mistress Salaz. "Preserved Corner has my salt and vinegar. Can't make khrin without it. We went together."

Ibram nodded politely, but took note. "And you, Master Bine?" he asked.

"I was with Master Guilhem over there," Bine answered. "Ordering a new brace of serviceware. Folk run off with them, you know. Leave the bowls but tuck the spoons and prongs into their purses or up the sleeve. It eats half my profits!"

"I'm always glad of your business, though," Master Guilhem said, with a grin. "As I will be when you rebuild."

"Light a candle about it," Harken Bine muttered, and his compatriots across the table grimaced at him. Master Bine harrumphed, a sound so dramatic Ibram had never before heard it in the wilds beyond a traveling theater. "I'd wager its only Nescata doing well out of this business now," Bine continued with an air of injured pride. He eyed Ibram from the side. "That'll be your man's doing, you know."

Ibram cocked his head. "My man?" he repeated.

"Doctor Berot has been kind enough to extend me a rent for the use of my apothecary," Mistress Corri said in a tired, but pleasant voice. "It was not so badly damaged as the other buildings."

"Doctor Berot is a man for all weather, to be sure," Ibram said. "I have the honor to serve his preceptory of course, but I'd be cut short if I called him 'my man,' I assure you, Master Bine."

Master Bine frowned heavily; his red hair bobbed when he shook his head. "I'll not say any more about it," he said. "Only that there's some folk at this table with more of a leg to stand on than others, and they who have the most to gain are made notable by their absence."

An agent might be grateful for even a cask of soured wine like Bine when its caustic properties brought forth the desired result. Ibram sighed and shook his head, leaning his left hand on the table. He reached out and grabbed the pitcher in the center of the table; it was light, but still serviceable. He began to pour out its contents into the members' cups, starting on his left.

"Is that how all you good folk joined together? It seems clear your businesses sustained each other," Ibram said with a covert glance about the table.

Mistress Corri touched her bandage again. The three cookshop owners calcified into grim statues. Only Mistress Dubidat and her husband seemed unaffected.

Master Guilhem smiled as Ibram poured, and picked up his cup. "I thank you, Master Ucalegon," he said. "Actually, the Pillared Circle fire alliance copied itself upon the tenets of the one in Builders Row."

"Oh?" Ibram asked.

"Indeed so," Mistress Dubidat said. She rested her right elbow on the table and massaged the side of her face with her fingers. "Bernat allowed me to see the document, and I shared the language with the others."

"No secrets between married folk," Ibram said.

Master Guilhem laughed. "Of course there are!" he exclaimed. "We're all of us entitled to a bit of privacy," he brought his wife's left hand up from the table and kissed her knuckles. She rolled her eyes, but Ibram noted a faint blush. "But there is nothing in that document to do with secrecy. It's fairly straightforward, after all."

"You were aided in its creation by the fire alliance in Preserved Corner, were you not?" Mistress Salaz asked.

Guilhem nodded. "The very same. No, young master, I'm afraid the terms of both fire alliances are quite standard. It's only in assessment of the damage that we differ. We have three members whose responsibility includes the building—those of us who own outright—and Pillared Circle have only two members who needed to do so."

So Nescata Corri and Soren Rennab had been the only two members who both lived and worked in their businesses. They would receive money for repairs, and be able to get back up and running the quickest. Indeed, Mistress Corri was already collecting on the disaster by renting her building to the sect. Ibram glanced at her neck. Or, perhaps, she would return to her work as quickly as her injury allowed.

"But you rent your space," Ibram pointed out.

"Within the building of my guildmaster," Guilhem said. "And as I live within it, the money would go to me."

Ibram smiled. That was what he'd forgotten. The Code of Enyabi the Younger stated that a subject of the empire had the right to dispense with their property as they so chose, but if the building was a *dwelling*, then all the monies involved would go to the folk who lived within the burned buildings, and not whoever actually owned the building. Of course, Salaz, Sembe, and Bine might have the money, but no right to the land, and Dubidat had lost twice over, unless she received funds from the alliance to recoup some of her losses. Mistress Vo Kaln would reap the insurance money there. They'd lost their livelihoods, regardless.

"Did you used to live in your evening courtyard, Mistress Dubidat?" Ibram asked.

"I did," Mistress Dubidat said. "Rather, we did, but I found I preferred my husband's house instead."

"It's cozy," Guilhem said. "Less cost to heat."

"I'm insured with the fire alliance for my goods and labor," Mistress Dubidat said. "I've workers to pay, no matter if my place of business has disappeared."

"And Mistress Vo Kaln?" Ibram asked.

"Owns the land and the buildings and clasps our futures in the palm of her hand," Master Sembe said. "Whatever we make back in money we all set aside a portion, but there's still negotiations ahead with that mob."

"Thanks to forethought and The Advisor," Mistress Dubidat muttered. She coughed and spoke more loudly, "And since it was the bakery-mill—"

"Now, we don't know that, precious," Guilhem said mildly.

"Well, where could it have started if not in the bakery-mill?" Master Sembe asked with air of a man who disliked repeating himself, but was unafraid to do it. "We all of us had our fire suppression tiles."

"All of you?" Ibram asked, and set down the pitcher.

"Of course," Mistress Dubidat said. "Who would be stupid enough to refuse to have them?"

"Especially after the disaster in Kandrilat," Mistress Corri said. She shuddered delicately. "The elder Mistress Vo Kaln's cousin came up from there, Ederetta, who does most of the contracts. She told me when she stopped by that they lost their entire manor."

"Absolutely insisted on inspecting all of their fire suppression systems, down to what door through which we should flee!" Mistress Dubidat said, with a shake of her head.

"Recently?" Ibram asked, diverted from his thoughts.

"Oh no," Master Bine said. "That rent collector only comes every other month or so. The younger ones all take turns collecting the rents. Their parents think it seasons them for adulthood."

"But not Master Rennab's evening courtyard," Ibram said.

"Well, of course not," Mistress Dubidat said. She waved her hand. "That old stick in the bog owns his building outright. They'd have no claim to enter!"

"It's why when he entered into the alliance, he insured his building, but we only insured the contents of ours," Mistress Salaz said.

"He insured the building but not the contents?" Guilhem asked, meaning Ibram did not have to. "I didn't know that."

"He said it was mostly his husband's property, and they'd made prior arrangements," Master Sembe said. "It's probably why he's out there with that agent, Berac Comoros. A friend of yours, Master Ucalegon, no doubt."

"I admit my mother has had him to dinner," Ibram said, and smiled. "Westerners are friendly folk."

"Well and good," Master Bine said. "But it's hard enough to be dealing with the Vo Kalns, much less the sect. And then the funerals on top!"

"Funerals?" Ibram repeated. "You mean for the bakery-mill's owners--Ozols?"

Master Guilhem nodded. "Tari and Desta Ozol were dear friends of mine," he said. "My wife and I made the formal identification. Their son, Ealar, was gathering a grain order in Polia when it happened, you know."

"I do recall that being mentioned," Ibram said. "He's returned, then?"

"He has," Master Guilhem said. "Your Master Comoros sent one of his own men to bring him home. The Builders Row fire alliance's portion will go to Ealar, now, to pay for the costs and the rebuilding, of course, but Philie and I can't just let him go through it all alone."

"Nor Rory and Kham," Mistress Dubidat said. She picked up her cup and drank deeply, and then set it back down with a sigh. "My candle dancers, you know. I don't know what they would have wanted, but I'll take charge of their bodies and see them granted a writ of travel for the Heavenly Crossroads, regardless."

The question of whether or not the two candle dancers had thought themselves going to the Heavenly Crossroads was another matter. He also wondered if a Vissilian Writ of Travel for a pair of heathens could get a soul into the realm of the divine anyways was also a bone of contention, but Ibram kept such thoughts to himself. It was kindly meant, after all. No way to send all the way to Tekdana for the appropriate funeral rites.

He excused himself from the table with a generous bow to all those still seated, and returned to his own table. Ahksell looked up at his approach. Ibram sat back down again and took a healthy sip of his warming cider.

"I've come up with a worst thought," Ibram said, and wiped his mouth clean on the sleeve of his gambeson. "What if—"

"Worse than a rogue alchemist involved in arson?" Ahksell raised a skeptical eyebrow.

"Now, we have no evidence of *that* at all!"

"Yet I cannot help but consider the possibility," Ahksell said.

Ibram paused. "What's the difference between an alchemaster and a rogue alchemist?"

"A rogue alchemist is a criminal but does not use alchemy in their crime," Ahksell said, "and the other is a criminal through use of alchemy."

That wasn't a bad division of criminal behavior at all. Ibram turned the matter over in his mind, and set it down as a little memento near the small table inside his memory room. Amota Evren would be pleasantly surprised at how crowded it was getting in there.

"There is no doubt that Erno Neilos was killed most mundanely," Ibram said. "I think we can rule out alchemastery."

Not that there wasn't a certain regret in the thought. On the first foot, an alchemaster might see the entire sect razed to the ground on charges of treason. On the second, Ibram had no doubt the experience might be very exciting.

"But why would anyone need to kill Master Neilos?" Ahksell asked. He gestured with his gravy-slick eating knife. A whip of sauce flew through the air out the window; Ahksell set down his knife.

"Money," Ibram said, and began counting on his fingers. The little bag of coin Ahksell had found weighed heavily in his purse. "Either to save spending it to keep Neilos silent, or to gain much more in his silencing. My faunt is on both. Blackmail is a long-lived crime."

"Master Neilos could have been a better man than that," Ahksell said. "He could have been on his way to tell us who the arsonist is, and that was why he was killed!"

"Dughlat had already gone to us, though," Ibram pointed out. "And, if it were true, then why did he not come up to see us with Master Dughlat? Or simply tell him who set the fire? If Neilos knew, that is."

Ahksell tilted his head, and then shook it. Ibram nodded. Ahksell sat back on his bench and blew air from his mouth as he stared out the open window. No fancy woven wire screens in this place, merely the open air and a supporting middle beam to close the shutters at night. Abruptly, he leaned forward across the table; Ibram leaned as far back as he was able. He held his cider cup up and away from his body.

"What?" Ibram asked. "What are you—hey now!"

Ahksell bolted up from the trestle table as the door burst open. Ibram twisted around. Attendant Zorion stood, panting, clutching the doorway in both hands. He cast his eyes left and right, and then beamed. Ibram fought the urge to hunch his shoulders like a strigi caught outside their burrow.

"Ahksell!" Zorion called out across the common room. "There you are! Mentor Hobon wants you to come and explain why you sent her a dead body."

He pointed behind himself to the open air and nodded encouragingly. A hush settled over the draughtshop, weighted by the impending explosion of speculation sure to follow their departure. Ibram sighed, and downed the remains of his cider.

❧ 7 ❧

It didn't take long to report their findings to Lady Azadiya, especially once Ibram took the opportunity to seize stylus, ink, and paper from one of her worktables, and take down Ahksell's testimony as the First Finder while they did so. She listened carefully as Ahksell relayed his impressions of Erno Neilos' room, and then while Ibram took his own turn explaining his reasons for conversing with the Pillared Circle fire alliance. The first draft of Amota Berac's report on the site of the fire lay open on her desk; Ibram recognized the spidery handwriting sloping to the right across the top pages.

"And there was nothing in the room's ethereal miasma to indicate Neilos was drugged, or in an altered state?" Lady Azadiya called down to them. Her footsteps padded across the ceiling over Ibram's head. "There are many ways to make murdering a man easier."

The evening was always colder up the living mountain, and Ladyship had all the windows open. Ibram was thankful for the heavy twill of his gambeson. The papers decorating her desk threatened to redistribute themselves in the breeze. Ibram walked over and began planting heavier objects on top of them, dividing Ladyship's cup of cold shay from its attendant plate of crumbs and pressing her portable furnace into service as well. He glanced up at another creaking of the floorboards.

"No, Mentor," Ahksell called up.

Ladyship's private rooms were more of a loft above her working office, accessible only to an alchemist capable of manipulating the physical world. Not even the servants could get up there without an exceedingly tall ladder. Beside Ibram, Ahksell shifted on his feet and finally sat down in the chair situated before her large desk. He resettled the pile of rugs draped along his own chair's back, and wove his fingers together over his stomach.

"So he was aware of his surroundings when he died—" Something opened and shut, and then thumped to the floor. Ladyship tsked, loudly. "And the lock was unharmed?"

"Utterly," Ibram said.

At least she had all her oil lamps ablaze and the glowbulbs hanging from her ceiling shaken into service. The night sky out of the office windows was beginning to show dangerous signs of moonlight beaming down onto the kitchen garden. Ibram stepped to the left and caught a drifting page of Amota Berac's writing. He placed a heavy silver ring he recognized as his own father's design on top of it.

"And neither bottles nor cups could I find," Ibram said. "According to the lady who runs the inn, all meals are taken in the common room, and she won't allow a morsel in the above rooms. Says it keeps down the vermin."

"Well enough. Neilos was in his right mind at time of death and opened the door for his attacker," Lady Azadiya called down from above. She sighed audibly. "Do you know, typically when the tower's cats leave dead bodies by the garden gate, they're easily disposed of in the forest."

"I'm afraid Master Neilos is too large to be a mouse, Ladyship," Ibram said.

He heard a wardrobe door shut, and then Lady Azadiya floated to the floor. She wrapped a green and gold woven shawl loosely around her back, and shook her long dark hair out from underneath it. Her layers of light green linen robes fluttered at her feet as she walked to one of her stuffed bookshelves and removed a stack of bound papers.

Ibram bowed with his hands over his stomach; she rolled her eyes as she waved him back up almost at the same time.

"Is this Neilos a rat, then," she mused as she crossed to her desk. "And his discovery is a warning?"

"It would be very difficult to remove the body from his room at the inn, and hide it," Ibram said. "Even if there were no witness outside his window, he couldn't go past the woman who owns the inn without being noticed at the least, and the way out through the window is ringed by other buildings."

"What was he doing before the fire, according to Shokan Dughlat?" Lady Azadiya arranged the fingers of her right hand as if she were holding a puppet's strings and flicked her first three digits upward. The plate of crumbs rose up from the desk and settled to one side.

"Before the fire?" Ibram asked. "They were fussing over the furniture in the back."

"And then Shokan said they began to put the chairs back out into the courtyard," Ahksell said.

"So they were not always in each other's company," Ladyship said. She picked up her shay cup and frowned at its contents. "Or did they need two sets of hands to transport the furniture?"

"I...will ask Dughlat about that," Ibram said.

"Where did he live?" she asked. She sat down at her desk, and settled her shawl around her.

"Cobblers Square."

"Could this owner you spoke to have been paid to turn a blind eye?" she asked, and adjusted the cream silk fingerless mitt on her right hand.

Ibram shook his head. "Possible, of course, but it doesn't seem likely. She only let us above stairs because we were on the business of the sect. As tenant inns in Cobbler's Square go, she runs one of the better establishments."

"And it would not due to gain a reputation for lawless behavior," Lady Azadiya said. She opened the stack of bound papers, and frowned at its contents, and then set it aside. With a fluttering motion like picking the strings of a harp, the heavy objects Ibram had laid over her papers drifted to a clear patch of her desk and settled into a tight grouping.

"To be sure, Ladyship," Ibram said. "The only item of interest in the room besides Neilos himself was what Ahksell found."

"Yes, the bag of coin," Lady Azadiya agreed. She turned to Ahksell. "Where was it?"

"Lodged beneath his bed," Ahksell replied, "in a little depression in the floor behind the back leg of the frame. It wasn't precisely hidden, but it wasn't obvious."

Ladyship crooked her little finger, and the silver ring flew into her palm. She placed it in a side drawer. "What did you glean from the purse?"

Ahksell straightened in his chair. "Master Neilos thought a lot of that bag of coin," he said. "Or it's more exact to say, he handled it a great deal before he died. The coin purse felt heavy when the introrse pendant identified it within his sphere of influence."

"There was enough silver in there for another set of rooms and a grand feast, besides," Ibram said. He took it out of his belt and tossed the purse to Ahksell, who caught it one-handed. "Who we need to speak with is the Vo Kalns."

"How so?" Lady Azadiya asked.

"If there is coin involved—and I mean to say, of the silver and gold persuasion—then they are the only family involved who have any amount of it," Ibram said. "They own four of the buildings involved in the fire, of which only three can be counted legally as dwellings. The three cookshop owners will be compensated for their loss, but the Vo Kalns were not part of the fire alliance at Pillared Circle. They retain ownership of the land, of course."

"Are they members of the fire alliance in Builders Row?" Ladyship asked.

Ibram cleared his throat. "If they are, it's through an intermediary," he said.

Ladyship nodded her head slowly in thought. "The Isconian's Hand was rented, but not a dwelling," she said, "since Dubidat lives with her husband, ah—"

"Guilhem," Ibram interjected. "Bernat Guilhem."

"On Builders Row and is covered twice for damages, regardless," Ladyship said. "Who has covered the Vo Kalns' loss of their buildings?"

"I can check that in the morning," Ibram said, "but I would think it would be covered in Amota Berac's report."

"Yes," she said. Ladyship picked up the nearest bundle of Amota Berac's writing and began flipping through the pages. "Ah, here."

She tossed two sheets of thick paper into the air, and then turned her wrist and showed Ibram her palm with the notched scar in the center. She snapped her fingers up and tapped the air. A soft breeze floated the papers into Ibram's hands.

"A layout of both evening courtyards," she said. "Study them."

Ibram bowed his head. At first glance, nothing seemed out of the ordinary in the buildings' plans. One doubled door in, and one single door out, with eight walls and slim alleys surrounding the bakery-mill. At the top of the Isconian's Hand, Amota Berac had scribbled out the words "Separate deposit, Runner's temple, portion of rent monthly."

"But we will also check in at the Office of Indemnity, first sign of daybreak, Mentor," Ahksell said, and wrinkled his eyebrows in Ibram's direction.

Ibram shrugged, tucked the papers under his arm. "May I look at the rest of the report, Ladyship?"

"You will have it once I'm finished," she said. "You mentioned earlier that the Vo Kaln family was interested in purchasing The High Climber?"

"Yes," Ibram said. "Might be cheaper to buy destroyed land than a successful business."

Ladyship hummed in agreement.

Ahksell frowned. "Surely not," he said, "what about all the loss in custom? Where will their former patrons go if they have to waste time rebuilding?"

"The cookshop owners did say they were worried the Vo Kalns were not going to rebuild their businesses at all," Ibram said. "It could be that they have designs on building to a grander scale than previously was possible. Which is why I want to go and speak to the family. If not them, then at least their representative in charge of rents."

"An interesting line of questions," Lady Azadiya said. "We shall have to see what comes of dinner tomorrow night. Ederetta Vo Kaln is to be one of my guests."

"Dining?" Ahksell asked. "You're going to host her?"

"Berac mentioned her as being involved in his negotiations." Lady Azadiya nodded. "It seemed as good an opportunity as any. It will be a small party an hour after they light the paths around the mountain. You will be there, Doctor Berot, and Berac. Ibram, also."

"I was going to go and find out from Hilbert what the Medicinal Corps has learned from Master Neilos' body," Ahksell said.

"Has he been tasked with the body?" Ibram asked.

"Doctor Berot finds Zorion very useful, actually," Lady Azadiya said. "He's more suited to be under Mentor Stadat's supervision, anyway. Their fields of study have more overlap. But you may speak with Zorion at dinner, he often comes down with Berot."

"Yes, Mentor," Ahksell said, and slumped his shoulders just a little.

"Now, what more can you tell me of the coin purse?" Ladyship asked. "Was it the only recoverable resonance?"

"Other than the dried lavin blossoms and the votive chain, there wasn't much Master Neilos seemed to be attached to," Ahksell said. "The purse felt heavy with expectation." He frowned. "Or maybe it was resignation, the spectrum was murky when I examined it."

"Give it here," Lady Azadiya said, and Ahksell opened his palm. She waved her fingers, and the coin purse lifted from his grip on a ripple of air. Her first and second fingers crooked as she pulled her arm backwards, and then snatched the small bag to hold it before her. Her eyes narrowed. "There's something of the soul remaining," she said. "But the anima has already fled. Yes, I do see the conflict."

Someday Ibram was going to learn how Ladyship knew these sorts of things. She had a delight in the more esoteric aspects of alchemy, the parts where the Preceptory of Yseult's refinement of the physical body met its manipulation of the anima. As a mentor, she no longer needed to rely upon downing any of their alarming collection of oddly bubbling, often smoking, potions. But it couldn't all be potables and practice, as there was no class or lesson in the Preceptory of Yseult that concerned itself with souls.

"I'll trace his movements today," Ibram said. Alchemy was all well and good, but he often found he preferred the mundane approach. To understand why folk did the things they did, all you had to do was follow them around until they told you. "Perhaps the answer will come of that."

Ladyship lowered the coin purse to her desk, and nodded. "The coins tells us nothing without understanding how it got beneath Master Neilos' bed. Merely how he felt about it."

"Given that he was strangled to death in such a relatively clean manner, Ibram said. "I would say whoever killed him came prepared to murder him, but perhaps hadn't quite worked themselves up to do so."

"Why do you say that?" Ladyship asked, and tilted her head.

Ibram cleared his throat. There were moments where he felt like Lady Azadiya had come to a conclusion before him, but thought it her duty as a teacher to wait until he brought the matter up himself. "The state of the room," he said. "I had a moment to think on it while we coming up here, and I don't think the room was searched at all. The items on the floor were knocked over in the struggle, and the clothing on the shelf was mostly left untouched."

"That's true," Ahksell said. "And the door was open."

"Suggesting that whoever killed Neilos left in a hurry," Ibram said, "such that the door rebounded and shook the wall, causing the runner's votive to bounce across the threshold."

"Which stopped it from closing completely." Ahksell nodded, and Ladyship leaned back in her chair. She seemed pleased.

"So the murderer kills Neilos—even perhaps searches the body—but panics at the thought of being caught," Ibram said. "The window was open in that room, it was only a matter of time before someone looked inside. And so, they run off without the purse."

"The time of day limited the amount of folk in the area," she said, "and the method would have made a great deal of noise, but of the sort that folk tend to ignore or excuse in tenant inns. We have a neat explanation for the murder of, perhaps, an accomplice."

"But we don't know that," Ahksell said. "If Master Neilos was an accomplice, then why is Master Dughlat still alive?"

"Maybe he killed Neilos," Ibram said.

Lady Azadiya pointed at him. "Nicely suspicious," she said. "He murders his co-worker. Why?"

Ibram ruffled the back of his head. "Perhaps he's the accomplice and Neilos was the witness."

She considered it for a moment, but then shook her head. "I think it's more pertinent to think through why Master Dughlat came up the living mountain at all," she said. "Ibram, thoughts?"

Ibram stood a bit straighter and settled his hands behind his back. "Dughlat tells his co-worker about the green fire, but not his employer."

"He explained that," Ahksell said.

"Yes, he thought it might come to nothing and didn't want to wait," Ibram said. "But if he was so uncertain, why would he travel all the way up the living mountain to see us? He can't believe the sect has nothing to do all day. No, in a choice between Master Rennab and Lady Azadiya, he chose the party most likely to investigate the matter. Therefore: he doesn't trust Master Rennab to act. Yet, he told Erno Neilos, maybe just to corroborate his own memory, maybe because he needed someone to cover for him, but now Erno Neilos is dead with money hidden in his room." Ibram spread his hands. "Someone has either been quick to lie to us, or slow to tell the truth."

"Oh now," Ahksell said. "That's not fair. Master Dughlat came to us!"

Lady Azadiya nodded slowly. "A helpful man might also carry some guilt," she said. "But I take your point. If the murderer is the same person who started the fire on Pillared Circle, then surely he would have wanted to kill the person who brought the fire to our attention first. Unless Neilos presented some kind of larger threat."

Ibram paused, and then nodded. "A fair hit."

"I believe it is," Ladyship said. "In the morning, go and find out if Master Dughlat lives. If he does, find out why. Also, I want to speak with Philendra Dubidat and Soren Rennab. Extend my invitation to dine tomorrow night as well."

"Do I get to eat?" Ibram asked.

She made a show of thinking about it. "If you perform your tasks adequately. Inform them that their spouses are invited. If they come, so much the better. If they don't, take two of the younger agents and have the spouses watched. I believe Esti has been haunting the educational sheds again. Give him something to do."

Ibram bowed, and Ahksell stood up. She lifted her head, and frowned at Ibram directly. Ibram paused, one foot already shifted to leave.

"The Vo Kalns," Ladyship said. "Clearly the majority landowners here." She tapped her fingers on the paperwork. "Where else do they get their money?"

Ibram blinked. "Soapmakers, so Amota Berac says," he said. "The landlady has allowed them to scoop up wood ash to turn additional profit. There's so much of the stuff they'll be able to make enough soap to last half the year. As for the rest of them...I could send a runner up to Third Mentor Nieminen's division? They keep notes on such things. Unless Amota Evren would know from what's in his archives."

"No, Nieminen was the right choice," she said. "But ask Evren about it. He would know with whom you should speak. The full clan, mind you, down to which version of the cadet branches we are dealing with here."

Ibram nodded. Lady Azadiya pulled Amota Berac's report towards her, and began to read. Ibram left the buildings' plans on a corner of her desk as he left.

☙❧

Below in the common room of the tower, the low couches and even parts of the carpeted floor were covered in folk who made their living in the sect. Lady Azadiya's tower was always awash in Learners and Attendants and, thus, doubly supplied with the agents and servants of the sect who managed the mundanities of life for their alchemists. Ibram leaned over the railing on the balcony and put his hand on the attached ladder for balance. He saw a knot of fellow agents his own age and rank passing around a leather flask by the central fountain. Attendant Zorion sat next to them, and politely refused every time the flask made its rounds past his elbow.

"He's down there if you want to speak with him now," Ibram said, and pointed.

Ahksell came to stand beside him and followed Ibram's leading arm. "I should think we must," he said. "It's not like more knowledge could make the situation worse."

Ibram chuckled. "There's the spirit that raised the Emerald Mountains."

"Ha ha," Ahksell said flatly, and grabbed Ibram by the shoulder. He dragged him along the long balcony and down the circular steps to the first floor. The Stinging Euphorbia once again attempted to eat Ibram's hand for lunch and was dutifully slapped back.

"Do you think they found anything besides the obvious?" Ibram asked as they managed their way through the crowded common area.

"If they did, Doctor Berot will know it first," Ahksell said.

Corbus, one of the newer agents from a delegation of Valantin in the east, raised his hand at their approach. He prodded Attendant Zorion's knee before returning to his conversation with Ibram's cousin Nesrine, who was seated on the lip of the fountain. She didn't seem to mind the splashing water, and was focused on showing a scrap of paper to the agent next to her. Attendant Zorion looked up, drawing Ibram's attention, and resettled his spectacles on the bridge of his nose.

"Hello again," Zorion said. "Did you explain about the body?"

Ibram glanced about once more. He was circumspect by nature, and what nature had not accomplished, nurture had further ensured. The water splashing down from above glittered with the reflected light from the translucent tiled roof; it also created sufficient noise that only those closest to another person might hear what was being said. Not that he supposed a murderer amongst their ranks, but still. No fool like an overheard fool, to be sure.

"That's why we were coming to speak to you, Hilbert," Ahksell said, while Ibram bowed shortly. His elbow jostled Ibram's left arm, and Ibram rose.

"I don't know why you brought it to the Hall of Tranquility," Zorion said.

It wasn't their doing—they'd only ordered the body picked up—but Ahksell nodded anyway. Ibram put his weight on his heels. Zorion was a literal man unless you were speaking about infusions or poisons or the ways what a man imbibed affected body, soul, and anima. Then, he could become positively poetic.

"We wanted to know the details of his death," Ibram said.

"His neck was cut open."

"Thank you, Attendant," Ibram said.

Ahksell jostled him again. "What Ibram means is, do you have any further thoughts? How long ago he might have died, and if he had been moved before we ordered him removed from the property, that sort of business."

"Well, we know that last bit," Ibram said.

"We do?" Zorion asked.

Ibram nodded. "Died by his bed. Scratch marks on the floorboards, and a disturbed mattress. Dying folk clutch things; the dead merely keep hold."

"Oh, I see," Attendant Zorion said. He settled himself more comfortably on the arm of the couch and crossed his arms over his chest. "Well, it was definitely the neck cutting that killed him, but the wire strangling him didn't help."

"Indeed?" Ibram asked. "What makes you say so?"

"Pattern of the blood on the clothes," Zorion said. "Doctor Berot said that a man would bleed differently if he'd had his throat cut while his heart pumped."

"So the murderer...just kept going, until the poor man was dead?" Ahksell asked.

Ibram nodded. It was the usual way to kill a man, but he didn't voice the thought. "Was that all, Attendant?"

Zorion thought a moment. "Oh, and his fingers got in the way for a bit. Before he died, you know."

"There you are," Ibram said, and Zorion nodded.

Ahksell cleared his throat. "Is it likely that the murder happened shortly before we encountered Master Neilos?"

"When did you find him?"

"Just past midday, really," Ibram said. "The mistress of the tenant inn was already in preparation for dinner."

And what a dining experience that would become, when word got out amongst the other tenants of a death in the building. Ibram eyed Corbus and Nesrine. Ibram was a measure above in seniority than them, on account of his travels for Lady Azadiya. It might be a good chance for his fellow agents to gain experience in information gathering. They weren't so distinctive that trailing after a few suspects would draw public attention. Corbus was a Valantin, with teardropped shaped eyes and his hair shaved around the back of his head with a thick black thatch on top. Nesrine's parents were from the plains of Merrilia, as Ibram's own mother had been. She wore her clan bracelet as a choker about her neck instead of looped over her wrist.

"I can only tell you what Doctor Berot thinks," Zorion said. "He came up from the temporary infirmary in the apothecary to look at the body, and declared the man had died much earlier in the day for reasons of temperature. It's actually very interesting. The healers say the body's changes in death are a reflection of not merely the state in which he died, but a direct product on environment."

"You are taking Berot's class as well?" Ahksell asked. "I thought you were going to stay within the realm of the internal."

There was a familiar eagerness in Ahksell's voice. One that had images of dry school texts piling up in the shelves of Ibram's memory construct. He wrinkled his nose, and gazed longingly at the leather flask in Corbus' hand as it passed by.

Zorion leaned forward with his hands on his knees. "I thought I was, as well," he said. "But after I had served my period of time in the tower, Mentor Hobon said that I had failed to consider the natural impulse of the body to heal itself. She suggested I had better research the conjunction of the anima with the regulatory processes of the physical realm, and introduced me to Doctor Berot."

"He went to a university before beginning his career in the sect, you know," Ahksell said, quickly turning his head to beam at Ibram.

"Ah ha," Ibram said.

Ahksell nodded quickly and then went back to his conversation with Zorion. "It's an unequalled perspective. Tell me, how are you accounting for the separation of thought and mechanical intent in the muscles?"

"At first, I thought a pipe of Shirin's Tincture might aid there," Zorion said, "but then I realized that a relaxant was too unfocussed."

Ibram sighed. Ahksell's eyes were alight with excitement. Zorion was leaning forward and waving his hands in the air as he described his current obsession. He'd lost sense out of them both for the evening, and it was a poor agent who didn't know when to withdraw from the field of study. He spied Amota Evren talking to Amita Sarrha in an alcove across the way from the common room. It would be best to speak with them, to share his own news and get an idea of Amota Berac's side of the investigation.

He bowed shortly to Ahksell and Attendant Zorion. "I must make my excuses," he said, "I see some folk I should speak with."

"Yes," Ahksell said, already partially on another plane. "Oh! I forgot to ask, how are the temperature tests for Kvaran's Basilisk going?"

Ibram took the requisite step away, and shook his head. He smirked at the oblivious pair, at least someone would have answers tonight. Or, if not, than a good time arguing. He reached over to grab Corbus by the shoulder.

"Busy tonight?" he asked, and smiled in the face of Corbus' growing resignation. "I've got just the thing to clear your heads after all that good ale I smell off your flask."

❧

Wrangling younger agents was slightly more rewarding than herding Attendants to and fro, but at least Ibram could relax in the knowledge that Shokan Dughlat was safely under watch for the night. Amota Evren had stated what Ibram already knew, that Mentor Nieminen's noble listings were the better place to check who might or might not be relevant to the matter at hand. Ibram left him with Amota Berac, arguing the merits of tolnic, which Berac favored, and Evren's preferred drink, sojin. He drifted through the crowd to the front of the tower.

Ibram evaded the Stinging Euphorbia as he climbed the few steps up to the terrace. Behind him, someone began a stamping beat; if they weren't careful, a dance might break out. He shook his head. If Ladyship had been a proper noble with a proper manor to run, the entire tower might have been given over to luxury and delight. As Fourth Mentor, however, Ladyship's administration was run directly from her tower from the lower circle of offices, to the second level of classrooms and storerooms, to the third floor laboratories that surrounded the central fountain. If it hadn't been such a wide stump of a building the tower would have been overrun, not merely from the constant influx of students and workers, but from the folk who made the tower their home.

Her messengers operated out of the little chamber closest to the double doors. Usually the positions were filled by younger servants, or agents who'd managed to anger Amita Sarrha during training. Ibram had not-so-fond memories of sitting in that small room, practicing his apologies on his fellow inmates, who had their own problems in mind.

Fortunately, the airing cupboard was full when Ibram appeared in their doorway, and he had his pick. He sent one messenger to Amita Sarrha's counterpart in the Third Mentor's division, requesting a full explanation of the Vo Kalns in the area, and then sent a second up to the Scribes' Bureau in the First Mentor's compound, with messages of introduction to Kenda Trading, which employed Master Finar's brother, and the Sect of the Iron Hand. He had no idea whom to contact there, but they were bound to have agents. Not even sects formed from the caprice of nobility would be able to act amongst the common folk without a proxy. The two youngsters were all too willing to carry his messages, else they'd be stuck rolling dice until Dihya dimmed the lights and kicked the loafers out.

Ibram stretched his neck, and winced as an answering crackle made his stiff neck whine with strain. He glanced about the tower, as three Attendants tumbled, shrieking with laughter, from the third floor ladders down to the basin of the fountain. They landed on its edge, arms raised in triumph. Ladyship did not come out of her office to investigate the resulting roar of approval.

Ibram rotated his shoulders, and then tucked his thumbs into his belt; he ran his thumb against the hilt of his sica. The night's festivities were in somewhat full swing, a lively house for a lively preceptory. He sighed, and tugged on the back of his hair. The noise sunk like needles into his head; he'd been up and about too much, perhaps. He might wait a quarter of an hour in the messengers' office on their broken-down sedan, a reply might come quickly and, if it didn't, at least the quiet might help.

❧

The sky was clear, for a wonder, sharp enough to see the constellation of Harman The Farmer and his starry plow glimmering above the tree tops. The air smelled of the trees and the promise of fresh rain, but the lamplighters had acquitted themselves fully in their duties. The way down the living mountain had been clear, and the same might be said for the rest of Lityen as well. It was bright enough that Ibram dodged a fair number of Talsconis' warders patrolling the imperial areas of the village on his way.

The road home wound ever so slightly off the main byways of Lityen, still nearest the roads paved by the empire, but down such streets that had been formed from endless carriages and stamping feet. Ibram did not bother to ring the bell; Kholdo would be in bed already, and there was no need to wake the rest of the house. He simply took a running start down the path leading around the house, stepped up onto the tree stump, jumped with all his might, and then clambered over the high stone wall which surrounded the main entrance and public courtyard.

He hung from the side of the wall for a moment, and then dropped carefully down on to the soft earth. Ibram stumbled back, shaking out his arms and rolling his shoulders. He chuckled—only a touch giddy from lack of sleep—and ran both hands through his hair. He stretched, barely holding in a deep groan, and let his arms fall to his sides. Not a bad run; it was a bit like being a small boy again, to be sure.

There was enough light from the clear night sky that Ibram didn't need to feel his way forward. It was in his mind to let the world slumber while he fended for himself. Dinner did not seem amiss.

The circular drive upon which he stood was empty, and the main doors were always locked by this hour of night. Ibram undid the buttons holding his gambeson closed at the neck, and tugged free the leather cord with iron keys hung around his neck. His parents' work-shop meant their lives were comfortable, but they still protected their valuables in the old-fashioned manner. No flashy expensive lightning locks or attuned stones for the Ucalegon-Cibulka household, just sturdy locks and thick doors.

Ibram let himself in quietly, and made sure to lock up behind him. The public courtyard, where Father and Ama did most of their busi-ness, always gave him a shiver at night. He hurried through, directly across the empty garden, and unlocked the second door, this time into the family courtyard. He turned around to face the kitchen garden in the center of the open courtyard.

His stomach grumbled at the sight of the leafy squashes all in a row; he patted it gently. Food was... Ibram frowned. He sniffed the air. It was clear, only the faintest whiff of smoke from the chimneys of his parents and Katka's bedrooms. He stepped out onto the terrace, and leaned out over the wooden railing, bracing himself on the post for balance. The stars above glimmered; he could see his breath in the chill coming off the Emerald Mountains. Ibram glanced to his right, and clapped his hands lightly on the railing. There might be some leftover flatbread from the dinner he'd missed, maybe a hunk of cheese he could snatch before it was turned into next day's meal.

He walked quickly down the righthand side of the terrace, past the sitting room for intimate guests, and then the family room with the largest fireplace where they took most of their meals and then down the short staircase to the kitchen, with its fireplace that connected to the family room. Embers cooled in the hearth, lending just enough light that Ibram could avoid the bigger obstacles in his path. He peered through the gloom to his left, where the door to Kholdo's sleeping chamber lay, but he heard no movement.

The thought occurred that he might have taken off his boots first, but there was no lapping up frozen milk. He padded closer to Kholdo's work table, and found better than he could have hoped. Crisped chiusti bread, twice-cooked to preserve for morning and cut into trian-gles, lay in a platter; they must have had the first batch for dinner. He found cheese beneath a cloth, and adding it to the platter, he spied a lidded clay pot near the fire, with a small wooden bowl and three spoons laid next to it. The spoons spelt out the first letter of his name.

Ibram leaned down to the remains of the fire, and delicately touched his finger to the side of the clay pot; it was warm but not boiling. He smiled over the rumbling of his empty stomach. He snatched up the cheese cloth, and opened the pot's lid; the smell of mouflon broth, and garlic shoots, ginger and chybollus puffed into the air on a cloud of steam. Kholdo had left him all the means to make tienasa. Ibram licked his lips, and set the platter down. He settled himself next to the hearth, crossing his legs underneath himself, and dropped the triangles of chiusti into the bowl. He picked up the middle spoon, and ladled broth on top of the bread, and then crumbled cheese over that.

Not so bad for a late night and no one to share it with. He stirred the hard cheese into the softening bread and brought the bowl up to sip the broth. He swallowed and licked his lips. Riant.

The door to the kitchen creaked open quietly. Ibram froze, bowl upraised, and carefully rolled his eyes sideways. In the doorway stood Katka, bane of all foundries and his own sweet little sister, with a candle upraised in one hand. Her tall frame loomed in the small light. She put her hand on her hip, bunching up her long shift that had clearly been made before all the practice at Father's anvil had broadened her shoulders.

"Ibram?" Katka whispered as loudly as possible. "Is that you?"

Ibram sighed and lowered his meal. He saw her peer at him, hunching forward.

"If you're a vagrant, you've picked a poor house to get out alive!" she said.

Oh for the love of *green fruit*. "Of course it's me," he hissed back. "Who else would it be?"

Katka snorted, and relaxed back onto her heels. She tossed her sleep braid over her shoulder as she came into the kitchen, letting the door creak shut behind her. "I thought maybe a cat had gotten in," she said in a more normal tone.

"A cat who wasn't leaving the house alive?"

"Be quiet!" she retorted, and raised the candle up. "You've made enough racket with those heavy boots. You'll wake Kholdo."

"No, I won't," Ibram frowned. "What are you doing awake?"

"You woke me, stumbling about on the terrace," she said, and knelt down next to him. Her long braid tumbled over her shoulder, and she shoved it out of the way. "And Lady Azadiya employs you for stealth."

"I have many fine qualities," Ibram said, and ate a large spoonful of tienasa, soaked bread dripping with broth and melted cheese.

Katka rolled her eyes, and grabbed up the platter in her free hand. "Come through to the table," she said. "You look like some kind of urchin."

Ibram glared and swallowed, but she had the rest of the bread and cheese. He groaned softly as he got up, and wrapped the cheese cloth around the clay pot to bring it in as well as his bowl. Ibram walked through the connecting door to the table first, and set his burdens down on in the table's center. His constant burden lay her items next to the clay pot and also a lidded jug of something she must have grabbed while his back was turned. She was balancing the candle on top of the jug, and caught the candlestand just as it began to tip over. Wax splatted across the wood.

"Take down those cups, would you?" she asked, as she settled down at the table.

Ibram fought back a yawn, but did as he was bid, and chose two of the wooden goblets Ama kept on a shelf by the fire. He returned and sat down.

"Is there enough for me?" she asked. She took the lid off the jug, blew dust out of the cups, and began to pour.

"I suppose," Ibram said. He got up, took a step away from the table, and looked about. The room was poorly lit only by Katka's little candle. He eyed the four corners of the room, and then surveyed the mantle of the fireplace.

"What happened to the oil lamps?" Ibram asked.

"Kholdo took them in for cleaning," Katka said.

Ibram sighed. "Well, that's just—we could have stayed in the kitchen, you know. Plenty of light there."

Katka shrugged and looked into the clay pot. She stole Ibram's spoon and poked about in the broth. "It's not comfortable."

"Well, we could have stood," Ibram said. He sighed, and brushed his hand down the front of his gambeson. His fingers caught on the button shield Ahksell had made for him. He pursed his lips briefly.

Well, a lack of light could be considered an emergency.

"Katka," he said. "Don't look directly at this."

"Directly at what?"

"Ahksell's gewgaw," Ibram said. He set his thumb directly over the bezel in the middle of the shield and closed his eyes. He pressed hard until he felt the sea glass sink into the metal and the whole button shield warm as bluish wavering light seeped through the seal of closed lids. The button shield turned hot and grew heavy; Ibram thrust his left arm out behind himself. "Quick, give me the pot lid!"

He heard the scuffle of Katka's feet bracing as she leaned over, and then his fingers curled around the glazed clay of the pot lid. Without looking, he slid the shield off the button on his gambeson and dropped it onto the lid. He walked forward to the end of the table as the light grew brighter.

"Oh, it's like being underwater," Katka said softly. "Can you see the waves?"

"I told you not to look at it!"

"I'm not!" Katka protested. "You're in front of me, so I couldn't anyway. But the light's so strong I can see around you."

Ibram reached out and, fumbling only a very little, found the chair at the end of the table. He set the pot lid down on the seat, and took two full steps backwards before opening his eyes. He blinked rapidly. Blue-white light filled the room, splashing up to the ceiling and flooding the area with a deep undulating glow that, he had to admit, was a little like looking at the bottom of a municipal fountain.

"Well," he said, and cleared his throat. "That should help."

Katka had his bowl of soup in one hand and his spoon in the other. She tilted her head. She gazed about the walls, a note of wonder glimmering in her eyes.

"I thought that was given to you for emergencies."

"It's only a test," he said, and sat down. "Give me my dinner."

Katka turned her attention from contemplating the lighting, and wonder was replaced by eye-rolling. She slurped from his bowl maliciously, and then handed it over. Ibram sighed, and began to make himself another portion. He crunched on a triangle of chiusti bread as he ladled broth over its compatriots.

"Why are you only now getting back?" Katka asked. "You were missed at dinner."

"Was Ama worried?" he asked.

Katka shook her head, and Ibram shrugged. He ate a bite of salted cheese. "See? You should only worry about me when Ama is worried. She always knows more."

Katka sighed, and set her elbow on the table.

"Are you still working on the fire?" she asked, yawning.

Ibram nodded. "I am," he said, and swallowed a spoonful of tienasa.

"Horrible business," she muttered. She leaned her head on her fist, and ate a triangle of bread, brushing crumbs from the bibbed front of her shift. "You came home reeking of soot."

"Some days that is the job," Ibram said. He leaned back in his chair and sighed, holding his bowl in both hands. The warmth felt good on his fingers.

"Ama never did anything like that," Katka said. Her wide eyes narrowed slightly. "Is it something you're allowed to speak about?"

Ibram shrugged. "I might speak as I find," he said.

Katka groaned. "Ugh, now you even sound like her," she said. "Can't you just say yes or no?"

"Yes," Ibram said, and thought it over. "Or no."

Katka snatched up her goblet and took a long drink. "This is why I never worry when you go about the sect's business," she said. "How could you ever come to trouble when you already are so much of a bother?"

Ibram grinned, and then yawned. He tipped the clay pot towards himself and squinted at the level of broth.

"Eat more," Katka said. She picked at a splatter of wax with her thumbnail. "You look green."

"I'm wearing green," Ibram said, even as he helped himself. "Anyway, there's not much to tell, to be sure. It's become complicated."

He set bowl and pot aside to try the drink Katka had brought along. He swallowed and grimaced, the sharp taste of small beer was never his favorite. He drank again, regardless.

Katka lifted her head, and leaned back, clutching her own cup in one hand. She tucked loose strands of her hair back into her braid with the other. Ibram watched her set herself to rights. She favored Father more than Ibram did; she had his red hair and soft eyes as well as the ability to be pleased in all her company. Ibram had merely gotten his stubborn chin, otherwise he was their mother's child in face and temperament. If that wasn't a sign from the heavens that they'd been apprenticed correctly, then he didn't know what was.

"How do you mean, complicated?" she asked.

Ibram shrugged. Should he tell her about the body? That someone was going around Lityen killing folk either by fire or by wire, or both? Not that it was a confidential corpse—hard to do when the procession up the living mountain was in broad daylight—but it seemed strange to simply announce a murder victim over a late night meal. Death with all its attendant legalities wasn't part of Katka's work, after all. Before he'd begun his apprenticeship, Ama had never spoken much about her job to either of her children. He swiped his thumb beneath his lower lip to catch a drip of broth. Katka made a face at him, exaggerating her injured patience. In the waving light, she looked like the old fire tale about the fisherman's daughter in the cavern of pearls.

"If you can't say, then what's the point of being mysterious about it?" she demanded. "It's of no interest to me, to be sure, but don't say I didn't try to uphold my end of the conversation."

"We could practice our Merrilian instead?" Ibram offered.

"Before bed?" Katka shook her head. "I'll have strange dreams."

Ibram snorted. He set his bowl down on the table with a sigh. "It's mostly just a lot of cross-talk," he said. "Talking and listening and remembering."

"You could put it in your memory map, or whatever Amota Evren calls it, I suppose," she said.

"I am getting better," Ibram protested "That's what all that work with Amota Evren is for, after all. The shelves in my mind are quite cluttered."

He'd spoken with Amota Berac and Amita Sarrha most of the night, going over the fire and the alliances. To Ibram, it mostly sounded like a cut and dried affair. No one seemed to have a motive, yet no one acted out of character. Competitors spoke disparagingly of the other's business. Folk worried about rebuilding and rent. Yet, there were five dead folk on their way down the First Road to the Crossroads, and someone must be held to account.

Ibram sighed and stirred his tienasa. "I have forgotten something," he admitted. "I had a thought earlier today—I had just spoken to a man about his fire damage and it called something to my mind, but then I spoke to Ahksell and it fled."

"Oh, I see," Katka said, and grinned. "His stream of thought has a strong current."

"No, it was only..." Ibram trailed away and shook his head. "Di na'shin sorela. Do ploune..."

"Oh now, come on, you're better at it than I," Katka said.

Ibram waved her off. "It was about the chalcan vitriol and then Ahksell explained the difference between a rogue alchemist and an alchemaster, and it flew from me."

Katka's eyes widened. "Why did you need to know *that?*" she yelped.

"Keep it down!" Ibram hissed. "You want to wake the house?"

"But why—"

"I only—oh, hush up," Ibram said. He cleared his throat and rubbed the center of his chest.

"Is there a danger of—of that?" Katka's eyes widened as she mouthed the word "alchemastery."

"No, of course not," Ibram said quickly. "Do you think I'd be home if it were?"

Katka clearly turned that thought over in her mind, and slowly relaxed. She frowned at the tabletop and then looked up at him. "Then what are you thinking of about? Chalcan vitriol?"

Ibram put his spoon in his now empty bowl, and took a slow drink of his beer. "It's being in those evening courtyards," he said. "Bound to have pests."

Katka snorted. "Well, you would know."

"I maintain a presence merely because—"

"The food is cheap and so's the cider?" Katka finished for him, batting her eyelashes.

"That, and the music is often good," Ibram said.

"I'll take a draughtshop player any day," Katka said. "Much less fuss."

"That *fuss* takes a certain level of skill, thank you." Ibram snorted and rubbed the side of his face. He yawned, and shook his head. He was too tired for this, but also too nervy to sleep. Besides, how many times had he missed family meals this month? It was somehow always easier to eat up the living mountain than return home in time.

"How is your artisan project going?" he asked. "It's the third...no, the four chains of competency now, yes?"

Katka's face brightened immediately. "I've plotted my third chain," she said.

Ibram smiled, and leaned on his elbows. "Already?" he asked. "I thought you were waiting for the next Harvest Moonrise Festival to—"

"No, that's only to display it," she interrupted, "if Father believes I've forged the links well enough and passed my test in rank. Now, you remember what I showed you?"

"The first is knots in twine," Ibram said.

"The first will be—yes, that's right," she said over him, and then laughed. She wriggled in her seat, and Ibram smiled down at the table-top, letting his weary head fall to his chest as he listened. "Because that's how I began learning the patterns in the filigree. The second I've decided shall be an anchor chain in copper in reference to the sect and our family's relationship to it." Katka paused briefly to finish off her cup. "The third...well, I've gone up and downstream on this decision. But it falls down to the fact that I want it to proceed thus, and Father only has to approve the design of the links."

"Is there any doubt he would?" Ibram roused himself, and poured out beer for the both of them.

Katka rolled her mouthful of small beer in her mouth as if it were wine, and nodded before she swallowed. "He might. I want to do a mesh chain, but in iron."

Ibram frowned. "Iron?" he repeated. "Hardly a jeweler's metal."

Katka groaned and snatched up a handful of chiusti triangles. She ate one, resentfully. "That's just what Father's going to say," she muttered.

Ibram shrugged. "He might not! After all, what do I know of your work? No more than you, mine."

Katka narrowed her eyes at him, and Ibram was forcibly reminded that they shared both a creative father and a crafty Ama. "You know well enough what to think of iron," she said.

Ibram paused and tilted his head to the side. "I should think in the rain..."

"My artisan's project is not going to rust!" Katka exclaimed, and then hushed herself and Ibram with a guilty look towards the kitchen door.

"If you already know the objection, then why use the offending metal?" Ibram asked.

"Because I want to," Katka said. "It turns this lovely dark color once it's burnished, and it's not like I wouldn't maintain the piece. Besides, why wouldn't I use it. There must be someone out there looking for jewelry that's out of the ordinary way?"

"Someone who can afford jewelry at Father's prices, but who can't afford gold or silver?" Ibram asked.

"We make folk items in bronze and copper," Katka retorted. "The piece should fit the customer's purse as well their neck."

"Or finger."

Katka giggled, and looked down into her drink.

"Is that what you were doing up this late?" Ibram asked. "Designing your examination project?"

Katka shrugged one shoulder. "Designing, redesigning, tossing all my little bits of twine and twisted grass to the floor, only to pick them up again."

Ibram rested both elbows on the table. "You are that worried?"

"I just...I want it to stand apart," she said. "Father's mastery chains are always our best advertisement, so who would notice my poor offering if I don't have something—something out of the common way to offer as well?"

"But it would be enough for your status as an artisan to sell your wares, would it not?" Ibram asked. "Father's mastery and your burgeoning skill, all striving together for the common customer?"

"Or the noble one," she said. "Or one of the alchemists high atop the living mountain. Or someone elevated and elegant in the Bureau of Currency." She shook her head. "I tell you, Ib-la, it's as easy to bring glory to the family business as it is to carry ice through the desert."

"Don't be silly," Ibram said. "You'll do it, regardless. There are always cold charms."

The corner of her mouth crooked. "I could use one as a pendant and sell it as protection from summer's heat."

Ibram laughed, which turned fast into an extended yawn. "Freeze a noble neck off," he mumbled, "and see how quickly fame finds you."

Katka sighed, long and low, and considered the bottom of her cup. "It's not fame, I want," she said. "Just a little...signature of my own. Like Ahksell and his gewgaw."

"To be sure," Ibram said, and gestured towards said bubbly light. "Something comes from something, doesn't it?"

Katka laughed. "Now I know you're tired," she said. "You're making less sense than usual."

He was too old to stick out his tongue or make a face at her. Besides, the lure of her bed was clearly pulling on Katka's shoulders, just as his own bed tempted him. Still, Ibram settled for the revenge of snatching up the cheese and remaining bread, and eating them out of Katka's reach.

8

Morning's hideously beaming light called Ibram forth from slumber, it seemed, almost immediately after his head had found his pillow. He stared up at the wooden beams of the ceiling and let his bleary eyes idly trace a cobweb connecting one wooden log to its brother. He felt the breeze from his window ruffle the top of his hair. He raised his head and stared blearily down the length of his body to his rickety writing desk and chair at the end of the bed.

He dropped his head back and groaned. There had been a fire in his dreams, green and gold flames sweeping up the sides of a barn on the Salt Plateau which burned but never collapsed. A man had stood within the barn, calling his name, but the door was locked with heavy chains at the top and bottom. So there Ibram had stood, flames singeing his hands and bare feet and the skin of his face, fruitlessly trying to kick his way inside.

Ibram pressed both hands to his face and took a deep breath. "If that was a prophetic nudge, O' Divine Yilka the Green, I have gained only one of your megrims in the assault," he muttered.

With a groan, he rolled himself up and out of bed, tossing aside his blanket. A strong cup of shay and a full plate would see him right. He stretched his back and sighed as it crackled. Puzzles delighted Lady

Azadiya, to be sure, but Ibram had less patience with them. He liked a good riddle, but he preferred his answers neatly and quickly delivered with a minimum of fuss. Preferably, with events that resolved matters to make dealing with the warders who littered their corner of the province like pocket lint from an absent-minded empire less of an aggravation.

He grabbed up his clothes, and dressed quickly: underlinen and stockings secured and trousers settled. He pulled his head free of his tunic, and stood for a moment, rolling his stiff neck on his shoulders. He spied his bells without tongues and his dice, not in their little pouch as he normally left them, but out and about as if ready for use. He didn't remember doing that.

He considered them as he buttoned his wool trousers. Prayer took more focus than he could conjure by himself to directly speak with the heavens, but Yilka the Green was his dedicated divine patron. Five folk had died now, and there might yet be a sixth murder in the works. His soul's connection to the heavens might be behind in the offerings this month, but Yilka the Green upheld opportunity as well as luck and work. She knew a busy man when she saw one; the issue at hand might be worth a roll or two. He picked up his four-sided dice and returned them to their little pouch, before untangling the chain connecting his silent bells and hanging the bronze bells between his fingers. He touched each one as if they might ring, closed his eyes and took a deep breath.

All he wanted was the tools to complete his task, not the easy answer—though if Yilka the Green felt it necessary, he wouldn't mind —and a fair wind to guide his heels on the hunt. Let the arsonist be found and peace settle where there had been chaos. A heavy silence fell, thick pressure behind his ears in a band around the back of his head; a ringing built in his mind, high and tight. The outside world grew muffled. He upended the pouch and the wooden dice thudded against the top of his shelf. Ibram waited until each die had stopped moving and opened his eyes.

The three green dice lay before him with only one white daubed point pointing upwards. Ibram sighed. Well enough. If he was only to have one favor from the goddess let it be opportunity and he would make his own luck. Footsteps flew down the walkway beneath his window. Ibram quickly untangled the clapper-less bells from his hand and returned them and the dice to the pouch. He snatched up his twill gambeson and then stuck one arm through the sleeve as he leaned out the sill and craned his neck down to the kitchen garden. Nothing stirred but the shoots of the carrots and salsify in Ama's kitchen garden. He frowned and began buttoning up.

The morning sun lay lightly across the kitchen garden, barely yellowing into warmth. He couldn't see anyone below, though doubtless it was one of Father's younger apprentices—Inzhu or Hedvi—running off along the first level terrace. Ibram patted down the diagonal length of wooden buttons on his gambeson. All present and accounted for, and nothing out of place. He brushed the fifth button over his chest, and then groaned. He'd forgotten to pick up his damnable button shield last night.

He belted his weapon and purses around his waist as he exited his bedroom and rushed out and down the stairs to the first floor. With any luck, the little thing had burnt itself out before Kholdo woke up to make breakfast. No telling what the old man would do if he went in to serve a meal and found the room suffused with a wavering blue light. Smash it with a cleaver? Chop it into a fine mince? Kholdo enjoyed surprises in the same way Ama appreciated visits from Warders. That was to say, not at all. The damning chorus of '*Ib-la, what did you do this time?*' began to swell in the back of his mind.

Ibram paused in a chilling flash of horror. Hang it, what if Kholdo looked into the light? Or attempted to pick it up? Ibram had been seeing double for a twelve-day after an accident helping Ahksell refine that gewgaw, and at the end its weight had trebled for no satisfactory reason. Kholdo was an old man! Who knew what that light might do to him?

He jumped the last three steps down to the first floor terrace with a resounding smack, and bolted for the family room. Ibram grasped the door handle, and then felt it twist beneath his grip. He pushed as Ama pulled and stumbled into the room, falling past her, and only a quick shuffle and twirl kept him on his feet.

He stared at the table. Father, Katka, and Inzhu, the second of

Father's apprentices, stared back. Ibram took a deep breath and braced his hands on his hips. He nodded politely and cleared his throat. Ama huffed behind him and brushed past to return to her seat on the opposite head of the table from Father.

Ibram cleared his throat again, as he took in the decidedly normal yellow light peering through the open windows down. "Good morning, everyone," he said. "I see breakfast is ready."

"And has been for at least thirty minutes, to be sure," Ama said. She pointed to an empty chair with a bowl already set out. "Sit down, then."

"What do we have here?" Ibram asked as he obeyed his mother while attempting to unobtrusively look about the room. His button shield must have shut down in the night. It didn't speak well for any rescue that required a long-term signal. He'd have to mention that to Ahksell after he found the thing.

"Well, it's certainly not a hair comb," Father said, and raised his eyebrows. He drew his hand down his long beard, neatly brushed, and braided with a leather tie.

"Ah, yes."

Ibram dragged both hands through his hair and shook his tangles free. He crammed the strands behind both ears and leaned back in his seat, casually glancing towards the corner of the room. Katka followed his gaze, and twitched her nose at him. She flicked her eyes deliberately down to Ibram's place at the table. Ibram wrinkled his forehead; she sighed.

"Forgot your boots, as well," Ama said, and smiled as she piled yellow cheese onto a slice of glass apple.

Ibram wriggled his toes against the floor, suddenly conscious of his stockinged feet. "I have had a very long night," he said, with all dignity.

Ama looked no more than her usual calm self, so Kholdo was probably not consigned to his sickbed, hands turned into mittens with bandages and sightless eyes weeping at the ceiling in the kitchen. Ibram allowed himself to breath more freely. That no doubt meant the Helping Hand was probably still in the corner of the room where Ibram had left it. He made himself more comfortable and reached for the clay pot in the center of the table. He smelled quash, nutty and with the sweetly sharp edge of trembleberries, as he picked up the long handled spoon inside the pot and stirred. He glanced down into his bowl, and there lay his button shield, sitting in the center of the clay pot lid from the night previous.

Ibram let go of the spoon. He picked up the bowl, and tilted its contents into his right hand. Where the button shield had touched, the clay of the lid was noticeably darker; he lay the pot lid on the table. In the cup of his palm, the button shield glimmered with a faint light against his fingers, but he felt no answering heat or weight. He slid it back onto his gambeson button.

"Kholdo brought it to us early this morning," Ama said. "He said he found it in a corner of the room, and thought perhaps I'd lost it."

"Gift from the sect, wasn't it?" Father asked. "It's too forgetful of you, Ibram, really. Tell him, Verena."

"He knows," Ama said. "And considering how many times he brought it up in conversation when he received that gewgaw, I'm wondering what prompted its use in my house? Did we repel invaders in the night?"

Inzhu snorted with laughter and covered her mouth immediately. Ama smiled at her, and then turned her sharp, twinkling eyes in Ibram's direction. Ibram rolled his head on his shoulders and sighed.

"The borders remain secure," Ibram said.

"Or at least no one else jumped that stump outside the west wall," Father said. "I really must get that dug up."

"Should I have rung the bell and woken everyone up?" Ibram asked.

"Oh, come now," Katka protested at the same time. "It's nice that Ibram didn't wake the house, isn't it?"

Ibram pointed across the table at her. "I was being helpful!"

"Helpful to a burglar as well," Father said. He stroked his beard, and ate his breakfast. "But, why did you use that device if you were so tired?"

"I was hungry," Ibram said. "There was much to do before I returned home. I suppose I was too tired to remember the little thing when I went up to bed."

"Nor I," Katka murmured.

"Well, why were you two up so late, anyhow?" Father asked. He picked up his cup and poured shay into it from a nearby pot. He set the pot down closer to Ibram. "There's always work to be done in the morning."

"Business obeys no schedule but its own up the living mountain and, as such, neither can I," Ibram said. He poured himself a cup of shay, and then ladled quash into his bowl.

Father raised his eyebrows, precisely as he used to when Ama had proffered that excuse to him when she had worked for Lady Azadiya. He let the matter go in the same quiet manner, as well. Ibram added a swirl of honey from the pot to his quash, and mashed it around with his spoon.

"Why didn't you just light a lamp?" Ama asked. "We have enough of them."

Inzhu tugged on Katka's sleeve and murmured something quietly to her. Katka reached out and grabbed the honey pot. She set it down by Inzhu's cup, and the girl spooned honey delicately over the wedge of bread and glass apple slices on her plate. Inzhu's parents knew Master Rennab, he believed. Or, at least, Rennab knew of the family.

"Inzhu," he began. "Do your parents know a Master Soren Rennab? Runs an evening courtyard in the village."

Inzhu patted the soft swirls of brown hair that covered her ears and shook her head. "I—I suppose so," she said. "They go to the same meeting as us, but you're only allowed to talk after it ends, and I go play with my friends then."

Ibram nodded. Ama watched him, and her eyes moved to Inzhu quickly. He obeyed the warning twitch of her mouth. Inzhu was only a child, after all. He might see about visiting her parents if he wanted better answers.

"Does he seem nice?" Ibram asked.

Inzhu shrugged. "I suppose," she said, and then wrinkled her nose. She ate her apple. "He's always tired."

Ibram drank his shay, and considered that. Something was bubbling at the back of his mind, but nothing he did brought the conclusion forwards. Maybe Amota Evren's memory constructions were impeding the natural flow of his thoughts. For a moment, he saw the gilded flames from his dream; he squinted and the vision cleared.

"There weren't any lamps to be had," Katka said, returning to the old conversation in the sudden silence. "Besides, it was rather fun. Like dining under the lake."

"Don't let Ahksell hear you say that," Ibram said, "or else I'll wind up trying to eat under water for one of his examinations."

Ama laughed and then turned to look behind her as Kholdo bustled through the adjoining door from the kitchen. He came in with his hands covered by cloths and set down a large metal kettle on the corner of the table. Ibram passed across the shaypot, and Kholdo took it with a narrow-eyed look on his face.

Ibram cleared his throat, and resettled himself in his chair. "I apologize for the button," he said.

Kholdo didn't make a noise of disapproval in front of Ibram's parents, but long standing tradition meant that Ibram heard it anyway. He coughed in discomfort. It would be fine. Ibram was fully grown, Kholdo couldn't make him peel vegetables any longer.

"That's as well as might be," Kholdo said, "since you didn't burn the house down, nor break anything when the pair of you fumbled around in my kitchen last night."

"Thank you for the tienasa," Ibram said. "It was most appreciated."

Kholdo rested on his heels in satisfaction. "You're very welcome," he said. "Though I might suggest investment in a traveling light in the future?"

"Perhaps on his birthday," Ama said, and cut another slice of her glass apple.

Kholdo busied himself pouring fresh boiling water into the shaypot, and she leaned away from any stray drips. Father spooned himself up another bowl of quash, while Katka spread butter on a piece of brown bread. Ibram raised his hands to his shoulders as Kholdo backed into the kitchen door and disappeared with a significant look on his face.

"He could simply have found a lantern," Father said, and Ibram dropped his hands to his lap. "The proper tool ensures success."

"But didn't you also say that innovation is the mother of mastery?" Katka looked up from her bread and butter.

Father sighed. "Is this about the iron again?"

Ibram drank his shay, strong, smoky, and unsweetened on his tongue. He glanced at Ama, who spread her hands slightly. Splendid, he'd missed Katka's proposal but arrived in time for the aftermath.

"Yes, it's about the iron," Katka exclaimed. "It's a perfectly acceptable metal. It shines up well, it's cheap—"

"It rusts, it smells," Father said with a curl to his lip that spoke to Ibram of fondness, but seemed to spark only frustration in Katka.

"Not if you take proper care," Katka said, and tore a bite off her bread. "Which you know I would."

"Now, you know I only wish to advise in this matter," Father said. "If iron is what you will use, then iron it shall be, and you have the talent to manipulate it, but using non-standard materials will carry its risks. Especially once we display your final product and people notice that length of chain in the collar piece."

Ibram took up a spoonful of quash and ate it. He shrugged. "Maybe they'll be intrigued."

"Curiosities are poor long-term investments," Father said, and shook his head. "No, what is best for business is innovation that people still recognize. Look at the stars of eternity I made for Lady Azadiya, one hundred platinum clips with black opal bezels no bigger than the nail on your smallest finger!"

"They saw the stars, but also the stones," Katka repeated with Father, while Ibram mouthed along. Those clips had been Father's first commission to Lady Azadiya, and featured in many of his stories, whether about business or craft.

Father laughed and shook his head. "So they do!" he exclaimed. "Whenever she wears them, I swear to The Wheelmaker our business grows times three. This is why it's important to strike the right balance."

"Enough to notice, but not enough to shock," Ibram said. "But doesn't that mean they won't pay it a second thought?"

Father shook his head. "Not at all," he said. "If it's truly of quality, then they will see that quality is your signature, and work will come to you accordingly."

Father nodded, which launched Katka on a different tangent about someone's order for mesh chains in bronze, and Ibram let their wrangling wash over him. He finished his quash, and then grabbed an apple from the bowl on the table. He bit through the iridescent skin and chewed, blotting the juice from his mouth with his sleeve.

He glanced down the length of the table to Inzhu, who was steadily working her way through her breakfast and nibbling on a piece of cheese from the wheel before her. Ama merely listened to the others in amusement. Katka and Father enjoyed a spirited debate over their shay, after all. He set down his apple in favor of his shay cup, and hid a sigh. It mostly seemed to Ibram that they were attacking the same piece of meat from different angles. Could a signature as subtle as 'quality' be rightfully called a signature at all? Surely a customer would assume paying for a skilled artisan meant all her work was of that high standard. Ibram fell decidedly on Katka's side in the argument, she needed something to stand out or else risk being ignored altogether.

Ibram tugged on the hair at the back of his head. "Father," he interrupted. "How do you stop the forge from setting the house on fire?"

Whatever Father had thought Ibram had been about to say, that clearly wasn't it. He broke off his conversation with Katka immediately in favor of gazing, wide-eyed, in Ibram's direction. Ibram felt his leg begin to tap in impatience, and gripped his knee below the table to still it.

"The fire suppression tiles, of course," Father said, finally.

Ibram shook his head. "No, I understand that, but didn't we..." He looked to Katka. "Didn't we have to throw water on the walls once? I remember, I was very young and—"

"Ha!" Father laughed and stroked his beard. "Do you still remember that? It was so long ago, you must have been, oh, six, if you were a day."

"Then I certainly never threw water on anything if Ibram was six," Katka said, and smirked over her cup.

"Oh no," Ama said, with a chuckle. "you gave it your best attempt with your little cup. I remember it well. You always wanted to do whatever he was doing."

"So that did happen?" Ibram persisted. "Do you remember why?"

Father nodded. "Yes," he said. "It was a problem with the mortar for the tiles, as I recall. I'd misjudged the mixture and as such it dried out too quickly. Completely negates its resistant properties. We had to damp cure the wall again to make sure it was at least good enough to support the suppression tiles so that they could do their work."

Ibram paused, and then frowned into his cup. The hot shay sloshed against the rim when he swirled the cup in his hand. There had been two explosions, and everyone had ignored the first one. When you lived in Lityen, you either became accustomed to bangs and blasts every now and again, or you left the village. The arsonist had counted on that.

He set down his cup and cleared his throat. "Ama," he said. "Please excuse me. I just now realized I have someplace I need to visit."

"Up to see Ahksell about getting your button shield fixed?" Ama asked.

He shook his head. "No, I—" he stood; his chair scraped against the floor. "Actually, yes, to be sure I will, but I need to see about a thought beforehand."

"Well then, by all means," she said, and laughed as Ibram rushed around the table to kiss her on the temple. "But put on your boots first!"

❧

Lityen was alive and very much about its business by the time Ibram reached Pillared Circle, despite the early hour. He skirted around the municipal fountain and down the second exit, and then turned right at the remains of the bakery-mill. A few days' time had not been suffi-cient to clear all the debris away, but on this side of the road, the builders of Builders Row had not been idle. Scaffolding rose up to the second story on some of the nearest buildings, and apprentices scur-ried up their ramps, toting buckets of tools ready for the repair work. A carpenter stood outside his shop, hammering wedges into an eight foot log to hew it into planks. His apprentices stood ready, and as Ibram passed by, were already tugging the latest plank into position to be smoothed.

It was good that he was here early, both so that he might check up on Nesrine and Corbus—and through them, Master Dughlat—but also because the thought rolling through his mind was best acted upon as soon as possible. Ahksell would have been no help—or at least, little to none. If Ibram was right—and he nearly always was, given enough time and tide—then what he was looking for barely remained on the plane of reality. In point of fact, he might be running off a short pier, but if any evidence remained, then he needed to act quickly.

He turned a corner and spied Masters Finar and Bine alongside Mistress Salaz, surrounding a tall, spindly table outside a hastily erected wintering tent, billowing blue-grey smoke through the ropes holding up the center pole. Ibram was surrounded by folk, all of who could clearly see him in his gambeson and torch brooch; he vigorously resisted the urge to groan aloud. What was Master Finar doing with those two? He had his own work! Far away in his caffa near the imperial buildings, where the warders kept everyone nice and loyal.

The cookshop owners each had a small wooden bowl in front of them, with a fat clay shaypot on an iron trivet in the middle. If they were not meeting deliberately, then it remained an opportunity for knowledge that Ladyship would not thank him for ignoring. He looked up and down the busy street, but not a helpful fellow agent could be seen. Amota Berac no doubt had them off running down officiates at the Runner's Temple in preparation for distributing the money to the fire alliance. Accordingly, Ibram swerved to investigate the possible early morning conspiracy.

He bowed shortly, but only Master Finar returned the courtesy. The other two frowned, but perhaps they simply were slow to properly wake. Ibram glanced about, but no one passing by the stained tent walls seemed alarmed by the smoke pouring forth from the tent, so he resolved to ignore it as well.

"What brings you all together on this fine morning?" he asked, and leaned over to sniff appraisingly. "Breakfast amongst friends is always a joyful party, to be sure."

"Just waiting for you sect agents to finish your reports," Mistress Salaz said.

Ibram nodded seriously. "It must weigh upon you," he said. "I am very sorry for it."

She opened her mouth and then closed it. "Well. Yes."

"What's this breakfast then?" Ibram asked, and nodded at the bowls. "It smells well enough."

"Smells like smoke," Master Bine muttered.

"Woodcutter's quash only, I fear," Master Finar said. He angled his own bowl so that Ibram could see the bits of stale bread and mushroom floating in the shay broth. "Otso managed to finagle the use of a cauldron and equipment from his landlady. It's quite good, if you're hungry."

Ibram nodded, and clasped his hands behind his back. "No, thank you. I'm glad Master Sembe has come to an arrangement with Mistress Vo Kaln," he said. "Am I to assume that Master Bine and Mistress Salaz have a similar tent in their futures?"

"If we can come up with the coin," Mistress Salaz said, with a sour glance behind her.

Master Bine rubbed both hands over his shock of red hair, and then poured more broth from the clay pot into his bowl. He picked it up and supped with barely a wince, though steam curled over his ruddy face. He set the bowl down with a snap and hissed through his teeth.

"Is Mistress Vo Kaln not being as generous to you two?" Ibram asked, and extended the quick step of a polite lie into the conversational dance. "I'm surprised, I've heard such good reports."

"I'm sure it's nothing so severe," Master Finar said, but Ibram didn't think he put his heart into the statement.

Master Bine sucked his teeth, but Mistress Salaz shook her head. "It's nothing to you," she said. "She wants something out of your Soren, but the situation is very different when it's *you* who wants something from *her*."

"Oh, now Carme," Master Finar began to protest, and again, Mistress Salaz shook her head. Really, Ibram might send her a token of his regard later on. He settled his weight on his heels and looked attentive.

"Well, look at us," she said, and flicked her left hand towards the ruins. "Barely through negotiations between ourselves—much less clearing up matters with Master Comoros and the sect—and does she move an inch in her demands?" She slapped her fingers on the table; the bowls wobbled.

"No," Master Bine answered sourly.

"No," she repeated. She drank her woodcutters' quash, and chewed heavily as she pressed her free hand to her left temple. Her clothes showed creases and her hair was leaning to the right on her head.

"I'm sorry, Carme," Finar said. "You're right, of course."

"It's disheartening," she said, and squinted down at her bowl. She cleared her throat.

A little silence developed. Around them, a few folk with ashes on their hems and rags covering their heads flooded around the table and into the tent. The lead woman pulled back the front hanging canvas and a strong waft of wild garlic and onion drifted out on a cloud of smoke. Ibram wrinkled his nose, and glanced about the table. He sighed and turned a critical eye to the tent.

"Can it really be called a cookshop now?" Ibram asked. He paused a moment for Salaz and Bine's confusion to allow them to focus on him. "Seems more in the guise of a festival stall, really."

Master Bine snorted, and then cleared his throat. "He's not got so much to rejoice in as that."

Mistress Salaz made a face that Ibram interpreted as agreement, or indigestion. Master Finar sighed and looked rueful.

"How did Master Sembe assemble his tent and equipment then?" Ibram asked. "I would have thought all his supplies were destroyed."

"Foraging, mostly," Finar said, and played with the rim of his bowl. "Hence today's offering."

Ibram waved his hand in the general direction of the tent. "But the shay for the broth? And all...this?"

The two remaining cookshop owners shared a look between them, all wide eyes and expressive yet silent mouths, and then Master Bine cleared his throat. Ah, the rewards of competition.

"Otso had already paid his rent for the month when the fire began," Bine said with a sniff. "He managed to convince Mistress Vo Kaln that he could have the use of her tent and some of her older household equipment on the strength of the remaining balance."

Ibram's eyebrows raised on their own recognizance, and he let them. So two of the three cookshop owners had been behind on rent. Philendra Dubidat had no claim to the money from the fire alliance beyond her own belongings. And Mistress Vo Kaln was allowing children to gather wood ash for the soapmakers.

"A charitable noble indeed," he said.

Mistress Salaz snorted. "She's not noble."

"Well, a cadet branch of a house..." Master Finar trailed off.

"There's too many of them," Bine said. "A cousin of a cousin of an aunt is barely noble. They only have the name through an accident of marriage. And, anyway, our Mistress Vo Kaln cares too much for the faunts and picaio. The great houses couldn't care less."

Ibram couldn't fault the claim. To most nobility the cost of something was like a bad smell in a temple, never to be mentioned. He rested a casual elbow on the table.

"So Master Sembe only has the tent for the remainder of the month?" he asked. "And then what happens?"

"He either pays his rent—the same rent for a building as for a tent!" Mistress Salaz began.

"Or else he's back where we two are, waiting on your Master Comoros to declare our claim legitimate before the imperial bureaucracy so that the Runner's officiates will disburse our monies," Master Bine finished.

Ibram tsked lightly, and shook his head. "It's a hard road," he said. "I'm sure Ladyship has you in her thoughts."

"Does she?" Master Finar asked.

Ibram discovered the urge to wince at his own choice of words, but suppressed it. He looked at Master Finar and affected surprise instead.

"Of course," he said. "Lady Azadiya is always interested in what goes on in Lityen."

"Is that what brings you down here today?" Master Finar asked.

Ibram shifted from leaning on his left arm to leaning on his right, so he could look the man in the face. The table creaked beneath him. He smiled.

"Naturally," Ibram said. "We all row together, don't you think? It's a Western thought, to be sure, but in times of crisis you need never look further than the folk up the living mountain. In point of fact, I was looking for you, Master Finar."

He hadn't been, but the sudden rapid blinking and slackened mouth on Master Finar's face was worth the price of omission. Master Finar's forehead wrinkled as he looked to his fellow diners and then Ibram.

"Looking for me?" he repeated.

Ibram nodded. "I wondered if you had heard from your brother lately? I mentioned his name to Lady Azadiya, and she found his wares interesting."

"You mentioned Achard to Lady Hobon?" Master Finar asked.

"That old peddler?" Mistress Salaz asked. "What would someone like Mentor Hobon want with him?"

"He's not a peddler," Master Finar snapped. "He travels for his company."

Ibram didn't twitch his head in her direction, but answered anyway. "Oh, Ladyship doesn't go past the imperial boundary much at all these days," he said. "She's ever interested in news of the world outside. And Master Finar's brother Achard has such a good relationship with the sects in the south."

Master Finar nodded once, and swallowed. Then looked down into his bowl and drank down his woodcutters' quash. He licked his lips with a quick slash of the tip of his tongue.

"Does he?" Master Bine asked. "Maybe I should have taken him up on his offers, then."

Ibram leaned away from the table and put his hands behind his back. "Oh now," he said with a smile. "You'll make Afsoun jealous, if that talk spreads."

They laughed, but it settled quickly and ended with Ibram smiling alone. He sighed, and tilted his head to the side, and then dragged his hair back behind his ear. Master Finar's forehead was beginning to show signs of permanent wrinkles.

"I'll be certain to contact you, when Achard sends me word," Master Finar said.

Ibram nodded. "I thank you, Master Finar. That would be very helpful. Now, is there anything I might do for you three, while we are all together?"

The trio looked amongst themselves, rather at a loss. Ibram stepped back from the table, and bowed shortly. It was past time he got to the bakery-mill, anyway.

"Ah well," he said, "good company is its own reward. I shall keep you in my thoughts, as you keep me in yours."

He'd planned to come down to the site, regardless, to see if Master Dughlat returned to his place of employment. If he did not appear, then Ibram would know how to proceed after all, and if he did show his face, then all the better for him to answer Ibram's questions. Besides, this way he might extend Lady Azadiya's invitations to dine to Mistress Dubidat and Master Rennab. She hadn't sent similar greetings to the cookshop owners, or the folk on Builders Row, but if Ladyship got nothing useable from the meal tonight, he expected to be sent down with another batch of invitations for a second night of revelry and subtle interrogation.

Ibram took a quick corner to avoid a train of mules pulling a stack of logs down the street. A small work party stood amongst the remains of the bakery-mill, shifting debris from one pile to another. Its stone foundations still outlined the plot of land upon which it had previously stood. The three conical grindstones remained, their tops driven through the floor by the force of the blast. The drag marks through the ash on the floor showed where the bodies had been removed; they were undisturbed. It looked as if folk were stepping around, rather than through them, as they cleared the area.

Ibram resisted the urge to whistle. Regardless of how—or who—had started the fire, all that loose flour in the air had worked a decidedly foul trick on the former owners. Not even the mules hitched to the grinders had been spared.

"Good morning!" Ibram called out. He walked in through what had been the bakery-mill's front entrance, and carefully made his way towards the work party.

A stout young man turned at Ibram's shout. He wore a simple bibbed work smock and red trousers, and his bluntly cut brown hair lay limp against his head. He watched Ibram approach with a dull interest. Philendra Dubidat came over to stand by him.

"Mistress," Ibram said, and bowed shortly. "May I make myself known to your friend?"

"Well, Ealar?" she asked gently.

The boy would be the surviving Ozol, then. Up close, he appeared younger than his height and stature had made him seem, and grief slackened his wide mouth even as it dulled his brown eyes. The young man nodded, and crossed his arms over his chest. He did not seem all that aware, though, in Ibram's estimation, that might have only been the unfortunate nature of their current situation. They bowed shortly to one another.

"Ibram Ucalegon, agent of the Sect of Seven Fires."

"Ealar Ozol. This is my family's..." Master Ozol pinched his mouth closed over his words and waved his hand out from his side. He took a deep breath and looked about to continue, but then merely looked at his shoes and breathed out.

Mistress Dubidat put her hand on the young man's arm. Ibram tucked his hands behind his back. He bent his head, and said, "May they be quickly through the Gate of Heaven."

That was what Vissilians said, and it seemed to help some, even if Ozol's mouth barely twitched upwards in acknowledgement. He swallowed and breathed in quickly through his nose, and then nodded. "Very grateful—I'm very grateful for the Sect's aid in getting me back home as fast as possible. How can I help you?" he asked.

This youngster now stood to inherit the bakery-mill. It was a fine situation if one was a monster, but it also followed that he stood to inherit a mountain of debts and a considerable loss of custom, if it were proven to be the bakery-mill at fault. Public opinion overwhelmingly favored that notion, if the talk around the markets was anything to go by. Young Master Ozol faced a steep road ahead of him.

Ibram tilted his head. In point of fact, he wasn't sure about that. "A question, Master Ozol," he said. "If you don't mind. You know my uncle, Berac Comoros, is helping the fire alliances with their reports and claims?"

Ozol swallowed, but nodded. "I was—I'm supposed to be involved," he said, "but I haven't felt equal to the task."

Ibram nodded. "No idea what to do with the place?"

Ozol shook his head, and then shrugged, and then shook his head again. His rounded shoulders wavered when he breathed. "Mistress Vo Kaln said she might buy the land," he said. "If I don't want it. Her family—there's a place further south that might need a baker, if..." He gestured around the ruins, and the folk who clustered about, but didn't meet Ibram's eyes as he looked around himself. "I could start again, somewhere else."

"We'd be sad to lose you," Mistress Dubidat told him.

"I was hoping to walk through your bakery-mill," Ibram said, as politely as he could. "The portion where it connects to the back alley in particular."

Ibram stole quick glances about the ruins, taking the damage in and making note for further study. The boy was right; there was little here to do but rebuild or sell the land. Looking at him, standing pale and disconnected, Ibram's instinct was that Ealar Ozol hadn't been involved in the fire. Best to be cautious, any road.

Ozol took a moment to process the request, and then jerked his head in a nod. "Yes, of course, you may," he said. "I, uh. I don't have any objections."

Ibram nodded. "I thank you, then," he said. "Could you tell me, young master, how your family arranged your fire suppression tiles?"

Ozol gazed at him for a moment, and then opened and closed his mouth. "Inside, along the back walls," he said. "As is proper."

"But none on the outside?" Ibram asked. "In the alleyways or anything of that sort?"

Ozol shook his head.

"Who made them?"

Ozol opened his mouth, and then looked puzzled. "The Preceptory of Afsoun, of course," he said. "Who else?"

Ibram smiled, and made sure it appeared reassuring. "Who else, indeed?" he asked. "Just a stray thought, young master. No need to think on it."

"What are you looking for?" Mistress Dubidat asked. Her face was all suspicion; her body language told Ibram to be on his best manners. Well enough, she was awash in burials and bills, and protective of an old friends' surviving child. The combination was bound to make anyone cranky. Still, it was good to run into her here, rather than be forced to chase her down later on in the day. If his search came to nothing, than at least he would carry some kind of knowledge up the living mountain.

He smiled. "It's nothing much," Ibram said. "I'll know it when I find it."

"Find what?" she asked.

"Had you heard of Master Rennab's great loss?" Ibram countered politely. "It seems a powerful blow to escape certain death by fire, only to die in your own home."

Both Ozol and Dubidat stiffened. Ibram rubbed a dull spot off his torch-shaped brooch. He clasped his hands behind his back.

"We had heard of Erno Neilos' passing," Dubidat said. "It's a tragedy."

"Was he truly murdered?" Ozol asked.

Gossip ran quickly, indeed. Ibram nodded. "I am sorry to report, he was. Can't think why, to be sure. Seemed such a nice man."

"He had no more brains than a fenek," Dubidat corrected him. "And he was as likely to jump at a prize as he was a shadow."

"Is that so?" Ibram asked.

"It is," Dubidat said. "You won't catch my servants shuffling off their work as he did, nor trying to pawn dross as gold off any wide-eyed pie-eater he came across."

"He wasn't so bad," Ozol said.

"I once caught him selling bread ends in that alley, just as if they weren't given as sops for the customers," she said, and shook her head. Her short red hair bobbed. "Rennab should have sent him away years ago."

Ibram nodded and kicked dust off his boots. "Thank you," he said. "That is good to know."

"Why do you ask us and not the folk in The High Climber?" Mistress Dubidat asked.

"Ah, now, Mistress, to learn more of that you'll have to accept Lady Azadiya's invitation to dinner this evening," he said. "A small party, just after they light the lanes up the living mountain. You might bring your husband along."

"I am invited to dine with Lady Azadiya?" she asked. She took a step back and raised her hand to feel at her collarbones.

"Indeed so."

"Lady Azadiya," she repeated, and patted her hair as though to comb it. "Fourth Mentor *Hobon*."

"The very same honorable soul," Ibram said. "She's been hearing such good reports of you and your efforts in this disaster, that she wished to meet you."

Mistress Dubidat gestured to her attire. "Oh, but I have nothing—"

"Ladyship doesn't stand on ceremony," Ibram interrupted, "so don't worry about appearing to any kind of disadvantage. Why, I have seen her sit on the floor in her finery and take a glass of water with the woodsman as if it were shay with Her Gracious Majesty. Now, do I return up the living mountain with your eager acceptance?"

He smiled and waited while she came to some fairly obvious conclusions very quickly. It was a little mean of him, to be sure, but a flicker of a laugh tingled in the back of Ibram's throat, regardless. No one in their right mind thought Philendra Dubidat, proprietress of The Isconian's Hand, would be able to refuse the invitation of Lady Azadiya Hobon, but it was well-known amongst the locals that Ladyship's invitations came only to those who she found interesting. Common gossip had it that that burden of expectation meant Lady Azadiya's guests either found themselves with an excellent firetale to mull for the long winter months, or a very short trip to Captain Talsconis' cells to await summary execution when the circuit judge came to Lityen. An exciting prospect either way, to be sure.

"My husband as well?" Mistress Dubidat finally asked with a slight catch in her tone. Whether it was excitement or fear, or simply she'd swallowed a fly, Ibram couldn't tell.

"If he is available," Ibram said. "No one understands the demands of a crisis like Lady Azadiya. She will accept his absence."

By her face, Ibram saw he'd shaded his emphasis on her husband's invitation with the right amount of force. One member of the duo might escape a good meal and an interrogation, but not both. Around him, the little work crew was taking ever so close of an interest to Ibram's pronouncements. He caught one's eye and smiled; she looked down at her handful of charred wood with renewed care.

"Do I have to come?" Master Ozol asked.

Ibram started and contemplated the question for a heartbeat. "No, young master," he said. "I think we can safely leave you to—I'm sorry, where are you staying?"

Ozol worked his jaw for a moment, like he was chewing the inside of his mouth. "Soren and Albin are letting me stay with them," he said.

"Master Rennab is very kind," Ibram said. "They're staying in Master Finar's business, are they not?"

Ozol nodded.

Ibram shook his head. "That must be an extraordinarily large caffa."

"Just a bed in their kitchen," Ozol said with a touch of humor. "But they've been very good to me. They let me be."

Ibram nodded. "Master Finar didn't mention you were staying there. That was kind of them."

"We thought at first that he could stay with us," Mistress Dubidat said, "but Carme and Otso lost their room at the Wyvern's Tail and so we offered them the loft before Ealar returned home. It's not big enough for three, more's the pity, so Soren made arrangements."

Ibram's eyebrows threatened to twitch. Soren now, was it? Or perhaps it always was, and Mistress Dubidat was feeling less than formal at the moment. Familiarity bred contempt when neighbors shared a wall. He made a show of being at ease, standing with his weight on his heels and his hands at his sides.

"It's good you and your neighbors get along in times of trouble," he said.

Mistress Dubidat snorted, and shook her head. Her face sharpened as she looked about her. "We don't get along," she said, "and anyone will tell you that. We're competitors. If someone doesn't eat at my tables, they'll drink at his, and I'm out the money to pay my rent."

"It must have rankled that Master Rennab has no rent to pay," Ibram said, and scuffed dirt from his boots off on his trousers.

"The cost of business differs for everyone," Mistress Dubidat said. "We were always scoring points off each other, stealing each other's entertainment and the like, but now we're in the same boat, aren't we? And all we have left to haggle over are these bones."

Master Ozol made a tight sound in the back of his throat and Dubidat's expression faltered. Her chin dipped as she coughed in discomfort. She patted Ozol's arm and pressed her lips together. Ibram tilted his head and saw movement in between their figures, on the other side of the building where The High Climber had stood. He bowed shortly.

"I understand completely," he said. "I think I've taken up enough of your busy time, though. I thank you for your permission, Master Ozol. Mistress Dubidat, I am certain to find you up the living mountain later tonight."

Dubidat's face smiled politely, even as her eyes remained watchful. "Of course, Master Ucalegon," she said. "I'll look forward to it."

"As will I," Ibram said, and walked around the pair to the back of the site.

The work crews clearing debris could not be helped, but they'd left the back of the bakery-mill relatively untouched—or at least, as chock full of wreckage as Ibram had seen before. He sighed through his nose, and cracked the knuckles of his right hand. The damage was near total, and somehow the recovery efforts made it seem worse.

He tilted his head, and brought the figure he'd seen moving about into his line of vision without obviously looking. Soren Rennab was seated at the table in the center of his courtyard, opposite sat Shokan Dughlat. They appeared to be going over a list together, if the bound ledger in Rennab's hands was anything to go by. A quick and merry whistle sent Ibram's attention skittering to his right. Corbus and Nesrine nodded at him from amidst a work crew attempting to shift half-burnt timbers into a safer configuration. Ibram nodded back slightly.

That Dughlat had survived the night was no surprise, since neither of the younger agents had scrambled through Ibram's bedroom window in a panic last night. It was also good to know that Dughlat had come to work, and felt no compulsion to stay abed, or run off into the west, never to be seen again. Ibram sniffed. Lucky, too smart for his own good, or too foolish for everyone else's equilibrium were all an equal possibility. Still, it meant Ibram could turn his attention to what had drawn him out of the dining room back home.

When he'd been ten, he had been introduced formally to Lady Azadiya, bright and unageing, and resplendent with Father's clips in her hair. Father was right, his craftsmanship was unequalled within the imperial boundary, and Ibram would lay a heavy bet that he had no parallel in Vanima province or anywhere else. The clips were tiny, the black opals glimmered as if possessed of their own interior light, and when Lady Azadiya wore them, it seemed as if she had caught a patch of the night sky and bound it within her hair.

"Ladyship," he muttered quietly. "I only ever saw the stars."

Sometimes the flash overwhelmed the function. He'd been saying to himself, over and again, there had been two explosions. But just as Dughlat had said, if you lived in Lityen, you grew used to the noise or you moved along. Ibram had been too used to the sound, and forgotten to ask what it portended.

He crouched by the long pile of debris that filled the former alleyway between the bakery-mill and the evening courtyards. The top layer was larger than the wreckage crushed beneath its weight. He grasped the upper plank with both hands; it snapped in two right along the deepest charred splotch. He tossed both halves behind him, and pushed the layers of wood and broken pegs and crumbled mudbricks aside until he got to a reasonable depth, closer to the ground. Dust and ash puffed into the air as he worked, coating his face and hands.

Ibram coughed into his elbow, and spit to clear the acrid taste from his mouth. He grimaced. As he delved further, the debris became more and more crumbled, as if the fire had burned hotter, or simply had more fuel to work with. He sneezed and wiped his nose on his sleeve. Around him, the sound of the work crew faded into the distance.

"What begins a fire?" he asked himself, or rather, the Ahksell in his head, earnestly explaining the ingredients necessary to strike sparks off flint. "What allows a fire to burn?"

Fire suppression tiles were designed to work in concert around large buildings. Father's foundry had an immense mosaic built of them facing the interior of the foundry, along the wall nearest the family's courtyard. They were imbued with the...well, Ibram wasn't certain what properties of the blue indicolite the clay tiles were imbued with, only that they required a constant maintenance as the temperatures rose in the forge. They reacted to the heat around them and, if they could not douse the flames themselves, then they could at least buy their owners time to escape.

Folk would have been given fair warning from the fire suppression tiles if the bakery-mill had blown first. They would have worked in concert, as they were intended to, unless they were interfered with. A scratch to a tile's surface might deplete their strength without much trouble. Likewise, the thick grout they were traditionally set into had no real protections.

Ahksell had questioned why, if it was a deliberate fire, the flames hadn't spread in a bright green wave, but had—by all accounts other than Dughlat's—been an orange and yellow inferno. Chalcan vitriol was in all sorts of places, for pests and the like, but also for the fireworks and stickums on Nikephoros' Night. The sellers around Book Row made a particularly fine example of Running Flames. They sold them cheaply because they were easy to make, nothing more than wire dipped in wax and wet minerals and then dried. Katka had loved them when they were younger. Ibram hadn't been paying attention yet again, letting what he did not know dominate his facts. He wrinkled his nose as he continued to dig.

He should have been paying attention. Amota Evren was always talking to him about his memory, and taking note, and being aware, and still Ibram had to wait while his damned unconscious worked itself out to the front of his mind. If he'd been faster, Erno Neilos would be alive to question. Now, Ibram would have to prove it on his own.

The sour odor of moldering destruction made him cough; he turned his head aside and breathed in and then out. Best to get used to it, the recent rains had turned all the burnt bits of wood into mush and threatened to decompose the unburned stuff into mushroom food. Ibram dug still deeper until his fingers hit something that bent and then broke apart. He sat back on his heels and rubbed out the smut and soot off his hands. Then he leaned over his bit of wreckage. He carefully pushed aside crumbling wood. Soren Rennab had substandard fire suppression tiles, installed by his brother-in-law. He had peddler's trash above his main entrance. Who was to say the mortar used in the back was better than that around the tiles which had crumbled so easily in the front? All grout was fire resistant to an extent, but if it were too dry to begin with, then there was no saving it, and grout exposed to all weather and time was worst of all.

There, on the lowest level of the debris, lay six pieces of broken, blackened wire, curled amidst grey cracked lumps of mortar and destroyed fire suppression tiles. He put his weight behind his next attempt at clearing his patch, pushing with both hands at the surrounding upper level of debris. It moved slightly, but enough that he could see a few more examples of what he'd thought to find. Wires, tiles, and broken mortar lay in a crushed grid before him.

Ibram pulled his handkerchief from his belt wallet, spread it out on a nearby piece of wood, and quickly pinched up every piece onto the fabric. He folded the cloth over the evidence as carefully as possible, and then placed the bundle back into the hard leather box. A terribly sequence of events spiraled in his mind's eye, but he still needed confirmation. Wires were one thing, but someone would have noticed a stranger marching behind the bakery-mill with a lit torch. That no one had come forward, shouting about a rogue lamplighter, gave rise to a motive for murdering Erno Neilos.

He stood quickly, ignoring the complaints of his knees. He coughed sharply. It was time to gather all this up and take it to Lady Azadiya. He raised his head and cupped his hands around his mouth. He could kill two birds with one stone, at the very least.

"Shokan Dughlat!" he roared across the space. "Come here this instant!"

Dughlat startled, rocking his chair backwards as he leapt to his feet. Soren Rennab followed him upright, and they both stared in

Ibram's direction. No doubt, the folk behind him shared the same bewildered expressions.

Dughlat made his way over quickly, as did his employer. They both stopped at the edge of the alleyway, and stared across the mess at him. Ibram dusted off his hands; the soot and ash barely moved. This theory just needed one more push, a small detail, that, now with Neilos dead, had grown large in Ibram's mind.

"What's the meaning of this?" Rennab blustered. "What do you need Shokan for?"

"Can I help you, Master Ucalegon?" Dughlat asked.

"You know Erno Neilos is dead?" Ibram asked. "Murdered in his own room at the tenant inn with none of his neighbors the wiser?"

Dughlat breathed in sharply, and took a step back. The lines of his face grew deeper with grief. His employer gripped his shoulder.

"I do, Master Ucalegon," Dughlat said. "Bad news travels quickly."

Master Rennab released Dughlat's shoulders and crossed his arms over his chest. "Why, in particular, are you asking us this question? The Runner's officiates—."

"What oil do you and Neilos use for the furniture?" Ibram demanded.

"I...what?" Dughlat turned, confused, to Master Rennab before facing Ibram.

"You told Lady Azadiya you and Master Neilos were repairing furniture in the back of the evening courtyard," Ibram said. "Scrapes and scratches, and the like?"

"Yes," Master Dughlat said.

"And what did you use?" Ibram asked.

"Linseed oil, of course," he said. "To recondition the wood."

Ibram nodded. "Very useful stuff, to be sure," he said. And it had a terrible habit of immolating itself without permission. "Master Rennab, I need Master Dughlat's help here." He pointed to the mess at his feet. "And then Lady Azadiya requires his presence up the living mountain."

$$❈ \quad 9 \quad ❈$$

Lady Azadiya looked up as Ibram entered her tent on the lower training field. She had her cutting board out, and a long knife in her hand. A pile of finely sliced wooly grass lay on the board, and another bunch lay soaking in a large bowl. She set down the knife, and swiped her palms clean of tiny white blossoms and bits of stalk. Her hands were already dyed a deep emerald that feathered to yellow between her fingers.

Amita Sarrha stood by her side, carefully observing a second large wide bowl with a glistening black snake writhing up from its fiery depths. A hideous spitting hiss burbled up from the eyeless snake's mouth as it elongated, fattening as though it were eating while it grew. It twisted itself around a wooden dowl that was already charred with flames; a second thin snake erupted over the lip of the bowl and curled outward in Ibram's direction. Acrid, mouth-puckering smoke plumed in the air. Amita Sarrha wore falconer's heavy leather gloves on both hands and held up a large heavy blanket. Behind him, Master Rennab gagged violently.

"We can—perhaps outside?" Master Dughlat asked in a strangled tone. "Master Rennab is particular about smells, you know."

Ibram touched his fingers to his nose, and tried not to breathe. He really should have known better, and waited outside. Nothing safe or pleasant ever happened when Ladyship entered the training fields. Lady Azadiya nodded at Amita Sarrha, who tossed the blanket over the snake and dowl. The blanket hung there like a forgotten tent, but did not burn. Smoke curled from underneath it like demonic tentacles.

"My apologies," Lady Azadiya said. "My counterpart in Afsoun asked me to conduct a test on an interesting new form of building security." The snake-covered dowl wobbled beneath the fire blanket, and then tipped sideways with a resounding crack. "Still unable to support its own weight. The smell is noxious, to be sure, but the implications are fascinating. Open up the back, wouldn't you, Sarrha? I think we could all do with some fresh air."

Amita Sarrha nodded, and turned to the back of the tent. Ibram cleared his throat. He bowed, hands on his stomach, and Ladyship tapped the air; he felt the answering touch on his forehead and rose.

"Ibram?" Lady Azadiya closed her hand, and a rush of air flew past Ibram's knees; the smoke dissipated immediately. "What are you doing back so soon?"

She tilted her head and raised her eyebrows at the two men he'd dragged up the living mountain. Master Rennab startled and bowed, followed closely by Master Dughlat. There they stayed while she considered the tops of their heads; a slight frown thinned her mouth. She moved her long, heavy braid behind her shoulders, and rearranged the sleeves of the fitted maroon Merrilian coat she wore over her grey trousers. The heavily embroidered buckles down the front of the coat glimmered when she brushed her palm at her hip.

"Ahksell is down with Zorion, examining the body, if you're looking for him," Amita Sarrha said. She folded the blanket in half and then tossed it to the floor.

Her greying dark hair was tied up in a bun. She came around the side of the table, and leaned back against it. She crossed her legs at the ankle, the one with the braced knee on top. Ibram handed her the small box of evidence which he had collected, and she set it none too carefully on the table. He winced.

"Delicately, please, Amita Sarrha," he said and patted the air with both hands.

That caught Ladyship's attention. She leaned back on the table and considered the wide box on the table. She sniffed the air delicately.

"Is that the smell of char?" she asked.

"Yes, Ladyship," Ibram said, and didn't ask how she distinguished it from the bowl of fire snakes. "Aunt, I'll go up to the Hall of Tranquility later." He jerked his thumb towards the two men. "I wanted Ladyship to speak with Master Dughlat once more, but Rennab insisted on coming along this time."

"Really?" Lady Azadiya asked. Her upturned eyes held a distinct glint of interest as she shifted her attention back to the tent at large. "So eager for dinner, Master Rennab? I assure you, I don't stand on ceremony, you might have sent your servant to confirm your acceptance of my invitation."

The sounds of the Learners on the training field running through their drills with the gar drifted inside the tent. Ibram wrinkled his nose at a particularly resounding clack of wooden staves. Rennab glanced up at his name, and Ladyship set both her arms at her waist to curl her hands and raise him up from his bow. He seemed to appreciate the formality. Rennab smoothed his hands down his tunic; he still wore the one damaged by the fire. Dughlat remained in his bow, but rose and stepped to one side at his employer's cough.

"Your agent seemed to feel it essential that he gather small items from my property," Rennab said, "and then abscond with my only remaining dayworker. I believe it's only natural that I might take an interest in the matter, Mentor Hobon."

"Ah, now, Master Rennab," Ibram said. "Who could tell in that alleyway what rubble belongs to who, anymore?"

"Has Ibram borrowed something important to you?" Ladyship asked.

Master Rennab opened and closed his mouth; his face took on a ruddy tinge about the cheeks. Lady Azadiya remained politely interested, but silent. Amita Sarrha snorted, loudly. Neither reaction seemed to please the man.

"I want to know what is going on!" Rennab finally demanded. "First my home is rendered unto Oblivion, and then Neilos is found with his damned neck broken, and now I find out that Dughlat here has been carrying tales to your court without my permission!"

Lady Azadiya turned to Master Dughlat. "How did Master Rennab learn about that?" she asked.

Dughlat swallowed before answering. "He and Master Finar were discussing Erno, and I wanted to—well, in light of his death, I thought it wouldn't be too long before you sent for Master Rennab and told him all. I didn't want him to go all the way up the living mountain unprepared with the facts, Mentor. It didn't seem fair, in the run of things."

It might not have been fair, but it would have been extremely useful. Ibram shook his head, caught Amita Sarrha's eye, and shrugged. He hadn't been around when the two men had spoken, after all; he couldn't be faulted every time something happened in his absence. It was a canny servant who confessed his own actions—which might, all unawares, contain some kernel of fault—and saved his employer embarrassment with one well-placed confession.

"Indeed so," Ladyship answered. "Well, what do you have to say about it, then, Master Rennab?"

Rennab stuck his chin out and Ibram strangled the urge to smack it. Whatever he had to say to Lady Azadiya could no doubt have been spoken later at dinner. Ibram had much to report, and very little time left to present his evidence to Ladyship. Corbus had followed his little party up to the preceptory, but Nesrine had not. Ibram hadn't yet found a moment to ask him why.

"Fourth Mentor Hobon," Rennab said, "I formally protest your questioning of my servant without my knowledge."

"He's not a serf," Amita Sarrha snapped. She uncrossed her ankles and stood away from the table. "A man comes up the living mountain to be heard, and Lady Azadiya has the duty to listen."

"It was the fourth day," Dughlat ventured.

Rennab pressed his lips together and shook his head curtly. Ibram shifted his weight from his left to right foot. He pressed his right hand over his belt wallet; he couldn't feel his handkerchief moving in the leather box, but he still didn't like to wait on presenting his findings to Lady Azadiya. He made a point of catching Amita Sarrha's eye and then looking directly at the box, but she merely tugged on the leather strap holding her knee brace in place and frowned.

Lady Azadiya moved to the front of the table. "To be sure, Master Rennab, I am not in the habit of ignoring folk with such interesting problems as Master Dughlat presented to me."

"I tell you there is nothing unusual in that fire," Master Rennab said. "By his own admission, he can't be sure the fire was green." His tone imbued the color with as much ridicule as he might in polite company. "He hit his head!"

"I did not realize Master Dughlat was given to such fantasies," Ladyship said, and picked lint from her left sleeve.

"He isn't," Master Rennab said. Sweat dewed his temples; he leaned forward without approaching the central table. "I'm not saying he fantasizes, I'm saying he was mistaken."

"Because he hit his head," Amita Sarrha said.

"Exactly," Rennab said with a decisive nod. "I have no intention of proffering a charge of—of arson, or negligence on the part of the Sect of Seven Fires!"

Ibram watched Dughlat's face stiffen into a mask, approximating the careful blankness of a servant who senses, regardless of fault, that blame is now to fall upon his shoulders. It was a good sort of face to cultivate, but Dughlat wasn't very good at it. Dughlat's wrinkles deepened; his mouth turned down at the corners as he breathed in deeply through his nose.

"I am relieved," Lady Azadiya said. "What made you think we feared such an occurrence?"

"I...well, the presence of green fire," Master Rennab stammered, caught off-guard.

"A good enough reason, to be sure," Lady Azadiya said, "but I never fear a justified charge, only one made in haste. I assure you, in return, Master Rennab, that none of my folk dreamed of harming your evening courtyard. I've had such good reports, I am sorry to say I never visited the place before its destruction. Sarrha, make a note, I should get out more."

"Ladyship," Sarrha said.

"But, then, Shokan's belief that he saw something strange in the fire... you don't think there is any merit in it?" Master Rennab asked.

Ibram had kept a careful eye on the man while he and Dughlat had dug through the rubble in the alley. Though he hadn't seemed enthused, he also hadn't twitched more than an aching back muscle when they had uncovered a satisfactory number of broken wires and—Ibram's favorite discovery—the corner of a wooden box, covered by shattered fire suppression tiles.

"Of course, I do," Lady Azadiya said. "He saw what he saw, and thus it is my duty to investigate. That is how it's done in Lityen."

"But there is no proof other than his statement!" Master Rennab said. He touched his sleeve to his temples, which had begun to glisten with sweat.

"And thus, he killed his co-worker," Lady Azadiya remarked. "So desperate he was to be believed?"

Master Rennab shuddered in affront; his mouth opened and closed. "Not in the slightest," he finally stammered. "Shokan is a good soul, never a mark of anger or hurt in his history!"

Ladyship spread her hands. "Then I am very sorry to admit to you, Master Rennab," she said, "that I feel it very likely Shokan saw green fire in that burning courtyard. Recent events being present in the mind, and all."

"And Neilos?" Master Rennab demanded.

"Erno did say he never saw it," Dughlat said. He bit his lip as attention turned to him in the tent. "He tried to convince me otherwise."

Ibram's weight shifted from his toes to his heels so swiftly he had already slammed his boots to the ground before he knew to control himself. The entire tent stared at him. Ibram cleared his throat.

"Is there something wrong, Ibram?" Lady Azadiya asked, her eyebrows raised.

He shook his head. "No, nothing's wrong, Ladyship. I am merely, like yourself, eager to seek and attain knowledge."

"Are you feeling well?" Amita Sarrha asked.

"Hungry for knowledge, Amita Sarrha," Ibram said. "Di eekent zicata."

"Riant," Ladyship said. She clapped her hands and heaved a great sigh. "Now, since we have established that Shokan Dughlat is neither a liar nor a ruthless murderer, I feel I must ask if this entire production, Master Rennab, is solely down to the fact that you used those horribly ill-favored fire suppression tiles from the Sect of the Iron Hand, rather than those turned out by the Preceptory of Afsoun?"

Master Rennab turned white and the flushed red. "How—I—"

Ladyship nodded. "Oh, my Attendants feel a bit, shall we say, *raw* towards our alchemical brethren to the south. To persist in the face of such incompetence is remarkable, to be sure, but a bit unseemly. Don't you agree, Sarrha?"

"Attendant Solari's report was illuminating," Sarrha said.

"My brother-in-law is not in the habit of selling shoddy merchandise," Rennab replied, stiffly.

"Not once he's passed through here," Ladyship agreed with a congenial nod. "And sold the goods he's brought from the south in return for our own Afsoun tiles. Now, far be it from me to deny a family the right to sell whatever they choose to each other. But it would take a great deal of the coins from your pockets if the fire alliance were to know about those tiles, would it not?"

Rennab's jaw worked as he chewed over what to say in answer. "It would," he said, finally. "As well as the penalty for the destruction."

"And the Ozols' deaths," Ibram said. He could see Amita Sarrha's evaluating eyes observing Rennab and then Dughlat. When she looked to Ibram he clasped his arms behind his back and shrugged.

Rennab shook his head and pressed his lips together. "On that I—" he swallowed. "No, I didn't have anything to do with that fire! The Ozols are good folk—they're my neighbors. They make my bread! I've known Ealar since he was so high!" He lowered his flattened hand closer to the ground, as if a child stood before him to be measured. "This cannot be my fault."

He seemed absolutely certain of that—or at least, desperate to believe it. And they had no proof that the deaths—aside from Neilos, of course—had been anything other than an accident of timing.

"He was in the marketplace when the fire began," Master Dughlat said. "I swear he was, Mentor. There was no one within the courtyard but myself and Erno."

Ibram considered the things he had found in the detritus of the alley, and bit the inside of his lip.

"How many folk knew about the tiles placed in the alley?" Lady Azadiya asked them. "Of their quality?"

Master Rennab shook his head again, and Master Dughlat spoke up for him. "Master Rennab and Master Finar, of course," he said in a gentle tone. "And Erno Neilos and myself. We have been there the longest, you see, and helped Master Achard Finar set the tiles in their place. None of the potboys or the other servers have worked there for more than a season or two; they would know nothing of it."

"How many did you place?" she asked.

"A full hundred," Dughlat said. "All he had left in stock. They were thinner and larger than the usual, so when we mixed up the mortar to set them into the wall, we had to spread the grout along a wider area. We set them into place ourselves."

"And tested them?" Amita Sarrha asked.

Dughlat shook his head. "There is always so much flour in the air from the windows of the bakery-mill... We were afraid to risk it. Erno dropped his knife cutting through a rope once, and struck a spark off the cobblestones. The backend of the coil nearly caught fire from the blaze up!"

So a hundred tiles—even substandard ones—had not reacted quickly enough to hold firm in the face of a spark or three. Ibram touched his belt pouch again. He raised his arm, and then dropped it back to his side; he had been attempting to curb his nervous habits. Even then, the tiles might have withstood the heat for long enough to raise the alarm, except for what he had discovered.

Lady Azadiya smiled, but Ibram said how her eyes flicked in his direction. "Master Rennab, I thank you for your time. As I also thank you, Master Dughlat. This is Sarrha—Have you met my agent in chief? Sarrha Pariamua, be known to Master Soren Rennab."

"I..." Master Rennab seemed confused, but began to bow.

Amita Sarrha bowed in return, and then leaned her hip on the table. "Shall I show Master Rennab around the premises?" she asked.

"A fine plan," Ladyship said. "In fact, why not show him and Master Dughlat the rest of the mountain? Through the relay system?

It's an unparalleled view of the lands west, Master Rennab. And it will give you some time to calm yourself before dining with me tonight."

"I thought I would return—" Master Rennab began, even as Amita Sarrha began urging him and his servant towards the open tent door. "Fourth Mentor—"

"Fear for nothing," Lady Azadiya called out as he left. "Sarrha will find you something to wear, or might send a message to Master Finar for you."

Amita Sarrha didn't turn back around to glare in Ladyship's direction, but the impulse was surely evident in her face, if Rennab and Dughlat's suddenly speedy exit was anything to go by. Ladyship watched them leave with vague eyes, clearly searching her mind for that one clue that answered her puzzles.

"I don't think he did it," Ibram blurted out. "Either of them. Neither, I should say."

Her attention won, Lady Azadiya sharped her gaze on Ibram's face. He shut his mouth. He coughed and resettled his gambeson. The corner of her mouth flew upwards.

"Do you...think he did it?" Ibram asked.

She shrugged one shoulder. "I should think it possible," she said. "When there is money involved, folk will do the most surprising things."

"Yes, but possible is not yet probable," Ibram said. "Isn't that what you always say?"

She tsked and then laughed. "My own words, used against me! But I suppose that is the plight of age," she nodded. "Now, what is in this box?"

"Larger fragments of what I found—here—" Ibram reached into his belt purse and withdrew his handkerchief. He held the folded bundle out to Lady Azadiya. "—when I searched the alleyway from the opposite side. The bakery-mill, I mean."

Ladyship took the handkerchief, and unfolded it in her palm. Her mouth pursed as she delicately touched one of the blackened pieces of wire. She squinted, and then frowned. Alchemists of Yseult drank all sorts of concoctions to flout nature's restrictions; as a mentor, Ladyship no longer needed to imbibe. Ibram wondered what she was seeing. Charred iron? Sand fired to glass?

"What were these attached to?" she asked. She looked up, and Ibram thought he saw her pupils contracting as she blinked rapidly.

He moved to the table, and began unpacking the box. "I have one thought on that, to be sure," he said. "But these—do you remember? Master Dughlat said it exactly right. When he mentioned the green of the flames 'just like on Nikephoros' Night'?" He drew out two other folded cloths, which he had borrowed from the workshops across the way. "In my search, we only looked at the rubble from the point of view of the evening courtyards, a terrifying mess, and the same on the side of the bakery-mill, but then I thought—there were two blasts. One to set off the other."

Ibram unfolded the longest cloth and sighed in relief. The tattered wires had survived the journey, and lay in their rows, blackening the rough fabric with soot and powdered detritus. "They're Running Flames," he said.

Ladyship laughed. "The children's toy?" she asked. "The one's they use—"

"—As candle fly tails, yes," Ibram said, and nodded. "You light the end as you let the kite lift up into the sky—'

"And it burns in multi-colored sprays to send your wishes to the heavens," Ladyship finished. "I've made a few myself, when I was a Learner. Dowse the wire in wax and powder, let it dry, and then set it alight and watch it glow."

She set her handful of wire bits down on the table next to the larger examples, and then pointed at the corner of the wooden box, still clinging to its tattered strip of rag. A chunk of plaster and fire suppression tile had fallen upon it, and retained enough power to preserve its destroyer. Ibram almost felt like sending the Sect of the Iron Hand a complimentary note.

"And this?" she asked.

"The remains of a wooden box," Ibram said. "If you'll recall, Lady-ship, Dughlat said he and Master Neilos were repairing furniture in the back before the fire began. They reconditioned the wood with linseed oil. He confirmed it again this morning."

Lady Azadiya sucked in a deep breath. "Oh, that is unfortunate. I take it this box was also in the alley way?"

"Full of the rags they used to wipe down the chairs." Ibram nodded. "All Erno Neilos had to do was wait until Dughlat had left the room, then slide the box of oil-soaked cloths outside into the alley and let them dry."

"After placing the ends of these wires within the box," Lady Azadiya said, "in recompense for that hefty purse of coin he had hidden in his room."

Her eyes narrowed. She and Ibram reached for the box at the same time. Ibram quickly drew back his hand to avoid touching her wrist. She paused and looked at him.

"It's very delicate, Ladyship," he said. "I nearly broke it, just moving the fire suppression tiles it was covered in. Those are still in the box I stored them in, if you wish to examine them?"

One side of her mouth quirked up. She flexed her right hand into a claw and pulled upwards; the box piece rose smoothly from its covering and hung in the air. Ibram took a step away from the table, and bobbed his head.

"This is good work, Ib-la," she said. "What do you think happened here?"

"The bakery-mill's tiles were all placed inside their building, but the evening courtyards had tiles on the outside in the alley. The High Climber is the weak point, their tiles were substandard. There they sat, too thin and covering too great of an area, in mortar that took on water when it rained, heated in the day, and froze at night."

"Weakening their bonds," Ladyship said.

Ibram nodded quickly. "I believe someone placed these wires along the grout lines of the fire suppression tiles in the alley. Everyone knows to be careful with linseed oilcloths. Drying them all together in a box in an alley had to be deliberate."

"Choked with loose flour in the air—especially when the grinders began working at that time of day—so that the air was filled with flammable particles. The linseed oil dries and ignites near the end of the wires," Ladyship murmured as she rotated the sooty box corner. The little bit of rag fluttered as she spoke. "It would have gone up in a flash."

"I believe the first blast we heard was a larger firework," Ibram said, and shivered. "Look, these two wires are still connected to each other at the top end."

He pointed down to the longest lengths he had discovered.

"And to something else," Ladyship said, and lowered her hand so the box corner returned to the table as well. She leaned over the table and drew a line from one wire along the short connecting wire to the next. "There's the remains of a tie here and here. The Running Flames were looped around something."

Ibram nodded. "Maybe something like a chain of Wanderer's Tears, or an Orilindan candle strapped on its side, even something custom designed for the purpose. It was fast enough to overwhelm the fire suppression tiles, and the strength of the flames caused the mortar to crumble under the blast."

"And then once the tiles on The High Climber were eliminated, there was nothing to block the fire from spreading," Lady Azadiya said. "The flames would have ignited the loose flour, and followed the paths of least resistance."

Ibram swallowed and clasped his hands behind his back. "What do you think, Ladyship?"

"Dangerously plausible, Ibram," she said, and drummed her fingers on the table. "What did Dughlat say? He helped you uncover these?"

"With Master Rennab supervising," Ibram said. "He showed no sign of guilt nor hesitance. Didn't even seem to understand what I was looking for."

"And Rennab? Did he say anything?"

"He mostly let me know how deeply inconvenient everything was. Wandered off to complain at Philendra Dubidat—very unsubtle folk, I could hear every word."

Ladyship's mouth quirked. "Anything interesting?"

"I'm very irritating, and they don't know how you put up with me."

She laughed, and then stood away from the table, just as Mila, one of the tower's servants, walked into the tent, hefting a covered basket before her like a talisman. She bobbed her knees perfunctorily, and stared up at the ceiling of the tent.

"Dihya's compliments," Mila announced, "and she says you missed the meal in the tower—"

"Oh, honestly," Ladyship muttered, but Mila continued, unabashed:

"—and thus you must eat here or else you'll have too much appetite for the dinner you insist on having below the stars of heaven violating all good sense to come in out of the rain. And she found the plums in the storage room you requested."

Ibram nodded while Mila deposited her basket on the opposite end of the table. She stepped back and away, bobbed up and down again, and left with a walk that was not quite a flounce. Lady Azadiya sighed, and began unpacking the basket.

"Really, it's too much," she said. "It's that lowland impulse in Dihya, you know. She prefers sunny days and gentle climes, and I ask you, did I make the mountain upon which we live?" She sniffed a baked roll dotted with cinnaks and tossed it to Ibram; he caught it. "No, I did not," she answered her own question. Ladyship unwrapped a crock and lifted the clay lid. Steam curled into the air before her face as she breathed in. She sighed with satisfaction. "Although, I cannot fault her choice of meals or cooks."

Ibram took a bite of the roll, and swallowed. "Should I find Ahksell, Ladyship?"

She nodded, and then cocked her head to the left. "What did you think of the bakery-mill's boy? Berac told me he was returned."

"Ealar Ozol is very sad, as to be expected. You should know Masters Rennab and Finar have taken him in for the duration."

Ladyship nodded, and surveyed the items littering her desk. "The rider Berac sent spoke to the farmers in Polia," she said. "The boy was certainly there, and evinced no stress or distraction. Given what you've discovered and the nature of the fire, I should think we might leave him to his grief."

Ibram bowed his head. "Yes, Ladyship."

Lady Azadiya reached out her hand, and a large folded piece of paper which Ibram had not noticed before, lifted off her chair in the back of the tent and came to her hand. She gestured with it.

"Your request has been fulfilled by Mentor Nieminen's staff," she said. "It seems there was some confusion about which Vo Kaln we meant, but it was soon sorted."

Ibram nodded. "There seem to be a dangerous lot of them, Ladyship. Is there...anything of interest?"

"It's too general for my taste. An additional inquiry has been made." Lady Azadiya dropped the paper to the table, between the two bowls, and considered another cinnak-heavy bun. "There's something to remember about a man with three mistresses and no wife, Ib-la."

"What?"

"He dies happy, and bequeaths the rest of us a very complicated diplomatic situation. Take my advice, and live straightforwardly."

Ibram snorted, and ate his roll. "Ladyship, I shall be guided by you in all things."

"Anyway," she said, waving her hand. "The bonfire that used to be Kandrilat tidied up their affairs nicely. Who knows where they would be else-wise. Do you know what interested me in particular?"

"No," Ibram said, swallowing hastily. "I don't suppose one of them started fires as a child?"

She laughed. "Sadly, no. The Vo Kalns who own the land here in Pillared Circle are a moderately prosperous bunch. The...grandfather, I believe, was a soapmaker who made his money with imported olive oil from down south. Sold it to the other members of his guild. They still have connections to the soapmakers, but they've branched out to land-lording. The Isconian's Hand used to be one of their old warehouses, before Philendra Dubidat converted it to an evening courtyard."

"Soapmaking and land ownership," Ibram said. "An odd combination."

"Well, they also have a pig farm."

"Delightful."

She hummed in thought. "With so many of the younger generation in Lityen, the challenge becomes finding occupation for them all. Or, if not an occupation, then a living. Did their renters know anything else of interest?"

Ibram paused in consideration. "Young Master Ozol informed me that Mistress Vo Kaln has offered to take the bakery-mill off of his hands, and, should he choose to leave us, her family has a need for a baker down south."

"Very generous," Ladyship remarked.

"One of the cookshop folk, if I'm remembering correctly, told me that they're involved landlords—or at the very least, they take an interest in preparing their younger generation for business. The Vo Kalns send younger cousins around to collect the rents. One of them escaped the fire in Kandrilat."

Lady Azadiya's head tilted, like a raptor sensing prey beneath her claws. She stilled for a moment, and Ibram composed himself in patience. She nodded sharply after a heartbeat or thirty, and Ibram loosened his shoulders.

She set the crock of soup aside, and began digging through the basket again. "Such a mess," she said. "Technical skill paired with such reckless disregard for life and property makes me anxious. This device —or devices—was too practiced."

Ibram crossed his arms over his chest. "Possibly why Neilos was killed."

"Oh, probably, Ib-la," she said. "Definitely the word is probably."

Ladyship's eyes drifted from the wires to the box and then back again. "Ahksell should be with Zorion in the Hall of Tranquility," she said. "Find him, learn what you can from the body of Erno Neilos. Afterwards, go to Book Row, and see if anyone has purchased Running Flames recently. They might have been purchased beforehand, but it would make more sense to buy them here rather than risk setting them off elsewhere."

"I'll need to speak with Corbus and Nesrine," Ibram said. "They were watching Dughlat last night."

She nodded, and then clapped her hands. "Well," she said, "at least dinner shall be lively."

❦   10   ❦

Yseult was the only preceptory in the Sect of Seven Fires that might strictly be called a fortress. Though the rest of the lot certainly maintained their own borders and ensured that folk could get from one place to another with minimal fuss, Yseult was the lowest, the oldest, and the most, perhaps, traditionally constructed, which in point of fact made travel within it a complicated series of gates and bottlenecks. Only the First Mentor lived in the big honeycomb mansion surrounded by a vast public courtyard and inhabiting in an equally formal and expansive family courtyard. The rest of the mentors' domains were located in rings below, divided by deep created reservoirs, packed earthen trails, and deceptively sweeping paved roads, often bisected by bridges or separated by flights upon flights of stairs.

Ibram was forced to climb up the mountain, like a mouflon trailing after its herd, to reach the First Mentor's compound, where the Scribe's Bureau stood and which had the most direct path to the hospital of the medicinal corps. He had yet to receive a response to the inquiries he'd sent to Kenda Trading and the Sect of the Iron Hand so he'd need to check for messages at the Scribe's Bureau another time.

Second Mentor Stadat's division lived in dormitories near wherein they worked: the Grand Hospital of The Wheelmaker, the biggest of its kind that Ibram had ever seen outside of the southern provinces. Spacious and serene, with three tiers of windows spanning its length to allow for sun and circulation of the air, a large and beckoning medicinal garden and fountain to provide sweet smells and fresh water, and every floor laid with tile mosaics. The wards bustled with healers of every description, from the crystal coaxers to the pill makers. Apart from their research, they mostly served the sect and its dependents, but Ibram had found the sect's stamp on quite a few potions and potables throughout the empire.

He skirted the front of the hospital entirely. He hadn't had occasion to visit the healers in years, and neither did he much mingle with the medicinal corps. They tended to make him touch things and wonder aloud why he hadn't turned green or floated away yet; it made a man nervous. It was barely drizzling, after all, and the fresh air felt good in his lungs. Instead, Ibram took the path that led directly through the sprawling gardens and around the side. He nodded politely to a few of the patients out testing the strength of their healing limbs as he passed.

It would have been better if he'd been able to simply grab Ahksell up and speak to Corbus and Nesrine immediately. He didn't think Neilos' corpse could tell him more than it already had. Death changed the body in numerous ways, but it couldn't be said to be unnatural, and being murdered certainly wouldn't change that. The dead didn't rise up and give detailed descriptions of their killer, in Ibram's experience. At most, they might find out if Neilos had his neck broken and then sliced, or if it were the other way around. That didn't seem helpful, and whatever had caused Nesrine to stay out in Lityen when her long night's duty had been accomplished was doubtlessly more important. Or, at the very least, something Ibram could hold over his cousin's head for a good long while.

Doctor Berot and his coterie worked within the Hall of Tranquility, which was carved into a basalt rock needle that rose twice as high as the surrounding deodar trees. Ibram approached via the seashell path, white with crushed freshwater mussel shells, and down the ramp behind the hospital. Ahead of him, the earthworks that bracketed the large arched entrance with the wooden plank awning were painted a bright blue with heavy metalwork lamps hung to either side of the doors, lit and glowing both day and night.

He shivered as he walked inside; the air was cold and dry, it made him glad of the heavy twill of his gambeson. There were no fires allowed in the hall, only glowbulbs and the occasional oil lamp, well-attended. Ibram washed his hands in the washing station tucked into the entry hall, and dried them off with one of towels stacked laid beside of the small copper basin. The low wooden beds laid out in rows to either side of the large center hallway were mostly empty, and only a few scattered groups of Attendants greeted him as he passed through the main room and into the back laboratories. He passed through the smaller connecting door and down a more narrow corridor lined with closed doors. The glowbulbs above his head swung idly on their hanging chain.

A nurse carrying a bundle of linen came down the opposite side of the hallway. Ibram raised his hand and stepped into her path.

"Excuse me," he said. "Can you tell me how to find Doctor Berot?"

She slowed but did not stop. "Second door on your right, as you're standing, young master," she said and swerved around him.

"Thank you," Ibram called after her.

Busy folk in the halls of healing. He turned back around and ambled to the correct door, as per instructions. A single knock produced an order to enter, and Ibram did so.

A lone window faced the door, its wooden shutter thrown wide and giving Ibram an excellent view of the light grey sky and sheer drop outside the Hall of Tranquility. There were no bodies in the small, cluttered room save for Ahksell and the doctor who were seated on opposite sides of his desk, sharing a pot of shay.

"Doctor Berot," Ibram said, and bowed with his hands on his stomach.

"Oh," Berot said, "it's Master Underwood, isn't it? Up, lad, up."

Ibram rose. "Ucalegon, sir," he said. "But you were very close."

Ahksell snorted, and then cleared his throat. He leaned back in his chair, and set his cup down on the desk. Ibram let himself further in the room. He felt no accompanying tingle that said Berot kept his office silenced, and made certain to close the door behind him.

"How are you finding the work down in the village, Doctor?" Ibram asked. He let go of the handle, and clasped his hands behind his back.

"The work?" Berot echoed. "Do you mean the burn victims?"

Ibram nodded. "I do," he said. "I believe you rented space in one of the afflicted's apothecary?"

Doctor Berot raised one eyebrow, and sipped his shay. "I did indeed," he said. "Mistress Corri's stocks were as welcome as the floor space in her shop. The patients, while most definitely uncomfortable, are recuperating as well as can be expected."

"I am glad to hear it," Ahksell said. "The fire was nearly uncontrollable. If we hadn't had the Water's Breath available to us, I don't want to think of how quickly it might have spread."

Doctor Berot nodded. "Oh yes," he said. "I can well remember the reports coming from regions with similar catastrophes. The numbers of the dead and wounded were sobering."

"And Mistress Corri?" Ahksell asked. "How is she?"

"Seemed in pain the last time I saw her," Ibram said.

"Well, of course she was," Berot scoffed. "No salve alive can take pain away on a permanent basis. But her condition is stable, and she is already helping my Attendants in their rounds with the other patients."

The urge to inquire whether or not salves were 'alive' was nigh insurmountable, but Ibram conquered himself. He coughed, and looked briefly down to his feet. He had a point to his inquiries, after all. He looked up, avoiding Ahksell's eyes.

"And her shop is mostly unharmed?" he asked. "I mean, it must have survived to be able to hold patients, but the fire blazed up so quickly..."

"Haven't you seen it for yourself?" Berot asked, with a wrinkle in between his eyebrows. "She has a kitchen for the mixing of resins and pills. The fire suppression tiles young Hilbert is so fond of protected a great deal of the interior."

Ibram smiled, and leaned back on his heels. "That is wondrous news, Doctor," he said. It also saved him a trip and another awkward conversation. "I thank you."

Doctor Berot cleared his throat, and nodded slowly. "Is that all you came up here to ask of me?"

"Lady Azadiya wished to know if you'd found anything out of the common way with our corpse, Doctor," Ibram said.

"Aside from the broken neck and torn skin?" Doctor Berot asked, with an air of amusement. He laid down his cup of shay and settled both elbows on the top of his desk. "No, not really. The clothes held nothing in their folds, and in his final acts, I do not think your Master Neilos grabbed much off his murderer."

"How do you know?" Ibram asked.

"There was nothing under his fingernails or in his mouth to say he might have scratched, nor even bit his killer, since there was obviously no way for him to turn around." Berot sighed. "It's a bad business," he said. "I am sorry to have seen it. What does Mentor Hobon mean by asking me to look the corpse over?"

Ibram stood by Ahksell at the front of the desk, and clasped his left wrist in his right hand behind his back. He wrinkled his nose at Ahksell, who minutely shrugged one shoulder in return.

"I suppose since your long seclusion in research is over that she merely wished to make use of the opportunity of your talent," Ahksell said. "It's not often we have a doctor as well as an alchemist in the sect!"

Doctor Berot grunted and drank his shay, though Ibram thought the man looked a little pleased to be flattered. Berot's very close-cropped hair was grey at the ears and temples, and his mouth and fore-head had study lines carved into them. He'd come to alchemy after the university days were behind him, perhaps, and joined up as an adult.

Ibram made note of the long seclusion, which for this sect meant at the very least a full year of dedicated work. When Ibram had been a child, Ama had told him stories of an Attendant who'd been shut up in a laboratory for so long the only way anyone remembered he was still alive was the servants, who reported that the meals they left by the door were routinely eaten. Generally, it was folk in the preceptories of

Govan and Mariae who went in for that kind of study, but academic folk were the same everywhere.

He widened his stance for comfort, and leaned back on his heels. "I thought Attendant Zorion said he'd fought the killer off?" Ibram asked. "Managed to get his fingers under the wire, or something like that."

Berot frowned and shook his head. "Fought off? No, not at all," he said. "What made—ah, no, I think young Hilbert misunderstood me. There was of course evidence of blood on the cheese cutter you sent with the body, but I believe you'll take an interest in this. Here, a moment..."

The doctor leaned down and opened a bottom drawer in his desk. Ibram heard the clunk of boxes being shoved aside, and then Berot rose up with a sigh of satisfaction and upended a cloth bag, the coiled cheese wire fell out onto his desk. Ibram leaned over and stared at it.

"This is what I meant," Berot said. His hand picked up the right handle of the cheese cutter and raised it in Ibram's sight. "Don't know if you can quite see it, but the splodges towards the handle, here and then here."

He pointed an exceptionally clean finger at a dried smudge on the wooden handle where the wire disappeared into the bored hole, and then to an equally dark smear of something on the wire itself. Ibram nodded, though the spots were small. He narrowed his eyes, and then glanced up at the doctor, who appeared to be waiting for some revelation to fall over Ibram like a wave.

"They're on the opposite handle as well, though differently placed," Ahksell said. "Doctor Berot showed me, when I came to speak with Hilbert."

"What are they?" Ibram asked. He backed away from the desk and stood up.

"What are they?" Berot repeated. He dropped the handle with a clatter, and shook his head. "Wheelmaker's knee, boy, it's blood! What did they teach you in the Bedris school? Numbers and noble metals?"

"I once learned how to weave a pine needle basket," Ibram said, with what he thought was admirable restraint. "Very handy for birthdays."

"Then I shall expect one," Doctor Berot said, "preferably filled with cakes. These marks, Master Ucalegon, mean that your killer cut themselves while murdering Master Neilos. I would say both hands, as well."

He curled his own hands in front of his chest, miming the grip on two handles, and then twitched both forefingers.

"I would hazard that the creases of both fingers were damaged," he said. "Given the thinness of the wire, I might even venture to say that they were deeply cut."

Ibram winced, and glanced at Ahksell, who nodded emphatically. "Then, I thank you, Doctor Berot," Ibram said, and bowed shortly. "This is good news."

Well, it was better news, more like. It wasn't like Ibram couldn't walk out to the laboratories strewn through the preceptory and find anywhere from ten to twenty folk with bandaged fingers. On the other foot, if they found someone connected to the fire—possibly who hadn't gotten rid of their blood-stained washing yet—and that person had bandaged fingers, then it was an additional mark on the tally of evidence.

"Unfortunately," Ahksell said, "it's been too long since the cheese cutter's owner held it. The resonance of possession has faded completely."

"Yes," Berot said, and tapped his fingers on his desk. "Otherwise, I would say your own previous observations were correct, Solari. The corpse was murdered in his home, and the third layer of animal resonance was entirely yellow. Caught completely by surprise."

There were a great many wonders of alchemy, in Ibram's opinion, that only worked in the immediate aftermath. It was incredibly inconvenient. He stepped back from the desk, and nodded his head at the cheese cutter.

"I should return the murder weapon to Lady Azadiya then," Ibram said. "If you've nothing left to do with it."

Doctor Berot nodded. "Yes, that will be fine," he said. "Do you know when the clerics in the Runner's temple will be coming to take charge of the body?"

"I don't," Ibram said. "My apologies."

"Then you may tell Mentor Hobon that we might store him here for a few days more," Berot said, "but our containments are all spoken for, otherwise, and there is no room in the cold storage."

Ibram nodded. This was why he avoided the Hall of Tranquility as much as was possible; there was just no enjoying so cold-blooded a building. Ahksell stood up as Ibram took another step backwards towards the door.

"I'll take my leave as well, Doctor," Ahksell said, and lifted the cheese cutter, bag and all, up from the desk with a single hovering claw. "I'm sure Mentor will be very interested to know about your theory as to Master Neilos' killing. Shall we send Hilbert back in as we go?"

"That would be very helpful, yes," Berot said. "He's a bit absent-minded, but I would say his infusions are promising, most promising."

Ibram held the door for Ahksell to leave first, and leaned in quickly. "What infusions?" he asked.

"Anti-inflammation tonic," Ahksell muttered. "Good for the hands, but tastes like chalk. Slight tendency to make you feel drunker than an apprentice brewer."

Ibram made a face. He plucked the cheese cutter out of the air, and tied it up securely within the cloth bag. Ladyship would want to have it placed with the other pieces.

❧

They arrived back to Lady Azadiya's tower in time to run smack into two unfortunate and immediate problems. The first, being that the Sect of the Iron Hand remained unmoved by letters of introduction. The second, was to learn that Corbus had gotten bored and run off back down the living mountain to find Nesrine. He'd at least left word with Amota Evren so that Ibram might follow. Junior agents left much to be desired.

11

They walked into Lityen with the afternoon sun riding the clouds above. Ibram took the opportunity to explain what he'd learned from Mentor Nieminen's papers. The air blew softly through the trees, chasing the harsh soap of the Hall of Tranquility from his nose and replacing it with the sweet, fresh smell of pine needles. There was a wild kicker bush nearby, peppery-scented; its dark branches heavy with little red berries.

"It almost feels like some kind of joke," Ahksell remarked as they passed through the main gate. "How many Vo Kalns can one well support?"

"One, but at least sixty cousins are needed to collect the fee to draw up the bucket," Ibram said. "I'd say it's fair to assume they need quite a bit of money to keep them all in silk and southern wine."

Ahksell snorted, and then shook his head. He continued onward to the inns and caravan courtyards that fed the main road through the center of Lityen, and Ibram followed behind. The folk who hung about these streets were often not from the village, nor its surrounds, and they were rowdy with the freedom of being let loose on a strange populace. Still the draughtshops and shayshops kept them in good humor, and it was never difficult to get past the throng when you followed an Attendant. At the very least, if an unwary soul crashed into Ahksell, Ahksell was never the one embarrassed.

"Where's Corbus?" Ahksell asked, with a quick glance behind him.

"His note said that he was going to see about Nesrine," Ibram said, and craned his neck to see across the crowd. "He said she made arrangements to meet him... Ah, just there." He pointed above and to the right. "The Nine Stars."

"The draughtshop?" Ahksell asked. "I know it."

He veered right, and Ibram went also. The sign heralding the draughtshop was freshly painted with yellow stars surrounding the green sphere of the world. The crowds were behaving themselves well enough, no doubt because warders more regularly made the road and its denizens their business. Away from the richer caravans and inns, folk tended to mind themselves. Here, they had to be careful the warders didn't mind them.

He caught Ahksell's elbow, just as they made for an opening between two noisy groups of folk, and pointed with his chin towards a clump of warders leaning over the front porch railing of The Churning Stew on the opposite side of the street. The sign above was a pot stirred by a ghostly hand, which was either a pun on Yseult or had a religious meaning. Ibram never could figure it out.

Ahksell looked at the warders and then down to Ibram; he raised his eyebrows. Ibram shrugged, and nodded at the warders again. One of them, he could see now, was Warder Dogani, whom he'd once spent a very uncomfortable night in the cells with, on account of the confusion between Lady Azadiya and the previous warder captain's sense of dignity. Ahksell sighed, but began shuffling through the crowd away from the patrol.

"They're not here to bother folk," he muttered.

"Look at them, they're leaning out like hunting beasts in a kennel," Ibram said, and tugged Ahksell a few steps sideways. "I don't like it when warders bunch up like so. It bodes ill for getting anything done."

"Some merchant lost their purse, and raised the hue and cry," Ahksell said, and sighed. "No doubt they're just making a show."

Ibram frowned. Ahksell was making his usual spectacle of himself, standing head and shoulders over most everyone in the street, while folk made way for the alchemist as best they were able. Not that he didn't have a right to do so, but warders had an uncanny sense for when folk would be happier to deal with them at a later moment in time.

The Nine Stars was a mere ten feet away—give or take a polite scuttle between pedestrians—when Warder Dogani shouted across the street:

"Hey there! Ucalegon!"

Ibram neither turned around, nor hunched his shoulders. Those were the actions of guilty folk, and proper agents of the sect were scrupulously trained out of such low behaviors. He merely tightened his grip on Ahksell's elbow, and continued to propel them towards the draughtshop. A stirring in the crowd at his back told him Dogani was probably following.

"What did you do?" Ahksell asked, and looked back over his shoulder.

Ibram rolled his eyes. "Nothing," he said, "this is merely a coincidence."

Ahksell allowed himself to be pushed up the steps from the street to the wooden footpath. "Do you owe him money?"

Ibram raised his hands to the heavens, and shrugged. "Not anymore."

"Begging your pardon, Master Alchemist," Warder Dogani said behind them. "A moment of your time?"

Ibram did not groan; he had his dignity. Ahksell came to a stop, and faced the street. Ibram opened his eyes wide at him, but Ahksell was unmoved. Ibram turned around and crossed his arms over his chest.

"Good day, Attendant," Warder Dogani said, and bowed politely.

He was his usual persnickety self, black hair neatly clubbed in the back, and his face and hands clean of dust. He waited a beat for Ahksell to raise him up, and then hooked both thumbs through his belt. His purple and black-banded gambeson looked exceptionally unmussed, even though the day was certainly moving onwards. Ibram resisted the urge to straighten his own clothes. He tucked his hair behind his ears; Dogani smirked.

"Good day," Ahksell said. "How might I help you?"

"Oh, it's not yourself we're interested in," Dogani assured him. "It's your agent."

"Ibram?" Ahksell stood a bit more straight and stuck out his chest; it was an inch when he was already a mile, but Ibram appreciated the gesture. "What business could you possibly have with him, and not with me?"

Well, that sentiment Ibram appreciated less. He frowned up at Ahksell, who shrugged back. Dogani coughed to redirect their attention. Ibram noticed the other warders had wandered off, save for one, who merely looked bored.

"Master Ucalegon's presence is required by Warder Captain Talsconis," Dogani replied, with a relish in his voice Ibram found uncalled for.

"What does he want with me?" Ibram asked. "I haven't done anything."

"Are you certain about that?" Dogani asked. He inclined his upper body as if he were imparting a confidence. "Because he is not best pleased with you, to be sure."

Ibram shrugged, and shook his head. "I cannot control how Captain Talsconis feels," he said, "that's for the Wheelmaker to decide."

Dogani rolled his eyes. "Just come along to the garrison house," he said. "If you're lucky you'll be out by the time they're baking bread for the Forty Martyrs."

Ibram clicked his tongue. "And yet I have so much to do today that I regretfully cannot clear my plate before I've spoken with Lady—"

"You have time to speak with the captain," Dogani interrupted. "And there is no reason to suppose what one agent has been commanded to do, another may not accomplish in his stead."

He stepped to the side and swept his arm out to the left. Ibram rolled his head back on his shoulders and groaned. He lifted his heavy head, and spread his hands.

"Dogani, what does he want me for?"

"Our lot is never to know, but only to accomplish," Dogani answered. He shifted his attention over Ibram's shoulder. "We'll return him up the living mountain in one piece, I assure you, Attendant. It's merely an invitation to speak with him."

Ahksell stepped down off the pathway, which forced Ibram to the right and made Dogani back up a full two steps. He nodded his head, and squared his shoulders.

"Well then," he said. "As Ibram is here at my disposal, and you require him so urgently, I shall accompany him to the garrison house. Since this is only a friendly discussion."

Dogani opened his mouth most probably to argue, but then threw up his hands and waved them both onward. Ibram bumped his elbow against Ahksell's as they followed him. He appreciated the little victories.

⁂

The garrison house for the Cohort of Peace was one of the oldest manors in Lityen, built more as a fortification than a town manor. Its shape only mimicked the popular honeycomb structure of the more elegant quarters. Here, where the warders lived and worked, buildings were utilitarian and the shops and tenant inns which pierced the area sold hot food at all hours, and cheap beds. It was a remarkably straightforward sort of place, even the rain gutters for the roofs were carved with less attention to detail than they were to function. Ibram imagined it was a security measure. The lack of banners and decoration made it a place where you truly had to know where you were going, if you wanted to get anywhere quickly.

Dogani ushered them into the main building with little fuss, and abandoned them at the door of Captain Talsconis' office. The captain's secretary, a solidly made warder missing a full third of her right arm, knocked perfunctorily on the door, before sticking her head in and announcing Ahksell's arrival. She then returned to her desk and the work upon it.

Ahksell looked to Ibram; Ibram shrugged. He tugged on the hair at the nape of his neck. Ahksell pointed towards the half-open door. Ibram scrunched his nose.

"Get in here!" Captain Talsconis barked from within.

"Settles that," Ahksell muttered, and walked through into the office.

Ibram was helpless but to follow. Captain Talsconis was up and out of his chair, and frowning heavily at Ahksell. He bowed perfunctorily and came back up again.

"Close the door," Talsconis said, flicking his sharp pale eyes to Ibram.

Ibram obeyed, and then came to stand by Ahksell's elbow. He clasped his hands in front of himself, and smiled. The lamps were lit in the mostly bare room, and the small high window to the left let in as much sunlight as possible. Still, Talsconis' office was dominated by his predecessor's desk, and the dusty bookshelf behind the single chair was the same.

"I see you have redecorated," Ibram said, and pointed at the furthest wall. "I wondered if you were going to bring the tapestry from your previous office to your new one."

Talsconis studied him for a moment. He was a blunt man, with pale blue eyes, lived-in features and a nose that had taken a few solid hits, but a body built like a bulwark. You could imagine him breaking down a door as easily as a stick of wood, and he had a voice to match.

"I'm not surprised to see you here, Attendant Solari," he said gruffly. "Where there's one of you, there's the other."

"And yet Warder Dogani only requested Ibram's presence in your office," Ahksell said.

"Because he's the one I wanted to talk to," Talsconis said. He sighed and sat back in his chair. "Unless you're a part of this, of course, and then I'm sorry to say that I'll be wanting to speak with you directly, Attendant."

Ibram cleared his throat and crossed his arms over his chest. "Why? I mean, I am always eager to work alongside Her Gracious Majesty's—"

"As much as you practice your patter," Talsconis said, "I should think you'd seek to actually say something once in a great while."

Ibram shrugged. "I might, if I knew why I was invited to speak."

"Attendant Solari," he said, after a moment's long-suffering consideration. "Did your magpie over here tell you about the note Kenda Trading sent my offices?"

"Why are they sending *you* notes?" Ibram asked.

Ahksell raised both eyebrows. "Hardly my magpie, Captain," he protested.

"Crow?" Talsconis offered. "Ferret?"

"I haven't touched anything shiny in days," Ibram said.

"Nonetheless, the result," Talsconis said, with a frown, "is that my warders are having to deal with an arm-for-hire trading on the name of the sect and the reputation of the Cohort of Peace outside the imperial boundary."

A bolt of outrage slammed into Ibram's chest, and left him gaping. "I sent a message! A personal inquiry!"

"Well, two," Ahksell said with a wince.

"Two personal messages, then," Ibram snapped. "Both regarding a directive by my own employer and merely—"

"Who else are you trying to contract with?" Talsconis interrupted, and put his elbows on the desk. "If I am about to get another snippy courier with tassels where his brain should be, telling me the Preceptory of Yseult is trying to undersell a sect in another province, then I need to know about it now."

"I asked who bought fire suppression tiles from the Sect of the Iron Hand," Ibram raised his voice. It seemed the thing to do. "Because their dormant talent and bloated self-regard have led to the deaths of four—"

"Five," Ahksell muttered.

"—*Five* villagers of Lityen! Who undoubtedly had better things to do with their anima than disperse it back unto reality! And Kenda Trading makes their wares available!"

"Are you proffering a charge?" Captain Talsconis asked with an abrupt snarl. "You want me to send word to my counterpart near Kandrilat, and have them institute an investigation?"

Ibram's mouth snapped shut so quickly he felt the tension vibrate from his teeth to his jaw. A heady silence fell, and Captain Talsconis settled back on his chair. He gazed at Ibram with his pale eyes, sharp beneath his rough brow.

"I make no charge," Ibram said, finally. He flicked his eyes towards Ahksell, who dipped his chin at him, and then away. "I only say that I am within my rights to ask a question. One of their salesman has been in the area...and might have gotten himself into trouble, after all."

"What kind of trouble?" Talsconis asked.

Ibram breathed in sharply and then cleared his throat. "The fiery kind," he said. "It's merely a thought I had concerning the tiles and where they were placed."

"You think the fire at Pillared Circle was arson?" Talsconis asked. By his tone of voice, it wasn't a true question, merely a request for confirmation. Talsconis had a sharp mind. He might have made a good sort of agent if he'd been employed before he fell in with the wrong crowd.

"I think a bakery-mill doesn't simply blow itself up," Ibram said. "Not even in Lityen."

"And yet you didn't think a company with contracts for a rival sect might find themselves distressed by your 'mere thought'?" Talsconis asked after a moment's consideration. "And seek out imperial advice?"

"Hardly rivals," Ahksell said with as close to derision as Ibram had ever heard in his voice. "But they made the tiles used at The High Climber, which Kenda Trading's man sold. I would say it warranted a friendly inquiry."

"Would be strange if they didn't seek to keep themselves out of it," Ibram said.

"The High Climber," Talsconis repeated, and nodded to himself a moment. "That's one of the two evening courtyards destroyed in Pillared Circle?"

"The only one not owned by the Vo Kalns," Ibram said. "It's a dwelling as well."

Captain Talsconis nodded once more, and worked his jaw, and then reached into his belt pouch and tossed Ibram a much-folded piece of paper across the desk. Ahksell took a step out of the way. Ibram caught the paper, two-handed, and held it within his palms. He frowned.

"Well, they've answered you," Talsconis said. "Or, me, more to the point."

"You?" Ahksell asked.

"The addressed complaint," Talsconis said dourly. "With about as much information as you'll be getting out of them, unless I miss my mark."

"You've read it?" Ahksell asked.

"Of course I've read it," Talsconis said. "It's written to me."

"Well, yes, I just mean... Can we leave?" Ahksell asked.

Talsconis stared at him a moment. "What's the second message your man sent?" he asked.

Ahksell's mouth opened and then closed. He frowned at Ibram, and raised his eyebrows. Clearly, he didn't wish to lie to the good captain. Nor did Ibram, of course, but it was the principle of the matter. To put a fine point on it, he'd sent three messages. Two by his own commission and one through Master Finar, who was merely inquiring as to his own brother's whereabouts. That message, perhaps, wasn't his responsibility.

Ibram curled his hands closed over the paper, and glanced towards the door. He turned on the ball of his right foot and set his heel down. Lady Azadiya wouldn't like it, though. She preferred equal terms with the warders, and to involve them only so much as was needed. To be sure, lying now might make for a difficult dinner later, when Ladyship had already invited him.

"I sent an inquiry," he said, while Captain Talsconis stared at him as if Ibram was about to bring a hammer down on his own hand, "to the Sect of the Iron Hand about the amount and time of their shipments of fire suppression tiles. To see if they aligned with the dispersal of Master Finar's brother, who is brother-in-law to Master Rennab, who—"

"Owns The High Climber," Captain Talsconis finished for him, in an even grumblier voice than usual.

"It seemed the thing to do," Ahksell said, with remarkable loyalty since he hadn't actually been informed at the time of what Ibram had dictated in the messages he had sent.

Captain Talsconis pinched the bridge of his nose, and took a deliberate breath. "The law," he said, once he'd released himself, "requires a peaceful and prosperous community."

"So do we all," Ibram said immediately.

Ahksell nodded. "And you will have that, as soon as we discover the arsonist and murderer."

"They are most probably one in the same," Ibram said. "No need for imperial oversight in what is strictly a local matter, covered by charter and license, and—ah—"

"Deed of land," Ahksell supplied. "The sect's stewardship of the lands granted by the charter remains firmly within its grasp. First Mentor E'garcid is always kept strictly informed."

Ibram's mouth twitched, but he controlled his burgeoning smile.

"Go away from me," Talsconis said, without changing expression. "If I receive another complaint from outside the imperial boundary, it'll be Ucalegon sleeping in the cells."

"What about me?" Ahksell asked.

"You wouldn't fit," Talsconis said.

"Lady Azadiya talks of nothing but your fairness," Ibram said.

Ahksell elbowed him sharply. "And the Sect of the Iron Hand are notoriously poor correspondents," he said. "I doubt we'll ever hear from them."

"That is what you hope, Attendant," Captain Talsconis said, and sighed deeply. "Send my secretary in when you leave."

⬥

The Nine Stars was still standing when they returned, but Dogani and his fellow warders were nowhere to be found. Ibram chalked it up as a victory, and led the way into the draughtshop. Corbus, if he knew what was good for him, was no doubt still within. The door was open and so were the good wooden shutters to siphon heat from the large fireplace in the back, where a large cauldron bubbled at the base. This close to so many caravans, the owner had enough coin to hang three glowbulbs from the rafters so the smoke was not as bad indoors as it might have been.

"Do you think it was Rennab?" Ahksell muttered. "I think it more and more likely."

Ibram sneezed as he came farther into the room. Murder, or a terrible accident that then led to a murder in order to cover it up again. It seemed likely, but felt wrong, somehow. Masters Rennab and Finar had opened their already crowded home to Ealar Ozol, when the smart action if either of them were guilty would be to express sympathy and stay far away from the grieving Ealar. And Rennab had readily admitted to buying substandard materials, purely on the basis of family ties. A heart as soft as that might bleed over a sharp crime. Ibram couldn't say a man was guilty simply on the basis that he competed with his neighbor.

"I don't know," Ibram said, finally. "Perhaps there's something we've overlooked."

The trestle tables in The Nine Stars' common room were not so packed with folk as they might have been, but a large group of caravanners kept the potboys occupied. In the back corner, Corbus raised his thin arm, and they crossed the room to meet him. Corbus stood, already reaching down to place his hands on his stomach as he bowed, and Ahksell waved it away. He sat down, placing his back to the room, and put both elbows down at the table. Corbus stayed, half-crouched, and turned his head, a little pleadingly, in Ibram's direction.

"Sit down," Ibram said, and followed suit with his own suggestion. He crowded Corbus next to the wall on the bench. "You've been around long enough to pay attention when an Attendant speaks to you."

"Ibram, don't be an ass," Ahksell said. "I thank you for the courtesy, Corbus, but it's not necessary every time you speak to me."

"Yes, Attendant." Corbus nodded politely.

He had that strained set to his teardrop-shaped eyes again, same as when he'd tried to explain Eastern grassland nomadic life to Amota Evren. Corbus said very little when he thought someone else was being inappropriately obtuse, but his face more than made up for it, if you knew how to look. Ibram was reasonably certain they were going to be having this conversation again at a later date.

"You don't have this problem with Attendant Zorion," Ahksell pointed out.

"We are in public, Attendant. And Attendant Zorion's not—" Corbus broke off immediately, and coughed.

Ahksell raised his eyebrows. Ibram removed his elbow from Corbus' ribs, and made a show looking about the common room. Corbus rubbed his side very ostentatiously, in Ibram's view. Ibram refused to register his outrage, and caught the eye of the potboy instead, who began walking in their direction.

"Where's my cousin?" Ibram demanded. "I told you two to watch the folk at The High Climber last night, not lag about all day."

"We didn't lag about!" Corbus protested. "I hung about that caffa they're living out of like The Wanderer in a hunter's trap. Nothing happened but that I got rained on for my troubles."

"And Nesrine?" Ahksell asked.

Corbus cleared his throat. "Nesrine took responsibility for Master Dughlat, Attendant," he said. "And when we met back up this morning, she said the same."

Ibram grunted, and then nodded to the potboy as he stopped by the corner of the table. "What can you serve the Attendant?" Ibram asked. "He's been hard at work all this morning, and deserves the best wine you've got."

"That's not necessary, you know," Ahksell said.

He turned in his seat, and smiled at the potboy. He was young enough to have to carry the pitcher with both hands; children had an unfortunate tendency to fall at Ahksell's feet in worship. This one was no different.

"We do have wine, Attendant," the potboy chirped. "Mama got it all the way from Gulrilat."

"Do you see, Attendant? I told you this was the right place." Ibram gestured to the potboy. "Wine all the way from Gulrilat. How much for a nice pitcher, child?"

Ahksell sighed. Corbus leaned over the table and rocked his own wooden mug. "They serve small beer and cold shay as well, Attendant," he said.

"Cold shay, then," Ahksell said, with a firm eye in Ibram's direction. "A pitcher for three."

"Yes, Attendant!"

The potboy scurried off, and Ibram sighed. "Cold shay."

"A sharp mind catches what the fogged mind disregards," Ahksell said.

"You need to stop visiting my Ama unsupervised," Ibram said.

Corbus cleared his throat, and drained the last of whatever had been in his mug. "Nesrine didn't want to waste time, but before we parted, she said she wanted to chase down something odd."

Ibram inclined his head, but Corbus only shrugged. He glanced between Corbus and Ahksell, and then back to Corbus. Ibram blew breath out of his mouth.

"And did she say what, exactly, she found odd?" he prompted.

Corbus had the grace to look chagrined. "She was in a rush, and I did not follow her."

Ahksell shook his head. "And then you both kept missing each other back at the preceptory."

"Well, we are here now," Ibram said, "and Nesrine is not."

He half-stood from the table, and looked out over the other customers. There was no one he recognized, not even obliquely. He stretched his neck to either side to see through the crowd.

"Did she give you any idea of where she might go?" Ahksell asked. "We could search the area."

"She did not, Attendant," Corbus said.

Ibram sat back down. The few customers who had noticed him standing turned away. A frantic bell began to toll. Ibram's breath caught; his chest froze.

Ahksell sprang to his feet, and took a step away from the table. "Is that...?"

He looked to Ibram. Ibram rose up, dragging Corbus by the scruff of his gambeson. "The fire bell. Come on!"

All three, they staggered through the crush of rising patrons and out onto the street. Folk rushed past, faces drawn with worry; their carts and stalls left unattended. Another bell rang out, then another, peal after terrified peal.

Ahksell grabbed a man running past, and forced him to a halt. The man struggled, spitting a curse, before looking up and up into Ahksell's face and subsiding. Ibram released Corbus and sniffed the air. He couldn't smell smoke.

"What is it?" Ahksell asked the villager. "Who raised the hue and cry?"

"I don't know!" the man yelled back. "Attendant, the fires—is it another bakery-mill? My house, I—"

"Oh, *hang it*," Ahksell swore and released the fellow, who stumbled off and disappeared back into the crowd. "Stay here!"

"What?" Ibram asked, but Ahksell had already grabbed the nearest support beam with his left hand, and with a scoop of air stirred in his right arm, flipped up and over into the air, landing on the porch roof above.

His boots landed heavily above Ibram's head. Ibram dashed into the road, and turned in time to see Ahksell let go of the wooden beam and slam hard down on his knees against the tiles. Ahksell struggled to his feet and ran for it. Ibram grabbed Corbus by the scruff again and dragged him back up the clear sidewalk, racing as they followed the sound of Ahksell's footsteps running down the roof of the wraparound porch.

"Hey!" Corbus complained, and wriggled in Ibram's grip. "I can follow well enough by myself."

"Shut up," Ibram said. Corbus stumbled; Ibram forced them both onward. "If you'd kept hold of Nesrine like this, we might not be missing her now."

"I'm sure she's fine!" Corbus exclaimed. They both ducked a hanging lamp. "Have a little faith in your own cousin!"

Above them, Ahksell's thundering footsteps disappeared. A clatter of roof tiles crashed to the ground; Ibram groaned. Pots and bowls banged under the sound of bells, the poorer folk adding their cacophony.

"Cangsa," Ibram hissed, and then forced them both out onto the street. He craned his neck upwards and spotted Ahksell on the roof of the next building over, leaning out and holding onto the support beam of a balcony for balance. Ibram ran for it. He released Corbus to get the blood flowing back into his own hand, let the man keep up or fall behind as he would.

"Attendant Solari!" Ibram roared, and even the crowd of folk escaping past him skittered back at the noise as it soared over the bells. "Come down this instant!"

Ahksell swung backwards, let go of the beam and twisted in mid-air. Ibram's heart stopped. He gaped as Ahksell's feet slipped from the roof tiles, hung apart as if they were on the separate steps in a stair-well, and then landed safely back on terra cotta. Ahksell braced his hands on his hips, and shook his head.

"I can see smoke!" Ahksell called down.

Ibram threw his hands out to the sides. "So can I, if you give me a minute!"

"Where?" Corbus asked, panting, behind him.

Ibram pointed a finger at the sky. "How many streets away?" he yelled.

Ahksell bent his knees and jumped higher than the roof brace— which was no less daunting for Ibram's having just observed it—and then pointed off to the northeast. A goose-shaped roof drain cracked in half when he landed back down.

"Two roads down!" he called out. "It looks like it's coming from behind The Crooked Tent!"

Ibram's thoughts flew along the map of Lityen in his mind. That was a lower-rent sort of establishment, but still respectable. No fires left unattended, nor reports of drunken routs.

"Charming," Ibram muttered. "Well, come on then," he continued more loudly. "Get down!"

Ahksell shook his head. "Meet you there!"

And he was off, bounding across decent folks' porch roofs and no doubt cracking tiles where ever he went. Ibram groaned, and lurched through the crowd. He swerved and shouted. A pair of carriages nearly sent him to the Crossroads before his time as he darted in between them. Already he thought he saw a few familiar warders on the streets, disturbed from their meals and pressed into service, stopping the surge of panicking folk and beasts from becoming a village-wide riot.

Ibram charged onward, arms pumping at his sides, ducking men and women alike, with only a choked curse or pant of breath behind him to let him know that Corbus was keeping up. This was an older section of Lityen where the streets leading away from the imperial road were more like alleys with pretensions of grandeur. Ibram cast his eyes up at the first intersection, but Ahksell was already a warehouse and a shayshop down from him. He winced as a falling roof tile clipped a gutter carved with a Wyvern's head and then down onto the street.

What did Ahksell think he was going to do? Blow out the fire like one big candle flame? Run back up the living mountain for The Water's Breath? Oh, that would have been handy, they never should have returned it to the storage shed.

The smell of smoke grew thicker, turning the air gray. Ibram coughed as he ran. The way through was often blocked by carts, or simply reinvented as a one-way avenue. Ibram skirted two such places before managing to find a way back to the source of the alarm.

He skidded into a small public area, the inn was constructed in reverse with a courtyard in front and an open space for stables to the one side. The fire wasn't behind The Crooked Tent, it *was* The Crooked Tent. Smoke billowed out from the open windows on the second floor, and something large and no doubt important crashed inside. The horses normally kept penned were screaming in fright, dragging at their leads as cursing grooms brought them further out into the street and away from the flames to safety. A bucket brigade was already in place, passing two sloshing buckets at a time. Ibram broke through the line and then stopped abruptly. He looked left and then right. Corbus crashed into his back; Ibram threw him off.

He drew breath and then coughed it out, and waved his arm in his face. "Do you see Ahksell?" Ibram asked, lifting his chin over his right shoulder.

Corbus blinked at him for a second, blank-faced, and then shook himself, before Ibram got the chance to. "No," he said.

"Hey there!" A woman called out. "Don't just stand there, heave a bucket!"

Ibram turned on his heels to face behind him, and saw the line of volunteers stretching far back down the street to where he could just spy the top of the burbling municipal fountain. A woman clutching a dripping burlap sack glared at him as she rushed past to slap the soaked bundle against the nearest spitting flame.

"Is there anyone left inside?" he yelled as she slipped past.

The woman didn't reply. He looked back to the bucket line. A girl towards the front passed her full bucket to the man next to her, and yelled, "We're all out! Only the mice left!"

Then where was Ahksell? Oblivion would take his hide if the fool was in there searching for folk. Ibram cast his eyes back up and down the street, and finally spied a very large mass of dripping laundry flying through the air, beneath Ahksell's upstretched hands.

"Oh for—Catha's *sodden* slippers," Ibram swore.

"Careful now," Corbus said. "Here he comes!"

The wet bundle swooped down as Ahksell met the line of bucket tossers, and scattered them. He ran up to the front of the inn, chest heaving for breath, and lowered his arms; the entire mass of assorted laundry dipped alarmingly.

"Whoa!" Ibram raised his own arms, as if that would help, and ran to Ahksell. "What's this?"

"No time for the—anything else," Ahksell panted as sweat poured down the side of his face. His dark skin was turning ashen; he gulped air and then coughed out the smoke. "Can you grab a few?"

"Riant," Ibram muttered. "Come along, Corbus!"

Ibram reached up and began yanking at the laundry; he came back with someone's tunic in his hands; he stood staring at the embroidery on its cuffs for a heartbeat, and then shook his head. Ahksell must have commandeered the entire neighborhood's laundry lines. Ahksell began slowly walking them all towards the front of the burning inn. In the corner of Ibram's eye, he saw Corbus take hold of a dangling cloak and start hauling on it as they moved. The bells continued their clamoring as they approached, but Ibram's breath in and out, dragging and rough, grew louder and louder in his own ears.

The heat from the fire prickled his front; he gathered up his tunic, and wrapped it around the lower half of his face as a mask. They were steps from the porch now, smoke poured from the open doors. Ahksell groaned, and the large mass of soaked fabric lowered and then heaved itself into the burning inn. Ibram stepped up onto the porch and ran inside. The common room was all smoke; the flames had eaten their fill of the stairs at the back. The mass of wet laundry in the air trembled. Ahksell pushed in front of him. He threw his arms wide and out.

Ibram lurched to the right, crouching, and peered into the smoke. The laundry had landed on the common room and was unraveling itself, like a great water flower unfurling over a pond. Soaked linen sheets and tunics, stockings and chemises draped themselves over every stick of furniture and burning timber, smothering everything in its wake. Behind them, Ibram could hear shouting and the slosh of water being thrown. Ahksell's entire body slumped and then bore itself upwards in a great release; he began to cough, and Ibram tore off his tunic-mask to smack it over Ahksell's face.

"Corbus!" he yelled, and the junior agent came in running. The heat of the fire made Ibram's skin tighten; he felt like a sausage in a pot. "Tell the bucket line to get the upper floor from the roofs next door! Through the windows!"

"Yes, Agent!" Corbus shouted, and ducked back out again.

Ibram tugged on Ahksell's arm. "Let's be off!"

"Do you see anyone?" Ahksell shouted back.

Steam and smoke enveloped them in a stinging cloud. The noise of the flames on the second floor was growing louder. A timber cracked above their heads, and they both instinctively ducked. Ibram kept hold of Ahksell's sleeve, just in case the idiot ran off again.

"There's no one left!"

Ahksell looked about the common room, draped in all the wet fabric he could have carried and beginning to dry dangerously if they didn't deal with the flames from above. He glanced at Ibram and then back again. Ibram pointed at the stairs, and shook his head.

"The stairs fell, you'll take the building with you if you try to jump it. Come with me, now!"

Ibram pulled and dug his heels in; Ahksell wavered. Wooden beams groaned overhead. A collective shout rose up from the outside, and Ahksell finally nodded. They dashed out of the inn and back into the street, coughing and colliding with each other, where a crowd of folk had organized, including some of the more junior agents of the fourth division. Ibram saw Esti at the ground floor of one line of buckets sending buckets up to the roof tops on the left, and Corbus directing volunteers on the right. Ibram took a more solid grip on Ahksell and yanked him closer to the main line of buckets.

It didn't do to insult an alchemist in public, but by all of Catha's quests, did they deserve it sometimes. "You utter—" Ibram coughed. "Do selu badosh—"

He smacked at Ahksell when he pounded on Ibram's back, and then stood away. Ahksell put both hands on his knees and hacked. He reached a shaking hand up and unwrapped the wet tunic from his mouth, and then stood, staring at it. Ibram released him, and stumbled backwards, breathing hard. He put both hands on his hips, and surveyed the disaster being conquered in front of him. The villagers had taken the chance on climbing the porch roof themselves, wobbling with buckets in their hands.

"Would you look at that," Ibram said, in between coughing.

Ahksell spit to one side, and then turned to follow Ibram's gaze, just as one of the villagers leaned back to throw water and promptly lost her balance. He pushed out with both palms flattened; the tunic flapped to the ground. The woman's yell of alarm halted in midair as Ahksell kept her from falling. She tossed the water through the window, the empty bucket to the ground, and grabbed for balance. Then she reached for the next brimming bucket handed to her. Her compatriot on the other side did the same, only his feet were decidedly not placed on the roof tiles.

"It looks better," Ahksell said, and nodded wearily. His hands kept position. "I should have... I was trying to get the linens up to the second floor."

Ibram nodded and dragged both hands through his hair; he tugged on the ends of it. "Fire was down below as well," he coughed. "All— needed to be put out."

Ahksell nodded again, and wiped his face off with his sleeve. They watched as water was tossed inside the building, and then the buckets were thrown down to the next person on the ground. The bucket brigade had a rhythm to the work now. Ibram could feel the tension in the crowd settling as the smoke continued to billow, but no more fire spread. He saw a line of villagers climbing up and over the roofs, striking out to get at the flames from the back.

Ahksell frowned down at Ibram. "Do you think, perhaps, Nesrine?"

He tilted his head to indicate The Crooked Tent, and Ibram nodded. "Have to take stock of the customers, I should think."

"You had better do it," Ahksell said. "I think I might be needed here for a while."

Ibram patted him on the back; Ahksell wavered forward, but straightened. Ibram slung the stocking he'd hung about his mouth and nose over his shoulder, and rubbed his face with his sleeve. He nodded.

"Back in a bit," Ibram said.

The wind was picking up, not enough to cause a disaster, but able to shift the smoke away to the south. The din of the bells continued, and Ibram pulled on his earlobes. A headache seized him, clawing its way up the back of his skull and sinking its sharp nails into his temples. He looked towards the folk corralling the horses, but they were too busy to speak with. To his right, Ibram spied a small pack of men and women, flitting around another group, who'd obviously caught the worse from the fire. Perfect, a captive audience.

He made his way over to them, and paused by the horses. "Owner?" he asked wearily. A groom leaning against the split rail of a hitching post spied Ibram's approach, and pointed to another tall man in a smudged kaftan in front of him. Ibram nodded and walked over to the owner, who turned at his approach, and bowed shortly.

"Agent," he said. "It's lucky for us the Attendant was in the vicinity."

Ibram returned the bow. "He has Yilka the Green's three heads turned, to be sure."

The phrase clearly went passed the man's understanding, but he let it go after a brief struggle. "May I be known to him?" the man asked finally.

"Ah," Ibram said, "perhaps later on. But you can certainly be known to me, Master...?"

"Master Shevault," the man replied. "I own this inn, or what's left of it." He spit to the side and kicked at the road. "It's what I get for buying cheap, that's what it is. Old hag was glad of my money—she knew she lived in a tinderbox! And now see where I am." He turned his bloodshot eyes back to squint at Ibram. "Are you here to see to the other agent, then?"

Ibram frowned. "What other agent?"

Master Shevault pointed behind himself. "It's just like that city down south," he said, voice hiccupping as if he couldn't help himself. "Kandrilat started with lots of little fires, so they say, and then the whole place went up like so much tinder!"

"We're not so unprepared, I assure you," Ibram mumbled. All his attention was centered on two skinny legs in wrapped grey trousers and stuck into heavy leather boots lying on the ground, surrounded by a quartet of young ladies. Ibram's eyebrows twisted upwards; his stomach plummeted.

"Nesrine?" he called out.

The body attached to the legs groaned. At least Nesrine was alive enough to make a racket. The young ladies parted to reveal his cousin, short wispy hair sticking out in all directions on her head, lying half-propped on a hay bale. Ibram patted Master Shevault on the shoulder as he hurried past, and then crouched at Nesrine's side.

"Hang it," he muttered. He held his hands out, hovering an inch from her shoulders. He didn't even know where to start; she was more makeshift bandage than woman—possibly due to the enthusiastic amateur nurses surrounding her.

"How'd you think I feel?" Nesrine slurred.

Her head sunk low on her chest. She seemed to be breathing all right, but she held her left arm close against her side. Ibram lowered both hands, ignoring the warning hisses of the young ladies surrounding them, and gently turned Nesrine's face upwards. He tsked. Her chin had a nice bruise coming up, and a smear of soot descended her cheek.

"What happened?" he asked.

She blinked rapidly, and then shrugged her right shoulder. She coughed raggedly, and then winced, holding her arm against her body. Ibram let her go, and then sat back on his heels. Nesrine's breath whistled. She grit her teeth against the pain, and began feeling at her belt with what must have been her good arm, poking her fingers into the nearest pouches.

"She was the first to notice the fire," the maid at his right said. "Raised the alarm—"

"And the most racket," her friend interjected.

Nesrine laughed, and then wheezed. "Saw a man at Dughlat's," she whispered. "Doing the same thing I was, only not so good. Followed him here in the morning."

She pulled a roll of paper from her belt purse, and held it out. Ibram took it, and frowned. The paper was torn and a little damp. He unrolled and turned it over, and inhaled sharply.

"The man you followed gave you a knock on your head?" he asked, with a sharp look. "The arm, too?"

She shook her head, and winced. "Tripped on a bag," she gasped, "trying to stamp out the fire. Couldn't chase him."

"Where's the bag?"

Nesrine merely shook her head again, and pointed to the draught-shop. A crowd of feet stamping with purpose broke through the noise; Ibram looked up, and saw a delegation from the nearest apothecary making their way towards them. Ibram nodded, and then stood up.

"All right," he said. "I'll leave you to get patched up, and then we'll show this to Ladyship."

Nesrine nodded, and relaxed back against her hay bale with a hiss. A slim young man carrying a wooden box came to her side and knelt, scattering the young ladies from his path. Ibram stepped aside, and returned to Ahksell.

$$\text{❧}\quad 12 \quad \text{❧}$$

Ibram tossed Nesrine's slip of paper onto Lady Azadiya's desk, where it landed face up. Nesrine sighed and settled more comfortably in the chair Ladyship had directed her to sit in. Her broken arm had been well-bandaged, and then strapped to her chest to restrict movement. She'd had her face cleaned, and her hair combed, but the bruise on her chin had grown up to her bottom lip. Ladyship stalked past him, and stood in front of her; she set her thumb to the space between Nesrine's eyebrows and took a deep, slow breath. Ibram felt a rush of air pass over his body.

"The locus point is undamaged," Lady Azadiya announced after exhaling, "but that bump on the back of your head is nothing to laugh at. What were you doing, Nes-la?"

Nesrine's entire face twitched as Ladyship withdrew her hand; the air pressure lessened. She shrugged, and winced. "I saw a man who alarmed me, Ladyship," she said. "Not in his face, which is nothing remarkable, but his manner."

"I see," Ladyship said. She nodded and crossed her arms over her green robe. "Tell me again what disturbed you, from the beginning."

Nesrine shifted against the rugs padding her chair, and bit her lower lip.

"Ibram set Corbus and I the task of watching over Master Dughlat and the owners of The High Climber," she began. "Corbus was to watch the caffa where they were staying, and I went to the building where Master Dughlat lives."

"Near the Crofters' Guildhouse," Ibram said.

Nesrine nodded. "He has a little room attached to the stew stall coming down the lane from the Water House." She cleared her throat. "There's no one there, but—ha—the widow who owns the shop; they seemed quite friendly. I took up the spot on the opposite side of the road, at the piemaker's next to the tenant inn. Good view of the door and they'd kept their shutter open that night."

"How long before you noticed him?" Ladyship asked. She lifted the paper from the desk, considered the portrait for a moment, and then sent the parchment to Ibram.

He plucked it from the air. Nesrine had a habit of stealing offcuts of paper from the allotments sent to the tower, and did a handy side business in drawing little pictures for a few faunts. Ibram frowned. She'd drawn the man she had spotted from the shoulders up, tilted to the right, but not completely in profile. The man in the picture had long dark hair and soft features; he wore a high-necked tunic.

Nesrine sighed. "I'd been in place about half an hour, Ladyship. I was sitting outside the shop on a little stool by the rain barrel, and I saw him on the porch of the tenant inn."

"He was staying there?" Ladyship asked.

"No, Ladyship," Nesrine said. "I thought so at first, and ignored him. He drew my attention because he kept moving. He'd go into the common room, and then come out to the porch, and then back again. Must have done it... Oh, six or seven times."

"Amateur," Ibram muttered.

Nesrine nodded, and winced; she touched her right temple lightly. The apothecary had given her something for a headache, but the crease between her eyebrows had yet to disappear.

"I ate my pie, and went inside the shop. Paid the owner to keep the shop open, and took up a place by the front window. He was still there when the tenant inn locked its door for the night."

"Didn't even pay for a space on the floor?" Ladyship asked.

"Squatted on the porch and then went inside," Nesrine said. "I won't say he huddled beneath the torches until the innkeeper put them out, but he lingered in the open for long enough that I got a good look at him. The man who owns the place told me he gave his name as Sophus Verco, and that he claimed to be traveling to an apprenticeship in Sevrelat."

"A potter with no kiln," Ladyship murmured.

"It's the man from The Sun Eagle," Ibram said. "He's been hanging about Pillared Circle. I thought he worked there."

"Have you spoken to him?" Lady Azadiya asked.

Ibram tensed, but shook his head. "I intend to do so," he said. "As soon as possible."

"I wish him presented to me," Ladyship said. "So release one fist so that you might grab as well as subdue."

Ibram frowned; he looked down at his hands and discovered he had, in fact, clenched them at his sides. He coughed and loosened his grip. Nesrine laughed.

"Did he take notice of your trailing him, Nesrine?" Ladyship asked.

Nesrine opened her mouth, paused, and then sighed. "I don't think so, Ladyship," she said. "I was careful where I walked, and never tried to draw attention to myself. I know he was surprised when he found me in his bedroom."

Strange folk rummaging through your underlinen was always a bit of a shock. Ibram snorted, and Lady Azadiya sent him a look. He coughed and straightened both his expression and his back.

"Did you find anything of interest?" Ibram asked, and tilted his chin up.

"Nothing much that you wouldn't expect a traveler to carry," she answered with a frown. "That wasn't what struck me—Oh, poor choice of words."

"How did you know it was his?" Ladyship asked, and quirked the side of her mouth.

"I asked the proprietor," Nesrine said. "Master Shevault said he'd been staying there for almost three weeks. No baggage but what he had on him. Gave his name as Karam Roko this time."

"Sounds fake," Ibram muttered.

"It most probably is," Ladyship said. "Please continue, Nesrine."

Nesrine nodded painfully. "He was drinking in the common room when I slipped up the stairs. I thought I had more time."

"And that is when he attacked you?" Ibram asked.

"Not exactly," Nesrine said. "We sort of stood there, staring at each other, and then he kind of lunged and I dodged, and he struck out at a box he'd affixed to the wall I stood in front of."

"A box?" Lady Azadiya repeated.

Nesrine outlined a large rectangle in the air, and then awkwardly dangled her fingers with her working hand. "With strings out the bottom," she said. "When I evaded him, he ignored me and yanked all three strings. I rolled clear of him, and saw the box fall. We reached the door together. I got him in the knee, and then by the arm, but..." She sighed. "I heard glass break, and then I noticed the fire."

Lady Azadiya tsked. "A recondite vial."

"A what?" Ibram asked.

"A bottle which can only be broken by placing something inside of it," Ladyship explained. "Fire boxes have them placed in straw, filled with a small amount of ignition fuel, generally wood alcohol. You pull the strings, a small pin strikes flint which drops with the char cloth to break the glass..."

"The bedclothes caught the flames. I chose to try and put out the fire," Nesrine said. "He escaped. When I tried to follow after, the fire caught so quickly I...I fell."

"Who would have such an object?" Ibram asked. "Where would you even acquire one?"

"They're a novelty," Ladyship said. "Less reliable than a stickum, but about three times the cost."

"Expensive plaything," Ibram remarked.

"They are indeed," Ladyship said. "Half the time they never light, or the stones fall from the wax on their own, and you are left with a dangerous mess in your bags. They were popular in the south, to be sure, but never made it up here. There was a workhouse in Hyperni province, as I recall."

Ibram tilted his head to his employer, and Lady Azadiya nodded. He settled back and let his shoulders relax. For such a far off place,

Hyperni province was casting quite the shadow. Though, he supposed it was large enough. Kandrilat had been its second largest city. The Sect of the Iron Hand, known for their shoddy tiles, nested in its valleys and now the province brought forth another sample of their substandard wares.

"Did the same sect—" Ibram began.

Ladyship waved her hand in the air. "No, no," she cut him off. "Utterly mundane workshop. The product of university folk. You know how they enjoy their little experiments."

Ibram raised his eyebrows, and Nesrine emitted a strangled cough. Ladyship ignored them, and tugged on the end of her braid. Her eyes fixed on a point only she could see. She sighed through her nose, and Nesrine's face fell.

"Apologies, Ladyship," she murmured.

"What?" Ladyship refocused. "Oh, not at all, Nesrine. You did very well. What we have now is more than we had previously. Ibram, take the portrait Nesrine drew and see if others recognize the man." She frowned. "I must consult Evren's archives. Be back in time for dinner."

"Of course, Ladyship," Ibram said. "I'll meet up with Ahksell at The Crooked Tent. Shall I send Corbus in to you now? He's been sitting with Amita Sarrha since we returned. He's probably roasted nicely by now."

"Well enough," Ladyship said.

"Nesrine," Ibram glanced her way. "Do you feel up to making copies of this? We have some offcuts left over from the bindery."

"I'm fine," Nesrine said. "And happy to do so."

Nesrine began to rise, but Lady Azadiya waved her back down. She resettled herself with a quick glance in Ibram's direction. Ibram shrugged slightly.

"I will need to speak to everyone," Lady Azadiya declared. "On your way out, Ibram, send for Berac as well as the loose paper. I can see the outline, but I very much dislike the design of this entire affair."

Ibram nodded and walked to the door, but on his way out, a thought occurred. He turned back to face the room and raised his hand.

"Ladyship," he said. "Your dinner?"

Lady Azadiya paused and blinked at him. "Oh yes," she said, and sighed. "I shall make it right with Dihya. It will have to be pushed back to tomorrow. Send someone for Sarrha and Master Rennab. I will extend my apologies for his detention."

Ibram bowed and turned to leave. Lady Azadiya called behind him. "In point of fact," she said. "What did you learn from the firework makers by Book Row?"

Ibram winced. He'd forgotten that.

Ahksell was still hanging about The Crooked Tent when Ibram found him, sitting on the lip of the municipal fountain and holding a large green apple, half-eaten. He bowed with his hands on his stomach, and Ahksell was so tired all he managed was a rude gesture and narrowed eyes to raise Ibram back up again. Ibram stretched out his back, and set himself down on the fountain as well.

He pointed his chin down the road towards the draughtshop. "Not overseeing the clean-up in person?" he asked.

"What happened to your button shield?" Ahksell asked. He leaned far to his right, near to overbalancing, and dug a small vial of blue liquid out from his belt pouch. He wrinkled his nose at it, and began breaking through the wax seal with his thumbnail.

"Hm? Oh." Ibram glanced down his front. "I used it up last night. Don't suppose you have a moment to re-imbue it with something?"

Ahksell shook his head and ate more of his apple. He swallowed, but gagged, and closed his eyes for a moment's deliberate breathing. Ibram nudged Ahksell's foot with the toe of his own boot. Ahksell sighed and looked down at the plugged vial in his other hand; he'd worked the wax free.

"It's awful stuff," Ibram said.

"You get used to it," Ahksell replied. He sat up straight on the lip of the fountain, and tossed the contents of the vial down his throat. He threw the empty glass down, and closed his eyes. He shuddered once, and licked his lips, before sagging forward and catching his elbows on his knees.

"Better now?" Ibram asked.

Ahksell wearily turned his head, and looked at him. His eyes glowed a brilliant green. Smoke coiled out of his mouth when he answered: "In a moment."

Ibram nodded, and interlaced his fingers between his knees. Ahksell breathed smoke a little while longer, and then grimaced at what was left of his apple. He made another attempt at eating it, layering over his previous bitemark, but only chewed.

"You have to swallow as well," Ibram said, "or it doesn't work."

"Tastes awful now."

"Well, next time finish eating before you rearrange the inherent nature of your insides. You've got six humors, keep them in balance your own way."

Ahksell rolled his eyes, and Ibram prodded him in the shoulder until he smiled. It was ever thus with Yseult alchemists, though usually Ahksell wasn't so reluctant. Food was a necessity considering all the anima they manipulated, but by Laumye the Blue's barnacled toes, if left to their own devices you couldn't convince half of the preceptory to eat without increasingly unsubtle blandishments.

Ibram spied a loaf of bread, untouched, on Ahksell's other side, with an empty crock nearby. He picked up the little clay pot and sniffed it, the heady vinegar made his face pinch. Chewed olive pits rolled against each other in the bottom, and so he tossed the pot aside again. Well, that was something. If he didn't finish the apple, there was a brinery somewhere around the section of the village; they could wander in search of the correct alley later.

Ibram leaned his elbows on his knees and considered the buzzing work crews being put through their paces by a few folk in recognizable green gambesons. He frowned. From where they sat, he couldn't tell if they were fellow agents or alchemists. He sighed heavily, and leaned back.

"I did, in point of fact, help with the clean-up. I also managed to do some investigating of my own."

"You did?" Ibram asked.

"Asked about the structure, and the tiles, and the like, before the man who owns the place had to attend to other duties." Ahksell took another bite of his apple and chewed loudly. "It's the Sect of the Iron Hand again," he said as he swallowed. "That's why the top went up so quickly."

"No need to think why he chose it, then," Ibram said, and opened his belt pouch. He held out the picture Nesrine had drawn.

"Who?" Ahksell frowned at the paper. A final wisp of smoke escaped from him as he spoke, but no more. "This is who attacked Nesrine?"

"She came upon him in his room and startled him," Ibram said. "Says he started the fire to get away."

Ahksell pulled a thin shard of porcelain from the fountain's edge on his other side and held it out to Ibram. Ibram took it from him, and looked at the piece. The surface was rough under his fingers, baked and dull on one side with a scraped glimmering sheen of something on the other. He held the shard closer to his face, and spied a stylized closed gauntlet stamped onto the dull side.

"How would Master Shevault know?" Ibram returned to the original topic. "The imperial inspectors merely record the presence of tiles, not where they came from."

Ahksell shook his head, and finished his apple. His dark skin was crusted with old sweat at his temples and where his neck met his collar; his green gambeson was smudged in ash down his front. He finished eating and tossed the core into the olive crock.

Ibram considered the sun shining above them, sailing through the clouded sky utterly unconcerned with what it shone upon below. Ahksell leaned on him, and yawned. He was a young Attendant, after all, and pulling on the strings of reality required not merely years of study but the careful building of endurance. Ibram bore up under the sudden weight.

"Is Nesrine all right?" Ahksell asked, and yawned again.

"She will be," Ibram said. "Broken arm, bump on the head, a trifle embarrassed at the attention."

Ahksell nodded, and frowned down at the portrait. "It's not a familiar face," he said.

Ibram shrugged with the shoulder not in current use, and frowned. "I have seen him about," he said. "Are we able to enter the building?"

Ahksell blinked rapidly and then blotted the side of his face with his sleeve. "The common room, perhaps," he said. "The stairs up to the sleeping quarters are too damaged, and I'm not certain the beams of the ceiling aren't going to come down on everyone's heads if we aren't careful."

He laughed tiredly, and patted his belt pouch. "Not that it wouldn't be an interesting test," Ahksell said. "Hilbert will be interested, regardless."

"Attendant Zorion does have many varied interests." Ibram nodded, though he had no idea what Ahksell was talking about. "I worried the structure might be too badly damaged," he said, "but Nesrine didn't have a chance to thoroughly search our arsonist—"

"Prospective arsonist," Ahksell muttered and twisted to release a knot in his back.

"Just the fellow," Ibram agreed. "Only we need to see his room. Maybe he left a clue or two."

"Note from his employer?" Ahksell suggested.

"If he can read," Ibram agreed. "It's not so common outside the imperial boundary, you know."

Ahksell snorted; Ibram studied the portrait again. No distinguishing marks; the man was damnably lucky. Most folk wouldn't give him a passing thought, much less remember him once he'd left their sight.

"And if he is employed," Ibram continued. "Though, I grant you, this is not the perpetrator I would single out as acting on his lonesome."

Ahksell nodded. "There would be more fires, elsewise."

Ibram leaned back and clapped his hands on his knees. "If you're up to it, I thought we might see what can be deduced from the draughtshop's remains. It's safe to enter, judging by the helpers I see scurrying in and out."

Ahksell straightened immediately, and raised his chin. "Of course I feel up to it," he insisted. "Ibram, what a thing to say."

"You're tired, I'm thirsty," Ibram defended himself with upraised hands. "I am only offering the option of coming along."

Ahksell rose from the fountain with a groan, and stretched his arms high over his head, bending back a little and then relaxing forward. He dropped his arms, and looked down expectantly.

Ibram sighed. He tucked Nesrine's picture into his belt pouch as he stood up.

The Crooked Tent had gotten off lightly when compared to the utter destruction at Pillared Circle. The roof still soared overhead, and the front of the draughtshop was reasonably uncharred. The terraced porch was more or less intact. Ahksell went directly to an older man slowly picking up debris and placing it in a bucket. Ibram took a moment to get his bearings by the door.

It was the inside which spoke most loudly of the damage. Ibram couldn't suppress a wince as he surveyed the burnt remains of the common room furniture. He pointed to the collapsed stairwell, and kicked aside a sodden bundle of fabric as he walked forward.

He glared up at the hole in the ceiling. The second floor railing listed out into the air. He bent his head and considered the remaining furniture. The nearest table looked only mildly burnt; it might bear up under his weight.

He dragged the table across the floor; the crisped edged crumbled in his palms. He grimaced. *Riant.*

Ahksell's conversation at the other end of the draughtshop stumbled, and then regained fluency. The man he was speaking with sounded like the owner. Ibram left them to it; he had other objectives. He bent down quickly; the table supports looked sturdy. Ibram stood and positioned it under the former stairwell, and then clambered on top.

One of the table legs slammed to the floor; Ibram's arms flew out to the sides for balance; he bent at the waist. The table rocked forward under his weight, and then back again. Ibram froze; he took a deep, slow breath, and carefully resituated his feet. He gauged the distance upward, and tensed.

"Ibram, what are you doing?" Ahksell called over.

Ibram leapt upright, throwing his arms in the air, and grabbed onto the exposed second floor landing. His right hand clamped hold; his left slammed into the railing, numbing his fingers immediately. Air whooshed out of his mouth as he dangled, feet kicking in the air. He grit his teeth, and forced his left hand to curl around the base of the railing.

The landing groaned as he pulled himself up. His weight dragged at him, shoulders bunching as he raised his chin to the wooden planks, and then just over them. He kicked out, and tried for a bit of a swing, so that momentum could bring him higher. Through the bars of the railing, he saw the blackened doorway where Nerine had surprised her prospective arsonist.

Old, soured smoke forced him to breath in shallow pants through his mouth. Ibram kicked his feet again, but only managed to knock his head against the railing. Oblivion could take every stick of wood in the place. His left hand throbbed, the nerves screaming in affront. He braced his right arm, and yanked up his left to grab the nearest bit of banister, and the entire pillar cracked off.

Ibram shouted, off-balance, and clutched the landing tightly. The piece of railing crashed to the floor. He looked down; Ahksell looked up at him, arms crossed. The draughtshop owner gaped next to him.

"You want the whole place about my ears?" the owner shouted. "Come down at once, young master! It's not safe!"

Ibram looked up and back down what he could view of the second story hallway, and then returned to the owner. "Ah," he said, "in point of fact, a friend of mine forgot his shoes. Verco or Roko, you might remember the name? Terrified of fire, of course, but they're very expensive things, leather and all." The piece of ceiling—or floor, he supposed—creaked in his grasp. Ibram cleared his throat. "I promised to get them."

"There's nothing anyone needs up there!" the owner yelled.

Ibram winced. Really, he wasn't that far above their heads, there was no need for such a racket. He swayed briefly, and resettled his grip.

"Would you like some help?" Ahksell asked with an unreasonably patient tone in his voice.

Ibram kicked the air, heels pinwheeling, and made another go of it. This time, he managed to land his left elbow on a clear patch.

"No," he gritted out as he pulled himself up and over. "Thank you."

He raised his leg onto the floor—definitely, now a floor—and the added leverage was all he needed. The railing broke apart as he rolled forward, and collapsed around him as he finally landed. He stared up at the damaged ceiling, and huffed for air.

"Just a quick look," he called down below him.

Ibram sat up, and carefully brushed ash and debris off his chest and out of his hair. He stood and walked back to the doorway he'd spotted before, making note of where his feet landed so that he might follow the same path backwards. The fire had crawled up the walls, made of thinner wood. The stench of burnt resin and smoke hung in the air, like a bonfire, badly doused.

He looked up and then down the hallway, but there was no sign of the bag that Nesrine had tripped over. The hallway had been damaged, and the window at its end was splintered and damp. Some enterprising soul must have been fighting the flames from the kitchen courtyard. The floor creaked again as he moved slowly and deliberately forward.

"Ibram, we can look later," Ahksell shouted behind him. "Master Shevault has a ladder, somewhere. Don't you?"

Ahksell was no longer addressing him; Ibram was free to ignore his remarks. He paused. The doorway had been bad enough, but the room itself was a husk of former furniture and destroyed belongings. This was clearly where the fire had begun. Ibram stuck an experimental foot out over what remained of the threshold, and tapped the floor. The embers disintegrated beneath his boot. He pinched his lips together between his teeth, and tried to find a patch of floor that might take his weight. Another portion of the wood snapped under his weight; he drew back his foot.

He sighed through his nose. He let his eyes drift from the right side of the room, where a great splotch of a burn mark stuffed with charcoal dust burst out across the wall and remains of a bed, to the left which had burned just as readily, if not as completely. Wires dangled from the opposite wall. He narrowed his eyes and leaned forward as much as he dared. It looked as if the man Nesrine had followed had set himself a trap, just as she had described. If discovered, he'd burn the evidence, as well as the discoverer and anyone unlucky enough to be napping when the fire caught.

A knot twisted in the center of Ibram's chest. Nesrine had been too quick for her attacker, but a murderer had lived in this room. Perhaps he might drop the 'prospective' from the arsonist's title. Perhaps he might go a bit further, and drop the arsonist altogether.

"I haven't found the shoes," he announced, just to give Ahksell an indication that he hadn't fallen out the back window. "The laces are here, though."

"The *what?*" Ahksell yelled back.

Ibram paused. Ah, he'd neglected to tell Ahksell about the Running Flames he'd found. He shrugged. Best to just continue.

"One moment," Ibram shouted.

He sidled left, wincing while the flooring protested his weight, and leaned as far into the room as he dared, and then a farther. He braced himself on the doorway, and stretched out his right hand. He swung and missed, swung and missed, and on the third time caught the dangling end of the longest wire. The fire had long since burnt away its wax and powder and whatever had held it against the wall. He tugged it free easily, and with it came its shorter neighbor, still hooked together as the wires in the alley.

Really, the sect needed to know who made the things. The durability was astonishing. He carefully leaned backwards, and rolled the wires together. They went into his fresh handkerchief and then into his belt pouch.

"You have had several moments," Ahksell said, much closer now.

Ibram jumped and caught himself against the doorway. The floor creaked like a dozen groaning voices. He twisted in place, and found Ahksell staring at him from the opening in the floor, half in and half out of sight, with both hands braced against the landing.

"What are you doing?" Ibram demanded. "Go back down at once."

"Of the two of us," Ahksell said, with both eyebrows reaching for his hairline, "I am far less likely to crash to my death. Now come back here immediately."

"I am seeking knowledge," Ibram kept his voice low. "Go away and I will bring it with me when I'm done."

Ahksell pushed up, and somehow rose higher inside the former stairwell, fully extending his arms. "What could there possibly be left inside that room worth you breaking your neck?"

Ibram pointed behind himself. "This is the room he occupied," he said. "It's a death trap."

"Aren't all traps deadly, technically?"

Ibram drew breath, stopped, and then shook his head. "No," he said finally. "Perhaps. I don't know, but I only require one more moment, and then I will explain everything."

"Fine," Ahksell said.

Ibram glared at him; Ahksell continued suspending himself in the air. They stared at each other. Ahksell began to glimmer with sweat at the temples again. Ibram sighed, and turned back to the room.

"Fine," he muttered. "To be sure, it's nothing to me."

He crouched down and craned his neck. It didn't seem like much had been left, after all. If it had been Ibram, he'd have put all his more dangerous belongings—papers, devices, and the like—on the same side of the room where his ignition lay. That way, he could be assured of its destruction, and it seemed the arsonist had followed the tide of Ibram's own mind. He saw nothing more personal than the remains of a wash bowl.

He let his eyes wander, and shook hair out his eyes. In the far corner, there was a small bundle under the bed, protected by the frame and the bed clothes, no doubt. Nesrine had said the bed had caught along with the floor and wall, but the floor had held where the walls had not. The frame was mostly tinder and wood ash for the soap-makers now. Ibram leaned forward to see the bundle more clearly. It looked odd, crumpled, but still intact...

Ibram blinked. It was a pact bag, made of heavy canvas and equally heavily waxed. How else would it have survived being in the very room with the fire? Some of them, if you had the coin to spare, had indico-lite dust worked into the fibers. Not as fireproof as tiles, nor as reliably waterproofed, but Amota Evren had several of them in his archives, protecting what he dubbed his items of 'particular interest.' Ibram had never been allowed to break their seals to confirm the contents.

He sighed through his nose. The bag was out of his reach. There was nothing for it. He got down on all fours, and began to carefully stretch out over the floor into the bedroom. He inched forward slowly, just like he were crawling over thin ice.

"Ib—Oh, why do I bother?" Ahksell muttered.

Ibram stretched his right arm out over the floor, and an enormous hand gripped him around the waist. His eyes widened; he shifted forward and found himself frozen.

"You are not going inside that room," Ahksell said.

Ibram pushed out with his knees. He felt his muscles flex, the pressure of the floor beneath his body; he strained forward and managed to do no more than wiggle in place. He reared back, and glared down the length of his body.

Ahksell stared at him, unimpressed. He was balanced on his left arm, with his right extended fully down the hallway. His fingers were clenched on open-air as he tugged whatever in the plane of reality connected Ibram to the chains of anima around him.

"Master Shevault says the ceiling could come down any moment," Ahksell said.

Ibram pointed above their heads. "The roof?"

Ahksell glared. "This floor!"

"I see a pact bag. It's damaged, but still intact," Ibram said. "It could be important!"

"So we punch a hole in the ceiling beneath it, and I catch it," Ahksell said.

Ibram blinked at him. "That's an excellent idea," he said.

"I have them, upon occasion."

"Well then, feel free to release me," Ibram said, and waved awkwardly at his midsection.

Ahksell flexed his arm, drawing it back a little; Ibram felt an answering tug at his waist. He rolled his eyes.

"Fine! Fine," he muttered, and scuttled back away from the door. He rose up on his heels into a crouch, and Ahksell's invisible grip disappeared.

❦

Ibram stuck the pact bag underneath his gambeson, carefully folding the burnt end, and buttoned himself while Ahksell paid Master Shevault for the damage to his ceiling.

"It's not right," Master Shevault muttered as he watched Ahksell count the coins into his palm.

"And another faunt for the damage to your chairs," Ahksell said. "For which I am very sorry. I do hope this aids in the reconstruction of your fine establishment."

Ibram came to stand by his elbow, and bowed shortly. "Fourth Mentor Hobon will be entirely grateful for your discreet aid."

They left the man sputtering, but compliant, which was really all Ibram asked of a draughtshop owner anyway. The clean up outside The Crooked Tent continued apace. Ibram allowed Ahksell to take the stairs down to the road first, and raised his arm to Esti, who was guiding traffic away from the rubble. A man behind him stood tossing charred splinters into a half-covered bucket.

Ibram pointed to Ahksell, and then himself, and circled his forefinger in the air. He'd be taking charge of the Attendant now. Esti nodded, bowed to Ahksell, and returned to pushing folk down the lane. Ahksell took another vial from his belt pouch, and thumbed off the wax seal. He downed its contents with a grimace, and pocketed the empty bottle.

"Ladyship wants me to search amongst the firework makers near Book Row," Ibram said, "to find out if any of the folk there recognize the man who Nesrine drew. If you join me, you might walk off that potion you just drank."

"It's only withy bark for my head. When did Mentor command you to do that?" Ahksell asked, as he walked down past the municipal fountain.

"When Nesrine showed us the picture," Ibram said, and patted the bulge of the pact bag trapped against his chest. "I was temporarily diverted checking in on you."

Ahksell's stomach chose that precise moment to growl like a barn cat confronted by a feisty rat. He pressed his hand to his stomach, and winced visibly. Ibram rolled his eyes.

"Come along, Attendant," he said, and jerked his head down the lane. "I sense pie in our future."

Ahksell laughed, and they walked onward. Book Row was on the other side of Lityen from The Crooked Tent, but that wasn't such a burdensome walk once they made it through the traffic which had slowed to behold the burned out draughtshop. This many walkers choking the roads should have felt like a festival, complete with fruit and honey sellers and dram stalls. Instead, folk whispered amongst themselves, and the air had a sharp edge to it. Ibram's shoulders tensed beneath his gambeson as they passed through a group of chattering villagers, who reluctantly parted for them.

Two fires in so short a span as a twelve-day was a bad omen. Worse, it was bad for business in the village. Already he could see groups of merchants gathering together their belongings in the inns and stable yards, preparing to head up and out of danger. If one too many caravan owners got it into their heads that Lityen was a bad bargain and made the attempt to take the older roads—perilous though they were—and skip Vanima province altogether, the sect wouldn't be happy.

"He must have had the box in place as a last resort," Ibram muttered as he evaded a passing wagon laden with clay jugs.

"What did you say?" Ahksell asked, and looked at him over his shoulder. He frowned. "Runner's corns, would you just get up here? It gives me a crick in the neck to have to keep looking behind me to have a proper conversation."

"You are the death of etiquette," Ibram said, as he obliged under orders and came closer to Ahksell's side. If not a step behind, then certainly still technically at Ahksell's shoulder, and definitely not beside or in front.

"Mentor says protocol is the panacea of small minds."

"That was because Mentor E'garcid refused to allow her to use the Third Mentor's south field as an obstacle course."

"They were only *little* trebuchets."

Ibram had no answer to that, if only because there was no such thing as a 'little' war machine, and certainly nothing capable of launching the kind of boulders Ladyship had specified in her proposal. There were times when one's employer became bored, no doubt owning to a long life and a never-ending thirst for knowledge. In Ibram's opinion, what that usually led to was a finer understanding of the term 'collateral damage.' It often made him wonder what the agents in the other divisions within Yseult did all day. He couldn't imagine Second Mentor Stadat leaving his bubbling cauldrons to slap a boulder in half, to be sure.

"Anyway, I was speaking of the tinderbox." Ibram frowned. "No, that isn't what she called it. The... A portable fire box, full of recondite vials."

"*That* is what began the fire?" Ahksell asked.

"He'd wired his room like he'd wired the alleyway behind the Ozols' bakery-mill, no doubt."

"He *wired* it?" Ahksell's voice spiked high on the last word.

"Keep your voice down!" Ibram hissed, and smiled at a passing wagoner. "Do you know of anyone who might sell such a box, locally? Ladyship called it a curiosity."

"She's correct in that. No," Ahksell said. "We certainly don't make them up the living mountain. I remember a visiting Attendant from the Sect of The Nine Stars made an exhibition of one while you were away on your travels. Used it to start a furnace."

"How thrilling."

"That is a—oh, I can see how that would work," Ahksell said. The only indication to show he'd heard Ibram was a slight softening of his voice. "A bit unreliable, and how did he use it in the alley? Surely, folk would notice someone running away."

Ibram shook his head. "He didn't—now, I should explain that later."

Ahksell hummed in agreement, clearly already onto his next thought. "They tell me that they're in use for festival days in rich houses, because of all the fireworks. Did you know in Bastilat there was even a city ordinance forbidding alchemists to celebrate within the walls?"

"It did burn down twice."

"Attendant Maqsi says the real celebrations are on the river, and they last for days. Ibram, did Nesrine happen to mention how big the box was, or how many ignition tabs she saw?"

Ahksell stopped the flow of traffic to mime the device Nesrine had described with both of his hands. One could not push an Attendant in broad daylight, of course. Ibram kicked him discreetly in the back of the bootheel. Ahksell dangled the fingers of his right hand down, and wiggled them

"They would have taken the form of strings," Ahksell said, wiggling away, "and most likely connected to wax caps which hold—"

"Attendant, this nice woman would like to pass by," Ibram said.

Ahksell dropped his hands immediately, startled out of his preoccupation as Ibram had known he would be, and looked about himself at the bare patch of street they both inhabited. His forehead crinkled in confusion.

"What nice woman?"

"Well, that's certainly no way to talk," Ibram said. He stepped up and prodded Ahksell in the ribs. "We shall leave immediately. Did you see that brinery? I think I spotted an entire jug of Garos with the top off—I swear you could see the caskfish disintegrating into sauce as it happened."

Still frowning, Ahksell allowed Ibram to guide him to the side of the street, and they continued onwards. The air smelled better the further distance they put between them and the fire. The brinery, sadly, was closed, but the bake shop was glad of Ibram's coin, and they continued on to Book Row. Ahksell devoured the slices of sausage and chunks of bread Ibram handed him, and nodded occasionally to show he was listening as Ibram apprised him of what Ladyship had said, and what Ibram had learned from speaking with Amota Evren the night before.

$\maltese$ 13 $\maltese$

"No one knows the man at all?" Lady Azadiya asked.

Ibram's report had been short, but thorough. He paused in unbuttoning his gambeson, and resisted the urge to squirm as he watched her pace her office. He shook his head instead. Ahksell shifted in his chair by the desk, and sighed heavily.

"He has a very common face," Ibram said. "And the wires I recovered from his room at The Crooked Tent were of great professional interest—apparently no one has ever seen braided Running Flames before."

Ladyship tsked. "Another importation," she muttered.

Ibram nodded. "And while the wires from The High Climber were *not* braided and several folk purchased Running Flames around the time that the bakery-mill caught alight, the only names recorded in their ledgers turned out to be entirely unrelated."

"Who?" Ladyship asked.

Ibram sighed, and flexed his aching feet in his boots. "Good families of Lityen, most of them containing young children celebrating their sixth year."

Ladyship tsked loudly once more. She crossed her arms and paced a short circle in thought. If the dinner had not been canceled, it would almost have been time to go down meet her guests. Ibram confessed, to himself at least, that he was grateful for the reprieve. He and Ahksell had been marching back and forth, practically from house to house trying to find someone who recognized the man who had attacked Nesrine and set those fires.

"Sophus Verco," Lady Azadiya muttered. "Karam Roko. What sort of pseudonyms are these?"

"Sounds Isconian," Ahksell said.

Ladyship chuckled, and then let a sigh escape her mouth. "I thank you not to tempt our luck. I'm far too old to be chasing Isconian saboteurs again."

Ahksell straightened in his chair; Ibram's eyes widened. He mouthed 'what?' at Ahksell, who appeared equally dumbfounded.

"When did you such a thing *before?*" Ahksell burst out.

She laughed, and rubbed her green-stained fingers. "I had to do something before I came here, Ahk-la," she said.

Ibram gaped like a fish, and then snapped his jaw shut. Lady Azadiya moved to the window, and began gazing pensively into the kitchen garden below. That seemed to be all she was willing to say on the matter.

Ahksell raised both hands in a helpless gesture. Ibram lifted his own hands in return.

"Plenty of folk recognized the face in Pillared Circle," Ibram said with a cough, as he resumed opening up his clothing. "but no one we spoke with could supply a name or even an employer. There's two roads that meet there, it makes for polite neighbors, but they don't pay attention to the crowds."

"But the man in the sketch was familiar," she said.

"Tella—she runs the little shayshop—said he looks like a man who comes into the village for the festival markets," Ahksell said. "But she's new to Pillared Circle, and can't claim prior knowledge."

"I've shown the picture to the other agents," Ibram said. He took the half-burnt pact bag from his gambeson and held it, unfolded, in the cup of his palm. Whatever was inside of it clinked against itself, but the bag was still too thick for Ibram to feel the shape of its contents. "You have twenty folk branching out from Pillared Circle looking for the man. Half of them have a picture, and the others have the face memorized, to be sure."

"Nesrine's skills might more rightly belong to another occupation," Ladyship said. "But I'll keep her."

"I told them not to approach, since it's clear he's dangerous," Ahksell said, "and they know to report straight back here. They're in pairs, so one might keep an eye while the other returns up the living mountain."

Lady Azadiya nodded, but mostly to herself.

Ibram eyed the open doorway. The usual bustle of the tower was muted, but he could still see folk milling about. He caught his heel bouncing against the floor, and stilled his leg.

"I should go back down the living mountain," he said. "The agents are skilled in their way, to be sure, but I would think having someone who'd actually seen the man we're looking for would be more helpful."

"Then send your evidence with a messenger next time," she said. "What is this you've brought back?"

She pet stray hairs back from her face; her hair was pierced with three golden sticks at the top and braided down the back. Trimstone and silver drops dangled from her ears. He looked again at the little removable pendants on her necklace. Father had followed very precise instructions to make those. By Ibram's estimation, Ladyship was arrayed with as many alchemical baubles as she was finery, and might arguably be as ready to set off a bomb as she was a scandal.

Ibram held out his handful of melted canvas. "Found this pact bag in the arsonist's room," he said. "I thought it might be important."

She frowned. "Is this what caused Nesrine to fall?"

Ibram shook his head, and then shrugged. "Possibly, Ladyship. It was the only thing to survive."

"Besides the wires," Ahksell said.

"Yes, them as well," Ibram said. "I think it must have indicolite worked into the fibers."

Ladyship crossed the room, and lifted the bag from Ibram's hand. She studied its ruined exterior, and the greying leather remaining, and sniffed the closed top. She wrinkled her nose, and raised her arm to put the bag in the direct light of the glowbulb. Ibram watched her tug on the remaining cord holding it closed; the twine promptly snapped off. She touched the broken end of the twine to the tip of her tongue; Ibram grimaced, mouth puckering, and averted his eyes.

"Is it anything important?" Ahksell asked.

"It could be," she said.

Ibram coughed behind his fist, and moved to one side. "Best to see what it is."

"Tastes of nothing unusual," she said. "Faint tinge of spice, perhaps." She snorted, and strode past Ibram to her desk. "It does not, in fact, carry indicolite within it. And it is not a pact bag."

"How can you tell?" Ibram asked.

"They're typically larger," she said, "for documents and such, and no responsible arsonist is going to keep documents about—nor would anyone looking to hire such a criminal sign their names to anything." She considered for a moment. "Not that I haven't met very stupid criminals, to be sure."

Ahksell stood at her approach and made room so that Ibram could join them at Ladyship's desk. Lady Azadiya held her free hand out and twitched her fingers.

"A handkerchief," she said.

Ahksell produced one, and laid it flat on the desktop; Ladyship set down the bag and the broken bit of twine. The contents again clinked together. Ibram glanced quickly between it and her.

"Do you think I've broken whatever is inside of it?" he asked.

"Possibly," she said. "Now, indicolite-infused pact bags are a province-wide export. One of those things they come up with for the jubilee of some unfortunate consul who needs to upstage the neighboring province. They're also typically stamped with the maker's mark within. Look, here, there is nothing."

She curved a line with her smallest finger along the bottom of the pact bag, where the wax had melted and the leather had burnt to a crackling cinder.

"It should have all burned," she said. "So why did it not?"

"It was under the bed," Ibram offered, "perhaps the fire only just reached it."

Ibram opened his gambeson wider and saw charcoal all along the front of his tunic. He winced. That was definitely going to deliver a talking-to at his door next washing day. Ahksell whacked him in the biceps.

"Clothe yourself," he muttered and made significant eyes in Lady Azadiya's direction.

Ibram rolled his vision ceiling-ward and began doing up his buttons. He refocused when Ladyship leaned forward over her desk. She frowned.

"Kicks the bag from the...where was it?" she asked.

"Under, but more to the middle of the bedframe," Ibram said.

Carefully, Lady Azadiya opened the burnt end of the bag. Ibram tilted his head to see the contents, and saw the others doing the same.

"Nesrine stomps upon it, then falls, which sends the bag under the bed," she said, and reached two fingers within the bag. She pinched out a thin dagger-shaped slice of clay, and raised it up.

Ibram flexed his right hand, his knuckles cracked. "And here we have the remains of a lovely set of fire suppression tiles," he said.

Ahksell reached out and began pulling other pieces out of the bag. A flurry of dust and tiny fragments puffed across the handkerchief as he laid out the clay tiles. A few had such delicate points—already cracked—that the tiny portions snapped at his touch, but other parts had thick edges which remained firm. He shook his head.

"Shoddy," Ahksell muttered. "I can't even understand how they survived the kiln."

"I suspect the Sect of the Iron Hand has little idea, either." Lady Azadiya turned the thin cracked shard over in her hand, and angled the unglazed side to the light. A chunky gauntlet within a circle was stamped not very neatly into the thick edge of the clay. Ibram leaned back on his heels and nodded curtly.

"The brother," he said. "Master Finar told me just today that he hasn't heard from him. Not until he reaches *Bromi*, he said."

"You think the arsonist is Master Finar's brother?" Ahksell said. He twisted his head and stared up from the tiles.

Ibram gestured at the desk. "Who else would know where to go?" he asked. "If he's selling the things to all and sundry, then he knows just where to strike."

"So we return to Master Rennab ordering the fire?" Ahksell said.

"On that, I have no opinion until I'm given one," Ibram said, with a twitch of his eyes in Lady Azadiya's direction at her scoffing. "But I will say I don't think we'll be hearing a reply from Bromi any time soon."

"What did the letter to Captain Talsconis from Kenda Trading say again?" Lady Azadiya asked.

Ibram retrieved it from his belt pouch, and unfolded it. He sighed heavily. "The representative—signed by the scribe of the second under-manager, whatever that means—in question has worked for Kenda Trading for a good twenty years in the capacity of traveling—dah, hadah, dah—has no spot upon his character," he read out. "Further, he has served the company with distinction...something about his lengthy and accustomed route full of happy customers... Securing its interests *even* while escaping the destruction of Kandrilat with his merchandise unharmed."

"Berac tells me of scavengers in Pillared Circle," Ladyship said abruptly. She set down her piece of tile to allow Ahksell to complete the puzzle. "And of groups of soapmaker's apprentices being granted permission to sift through the rubble."

Ibram opened his mouth to answer as she moved past them to the open window, and frowned. He refolded the letter and tossed it to the desk. Ibram could see enough of her face to know she was scrutinizing something down below, whether that was one of the sect gardeners or a fly on the garden wall he couldn't say. He pulled on the hair at the nape of his neck, and rocked on his feet.

"What about the shards here, Ladyship?" he asked.

She tsked without looking away from the window.

"At the fire site, yes, they were gathering wood ash," Ibram answered her question. "I chased some off myself, before I was told they had permission from Ederetta Vo Kaln to collect from the debris."

She pursed her lips. "Nothing bigger? Berac informed me of the reward."

Ibram raised his eyebrows in Ahksell's direction; Ahksell shrugged.

"I don't think they could go so far in as I could, Ladyship," Ibram said and kept his sighs to himself. "There were none about when I did my own digging."

Lady Azadiya turned in a circle by the hanging glass bulb of mauve smoke, and then looked back out her nearest window to the kitchen garden. She flicked the latch holding the woven wire screens together open and closed with her thumb. The light outside was dim.

Someone knocked on the threshold of the open doorway as they entered. Ibram swung around, and fell back a step. Dihya stood in the room, just past the lintel. She was Ama's age, having been employed out of an Old Lityen farming family around the same time as Ama had been dragooned, and her short frizzy brown hair was shot through with grey. She raised her chin; Ibram brushed down the front of his gambeson reflexively.

She nodded swiftly. Dihya wore her usual thick wool tunic and heavy trousers, as old-fashioned as ever. She complained endlessly about the temperatures of life up the mountain and always dressed accordingly. Her pale orange tunic was buttoned up to its square neck, and then tied at the waist by the rope which held her belt and keys of office; her green trousers ended at her booted ankles. She bowed, hands on her stomach, but didn't wait for Lady Azadiya to wave her back up again. Instead, she held out a sheaf of papers bound in ribbon.

"Third Mentor Nieminen's compliments," Dihya said, and made no expression when the papers lifted from her hands and drifted across the room. "Also, Captain Talsconis is here to speak with you."

"Talsconis? Why? I sent Esti to tell him about the delay in my dinner." Ladyship unknotted the ribbon, and tossed it over her wrist. "Thank you," she said, as she began to read the top sheet.

Dihya interlaced her fingers in front of her and shook her head. "Says it's about the party, and that it cannot wait."

"Is he in good spirits?" Ahksell inquired.

"Very tired spirits, I believe, Attendant," she said.

"He's had enough time at his post to lose sleep over it," Ladyship said. She turned the first page over, and tossed it to Ibram. "Well, if he is here, then we must see him."

He looked at the paper, though he kept one ear on the conversation. It was a list of business transactions between the Vo Kalns and the sect. The exchanges began as simple foodstuffs, a certain percentage of the proceeds of the Vo Kalns' farms. All perfectly normal. Since the sect owned a great deal of the land within the imperial boundary, they charged rent accordingly.

Dihya was still speaking; Ibram made an attempt to listen as he read.

"Berac has arrived for your meeting," Dihya said, "but Doctor Berot has not."

"I can see him tomorrow," Ladyship said. "It grows late."

Ibram heard the rustle of paper, but nothing came into his own hands. He looked up to Lady Azadiya, but she was still reading. Ahksell held out his own hand and flexed his fingers; Ibram felt a tug on the paper and let it go.

"Should I show the captain up?" Dihya asked.

"Yes," Lady Azadiya said.

Another page drifted atop Ibram's hands. The amounts exchanged began to dwindle quite rapidly. The Vo Kalns at first had traded in goods and service—bills of sale to the kitchens and contracts for arms-for-hire in equal amounts to the rents, but then the family began to send no more than a token to the occasional festival presentation. Ibram frowned. They'd purchased land from the sect—their own farm —as of five years ago. That might explain the sudden withdrawal of business, but not the windfall of coin the preceded it. If the Vo Kalns had done well in the village, Ibram would have heard about it— Well, Ama would have heard about it, and then Ibram would have, second or third-hand. If the money didn't come locally, then how had it appeared in their coffers?

"What do you think Captain Talsconis wants?" Ahksell asked. A little time sitting down had done wonders for his constitution; he looked much better than he had before.

She raised her eyebrows in his direction. "To complain," she said.

The space between Ahksell's eyebrows crinkled. Dihya sighed heavily, but bowed and left quickly. Ladyship adjusted her grip on the Mentor Nieminen's message, and began to read. Ibram coughed, and then pointed to the opposite side of the room.

"Should I fetch a chair?" he asked.

"Hmm?" She tilted her face upwards. "Oh, no, thank you."

Ibram felt a rising pressure from the floor, as if water was climbing up his calves. He wavered and dropped his arm. Ahksell grinned and shook his head; Ibram mugged at him. So what if it didn't hurt him, running up against the ropes of reality was disconcerting for most folk. Ibram's hand hit some immaterial barrier and then fell through. The pressure rose past his knees and stabilized. Lady Azadiya sat down on the air. Her finished pages hung at her knee.

Captain Talsconis came up to the office by himself a few moments later. He'd worn his badge of office for the occasion and his clean blue tunic was edged in silver. He'd cut his hair after their encounter, and the barber had been careless; there was still a fading red line at the side of his neck just below the bristles of his brown hair. His battered face remained unimpressed with the sight of Lady Azadiya floating at her leisure, but his eyes widened ever so slightly.

Ibram cleared his throat, and bowed politely. "Captain," he said.

Talsconis grunted and waved his hand at him. Lady Azadiya looked up from her reading, and he bowed, with his hands on his stomach. She stood with a smile, held her arms outstretched at her sides, and curled her hands into delicate fists. The captain rose immediately.

"Should I close the door?" he asked, gruffly, already half-turned.

Lady Azadiya paused in gathering up her reading, and shook her head. "Oh there's no need," she said. "No one can hear us."

Talsconis turned back around with an irritable grumble. He frowned when Ibram helpfully pointed to the noise suppressing tiles above the door.

"Ahksell, do you still have those first few pages?" Ladyship asked.

Ahksell stood. "I do, Mentor," he said.

"Well, here," she said. She looked over another page, and briefly pursed her lips in thought, before sending it Ahksell's way. "Captain," she said, still reading, "my housekeeper tells me you had something you wished to discuss? If it's Ibram's habit of sending messages, I am afraid it was I who taught him how to use the Scribes' Bureau. The fault is mine entirely."

Captain Talsconis' body rocked with a brief chuckle, like a rusted chain turning over a new link. "He told you about that, did he?"

"How could he not?" Ladyship asked. Her braid fell over her shoulder, and she twitched it back. "It was almost the most exciting thing to happen to him all day."

Another noise that didn't know whether it was a chuckle or merely a soft complaint. Talsconis shook his head. "Another fire," he rumbled. "I don't like it."

"Neither did Kandrilat," Ladyship said, and made a point of looking the good captain directly in the eyes. "Interesting place, Hyperni province, don't you think?"

Captain Talsconis matched Lady Azadiya's stare, and nodded slowly. After a moment, Lady Azadiya looked back down at the papers in her hand, and Talsconis appeared to be weighing his next statement. Ibram frowned. He'd missed something; he didn't enjoy the feeling.

The moment—whatever it had contained—passed, and Lady Azadiya tilted the papers up and back, and then squinted.

"Ah," Ladyship exclaimed. She beamed with satisfaction at whatever point of interest she had found and declined to share. "I must send a gift to Mentor Nieminen."

"Why would that be?" Captain Talsconis asked before Ibram could.

"Lamy has her rough edges," Lady Azadiya said, "but she keeps a good record."

She flicked the page in front of her, and smiled tightly. "I shall have to visit tomorrow and thank her."

"Not that I'm unappreciative of the invitation to dine," Captain Talsconis said, in a clear attempt to change the subject, "but I wanted to know who invited me."

She tilted her head. "Oh?" she asked. "Ibram, call for Evren, he's been forgetting to announce me in messages again."

Ibram clasped his hands behind his back and nodded seriously. "Yes, Ladyship," he said. "I'll take the messengers through your full list of titles personally."

Ahksell shook his head as he held out his few pieces of paper. She handed him the rest of the stack, and he held the bundle in both hands. Captain Talsconis cleared his throat, and pressed his mouth flat.

"I mean," he said, with the grumblings of a bark in his voice. "Whether I am here at the personal request of Lady Azadiya, or the professional behest of Mentor Hobon. Because if it's the first part, I regret to inform her that I'm a man with many duties yet ahead of me."

Ibram assumed Captain Talsconis wished them all to forget that he was a man of many duties, who none the less had taken the trouble to complain in person about being distracted from them. It might have been the courteous thing to do. Imperial officers had very complex relationships with duty, after all.

"Is this not why we have subordinates, Captain?" Ladyship asked. "I know even now my agents are out and about, doubtless protecting Lityen from the scourge of sobriety. We can do no more than bless them for their diligence."

"And that is another thing," Talsconis said. "My warders have spotted no less than five of your arms-for-hire roaming the streets like a pack of mutts. What are they searching for?"

"Excitement, to be sure," she replied. "The sect has delivered me a full brace of agents who grow bored without regular exercise."

"An answer a noble might give," Talsconis said, with some exasperation, "but a Mentor will soon discover that so imprecise an response might attract my personal attention."

Which was, of course, exactly what Lady Azadiya had wanted, though Ibram wasn't certain of the reason just yet. He smirked down at his boots, and ignored Ahksell clearing his throat. He resolved not to ask until the warder had left.

"Am I thus to be torn asunder," she replied with a sigh. "Is there no friendship in duty, Captain?"

"There isn't when my dining companions are all sifting through the remains of their own pyres," he said. "If I've got to send Claes down for reinforcements, I'd like to know now before she gets too comfortable with your arms-for-hire."

"Agents, please," Ibram said, and pointed at himself, helpfully. "I'm thoroughly employed."

Talsconis cut him a look. "Turn out your belt pouches."

Ibram spread his hands, palms upward. He hadn't borrowed anything in days; items found in burnt out wreckage most assuredly didn't count. Lady Azadiya snorted in amusement, which sent a ripple of surprise through Captain Talsconis. He lowered his eyebrows and stared at her, swiftly glowering as if his reputation depended upon it.

"Well, Mentor?" Talsconis asked.

"And so it is decided for me," she said. She waved her hand at him, and light glimmered on her rings. "Such is the way of all imperial favor."

Ibram flicked his gaze between Ladyship and Ahksell and then back again. It didn't seem likely that she would show her hand to the warders until it came time for them to cart off the guilty to their holding pens. And she had read something in Mentor Nieminen's letter that had pleased her. He could just about see the pages on the desk from his position.

Ibram tapped his boot against the floorboards, grimaced at the noise, and pressed his heel down hard. He needed to speak with Master Finar again, especially now. If they could just separate Finar and Rennab, then they could find out exactly how long Finar's brother had been in the village. After that, Ibram could join the hunt down in Lityen, and secure the man for trial. Easy as blinking.

"You are here for the same reason as my other guests—well, you would have been had we not needed to postpone," she said, and resettled her glass cloth overdress and the complicated necklace that covered her collarbones. "I like you better than the captain of the Cohort of Vigilance."

He laughed at that, a splintery note of surprise that ended almost as soon as it escaped his mouth. "Snubbed you, did she?" he asked. "She does that."

"Regrettably indisposed for ten years and counting," Lady Azadiya said, and touched her thumb to the mongoose on her signet ring. "Our dear Third Mentor tells me she has her good points, however."

Talsconis nodded, and pursed his lips. "And that is all?"

Ladyship waggled her hand in the air. "Nothing too strenuous, to be sure," she said. "A good meal, intriguing company..." She paused and looked at him from the corner of her eye. "Perhaps a small amount of leniency in any jurisdictional matters that might reveal themselves at the end of the night?"

Ibram frowned. So far, they hadn't uncovered anything but local matters. Business like that was the province of the sect, not the imperial cohorts. They had more than enough agents involved already.

Captain Talsconis rocked up and then down on his boot heels. He smirked and crossed his arms over his chest. "Now it comes out," he said.

"Captain," she said, "you know as well as I do that if my agents—that is to say, those assigned to my division—uncover anything criminal, I am bound by law to turn those criminals over to your cells and the mercy of the Vissilian court."

"You could hold a man on the ceiling as easily as I could throw him in a cell," Talsconis retorted.

"Your faith in my abilities is touching," Ladyship said. "But at present, unworkable. Is it so strange, that I would want to couple my duty as Fourth Mentor with the natural conclusion of sending him off with you?"

"And to that," he said, with an accompanying jab of his finger. "You don't have to drag me up and down that blasted relay system of yours. One of these days I'm going to pitch right off the mountain!"

On that score, Ibram was forced to agree. The entire blasted process of perpetual wheels and relays gave him nerves. Of course, nothing unnatural might exist and thus, they were perfectly convenient amenities—just as the sewers that dealt with waste and the municipal fountains that watered the villages—but Yilka's megrims, what a way to travel.

Lady Azadiya scoffed. Ahksell leaned back in his chair, and Ibram settled on his heels. They were off again, and it would be quite some time before Captain Talsconis was placated, and they were allowed to leave.

❧   14   ❧

The next morning dawned with a crack of thunder and a dense drizzle of rain that painted Lityen in nothing but grey clouds and mud. Ibram woke with a fuzzy head, and a crick in the neck. The kitchen garden was a swamp by the time he came down to breakfast, and the cold seeped up through the floorboards in a cloud of mist.

Ibram paused with both hands on the threshold to the family dining room. They were all there, Father and Ama, Katka and the apprentices. Ahksell raised his hand in greeting.

Ibram frowned. Ahksell nodded. He pointed down the table to Ibram's spot, where a cup of shay gently steamed.

"Good morning, dear," Ama said, sounding entirely too amused.

Ibram cleared his throat and rubbed the back of his neck. He nodded. The shay did look good.

"Have to sit down to drink it," Father said.

Father was wise. Ibram went to his chair, and sat down. He brought the shay cup close to him, and breathed in deeply. He took a sip, and it was perfect, warm and smoky, soothingly bitter and faintly spicy. He sat back in his chair with a sigh.

The apprentices giggled to each other. Ibram ignored them; the shay was calling. He tipped the cup back and swallowed half its contents. His legs splayed out underneath the table.

"Feeling any better?" Katka asked.

Ibram clutched his cup to his chest, and rolled his head on his shoulders. "I will," he muttered. "Given an end to all this mess."

Ama cleared her throat. "Nothing unusual in that feeling," she said. She dug her spoon into her bowl of quash. "A good meal and you'll be on your way."

Ibram drank the rest of his shay, and poured himself another one from the pot immediately. He set both pot and cup down, and then eyed the cauldron of quash in front of him. His stomach grumbled. He pressed his hand over his belly and grimaced.

Ahksell laughed at him from the other end of the table. Ibram sniffed and turned his head to squint at him.

"What are you doing here?" he asked. "Did they forget to feed you up the living mountain?"

Ahksell grinned, and leaned on his elbow. His bowl of quash was supplemented by a healthy-sized glass apple and a hunk of pale yellow cheese.

"I thought an early morning might help in our search," he said.

Ibram shrugged, and then groaned as he leaned forward to spoon quash into his bowl. It might help, at that. Certainly, they couldn't do worse.

"Search for who?" Katka asked. "The person who's been setting all these fires?"

"How do you know anyone's been setting fires?" Ibram demanded.

Katka blinked innocently at him. "Because I never thought fires set themselves?"

Ibram dragged the shay pot over to his plate, and kept it there, close at hand. He had a feeling he'd need the fortification.

☙❧

There was something in the Writ of The Advisor about adversity they read out on the Empress' birthday. Something about solace and cheer in dark places. Ibram reflected on that vague couplet while he and

Ahksell hopped from terrace to porch and in between stanchions to keep dry like the rest of the poor fools whose business kept them out and about in the rain.

"Tell me there's news that brought you down the living mountain," Ibram grumbled as he tugged his sodden cloak's hood back over his head.

Ahksell laughed as he sighed. "I wish I could," he said, and splashed through a dip in the street.

Ibram jumped the distressed pond Ahksell had created. "Then where are we going?"

"Master Comoros has set up in The Steady Spout to look for the man who attacked Nesrine," Ahksell said. "Or, that's what Mentor Hobon told me. I thought we might go and see if there's any way we can help in the search."

"You mean by replacing one drenched agent for one merely soaked," Ibram said.

At least it was an old part of Lityen they were aiming for. Ibram shook rain drops from his cloak, and wrapped it around himself again. The spitting wyvern drain spouts placed at the corners of the stable yard they passed poured down into the barrels placed outside in the street, already more than half full.

"Well, I won't say it hadn't crossed my mind!" Ahksell called over his back.

Ibram swung wide around the corner of the side street near Marshall's Rest, and spied their destination. The Steady Spout was a shayshop equidistant from Pillared Circle and The Crooked Tent, built ramshackle between two older and more sturdy buildings. It made sense for Amota Berac to govern the search from there.

"Did you see whatever it was Mentor Nieminen sent Lady Azadiya last night?" Ibram asked under his breath.

Ahksell shook his head. "No time," he whispered back. "No clue what bit she was looking at, anyways."

Ibram sighed, but nodded. No doubt she would let them know in good time. It didn't make him feel any better about not knowing, to be sure.

"What about the parts you did read?" he asked.

"Looked like more information on the Vo Kaln cousins," Ahksell said, and then straightened his back.

Ibram shut his own mouth and kept pace behind him. He could see straight inside as they arrived at their destination. The window shutters had been flung wide and the door cocked open. All the builders and carpenters' apprentices who claimed The Steady Spout for their daily meal had cleared out, leaving only Amota Berac and Amita Dervla at the trestle table, and a small gang of older agents lining the right hand wall to keep the owners attentive.

Ahksell entered the shayshop first, and then stepped to the side to admit Ibram. They both took off their cloaks and shook them in the corner of the room. A chair scraped further inside. Ibram looked up at the sound of footsteps.

"Good morning, good day!" caroled the owner, a plump little man with a large red mustache and very little hair anywhere else. "Attendant, Master Alchemist, you do me a great honor."

He bowed deeply, barely wrinkling the stiff dun apron that covered him from neck to ankles, and Ahksell hunched his broad shoulders and waved him back up almost immediately. He cleared his throat several times, and shifted his eyes in Ibram's direction. Ibram draped his cloak over his arm, and then crossed both arms over his chest. He smiled and nodded.

"No, yes, good morning to you as well," Ahksell said. "Can I —Ibram—"

"Oh, yes, you are here for your party," the owner said, and clasped his hands together. He beamed. "It's been quite the morning, I tell you, quite the time. I should think we're eager to help, of course. Anything for the Sect of Seven Fires."

"Yes, of course," Ahksell said, nodding along. "That's wonderful, but we should perhaps—"

"A cup of shay!" The owner exclaimed and patted the air in front of Ahksell's chest. "Yes, for you and for your man. And a good bite to start you on your day. Come this way, if you will."

The owner burbled off, and Ahksell trailed after, tossing Ibram his cloak. The wet wool smacked him in the face. He flinched, and just managed to catch it before the cloak hit the rush-covered floor. Ibram looked up towards the counter at the back of the shop. Huge round loaves hung from the rafters behind the counter. A large boiling samovar bubbled away next to a stack of wooden cups, and an enormous, partially destroyed, round of bread half covered by a towel near a crock of butter with a knife stuck in it.

Amota Berac raised his arm without shifting his attention from whatever he was studying with Amita Dervla. Not that it was possible to avoid their table, since it was the only one in the room. Tono and Juanma lifted their cups in Ibram's direction, and cousin Japhet clapped him on the back as he passed. He smiled and shifted his bundle of sodden cloaks out of their path.

"What brings you and young Solari out here?" Amota Berac asked.

Ibram looked over his shoulder. He and Dervla were consulting a map of the village, drawn in charcoal on the trestle table itself. Amita Dervla's cup was standing in the middle of the Cohort of Peace. She lifted it and drank, while turning in their direction on the trestle table bench.

"Good morning," Ibram said, and she nodded back.

Ahksell had taken over the head of the trestle table, where there was just enough room to sit near Amota Berac and legroom for his tree stumps to sprawl in. Ibram stood waiting while the water from the cloaks seeped into his gambeson.

Amita Derval set down her shay cup. "Put them on the hooks," she said, and pointed behind him to the wall.

Ibram turned. "Ah."

He hung the cloaks, and returned, sitting down next to his aunt. He rested both elbows on the table, and sighed. The owner bustled back down to the table, setting thick wooden cups of shay down nearest Ahksell, as well as a large wrapped bundle, which he revealed to be freshly sawn planks of bread slathered with glistening yellow butter. He set two ridged spoons—which did not seem as if they got much use—on the table, and sat back. He beamed at them all, mustache bristling with good humor.

"Yes, yes, a healthy start," he said as he went away back behind his counter.

"No wonder this place is so popular," Ibram muttered.

"Is there something in particular you wanted?" Amita Dervla asked, distantly amused. She had a way about her that seemed like she was only waiting for strangers to catch on to the joke, but Ibram had never seen her share.

"Merely to see how the search was going," Ibram said. "I have seen the man in question, after all."

"Has there been any progress, Mistress Prohaska?" Ahksell asked.

Amita Dervla shook her head. "I think we might have informed Lady Azadiya first, young Solari, rather than waste time marking off points on a badly drawn map."

Ahksell cleared his throat, and sipped his shay. "Yes, Mistress," he said, "Of course you would."

Ibram winced. If there was one thing Ahksell and Ibram agreed upon, it was the singular delight of working amongst folk who aided and abetted them when they were too small to refuse the honor. Ibram never felt so young. Amota Berac clapped Ahksell on the shoulder. Amita Dervla grabbed a steaming cup by the lip and set it down in front of Ibram. He sniffed it, and then eyed the bread Ahksell was towing closer to himself. Amota Berac's arm broke his line of sight; he tapped Pillared Circle on the makeshift map.

"Foolish to think he'd come back," Amita Dervla said, and sighed. "We've had Dobrila and Corbus watching that caffa Finar owns all night."

"He did return several times before," Amota Berac reminded her.

"Yes, but that was before the mess at The Crooked Tent," she retorted.

"There's too many places he could go to ground," Berac said. "We're a village built for travelers, more's the pity."

"Is there any thought that he might try joining a caravan and heading west?" Ahksell asked. He excised a small piece of bread from the wedge in front of him with his spoon, and popped the morsel into his mouth.

Amita Dervla shook her head. "We have Nesrine at the first gate up the mountain road. If she spots him, it's all over."

"Besides, Master Finar said his brother Achard doesn't have

connections up there," Ibram said. "If he's running, then I would say he'd go for his familiar trade routes."

"Why do you say that?" Amota Berac asked. "He's more likely to be recognized, no matter what professional contacts he has."

"Yes, but he's not a professional fugitive, is he?" Ibram asked. He yawned unwillingly. "I had a lot of time to think last night. About what I might do if I needed to escape a hive I had kicked over, and what this man might do now, and he hasn't behaved properly at all."

"Yes," Ahksell said, with a twist to the corner of his mouth. "He's been a very rude arsonist."

Ibram did not roll his eyes, but he made note of that comment for a later moment. "I mean, he's not used to this. He wanders around Lityen touring the scene of his crime for days, and then kills his accomplice, and never once leaves? He should have set his fire and gone about his business. Why hasn't he? What's keeping him here?"

Ahksell floated the second chunk of bread and butter across the table to him; Ibram plucked it from the air and bit down on the end most thickly spread with butter. He smiled, chewing. Crumbs fell to the table. Amita Dervla flicked him on the temple.

"Manners," she said.

Ibram swallowed hastily, and licked butter from his lips. "I am only saying that his behavior means something."

"He could be worried for his brother," Amota Berac said.

"If he was worried about his family, then why would he light their home on fire?" Dervla asked, and scratched her fingers through her light brown hair.

"For the money," Ahksell said, and looked briefly ill. "Or perhaps he didn't care about them."

"If it was for money, it would make some sense." Ibram mused, "After all, none of the family was at home. Only Erno Neilos and Shokan Dughlat were there."

He looked down at the map his amitai had drawn across the worn trestle table. It wasn't, perhaps, the most accurate measurement of distance, but it would do. Amota Berac was right, there were far too many boltholes in the village. Usually, Ibram enjoyed that fact, but now he wished for roads as straight as a temple's pillar and closed doors by the bushel.

"What about the little hut Dughlat lives in?" Ibram asked, and reached over to point his bread at the smudged Crofters' Guildhouse. "Could he be holed up there?"

Amita Dervla shook her head. "We moved Dughlat out, and installed Zhyrgal in his place."

Ibra winced and covered it by taking another bite of bread. "When did he get back?" he asked, and then reconsidered the question. "He actually agreed to go sleep in that shack?"

"He made do," Amota Berac said. "He's been wanting a quiet place to recite his poetry any road."

Ibram sucked his teeth clean, and licked his lips. Ahksell returned to spooning up bites of bread with his ridged spoon, painfully correct in all his table manners as usual. His dark fingers scratched the wooden handle, and then he lay the spoon down.

"Why can't we simply ask Master Finar where his brother might be hiding?" Ahksell asked. "Surely, that would be the quickest way forward."

"It would be quick," Amita Dervla said, "but not necessarily the easiest path forward. It hasn't been completely confirmed that the man who attacked Nesrine is Master Finar's brother—that's only our assumption based on the tiles found in his room. It's entirely possible the men are unconnected."

"Not a great family resemblance, to be sure," Amota Berac said.

"I don't look like Katka," Ibram pointed out.

Ahksell made a considering noise. "Yes, I suppose," he said, and slowly picked up his spoon again. "But why not simply show Master Finar the picture and have him confirm it? Or deny it?"

"Better to ask for a reference after we have the man in hand," Ibram said. "That way Master Finar has no chance of lying to us and then signaling his brother somehow that he's been identified and sought after."

"Well, he must know he's sought after by now," Amota Berac remarked. He stretched his thick arms over his head and then dropped his arms with a sigh. "Ladyship wants us to watch Masters Rennab and

Finar for the time being, so that the normal course of their day is unencumbered—it might lull our man into approaching."

"I see," Ahksell said, though Ibram couldn't say he sounded happy about it. "But how else can we find him?"

Ibram crammed another fourth of bread and butter into his mouth, and washed it down with shay, which had cooled sufficiently to be drunk. He swallowed, and watched Amota Berac and Amita Dervla consider the map again. The agents lining the back wall spoke wearily amongst themselves. He heard Japhet complaining about a hole in his boot, and tilted his head back. The roof beams were old, but clean, no old spider webs dangling dust in The Steady Spout, but the rain seemed to hit the roof just as fiercely as it had when they had entered the shop. He hoped the wood slat roof tiles he'd spied when they walked in—

Ibram sat forward. "The tiles," he said.

"And then if we station Japhet here—What, Ibram?" Amita Derval asked.

"The tiles!" Ibram said again, and leaned towards the group. "That's why he—let us call him Achard—that is why Achard Finar chose The Crooked Tent!"

Ahksell's eyes widened. He pointed his spoon at Ibram. "They had fire suppression tiles from the Sect of the Iron Hand, too! He must have sold them to Master Shevault—"

"No," Ibram spoke over him. "The previous owner—Master Shevault complained to me about the purchase, so *she* was the one who bought from Achard Finar—"

"Because he constructed an elaborate fiery escape that he knew would stop anyone from following him, if he was discovered!" Ahksell's voice rose triumphantly. He grabbed up his shay and took a victory drink.

Ibram grinned. The sodden atmosphere in shayshop felt a little lighter. Even Japhet's mournful voice was but a murmur.

"So he doesn't have to return to his brother, he might have gone to ground in an establishment where he's sold tiles before," Amota Berac said. "Just as he did previously."

"But can we rely on finding another draughtshop under new ownership just on the off chance Achard Finar can plan a suitable exit *and* lodge under an assumed name?" Amita Dervla asked. "It seems unlikely."

"But there's a chance," Ahksell said, and hunched forward, ducking his head. He smiled at her, teeth flashing. "I am not here in any official capacity of course, but if Ibram is tasked with looking into where those tiles might be sold and I am merely in the area as a helpful... helper, then perhaps it might be worth looking into?"

Ibram tugged on the hair at the base of his neck, and drummed his toes on the floor. It did seem like a good idea, an idea for action rather than waiting about, as good as the shay was. Amita Dervla cocked an eye at Amota Berac, who pursed his lips and cocked his eye right back. She waggled her head left and right slightly. Amota Berac nodded, also very slightly.

"An excellent suggestion," Amota Berac said finally. "Or at least a matter worth looking into."

He raised both hands as they both of them scrambled up from the trestle table. Ibram stuffed the last of his bread in his mouth, and then snatched up Ahksell's wedge before the fool left it in the name of good manners. He chewed furiously, backing away from the table.

"Ibram says thank you to you both," Ahksell said as he skirted around the side of the table. "And I do as well. We will report back with our findings!"

"We will!" Ibram said around his mouthful.

Ahksell grimaced. "Oh, please just keep chewing," he muttered as he grabbed up both their cloaks and headed for the door.

❦

An obstacle became apparent, almost as soon as they had left The Steady Spout, and certainly by the time Ibram and Ahksell had finished their second breakfast. To wit, they had no way of knowing to whom Achard Finar had sold tiles from the Sect of the Iron Hand, or when he had done so, if the blasted place had indeed changed owners. Not without asking everyone in Lityen, Old Lityen, South Lityen, Lityen Hill, or even Lityen-By-The-Blue-Hole, which Ibram maintained would be a lovely place to go to ground, even if you didn't actually need to.

Showing the man's portrait indiscriminately hadn't done any good, especially since the other agents had already been doing that for hours. If it had been working, they all would have been waving Nesrine's artwork around less. Ibram ducked his head out of the awning they currently sheltered under, and eyed the dark grey sky dubiously. Rain splashed against his forehead and rolled down the bridge of his nose. He leaned back where it was dry, and shook his head.

"Knock it off," Ahksell said, "You're getting me all wet."

Ibram shook out his hair once more for good measure, and then crossed his arms underneath his cloak. The rain splattered down into the puddle that had once been the street, lapping almost overtop of the stone flood blocks that were supposed to keep folks' boots dry crossing between buildings. He leaned back against the wall, and curved his head in Ahksell's direction.

"We could ask his brother," Ibram said.

Ahksell, hunched beneath the greying soffits of the awning, grimaced and shook his head. "Without alerting him to our interest? Besides, it's still only a conjecture."

"A pretty safe one, if you ask me," Ibram said.

"Lots of folk might have those tiles," Ahksell said. "We saw no evidence of seller's materials."

"That was a sample bag," Ibram said, "or I'll eat my right boot."

"When we found it, you thought it was a pact bag."

"Just because I admit when I am wrong, doesn't mean I'm not more often correct!"

Ahksell scoffed and considered the rain for a long moment. He sighed through his nostrils. "And Mentor doesn't wish Master *Albin* Finar to know of our suspicions about Master *Achard?*"

Ibram nodded. "She does not."

"Well then..." Ahksell's arms flapped at his sides. He blew out his breath. "I—We should cross the street. Let's go back to Pillared Circle, regardless."

"What for?" Ibram asked.

Ahksell stood away from the wall, and turned left, making for the break in the railing where they might jump across the flood stones. Ibram sighed, but followed.

"Do we know anyone else who might have these tiles?" Ahksell turned the hood of his clock up and over his head; Ibram did the same, not that it mattered much. "Maybe The Isconian's Head?"

Ahksell stepped across the little river developing between the walkway and the road, and onto the first stone. Ibram jumped after him, and then paused on the middle stone for a moment. Cold rain and wet clothes, and the smell of damp wool and fresh mud rising up all around him. Ibram was owed a pint of cider for this, mulled with fruit.

"Not Dubidat," Ibram said, with a quick shake of his head. "I saw none when we searched her evening courtyard. Besides, I don't think they got along well enough."

"And I thought a merchant might dare anything," Ahksell said.

He hopped off the last flood stone and onto the walkway, and then paused while Ibram caught up. Ibram pointed right, toward the next intersection of alleys, and Ahksell nodded.

"I wouldn't try anything with Mistress Dubidat, and most especially with that husband of hers," Ibram said, as he dodged a little girl with her brother, running past with a sloshing bucket held between them.

"What's wrong with Master Guilhem?" Ahksell asked.

Ibram wrinkled his nose. "He's too polite."

Ahksell laughed. "How is that a bad thing?"

"I don't like it when folks are too nice to me," Ibram said. "Speaks to a guilty conscience."

"Well, you would know."

The rain had forced everyone in doors. Ibram raised his hand to his shoulder and flicked his thumb at Ahksell's back. Ahksell bowed his head as they crossed from the one porch to its neighbor via the alley.

"I still think..." Ibram sneezed, barely managing to turn his head in time.

"What about the three who sold food next door?" Ahksell asked.

"Yes, I thought about them, too. You said they all had tiles from our sect, correct?"

Ibram cleared his throat. "That's what they told me," he said. "Nothing's been recovered from their ruins to make them liars."

"At least Mistress Vo Kaln's not about to let her properties use substandard goods," Ahksell said. "Oh, wait, the apothecary—ah, Mistress Corri. Does she use our tiles?"

Ibram blinked. "Do you know, I forgot about her?"

Ahksell turned around; Ibram stumbled to a halt. "I thought you spoke to her?" Ahksell asked.

"I did!" Ibram pulled down his hood, and ruffled the back of his head. "Not that she said much. She's wounded, you know. People in pain are not so chatty as you might think."

"So there's been no interview at all?"

"I spoke with her once! Doctor Berot has spent the most time with her," Ibram said. "He rented the space for the folk who were injured putting out the fire, if you'll recall."

Ahksell swallowed, and nodded. "Well, maybe Achard Finar tried to sell to her?"

Ibram tilted his head. Ahksell opened his mouth, and Ibram held up one finger. The rain sputtered above them; the wind blew it sideways for a discomfiting moment, and then settled.

"She...no, give me a moment," Ibram muttered.

"Come along," Ahksell said, and began towing Ibram down the walkway. "Think as you go!"

❦

The rain wore itself out to a frizzling mist by the time they'd walked to Pillared Circle, leaving behind a chill and an inch of standing water in its wake. Ibram scraped mud from his boots off the side of the municipal fountain, and wrinkled his nose. Wet wool and village dirt were never a pleasant perfume, and Ibram felt liberally doused in the odor by now. Next to him, Ahksell cleaned his own footwear and popped his back as he stretched upwards.

Ibram huffed and turned away from him to look about the open area. It was clear of traffic for once. Most of the work crews had abandoned the ruined buildings, but a few brave souls were beginning to venture forth from the surrounding shops.

"Since Mistress Corri inherited her apothecary and home," Ibram said, "it stands to reason that of the six members of the fire alliance, she and Master Rennab were bound to gain the most profit."

"Are you certain of that?" Ahksell asked.

Ibram rolled his head, and glared briefly over his shoulder. "Would you stop?" he asked. "I remembered the conversation with Doctor Berot. *Our* conversation with Doctor Berot!"

Ahksell spread his hands. "I'm only saying..."

"Oh, you're only saying," Ibram muttered.

"Maybe we should both be taking tutelage under your uncle Evren for our memories," Ahksell said.

Ibram sneezed, and then snorted. Ahksell was far too amused for someone so incredibly wet. Ibram sniffed, and then scrubbed his hand though his hair; he winced at the tangles from his cloak hood.

"Anyway, you said you remembered that Doctor Berot—"

"Told us that the reason the apothecary had survived was that she had Afsoun's fire suppression tiles on her building, yes," Ibram said with a nod. "Which means Mistress Corri will, one, not gain substantially from the event, and two, that she did not purchase tiles from Achard Finar."

"But she might have refused him," Ahksell said. "What about the others?"

"They have nothing to do with the construction of their dwellings," Ibram said. "They don't control who installs what safety measures to the buildings themselves."

He began walking across the circle towards the apothecary. Already, he could see a few Attendants circling the doorway. Ahksell's footsteps resounded after him.

"And they never mentioned the brother?" Ahksell asked.

Ibram dropped back so that Ahksell walked in front of him. Ahksell grimaced, and slowed to walk beside instead. Ibram lagged back, and Ahksell pinched his elbow. Ibram walked alongside him.

"If they did recognize him," Ibram said, "they lied when shown the picture. And Amota Berac can be very intimidating, when he needs to be."

Ahksell hmphed. "So, really, the only person gaining substantially is Master Rennab, and if we can confirm—"

"Well, no," Ibram said as a late-blooming thought unfurled in the front of his mind. "That would be Mistress Vo Kaln, wouldn't it?"

Ahksell paused. "What do you mean?"

"She owns four buildings caught in the fire, whereas Rennab only has the one."

"But she won't collect any greater measure of insurance," Ahksell said. "Because only Mistress Dubidat lived outside the building. The rest dwelled within."

Ibram nodded slowly. He eyed the apothecary, whose front porch was festooned with expensive hanging glass bottles full of colored liquids in variegated forms. The building itself was fairly old, and even a little shabby, but the baubles in front enticed customers to enter, regardless.

"Ladyship has been requesting reports upon reports about the Vo Kalns," Ibram said, and then tugged on the hair at his nape. "All about the family's structure, and their legal rights, and the like."

"Yes," Ahksell said. "Third Mentor Nieminen has been very helpful —she always is with the local noble families."

Ibram clicked his tongue, and then turned to Ahksell, and raised his hand. Ahksell stopped walking obligingly.

"I think we should go in there," Ibram said, and pointed at the apothecary. "And ask about Master Finar—and show her the picture again, regardless of whether or not she's seen it before—but then I believe we should go back up the living mountain."

"Back to Yseult?" Ahksell asked. "Why?"

"I think we should ask Ladyship to see the report she read," Ibram said. "The one she did not have time to tell us about."

Ibram took a deep breath, and let it out again. He didn't think the smell of smoke would ever leave Pillared Circle completely. The stench had worked its way into the buildings themselves, even to the land beneath. The apothecary could repair its roof, but Mistress Corri's burns would scar. Another thought took shape next to the first, he might have called it the first thought's cousin. He placed both blooms in a kitchen garden in his mind's manor to let them grow.

⚜

The training fields were awash—literally—by the time they arrived at Ladyship's tower. The ditches dug alongside the split rail fencing were beginning to overflow their banks. They hurried past a platoon of servants unclogging the drainage grates that fed the reservoirs with long-handled rakes and shovels, and ducked inside the tower.

"I think Dihya's going to get her wish," Ibram said as they pushed through the unnaturally light stone doors.

"What wish?" Ahksell asked.

The damp heat enclosing the tower was stifling after the brisk mountain air. Owing to the weather, the common room in the center of the tower was choked with agents, servants, and alchemists, all vying for space on the low couches and short tables laid out near the central fountain. Sailing lights had been lit, moored to the beams holding up the balconies above, though the transparent tiles and cunningly placed mirrors were still reflecting the pale storming light from outside.

Ibram laughed. "Ladyship's dinner will have to be moved inside."

"Nonsense," Dihya said behind him

Ibram jumped, and slid into Ahksell's left side. Ahksell snorted, and pushed him off. Ibram wheeled about, and bowed shortly.

"Dihya!" he exclaimed. "Exactly the housekeeper I wished to see."

"Indeed," Dihya said, with a raised eyebrow.

She gestured behind herself, and a small boy stepped forward, holding out his arms. Ibram whipped his cloak from his shoulders immediately, and tossed it to the servant. The boy caught his wet cloak, and then Ahksell's, and scurried off with them. Ibram stood with his arms away from his body, damp to the skin.

"Is Mentor in her office?" Ahksell asked.

"She is not, Attendant Solari," Dihya said.

"Training?" Ahksell asked. He drew his hand over and down his scalp and then returned upwards and rubbed his face.

Ladyship cordially detested the rain, and occasionally enjoyed reminding herself of that fact by going out and conducting training sessions for the older attendants in bad weather. But since the training fields had become a coastline, Ibram had expected to find her upstairs wrapped in one of her silk robes, formulating the next portion of her treatise on enigmatic physiognomy in unreal xanthosis.

"Mentor Hobon is in the composing laboratory," Dihya said. She smiled thinly. "And I am informed that the next agent who returns from the village is to report to her immediately."

Ibram cleared his throat. "Which would be me?" he asked, and pointed at himself.

"Indeed so," Dihya said, and clasped her hands in front of her. "Off with you. Attendant, if you'll give me your gambeson, I'll see about a change of clothing for you."

She hustled Ahksell away, despite his attempted protests. Ibram considered his own gambeson, sagging to the left from all the water, and sighed.

"Not at all, Mistress, quite comfortable," he muttered as ran his finger underneath his collar and undid the top button.

He walked up the wide staircase on the right to the second floor and then three doors down to the composing laboratory. Ibram ducked his head through the doorway and bowed. Lady Azadiya noticed him, and waved him further inside.

The window shutters of the laboratory were flung open. Ladyship and Attendant E'garezzo stood behind a short, but wide, working table with a sliding scale made of brass and strung with polished glass pebbles between them. Attendant E'garezzo lifted a container full of a brilliantly white liquid—from the stench, something corrosive—and poured a thin stream onto a small wire box placed in a dark wooden bowl. The box began to smoke; the pebbles turned orange and clacked apart.

Ibram backed up a half-step, and clasped his hands behind his back. "I bring news, Ladyship," he called out.

Ladyship tsked, and eyed the smoke with an expression of personal affront. "I don't want news," she said. "I want Master Finar. Go and bring him here."

"That's fortunate, to be sure," Ibram said, while attempting to breathe less, "because I don't truthfully have any." He coughed. "Which might make capturing him rather difficult?"

That brought her attention off the now fully corroded wire box and the vibrating scale. She moved around the side of the worktable, and came to stand by the door. Ibram took the opportunity to step back towards less foul air.

"What do you mean?" she asked. "Surely, he's at his place of business this time of day. It's only raining."

"His place—do you mean Master Albin Finar?" Ibram asked. "Runs the caffa? I thought we were to leave him alone in case his brother attempts to contact him."

Ladyship shrugged with her hands. "Berac has fine ideas. He is perfectly capable of finding the brother on his own. I, however, require more information, and for that, I require Master Albin Finar."

"Yes, Ladyship," Ibram said. He put one foot out the door, paused, and then turned back. "I was going to ask to read the report Mentor Nieminen sent you?"

"Hm?" Ladyship glanced up from her study of the brass scale. "Oh, no need for that. When Albin Finar becomes cooperative, it will be explanation enough."

✿   15   ✿

Ibram tucked his hair behind his ears, and sighed. He wriggled his shoulders beneath his borrowed gambeson. It was too big, one of the older one's directly from the sect's stores, but at least it was dry. Even now, his boots squelched when he walked.

"Is Master Finar prepared?" Lady Azadiya asked.

Ibram nodded. "Yes, Ladyship," he said. "Or at least, he's willing."

"Half of a whole, better than none," she answered.

"I just... Is this truly the only way forward, Mentor?" Ahksell asked. He was tucked into one of the more comfortable chairs in Ladyship's office, reading the last page of Mentor Nieminen's report.

"No," Ladyship said. "But it seems the quickest resolution, and the one far less likely to result in further damage."

Lady Azadiya settled her gauzy glass cloth robe over her green silk dress and buttoned the three shimmering buttons that held the robe closed at her waist. She readjusted her matching fingerless mitts, and turned from the window overlooking her kitchen garden as Dihya entered her office.

"Are they all assembled?" she asked.

"They are indeed," Dihya said with some heaviness in her voice. She clasped her hands before her.

"In what order?" Ladyship asked.

She thought for a moment. "Sarrha arrived first—I was in the back, arranging for Uncas to bring out the mouflon pie, but Mila tells me she came with Masters Rennab and Finar. I believe she showed them the observatory on the Outer Bank. They sent their servant Master Dughlat to the kitchens."

"In good spirits?" Ahksell inquired.

"Not very, Attendant," she said. "But he's equal to the moment. He's got a plate of our dinner coming his way now, though, and has got his breath back."

"Settle him between the gardeners," Ladyship said. "They're tall this season. I don't want him to feel like he might run off if he takes it into his head."

Ibram bounced on his feet. Now that the plan was in place, he would rather it were already in play. Achard Finar was at large, after all, and he was the unfortunate fulcrum of the entire affair. They could only take the dinner so far, and gain so much insight into the guilty party without him.

Dihya was still speaking; Ibram made an attempt to listen. "Then came Captain Talsconis, and his Warder Claes," Dihya said. "As instructed, I gave him his ale and set him near the fountain in the common room. He expressed a wish to see you in private before eating."

"Goodness," Ladyship murmured.

Ibram heard the rustle of paper. Ahksell had turned the final page, and shook his head. He raised both eyes to Ibram; Ibram nodded back. It was the sort of mess a man might see on a traveling player's stage. Ibram was, of course, not a betting man, but he thought perhaps Lady Azadiya was taking the opportunity of working her frustration out with this little gambit.

"Philendra Dubidat arrived with her husband," Dihya said. "Mistress Vo Kaln has just now made her appearance."

"Alone?" Ladyship asked.

"Quite so," Dihya said.

"Where did you stash them?" Lady Azadiya asked.

"In the common room below," Dihya said. "We set out the wine as requested. They've just about run out of things to say to each other."

"Anything of interest?" Ibram asked.

"Nothing like it," Dihya said. She smoothed her hand down the line of embroidered buttons holding her blouse closed on the side. She, at least, had a good option to dress for dinner. "Captain Talsconis' mere presence is enough to keep them polite as a burial ground."

"Tell Mila to round them up and send them down the hill for dinner," Ladyship said. She patted the twisted gold strands of her necklace and untangled the chalcedony pendant. "Keep Sarrha with them, and make sure my helpful staff have their ears open for enlightenment." She smiled. "And quietly inform Captain Talsconis he may join me in my office at his earliest convenience."

"Why quietly?" Ahksell asked.

She raised her eyebrows in his direction. "Ahk-la," she said. "I want my guests to know the dear captain has my full attention as a good subject of the empire. What better way for them to find out than by attempting to be discreet at an intimate dinner?"

Lady Azadiya enjoyed a well-planned entrance. Ibram doubted anyone in their little party was unaware of the statement she made, strolling down to the table with Captain Talsconis at her side. The others, of course, had been forced to mill about on the training field, getting their shoes and hems wet on the torn grass. The rain might have ceased by midday, but its effects lingered. By the looks on some of their faces, they were feeling a chill.

The servants had arranged an open canopy in the nearest training field, held in place with five long torches. When Ladyship stepped beneath the canvas, golden threads shown in her robe, glittering in the warm light of the sailing lamps. Ahksell and Ibram trailed in upon Ladyship reaching her seat at the head of the table, and then separated on opposite sides of the table. Captain Talsconis stumped his way over to a seat at Ladyship's right; no one disputed the claim.

Amota Berac was not to be found, which meant he'd either made his excuses previously, or that he'd been detained by something far more interesting. It looked like Amita Sarrha and Ibram would have to uphold the honor of Ladyship's contingent of agents by themselves. He hoped they served a good cider at this fest.

Ibram caught Dihya's eye and shrugged minutely. She pointed discreetly with three fingers towards a chair at the furthest end of the table, and Ibram made his way to stand behind it. Across from him stood Master Finar. He smiled, and Finar smiled back, but he didn't quite meet Ibram's eyes. He looked nervous; Ibram couldn't blame him.

Ibram nodded to Bernat Guilhem and Philendra Dubidat to his right and surveyed the covered table. White linen had been stretched over the top and pitchers of drink lay in a row down the middle. Glass goblets had been unearthed, blue with gold flakes swirling as if their bowls were already filled. There were plates instead of trenchers, set with serviceware, which meant they were dining like Vissilians. He felt his mouth quirk to the left, and controlled himself. When Ladyship ate informally, the servants usually handed forks out for those who needed them, and allowed the rest to eat as they pleased. It was far more relaxing, but that was the difference between work and play, sadly.

Lady Azadiya smiled as she sat down in her chair, and readjusted her clothing. "What a delight to see that my invitations bore such fruit."

No one quite grumbled at that pronouncement, but then none of her guests seemed too relaxed either. Rennab and Dubidat seemed worried and tired, but only Rennab showed any sign of true strain. Master Finar visibly attempted to calm himself, which made him look even more anxious. Master Rennab's entire jaw was clenched so hard he was about to lose a tooth. Master Bernat seemed cheerful, but Ibram put no store in it.

Now that Ladyship had seated herself, the others were allowed to take their places as well. Mistress Vo Kaln made what she doubtless considered a graceful descent into her chair beside Amita Sarrha, who had taken command of the place nearest Lady Azadiya to her left. Warder Claes was at her commanding officer's elbow and next to her sat Ahksell, and then Master Rennab followed by his husband.

"I'm told you took in the Ozol heir, Master Finar," Lady Azadiya said, and Master Finar jumped. "That was kind of you."

"It was—it's the only thing to do, Mentor Hobon," Finar said, with a brief, fortifying glance to his husband. "Tari and Desta were great friends of ours, and Ealar... When something so cruel happens as—as all this, what else can you do? He must go somewhere, let it be to people who know what he has lost."

Master Rennab nodded, and took Finar's hand. "He may stay for as long as he wishes," he said.

"Smartest thing you've said in two years, Rennab," Mistress Dubidat said.

Lady Azadiya laughed, and her guests remembered their company. Talk settled down to politenesses. Hallie and Esti took a slow turn about the outside of the tent. Usually, Ibram was amongst them, one of the agents who even now stood loosely outside the canopy, watching the guests eat and keeping an eye on whose hand might be falling too quickly to their knives. It was a rare treat for him to dine in public, though they'd all done it a fair amount in private, when Lady Azadiya dined within her tower.

Ibram frowned. He had three cups in front of him, the wine glass he recognized, but the other two seemed unnecessary. At any moment, he was going to be forced to remember which way to hold his fork. Was it prongs up or down? This was a nightmare. He could only hope the food made up for it.

"Mistress Vo Kaln," Amita Sarrha said. "I'm told you know the area around Ammoni quite well. I traveled there in my youth. Very pretty sort of place."

"Why yes," Mistress Vo Kaln said, sounding a bit surprised to be spoken to. "We're a rather extensive family, you see, but we believe in keeping close. I have never been there, of course, but several of my younger cousins who are now visiting live down there."

"They're not of your generation?" Sarrha asked.

"Oh, their parents are," Mistress Vo Kaln said. "We all of us found common cause early in life, and made efforts to keep in contact. We abuse the Scribes' Bureau horribly, passing messages back and forth. I don't know how much we spend in paper!"

"A family should be close," Sarrha said blandly.

Ibram's head twitched. Family near Ammoni? Amita Sarrha laughed, but it was too practiced and polite; it made his skin itch. Ibram could see the servants bustling around a separate table set up for the dishes to be served. The smell of sauced mouflon and flatbread drifted out as they uncovered their platters and baskets.

He bit the inside of his bottom lip, and tried to stretch out his back unobtrusively. It wasn't a merry party, but it was polite enough. Ahksell was already trying to engage Warder Claes by loudly describing the portable fire box Nesrine had mentioned, even though he himself hadn't been there when she had described it. Claes seemed confused. Amita Sarrha yawned. Mistress Vo Kaln picked up her goblet of wine and drank deeply.

"I wonder about these small workshops," she said. "Do they understand the consequences of their actions when they make such devices? Such exploits should be left to the alchemists, surely."

If she was attempting to curry favor, it had no seeming effect on Lady Azadiya, who tilted her head in consideration, and then shook it slowly.

"I'm afraid I have no real experience of them," she lied. "I must rely on your knowledge, Mistress Vo Kaln. Ahksell, did you know these boxes were not of alchemical origin?"

"I did not, Mentor," Ahksell said.

"Have you used one, Mistress Vo Kaln?" Master Finar asked, a bit too harshly.

"You flatter me, Mentor Hobon," Mistress Vo Kaln said, after a brief pause. "I do have some small knowledge, through my cousin, you understand. He owns a farm, and rented a portion of the land to a group of academics. They used one in an experiment and scared the life from his pigs."

A polite laugh rippled through the party. Mila circled the table, refilling glasses. Across the way, Master Finar took a deep breath, and caught Ibram's eye. He nodded, almost imperceptibly.

"Has your brother reached Bromi by now?" Ibram asked, just loudly enough.

Finar nodded. "I believe it should be no more than a day," he said.

"When he responds to my message, you will be the first I inform, Master Ucalegon."

"What's this about the village of Bromi?" Mistress Dubidat asked.

"Albin's brother travels there," Rennab answered. "He's on his route, carting junk to and fro."

"You are harsh on your brother-in-law, Master Rennab," Mistress Vo Kaln said, with a sideways glance at Lady Azadiya. "Your husband cannot be in favor of it."

"He sells sundry goods up from Hyperni province," Master Finar explained to the party. Captain Talsconis barely acknowledged him, and only leant to the side so that Dihya could present him once more with his ale cup. Lady Azadiya always remembered the preferences of her habitual guests.

"Ammoni lies within Hyperni Province, does it not?" Ladyship asked. "Who does your brother work for?"

Master Finar blinked once at her, startled, and then remembered himself. He and his brother truly resembled each other very little, at least according to Nesrine's portrait. He was boney where Master Albin was plump, but there was a set to their eyes, a similarity of expression now that Ibram knew enough to compare the brothers.

"He is employed by Kenda Trading," Master Finar said. "Our parents apprenticed him to the company years ago when he and I were children."

"He is the elder brother, then?" Ladyship inquired further. "I am aware that the eldest child in the family of the Kilk persuasion generally leaves the family for work, and to send funds back."

"He is," Master Finar replied. "By five years. He's always had a great sense of responsibility."

"I believe he sold you your fire suppression tiles," Lady Azadiya said, and raised her wine glass for a delicate sip. "Where did they come from again, Ibram?"

"The ones I recovered from the alleyway were produced by the Sect of the Iron Hand," Ibram said on cue.

Captain Talsconis leaned forward, and moved his ale cup out of the way. "Not a crime to buy another sect's goods," he said.

Mistress Vo Kaln's laugh was thin, but attempted to sparkle. "No indeed," she said. "Or else how would any of us make our living?"

"I will be sure to recommend that my counterparts in Afsoun keep a check on their pricing," Lady Azadiya said.

"Oh no, the cost is nothing," Mistress Vo Kaln hastened to reassure her. She touched her hand to the old-fashioned cap surrounding her bound hair. "We have always used the tiles produced here in Lityen."

"They saved much of the building," Philendra Dubidat said, with a grimace. "Even if the blast overwhelmed us in the end."

"Two blasts," Ahksell said. Mistress Dubidat frowned in confusion, and he explained: "There were two explosions. One to get rid of The High Climber's fire suppression tiles—as meagre a defense as they were given from where they were made—and the second to produce the most damage."

"What do you mean?" Captain Talsconis asked. His eyebrows lowered; his sharp eyes flicked up and down the table.

Lady Azadiya leaned in his direction. "I'm afraid that as much as I support any alchemist's right to pursue their ambitions, the Sect of the Iron Hand is..."

"Infamous," Ahksell supplied.

"*Infamous*, you see, Captain Talsconis," she explained. "It's a newer sect, formed around the young scion of a rather cadet branch of an already middling noble house. Incredibly enthusiastic, but not much else to go on." She paused. "Well, there's certainly a lot of money going into them."

"Shoddy goods?" Captain Talsconis grunted.

Mistress Vo Kaln sipped her wine, and shook her head. Mistress Dubidat and her husband soon followed suit, as if a spell keeping them from their drink had broken.

"Why would anyone purposefully buy inferior materials—how would that even be accomplished?" Master Finar asked. "He sold them to us cheaply in order to help in our business. I've got them at my caffa as well. They're—"

He stopped speaking abruptly; his eyes widened. Down at the end of the table, he was attracting a great deal of notice from Mistress Vo Kaln.

"You do seem to have problems with the grout," Ibram said. "Tiles go loose after a while. Seen it before when the water level gets too high."

"That's true enough," Master Guilhem said. "Remember last rainy season, when I helped you and your dayworkers patch up that corner round the back of the building?"

Master Rennab nodded, and held up his glass for a passing servant to fill it.

Boots scraped on gravel, running fast. Ibram looked left, and squinted; the torchlight was enough to ruin his night vision, and the glowbulbs had yet to be lit on the path. He tensed, closing his hands on the edge of the table, and made to rise. Dihya stepped in his line of sight, and poured water into his cup.

"Be settled," she hissed at him, ducking her head behind her outstretched arm. "Once you're seated, you stay there."

"Is there something the matter?" Master Finar asked.

"Nothing in life," Ibram said. He stretched himself up over Dihya's arm and smiled.

Master Finar's forehead lowered. He also glanced out from the canopy.

"You're joining us at the table, Master Ucalegon," Bernat Guilhem said jovially. "I'm glad to see you again."

"It's a charmed moment for me as well, Master Guilhem," Ibram said. "How go the repairs?"

He leaned away from Dihya, arching against the back of his chair. There was a figure charging up the gravel path, getting closer every second. Ibram half-rose from his chair, and Dihya moved in front of him once more.

"Let one of the *others* handle it," she murmured, and then continued up the line of guests towards the head of the table.

"Very well," Guilhem said, not appearing in the slightest way bothered that Ibram had yet to look at him. "I thank you for passing on the invitation to dine with the sect. I've always wished to see the buildings up the living mountain."

"They're built to last," Master Rennab said, from the other side of the table. He sighed deeply. "Unlike some I can think of."

"You'll be fine as spin-lace," Mistress Dubidat retorted.

The conversation turned to neighborly grief, which normally Ibram was careful to take note of, but the runner was still gamboling up the hill like a hunter was snapping at his feet. Ibram tapped his heels on the grass, and licked his teeth beneath his lip. He grabbed his water glass and drank deeply. Master Finar watched him with concern.

"I hope everything is all right?" Finar asked.

Ibram shrugged, and put down his glass. He readjusted his seat, leaning to the right so that he could look at Finar and the gravel path at the same time. He caught Warder Claes' eye across the table, mostly because he was attempting to catch Ahksell's attention, and waggled his eyebrows at her. She looked away with barely a twitch of her lips. Ahksell frowned at him. Ladyship had engaged Mistress Vo Kaln in conversation, but it was low enough that Ibram could not quite hear what she was saying. That was all well and good, since he had his own conversational partner, and he had the welcome feeling that something was about to draw his attention away from Ladyship's plan.

"Are you certain your brother might make his way to Bromi soon?" he asked, loudly enough to be heard at the servants' table, and turned half of his attention back to Finar. "Only I could swear I saw him just yesterday."

Finar's eyes widened at the signal. The running grew louder. Whoever it was had gotten close enough for Ibram to see the flapping tassels on his sleeves. It was a young man, maybe no more than fifteen; he still wore a half-apron splotched with old stains. Someone from an inn, perhaps?

"My brother?" Finar asked sharply, and then laughed uneasily. "I don't know what you mean."

"He's traveling, no doubt," Master Rennab said. He was much less uneasy. In fact, he sounded downright irritated. "Slippery as a devil in a pond."

Ibram nodded, and watched the runner's approach. It was a little ahead of Ladyship's schedule, but it seemed appropriate to rush in the face of oncoming news. He dug into his belt purse. A potboy, perhaps, someone easily dispatched and eager for a coin or six for an evening run. The nearest agent caught him by the elbow, sending the boy stumbling, before he was dragged off to the grass for a quiet interrogation.

"Traveling salesman are all alike," Ibram said, as he flipped open the top of his purse and pulled out the roll of paper. "Makes it easy to forget a face. That doesn't happen when you're family, though, I suppose."

Finar's smile fluttered about his mouth and disappeared. "No, not really... Master Ucalegon, what are you looking at?"

Ibram jerked his head in Finar's direction, and raised his eyebrows. The agent—looked like Hallie—had sent the boy to the table surrounded with servants. There might be a sour bun in the young master's future. Ibram tossed the paper onto the table. He held it open with two fingers, and made certain that Nesrine's portrait of the dark-haired man was fully visible.

"Would this be very like him?" he asked. "Tall fellow, has a room at The Crooked Tent."

"That draughtshop that burned to the ground?" Master Guilhem asked. "Philie, did you hear that?"

The back of his neck tingled and tightened as the agent hurried past behind Ibram. Hallie was on her way to the head of the table. Conversation was beginning to quiet down.

Master Finar's mouth dropped open, just enough that Ibram could see the edges of his teeth and the curl of his tongue. It was a hard thing to publicly lay out your own brother's possible corruption; Ibram didn't blame him for the discontent in his gaze. He admired the pause, planned though it was, while they waited to see who else would identify the man. Master Rennab frowned heavily. He looked from Finar to the paper, and then leaned across him in order to glare more readily at the portrait.

Rennab transferred that glare to Ibram. "Yes, that looks very like him," he said. "Where did you get this?"

"I have a cousin who dabbles in the arts," Ibram said. "What's his name again? Amon? Ambur."

"Achard," Master Finar said. He smoothed his left hand over his right. He really was quite good. Concern was starting to steal the color from his cheeks.

From the corner of his eye, Ibram saw Hallie lean over to whisper to Lady Azadiya, who tilted her head away for a private conference.

Mistress Vo Kaln looked uncomfortable. She leaned across her place and glared down the table.

"It's not what you think," Master Finar burst out, loudly enough to startle the rest of the table. Bernat Guilhem began whispering furiously to his wife, who pressed her hand to the front of her chest. "I'm sure it isn't."

"Albin?" Master Rennab prompted him again. Ladyship had asked them for a bit more chatter than Master Finar seemed currently capable. Still, Ibram felt equal to helping matters along without him.

Ibram grinned. "Oh, I never think," he said. "Saves time."

He left the paper where it lay, and rested his elbows on the table. Ibram glanced to his right. Lady Azadiya smiled and fluttered the fingers of her right hand. The portrait of Achard Finar ruffled up from the table, and drifted to lay before her.

"Is it a good likeness?" she asked, and turned the portrait to face the rest of her guests.

"I..." Mistress Dubidat shook her head and turned pale, and then flushed red. "I think so?"

"It *is*," Mistress Vo Kaln said in thunderous tones. "He asked for an interview once, to provide my buildings with tiles. It's a very good likeness. Master Finar, how—"

"Ibram," Ladyship interrupted. "I'm afraid something interesting has occurred in the village. Hallie will tell you on the way to the relay station."

Ibram jumped up from the table. He gripped the hilt of his sica, and nodded. Ahksell blinked at him and then twisted to catch Ladyship's eye.

"Mentor, may I..." he asked delicately. The table buckled slightly beneath his hands. "I mean, if it's *interesting*."

Lady Azadiya paused. The guests at her table sat in silence. Claes made a move to rise, but Talsconis sent her back down with a swift shake of his head. Master Finar had turned a greenish shade of pale. Hallie moved from Ladyship's side, and strode to Ibram.

"Oh, very well," Ladyship decided, and smiled indulgently. "Bring me back something talkative."

Hallie led them to the relay station, but no further, leaving it up to Ibram to guide Ahksell to where Amota Berac was holding up a wall with Amita Dervla, loitering beneath the collapsing awning of the wraparound porch of The Star and Spice. The night air threatened rain if they lingered much longer, with that chill warning that spoke of a long and miserable drizzle. The roads were already half-muck and puddle. Ibram noted Tono and Juanma sitting on a few barrels on the opposite side of the street, their cloaks hid their green gambesons and sect brooches from view. Ahksell's head jerked in their direction, but he didn't greet them.

"Lityen Hill?" Ahksell muttered as they approached the mouth of the tributary street where it joined the main road.

Ibram nodded, and then shrugged. The entire hamlet wasn't more than half a mile down to Pillared Circle, after all. Nothing much more than a collection of storehouses, warehouses, a bathhouse and a draughtshop, and a few small places that were rightfully draughtshops but called themselves tenant inns. What shops there were mostly existed to provide a space for the tannery at the top of the hill to offer up their finished goods. At this time of the evening, the draughtshops would be expecting their customers, ripe from the tannery and eager to forget how much they stank. A thin stream of customers already threatened to become a river, and then, a flood.

"No, we've got him sighted," Amota Berac was saying as Ibram and Ahksell walked up to his back. "If we can keep him there, we'll have him boxed in neatly. Just a matter of making sure he doesn't duck back into the kitchens or jump out a window."

"Who do we have stationed inside?" Ibram asked.

The buildings across the way formed a solid bulwark of wooden beams, easily crossed by rooftop, and sadly, easily burned to a crisp. A few horses stood at a trough nearby a table of drovers drinking their evening away. There were lamps on this road, not more than a torch set up by the buildings' owners, but enough that he could see more of the street.

Amota Berac jumped slightly, and then glanced over his shoulder, the picture of a man caught mid-conversation. Amita Dervla clapped him on the shoulder, and then shrugged. She gestured back down the road as if Ibram had asked for directions.

"Roswitha and Kenzou are within." She pointed overheard. "Rotem and Nikora are watching the windows from the roof."

"So we might not need the unsubtle approach," Amota Berac said, and relaxed back against the wall. "Take him while he's in the common room and none the wiser."

"What's all this waiting about then?" Ibram asked. "Drawing lots to see which of us looks the most unthreatening?"

"We don't have to, now that you're here, Little Ibram," Amita Dervla replied. "Bait or beater?"

Ibram popped her a polite bow, and held out his arms. "I stand ready to entrap or pursue, as needed."

"Mentor released Ibram and I for the capture." Ahksell sighed. "Perhaps he'll come quietly. We're a bigger group than only Nesrine, after all."

"Is that why you're all waiting outside?" Ibram asked.

Amota Berac's face turned wooden. The light from the nearest torch threw a shadow across his forehead. "It's always necessary to plan," he said. "Better to wrap a boar in wool than face him naked."

Ahksell blinked rapidly. Ibram leaned into his shoulder. "It sounds better in the original Merrilian," he said.

"I would hope so," Ahksell said. He cleared his throat. "Well, if it must happen, then how can we help? Mentor can't keep her guests at table forever."

"Do we have confirmation on the face?" Amita Dervla asked Berac, who waggled his right hand. "First thing is to get young Solari under cover—"

"We could disguise him as a pillar," Ibram offered. "He's tall enough."

Amita Dervla talked over him. "—and then settle Ib-la on the porch outside the tenant inn and—"

"Which one?" Ibram asked, and raised up on his toes for a better look across the street.

"The Orilindan's Refuge," Amota Berac answered, and tapped

Ibram's stomach with the flat of his hand. Ibram coughed and leaned back.

"Cheap and decidedly uncheerful, despite the name," Ibram said, as he rocked back on his heels. "Stinks like the Abyss, inside, actually."

"And no convenient shared courtyard in the back to box him in," Amita Dervla said.

"How do you know that?" Ahksell asked. "About the smell, I mean."

"Had a drink or three in there on account of that mess with the smugglers and Axan's Trading Company," Ibram said, and waved a hand under his nose. "Lots of tanners stop for their nightly meal, most of them not too fussed about who pays for it."

"Have you gotten drunk in every building within walking distance of the preceptory?" Ahksell demanded.

"*No.*" Ibram raised his chin. "Sometimes Father lets me ride Gilma."

Ahksell rolled his eyes, and crossed his arms over his chest. Amita Dervla snorted with a certain flavor of weary disgust she had only ever truly let bloom around the younger agents. Ibram shrugged.

"It's come in handy, has it not?" he asked.

"What's it look like in there," Amita Dervla asked. "If he runs, we need to contain him."

She sounded like she hoped Finar did make an attempt at freedom. Ibram couldn't blame her. He nodded, and studied the front of the inn again. He brought up his own sense of direction, picturing a tapestry on the wall of his bedroom as Amota Evren had taught him. Himself at the table nearest the bar counter, listening to folk complain about their employers and their spouses. Bad lighting, single staircase up and down, typical layout for a tenant inn with a reliably edible kitchen.

"Old as the tannery. Firepit in the center of the room," Ibram said. "Only an alley in back."

"For supplies?" Amita Dervla asked.

Ibram shook his head. "Mostly for garbage and barely more than a trough. A single man might walk it, if my memory serves, but it connects with the tannery."

He wrinkled his nose. No fugitive would be that desperate, surely.

"He's calling himself Rymand Rockfish at the inn," Amota Berac said. "Shouldn't we use that until his true identity has been confirmed? The potgirl who took his bags upstairs heard it when he made arrangements with the proprietor."

Ibram snorted. "No one is called 'Rymand Rockfish'."

"He is," Berac said. "Or whatever he was using when he attacked Nesrine."

He shrugged, and Ibram sucked his teeth. What was in a name when there was a body to catch? He closed his hand around the hilt of his sica, and sat back on his heels.

"Sophus Verco," Ahksell said. "But it's Achard Finar, in point of fact."

"Really now?" Amota Berac leaned on his left shoulder, and returned to staring out onto the street.

"His brother confirmed it," Ibram said. "Turned pale as milk when he saw that portrait; he's with Ladyship now."

Amita Dervla snorted. "I wish him joy, then," she said.

Ibram frowned. "When do we move on him? Is the signal given?"

Amota Berac sighed, and rubbed the side of his head. "I was about to go inside and ask for a bowl of something hot."

"Quash with potatoes, if memory serves," Ibram said.

"Is there an upstairs?" Amita Dervla asked. "Private rooms?"

Ibram shook his head. "A shared space for sleepers, I think," he said. "I never had cause to leave the common room."

Amota Berac paused, and then resettled himself so that he face Ibram completely. "Ladyship tells me you saw him hanging about Pillared Circle a few days ago?"

Ibram nodded. "A number of times," he said.

Amita Dervla's mouth crooked sourly as she leaned her full back against the wall. Ahksell took a few steps backwards down the porch, further out of sight from the street, though he had to hunch over to do so.

"If he set the fire," Dervla said, "he's got a certain interest in keeping an eye on its investigation. If he's called out by someone who recognizes him, he has an excuse to be present and an accomplice to provide cover."

"Ladyship has nothing to say on whether or not Master Finar is involved with whatever his brother is tangled up in," Ahksell said. "Or, at least, not so involved."

"Anyone who uses the excuse 'it's not what you think' is most certainly innocent," Ibram said.

"He was very distressed and very helpful." Ahksell swatted him on the shoulder. Ibram shrugged. Amita Dervla observed them narrowly. She'd bound her light brown hair tightly to her head; it made her look like a hawk who'd been rudely awakened.

"If young Solari is willing," she said, "we can settle him at the draughtshop with a few agents. Additional cover and someone who can identify whoever we flush out."

Amota Berac shook his head. "He's too tall. Rockfish or Finar— what have you—will spot young Solari faster than you can spit. He'll run the other way."

"Close the trap sooner," Dervla said, and shrugged. "Put Ibram on the inside. He's been there before, less likely to draw suspicion."

"Are Kenzou and Roswitha inside disguised?" Ibram asked.

"No," Amota Berac said. His eyes narrowed. "You'll go to their table, pretend it's a prearranged meeting, and then give the signal."

"So I'm the bait, then," Ibram said. "Finar sees me, he jumps up and starts for the door, and straight into our hands outside."

He stepped around Amita Dervla on his way to the street. Ahksell's hand clamped down on his shoulder and yanked him to a stop.

"That's a horrible idea," Ahksell said. "You can't even fish."

"What does that have to do with anything?" Ibram asked. He shook himself free of Ahksell's grip, and straightened his clothes.

"What if Master Finar goes upstairs?" Ahksell asked. "What if he has another one of those portable fire boxes?"

"No time left to wonder," Amita Dervla said. "We've waited long enough."

"I'll go in as well," Ahksell said

"He'll run," Amota Berac said.

"And I can stop him," Ahksell said.

"So can I," Ibram said, "and with less ruckus—not that I don't love the shouting and the exclaiming whenever you lift someone overheard."

Ahksell groaned.

"And are you quite recovered from your adventures at The Crooked Tent, Solari?" Amota Berac asked, a little more gently than he might to an alchemist he hadn't had a hand in fetching up.

"Esti tells us you knocked back a nice dose of Nikephoros' Oil," Amita Dervla said. "Running across rooftops will do that to your paths of concentration."

"Esti should mind his own business," Ahksell retorted. He cast his eyes up and down the intersection.

Ibram shook his head, and bounced on the balls of his feet. Time was frittering away like flour in hot oil, and they were just standing around, debating. He cracked his knuckles.

"Nesrine made Finar nervous," Dervla said. "According to the potboy we sent up the living mountain, he's been acting like a man waiting on a sweetling all night. If he is actually waiting for someone, they haven't come—best we get him now, and let Ladyship sort out the rest of it."

That explained why they hadn't snatched him immediately. No matter, Amota Berac's caution was Ibram's opportunity. Ibram rubbed his wrists, first left and then right, and nodded. He stepped forward down the long curving porch, and glanced up over his shoulder. "Back in time for supper," he said.

❧

He kept the bounce out of his step as he crossed the street. A thin seam of stars had broken through the mass of clouds overhead, but no moonlight. If Ibram had not known where he was going, the irregular torchlight might have been a problem, but the flow of villagers was easily discernable. Not many went his direction, but that was to be expected. There were other inns and draughtshops open for business, after all.

He felt eyes upon him from the moment he stepped free of the porch and made his way beneath the sodden timbered awning of The Orilindan's Refuge. The door was shut against the weather, but swung open easily at his two-handed push. He breathed lightly as he crossed the threshold, the air certainly smelled as he'd remembered. Nothing like the run-off of a tannery to make armored turnips and yesterday's mouflon quash entice like pies at a feast.

He made a show of stomping mud from his boots in the doorway and swiping at his arms, in order to get the lay of the room before committing to walking through the common room. The Orilindan's Refuge wasn't as wide as it was tall, with room for three long trestle tables to the left of the center fire pit, and a single bench and table shoved next to the bar counter on the left. The central fire supplied most of the light in common room, with a single guttering lamp nailed on the wall over the counter and another just inside the front door.

Ibram's vision dazzled. He squinted, and water gathered at the corners of his eyes. Folk tended to crowd on the right here, but the space before the stairs up to the shared sleeping room had a few somber eaters at a table near enough at the end of the counter. A dozen or so men and women sat drinking away their worries, and eating their dinners in quiet company. Achard Finar was either tucked away in the corner, or upstairs; Ibram couldn't spot him.

Ibram sidled to his left. Kenzou and Roswitha had sat themselves in the corner of the nearest trestle table to the door. Roswitha faced into the common room, her slim fingers tossing nut shells onto the floor, while Kenzou faced out. Ibram concocted a small scenario in the back of his mind, a few lines of conversation to bracket Amota Berac's signal in a comforting reasonability.

Kenzou was just finishing off his ale, and set the mug aside as Ibram approached, licking foam from his mustache. Ibram raised his arm in greeting, and a man sitting at the furthest table broke for the stairwell, violently shoving himself free of the trestle table. The man slammed into a server and sent the boy spinning to the ground. He had a soft face and dark hair, and the fingertips of his hand were bandaged.

"Finar!" Ibram roared, as the room erupted into hollers and confusion.

He rushed across the common room, caught his boot heel on the stone edge of the fire pit and managed the turn just as Finar reached the bottom stairs. Ibram heard Roswitha shouting behind him as he kicked chairs out of his path. A woman shrieked. He raced forward, boots thundering on the floorboards as Finar jumped up two steps on the stairwell, momentum propelling him to the third. Ibram leapt with his arms outstretched and caught the flapping edge of Finar's tunic in both hands. He yanked hard, and Finar's feet slipped; he slammed belly-first into the stairs with a choked bellow and Ibram fell on top of his legs, turning his face to the side in time not to slam his own nose on Finar's thigh.

Finar yelled and kicked backwards; Ibram groaned behind gritted teeth, shuddering at each slam of Finar's heels into his chest and stomach. Ibram dragged them both down the steps, grabbing at handfuls of Finar's tunic as he drove his knees into the wood to brace himself. He reared back, almost lifting them both clean off the stairs, and Finar's left foot caught him solidly in the stomach.

Ibram gagged. His head swam and for a brief, horrible second his entire body froze with a hideous wavering affront as his breath was shoved from his body. His fingers loosened of their own accord. Finar began to wiggle free, slipping out of Ibram's grasp and making for the next step to freedom. Ibram wheezed, and then Roswitha shoved a broom handle into Finar's side through the stair railing.

Finar shouted and twisted right; Roswitha lunged again and pinned him in the belly against the wall. Finar froze, eyes bulging; his face was splotched red and white, a furious sickly sweat dripped down his forehead. Ibram consigned his lungs to the heavens and coughed miserably, he settled on the step below Finar and rested on his aching knees.

"Truly, Master Finar," he said, and then hacked to the side. His chest tightened as he forced his lungs to admit they could still function; his entire body flushed with heat. "You should—oh, this *will* bruise—never attempt to run away in a building without a proper exit."

"Recipe for disaster, really," Roswitha said.

"Where'd Kenzou get off to?" Ibram asked.

He risked a glance over his shoulder to the suddenly quite silent common room. Significantly fewer folk than had been present before the struggle stared back at him. Ibram sniffed and drew his sica, miraculously undamaged in the scuffle and now of more use. He set its point directly on Master Finar's kneecap; Master Finar swallowed heavily, and lay very still. He'd attempted some type of disguise, mostly by cutting his hair which now revealed his ears fully. A smart choice for a man of the Kilk faith, to be sure, though Ibram might have suggested a hat, or something like it, to conceal his face as well. It would also have probably been better not to run.

"What—what—I," Finar stammered.

"I'll thank you for not moving," Ibram said, raising his voice, "until I've caught my breath a little."

Finar's eyes bulged from their sockets. He and his brother didn't much resemble each other, but they had the same form of expression. His chest rose and fell rapidly. "This is—"

"Ah!" Ibram said, again loudly, and then flicked his dagger, letting it slice a hole in Finar's trousers. "We are resting now! Keep your breath to cool your quash."

Roswitha jabbed the broom handle a trifle more solidly into Finar's stomach. He made an oof-ing sort of sound, and then lay still.

"Kenzou went for Amota Berac," she said. "They should be charging to our rescue at any moment."

Ibram nodded. Yilka's megrims, his chest ached. If he'd cracked a rib, he'd never live it down.

"*Riant*," he said.

The amitai took charge of Achard Finar almost immediately. Roswitha abandoned him as well, leaving Ibram to Ahksell's disappointed looks and pointed reminders that *he* could lift a man entirely over his head without fear of getting his ribs kicked in. He refused to accept Ibram's own entirely sensible rejoinders that Ibram was perfectly fine, and quite capable of tackling anyone he so chose admirably—as in point of fact, they had the malcontent in custody. Ahksell was free to witness him walking ahead of them even as they discussed the situation.

Thus engaged, they all marched the prisoner up the living mountain, surrounded by agents. Finar said nothing the entire trip, staring at his feet or his hands by turns. His jaw worked occasionally, as though he were chewing his cheek. By the time they made it back to the

Preceptory of Yseult and Lady Azadiya's tower, Ibram had drunk a half-measure of powdered withy bark shaken in water, and a full vial of mashed Haluppu-tree seeds soaked in wine while Ahksell had stared pointedly at him, often tapping his foot. Ibram refused to be cowed, but accepted the pain remedies as they appeared; his chest and stomach ached too much to argue, anyway.

"I think it's safe to say we've absolutely ruined Lady Azadiya's party," Ibram said, as they walked at the back of the pack towards the training fields. "And Master Albin will probably be beside himself again."

The glowbulbs and lanterns had been fully lit by now, obscuring the sky above, but decorating the paths all over the sect with trails of green and purple and blue lights. It destroyed Ibram's night vision, but he couldn't argue that an easy and well-lighted path wasn't a boon for a wounded man. Haluppu-tree seeds were very relaxing, to be sure, but the wrench in the right side of his neck might as well have been permanent for all the good they seemed to be working. Ahksell turned his face down from studying the nearest swaying glowbulb, and frowned at him.

"You think they're all still there?" he asked. "The night's growing long. I was just considering where Master Comoros would want to stash Master Finar while we all take the time remaining for our recovery."

He gave Ibram a very pointed look, which Ibram refused to accept. He stuck his thumbs through his belt, and did not groan as the movement jostled what seemed like every disgruntled muscle in his body. Ahksell sniffed, loudly.

"And I think you underestimate Lady Azadiya's interest in a certain someone's reaction—" Ibram raised his voice, "—to seeing Master Finar's arrival in our charge!"

Achard Finar's shoulders definitely flinched at that. He stumbled, and Amita Dervla hauled him back into place by the back of his tunic. They'd lost a fair few of the other agents to nighttime patrols as they'd entered the preceptory, but she, Amota Berac and Roswitha, as well as Kenzou had continued onward. Roswitha carried the sack of personal items they'd recovered from the sleeping room at inn.

"For his own part, I'm sure Amota Berac is as eager to have the whole mess over with," Ibram said, a touch more quietly. "Think of what the reports will look like when this is over."

"Yours will be very interesting reading, to be sure," Berac called back over his shoulder.

Ibram winced, and Ahksell began digging into his belt pouch. Ibram smacked him lightly on the shoulder.

"I'm fine!" he insisted. "Put it away, all I need is a good night's rest."

"And a wooly grass poultice or nine," Ahksell said.

"You are not my mother," Ibram said.

"Just wait until she hears—"

"No," Ibram interrupted. "She is in bed! You shouldn't—shouldn't disturb her sleep like that. And furthermore!" He leaned forward as they walked, pitching his voice to be heard. "We should be focusing on how this man in front of us convinced his entire family to set their livelihood ablaze, and caused the deaths of five upstanding folk."

Achard Finar twisted to right and then left, trying to glare behind himself and walk at the same time. "I'm not involved in any such thing!" he yelled. "Can't a man eat his dinner in peace?"

Ibram shrugged, even though he immediately regretted it. "Shouldn't have run," he said.

"It does seem strange," Ahksell said.

"Who wouldn't run when a barbarian arm-for-hire comes after him?" Finar exclaimed.

He stumbled as they cleared the last small hill and passed through the gate into the training field. Ibram could just about see the peak of Lady Azadiya's tent, and the beckoning lights within.

"All I did was walk in the door," Ibram said. "I was only there for a nice meal."

Finar twisted back around with a huff, and struggled a moment in Berac and Dervla's grip. It didn't free him, but perhaps the act made him feel better about his situation. They marched through the damp grass and up to the tent, where everyone was still seated, but no one was at their leisure.

Berac and Dervla halted at the head of the table with their quarry firmly in their grasp. Roswitha and Kenzou went left and Ibram and

Ahksell walked to the right of the tent opening. Master Albin Finar stared up at his brother from his seat, and Ibram felt a small twist of sympathy deep in his chest. It was a hard moment for the brothers. He didn't blame him when Achard Finar looked away.

"Ladyship," Amota Berac said. "May I make your arsonist known to you?"

A particularly heavy sort of silence lay over the group assembled at Lady Azadiya's table. The remains of a fine dinner lay out on the table, with fruit in bowls at either end. Ibram looked through the side opening of the tent; the food preparation table was crowded with servants and younger agents, eating their own meals. Their liveliness was all the more loud for the silence in Ladyship's tent.

She sat back in her chair with a glass goblet of wine delicately raised in the air, staring down the length of the table at her newest guest with a blank face and sharp eyes. Dihya stood just behind her. Captain Talsconis fidgeted in his chair, set down his ale cup, and put both arms on the table. He leaned forward over his plate; his face turned red.

"What is the meaning of this?" Talsconis barked. "You're telling me this man is responsible for the fire at Pillared Circle? Claes!"

Warder Claes pushed her chair back, and braced herself on the table to stand. Philendra Dubidat inhaled sharply, and clasped her husband's arm. He covered her hand with hers.

Lady Azadiya set her goblet on the table. "I should think he is," she said, "but there's no need for Warder Claes to stir herself. My agents have him well in hand." She raised her voice slightly. "Dihya, find Master Achard a chair. He looks uncomfortable."

"Of course, Mentor Hobon," Dihya said, and went to the next table.

"Now, the usual chain of protocol involves my personal scribe, I believe," Lady Azadiya said. "But as Evren has doubtless retired to bed, I believe we might continue and simply recount these events in the morning. I must tell you, Master Finar, that I am tremendously excited and curious to make your acquaintance."

Ibram shifted his weight on his heels and kept his hands loose at his sides. There were forks and knives and all manner of throwable items on the dining table, and several guests looked like they were strongly tempted to take aim. Ahksell frowned down at him on Ibram's right, but Ibram shook his head.

"Do you mean to say..." Philendra Dubidat found her voice, but it cracked halfway out her throat. "Albin's brother set the fire? Were—Soren, did you put him up to this? You disgraceful—"

Albin Finar put his head in his hands.

"Don't you dare accuse me!" Rennab shouted, and reared back in his chair. "I am just as shocked as anyone!"

"How can that possibly be?" Mistress Vo Kaln asked. Scorn sharpened her voice into an ax. "Is this because I offered to purchase your building? Did you think I would pay more out of sympathy?"

Achard Finar's head twitched at the sound of her voice. Ibram noticed the contempt curling about his thin mouth and the sharpening of his eyes. Ibram stretched his neck along his shoulders, and winced at the popping noise his spine made. Lady Azadiya's eyes flicked towards him. Ibram stopped stretching, and stood tall; she waved him back.

Ibram sighed through his parted lips. He widened his stance, and thought relaxing thoughts at all his aches and pains. They'd said something about mind controlling matter in school; it had to be relevant someday. Tomorrow, he was going to be stiff as a plank unless he found that jar of symphis cream Ama had made last year.

"I am..." Master Albin Finar stopped and then breathed out. He raised his head and dug his knuckle beneath his eye. His husband took him by the elbow, but Finar shook his head and then pulled himself free. "I am tremendously remorseful, Mentor Hobon. I had no idea that anything—well, that doesn't matter now, does it."

He swallowed, heavily, and went to stand beside his captive brother. Ibram stepped forward, and Lady Azadiya waved him back. They all watched while Albin Finar reached out and touched his brother's arm, and then his exposed ear. Achard's entire face flinched, and then stilled with an obvious effort. Albin cleared his throat.

"Didn't know what?" Talsconis asked. A bit of a flush highlighted his cheeks. He shifted in his chair, and sat forward over the table, placing an elbow near his plate for balance. "Didn't realize how many of your neighbors you might kill when you got your brother to set your husband's evening courtyard on fire? How much will you make out of this now? Enough to expand your caffa?"

"No!" Albin Finar exclaimed.

"No, not as such," Lady Azadiya said. "And he certainly had nothing to do with the fire that overtook The Crooked Tent."

Mistress Vo Kaln sat back in her chair, and glared silently in the Finar brothers' direction. Captain Talsconis turned to Ladyship, and took a deep breath, much like a bull in a field whose just spied the gate left open. She watched him courteously, and he shook his head without speaking.

Ladyship smiled. "Now, a bit of a return to past business," she said. "But we are all certain this is Achard Finar?"

"Of course we are, Mentor Hobon," Mistress Vo Kaln said. "Who else could it be? Obviously, he has done this to take care of his brother, in light of Master Rennab's failing business. Acting on his own, he wanted to make certain Albin was taken care of, and these murders are the result."

Achard trembled where he stood, a fine tremor from his shoulders to his legs. Ibram caught him swallowing from the corner of his eye, and saw Achard glance once to Albin, before staring straight ahead once more.

Lady Azadiya hummed lightly. "Is that the reason?" she asked.

"To take care of family?" Mistress Vo Kaln asked. "How could it be anything else? Master Finar himself said he's the younger child. Achard clearly feels some sense of responsibility for him—selling him tiles cheaply, concern for his welfare in his husband's failing business."

"I do not have a failing business," Master Rennab snapped.

"Well, not anymore," Mistress Vo Kaln said. "Now your brother-in-law has taken it upon himself to relieve you of that burden."

Ibram kept his attention on Achard. He was certainly paying attention to Ederetta Vo Kaln.

"He could be deranged," Ibram offered.

"Or angry at someone," Ahksell suggested.

"He might even have been paid," Ibram said.

"Oh, now that is a very interesting idea," Lady Azadiya said.

Dihya arrived with Master Dughlat, who carried a chair before him in both hands. They set it down by Achard Finar, and then moved to stand near the head of the table by Lady Azadiya. Amota Berac bound Achard Finar to the chair at the wrists and ankles. Albin Finar remained standing.

"How so?" Captain Talsconis asked.

"Well, you see, it leads me down such fascinating avenues of thought," Lady Azadiya replied. "Dervla, did you find anything at Master Finar's lodging?"

"We did find a very heavy purse in his belongings, Ladyship," Amita Dervla said. "He hadn't the opportunity to wire their communal bunkroom to light up as he did the private room at The Crooked Tent. Roswitha has all his belongings."

"You have to wonder what type of work a man does to bring in so much coin," Amota Berac said.

"Stolen from his employer no doubt," Philendra Dubidat sneered. "I put nothing past this one."

"You put nothing past anyone, you—" Master Rennab began, then swallowed whatever he was about to say at the sound of Ladyship clearing her throat.

"To return to the subjects in custody. Master Finar," Ladyship paused and then frowned. "I apologize, I realize you are both of your majority, but do you mind if I refer to you as either Master Albin or Master Achard? Only for clarity, to be sure."

Silence mushroomed in the conversation until the brothers realized Ladyship was perfectly serious and waiting for their reply. Mistress Vo Kaln's quiet noise of scorn would have been lost if anyone else had chosen to speak in the interim. Mistress Dubidat glanced at her askance, and then nervously turned her eyes towards Lady Azadiya.

"I don't mind," Master Albin said finally.

Master Achard said nothing. He nodded once, and then stared at his lap.

"I thank you," Ladyship said. She touched her signet ring with her thumb, and leaned forward in her chair. "Now, it's a cold night and so I believe a few points of correction are in order."

"Correction?" Master Guilhem asked.

Ibram blinked. He'd almost forgotten the man was present. He and his wife held hands on the table, gripping each other tightly. Guilhem leaned back in his chair when Lady Azadiya nodded at him.

"To be sure, Master Guilhem," she said. "In alchemy, as in trade, precision is everything. A false accounting does no one any good. Wouldn't you say?"

"Yes, of course," Mistress Dubidat answered for the pair. She glared across the table at her former neighbor; Soren Rennab glared right back.

"To begin, Master Achard," Lady Azadiya said. "You are Achard Finar, brother of Albin and brother-in-law to Soren Rennab, formerly of The High Climber?"

Master Achard's tense jawline seized and then jerked to the right. He sucked his teeth, and his eyes darted left and then back to the head of the table. Amota Berac prodded him in the back.

"I am," he ground out between clenched teeth. "Mentor Hobon, I protest this ill treatment! I was assaulted by your arms-for-hire!"

"Agents," Amita Dervla said. "We prefer *agents*."

Lady Azadiya sat back in her chair. "Assault?" she repeated. She rested her elbows on the arms of her chair and interlaced her fingers. "I have a young agent, Nesrine Waqaban, in my division. She is currently in bed, sleeping away the damage of smoke inhalation and the breaking of her arm in The Crooked Tent. My inclination is to make her known to you, but I believe you have already introduced yourself."

"Achard, you *didn't*," Master Albin hissed.

Master Achard pulled against his restraints. "I am a common merchant," he said. "I trade alchemical goods up and down the empire and I am being held against my will by—by a competing sect! You, there, warder, I want it taken down! I am proffering a charge!"

"Claes, make a note," Captain Talsconis said without looking away from the prisoner.

"Sir," Warder Claes responded.

"Only one?" Ladyship asked. "I find that interesting, don't you, Mistress Vo Kaln?"

"I—I do, Mentor," Mistress Vo Kaln said. A wrinkle developed in her forehead. She touched her goblet, and then pulled her hand away, leaving the wine undrunk. "When I think of those poor people in the bakery-mill!"

She touched her sleeve to her mouth, and turned her head. Lady Azadiya watched her politely, but when nothing further came out of her, she turned back to the table. Ibram clasped his hands together, and coughed. Ladyship directed her attention towards him.

"Yes, Ibram?" she asked.

"Master Achard was found with several ledgers for Kenda Trading, which has their main office in Kalisbrite, a town in Hyperni province. They broker sales for the Sect of the Iron Hand. Found a few more fire suppression tiles with him, and the place where he was lodging had an entire back wall of the ugly things. Already cracking."

Master Achard glanced to him, and then Rennab, and went back to glaring at Lady Azadiya.

"I sold them those tiles at the price of their worth," he said. His lip curled derisively. "Bad enough I had to justify my earnings at the end of every trading route, but what is it to you?"

"The highest quality tools for the most lackluster achievement," Ahksell said. "They couldn't even keep a waxed bag from burning. We found them in his room at The Crooked Tent and all over the alley in between The High Climber and the bakery-mill."

"Also a great deal of Running Flames," Ibram added. "That would be the green flames you spotted, Master Dughlat."

Master Dughlat took a deep, convulsive breath and shook his head. Dihya took him by the arm.

"I wish I hadn't," he muttered. "I wish to the Wheelmaker, I had held my breath and kept my thoughts to myself."

"Oh, but then the Ozols would still be dead," Lady Azadiya said. "And Mistress Dubidat's candle dancers, all four of whom deserved to be breathing just as much as anyone here. I think there's a need for restitution in that, Master Dughlat."

"But Erno would be alive if—" Master Dughlat began.

Ladyship waved the assertion off. "And, to be sure, no telling if Erno Neilos would have survived. Which one of you bribed him, by the way?"

"I…what do you mean?" Master Albin stammered.

"I hate to bring bad news to any of my neighbors, but I am sorry to inform you, Master Albin, Master Achard," Lady Azadiya said gently. "That there is no way that Master Achard could have acted alone when he caused the fire at Pillared Circle."

Albin Finar stepped back with a sharp noise of betrayal and denial. Ibram had no doubt it was real, after all Lady Azadiya had given him no reassurances in return for his aid but that his brother would be returned to him alive and undamaged. She had been matter of fact in her suspicions, and why she needed him to confirm his brother's identity, but she had not been comforting. Ibram considered the brother; Achard Finar's entire body seemed turned to stone. He stared at Lady Azadiya intently.

"You knew your brother was in the village, did you not, Master Albin?" she asked.

"Don't say a word, Albin," Master Achard hissed.

"I—I did," Master Albin said, and repeated what he had told Ladyship in their interview that afternoon. "He told me news had flown about the disaster in Lityen and that he had returned as quickly as possible."

"Quite a feat for a man who had left the area so long ago," Ladyship said.

"Indeed," Master Rennab said grimly.

"He thought it was the tiles," Master Albin continued. "He told me, he thought the blasted things had—he said he'd been hearing reports that they didn't work right, and that he worried that if it were known that our tiles had failed—"

"You'd be in dereliction of your own agreements with the fire alliance," Mistress Dubidat snapped. "And so you are! May you fall to Oblivion for the lies you've told and the damage you've done."

"No need for rancor at my table, Mistress Dubidat," Lady Azadiya said. "Have another cup of wine instead. Dihya informs me it's fortifying."

Mistress Dubidat wasn't stupid enough to tell Ladyship where she might pour her own wine, but it was a close run thing. Ibram tsked and sidled a little further down that side of the table.

"It is a little hard to believe that's all he knew," Master Guilhem said apologetically. "I mean to say, we never saw Master Achard about the place. Didn't you suspect anything when your brother didn't help with your recovery?"

Albin shook his head morosely.

"I told him I wanted to stay out of the entire affair, to make sure no one suspected it was the tiles I sold to him," Master Achard burst out. "It was only myself involved!"

"Then why burn down the evening courtyard?" Lady Azadiya asked. "And not the caffa. It's in the imperial district, after all. The property is worth far more, and most of the buildings are made of stone. Albin would directly profit."

Master Achard leaned back in his chair as best he was able while tied up, and breathed in slowly. Master Albin rubbed the lower half of his face, and went to sit down by his husband, who put his arm about his shoulders.

"Erno Neilos was a man who'd sell sops to a sow if he could get away with it, am I correct in that?" Lady Azadiya asked.

"You are," Philendra Dubidat answered her, since neither Rennab nor either Finar seemed up to the task.

"I am thinking he left that box of linseed oil soaked clothes in the alleyway for a great measure of coin—which we found, by the way, in his room. Wonderfully good at hiding things, was he not, Ibram?"

"Held on like grim death, I'm sure," Ibram said. He pointed to Master Achard's bandaged hands. "Cut yourself on that garotte, didn't you? Doctor Berot will be pleased to make sure infection doesn't set in if you'll let him take a look."

"This is monstrous!" Mistress Dubidat exclaimed. She began to struggle up from her chair. "Ealar is staying with these—these people! They murdered his parents!"

"I have murdered no one!" Master Albin exclaimed. "I would never!"

"He hasn't done anything wrong," Master Achard shouted. "I did it alone!"

"For your own insurance money?" Master Guilhem asked gently. "I'm sorry to say, it doesn't make sense."

"They knew nothing," Achard insisted.

"But the only way for The High Climber to burn and for Albin and his husband to profit," Lady Azadiya said, "would be if they made every seeming attempt to satisfy the terms of your fire alliance, while in fact providing the very means for its destruction."

"Linseed oil soaked rags," Captain Talsconis said and shook his head. His sharp eyes dulled for a moment. "Drying up in an alley choked with loose flour—They must have gone up like a pillar."

"And surrounded by Running Flames to loosen the substandard grout," Ibram said. "Once the tiles cracked to the floor, what little charm they had left to them wouldn't amount to much."

"And the heat of the blast overwhelmed everyone's own protections," Master Rennab said. His voice shook. "Because of our evening courtyard."

"The family is given a grand amount of money," Lady Azadiya said, "Everyone else gets less, but still enough to move along with, and no one is the wiser."

"Except for Erno," Master Dughlat said in a hollow tone.

"Yes," Lady Azadiya said. "I am very sorry about your friend."

"I must go," Mistress Dubidat muttered. "I must go and collect Ealar at once."

"Sit down, Mistress," Lady Azadiya said, and Mistress Dubidat froze, half a step from the table. "Let the boy sleep a little longer. I am sure nothing will happen to him tonight."

Mistress Dubidat's face was piebald in outrage, sweat bloomed at her temples. "But these—"

"Sit down, Philendra!" Mistress Vo Kaln snapped. "This doesn't concern you!"

Mistress Vo Kaln glared at her until Mistress Dubidat obeyed. She flounced into her seat with ill grace. Ibram had to admire the charitable impulse even as he was forced to wait out her temper.

Lady Azadiya hummed in agreement. "Thank you," she said. "Always helpful to have a landowner in charge, is it not?"

Ibram's mouth twitched. Mistress Vo Kaln looked pleased. She smiled and sat primly in her chair.

"In matters such as these, I am sure you understand the need for a steady hand, Mentor Hobon," Mistress Vo Kaln said.

"Oh, I do," Lady Azadiya said.

She looked from Master Albin to Master Rennab, and then to Master Achard. Her left eyebrow twitched. Master Achard flexed his arms and shoulders, pushing against his bonds. He shook his head once, hard, and glared down the length of the table.

"I'm afraid an opinion stands against you and your family," Lady Azadiya said. She met Achard's eyes squarely, and then deliberately slide her gaze to her left. "It's a matter of what evidence is revealed now."

"We're ruined," Master Albin said. "I would never have agreed to this. Philendra, you know me! You know us, we are not such folk. Where would we even have the money to give to Erno for such an act?"

"It is a lot of money for a traveling salesman to have on his person," Ibram said. "They tend to travel lightly, and return the money to their employers by turning it in at smaller offices in connected towns."

"You can transport a great deal of profit through those companies," Talsconis said. "Easy to hide a higher amount of funds."

"Achard," Master Albin asked, quietly. "What have you done?"

Master Achard licked his lips. Ladyship waited. Achard breathed in and out, and then nodded, almost to himself.

"The problem being, of course," Lady Azadiya said, "is that the fire —besides being green at one point which is how this entire affair began—well, you must understand. Setting a fire takes a certain amount of skill—professionally speaking, I would even call it a kind of art."

Master Achard grunted; Amota Berac prodded him in the shoulder. "Answer," he said.

"Yes," Master Achard bit out.

"And you work for Kenda Trading," Lady Azadiya said. "Do you not?"

"I do," Master Achard said.

"In Kalisbrite, a town just outside the imperial boundary of the Sect of the Iron Hand wherein lies the village of Ammoni, and whose nearest city was—as of a mere handful of years ago—the spires of

Kandrilat in Hyperni province," Ladyship continued as Master Achard turned pale and then grey and slumped against his bonds.

"Kenda Trading is very proud of Master Achard," Ibram said, unprompted. "Do you remember the message they misdirected to the Cohort of Peace, Captain? He did wonderful things for them in Kandrilat—saved his entire stock from the blaze."

Captain Talsconis was a man in the grips of a terrible thought. He drank his ale, and set the cup carefully on the table. He nodded slowly, and regarded the end of the table.

"What do you mean by this, Mentor Hobon?" he asked.

"Only that so many things seem to be popping up in Lityen from Hyperni province these days," Lady Azadiya said. "Master Achard's business stems from there, his brother no doubt has visited, and of course, Mistress Vo Kaln's family has a great many holdings and property in Hyperni as well."

Mistress Vo Kaln jumped as if she had been kicked, and the entire table shook. She coughed to clear her throat, and shook her head, and then brushed her fingers along the embroidered family badge still decorating her shoulder.

"Yes, yes we do," she said, "farms and such, just as we have here. Oh, the terror of the fire in Kandrilat. One of my cousins barely escaped with his life!"

"Yes, I believe you own Kenda Trading as well," Lady Azadiya said, and drank the last of her wine. "Amazing how that company keeps intruding on my village."

Ibram felt a tug on his ear. It was time. He walked around Ahksell's back, and stopped just behind Mistress Vo Kaln's place at the table. Without raising his arm too high, he twisted his first two fingers together in Hallie and Esti's direction. They closed in at the head of the tent. Dihya took Master Dughlat to the next table, out of the way.

"I—no, you're mistaken, Mentor," Mistress Vo Kaln said. "It's a concern of my cousin, Faldrimm."

Lady Azadiya tsked. "Would this be the same one who rents land to those academics who make portable tinder boxes? Ibram where did we find one of those?"

"Nesrine saw it in The Crooked Tent," Ibram said. "Then it

exploded."

"Master Achard, however did you acquire such a curiosity?" Ladyship asked.

"On a return trip to Hyperni province," Achard said.

Ibram couldn't see her face, but Mistress Vo Kaln's shoulders were as tense as a clothes line. He shifted his weight, and winced as moving aggravated his bruises. Beside him, he saw Ahksell palm a vial of something out of the corner of his eye.

"And you lost a manor in Kandrilat, did you not?" Ladyship continued. "The main branch of Vo Kalns, I mean. Terrible tragedy, and in the midst of that legal dispute as well."

"Too many mistresses," Ibram murmured.

"It was an awful, sordid affair for everyone involved," Mistress Vo Kaln's voice sharpened in her displeasure. "But I am certain we would have worked matters to a satisfactory conclusion, had the case before the Court of Chancery not been dismissed."

"On account of the fire then," Captain Talsconis said. "I remember the jubilee the Empress proclaimed to allow those afflicted by the disaster to recoup some of their losses."

"The luck of providence," Mistress Vo Kaln snapped.

"It follows you," Lady Azadiya said. "I wonder anyone dares to roll dice in your presence. Doubtless you'd make off with their winnings, no matter who was playing."

"How dare you!" Mistress Vo Kaln lurched to her feet.

Ibram placed his hand on the back of her chair. "Please remain seated," he said.

Ederetta Vo Kaln turned to him, wisps of hair loosened from underneath her cap. He dipped his head politely, and waited. She sat slowly, and only turned back to face the table at the last moment.

"You see, although I fully understand your insistence that Master Achard acted alone and so that you—I mean, *he* might be able to 'take care' of his family," Lady Azadiya continued as if she had not been rudely interrupted. "I have always made it my guiding principle to ask who stands to gain the most from any unfortunate interaction. Helps immeasurably when the Learners have been given corrosives, you understand. We lose four tables a year!"

She leaned on one elbow and beamed down the table to Master Achard, who swallowed heavily. His badly cut hair lay limp and sweaty against his skull.

"Four tables?" he murmured, coughed, and then cleared his throat. "I understand completely, Lady Azadiya."

"Who do you believe has the most to gain?" she asked. "Your brother and his husband, who comfortably own two businesses and enjoy good health and a certain amount of ease with their neighbors. Who take in orphans while in the midst of great personal upheaval and tell me the truth at great personal risk?"

Achard laughed weakly, and shook his head. He had a handsome smile, but it was marred by the tremble in his face. The entire table sat and stared at him or Ladyship by turns.

"No, I do not," he said.

"Then might it be someone—perhaps a few folk, even—who own a great deal of land in an area that sees a great many customers? Who have found money in recovering wood ash from ruined dwellings and selling it to their family in the soap makers guild? Who have drawn new and very favorable contracts for dependent businesses? Who offered to buy a ruined evening courtyard and the bakery-mill behind it, as it adjoined the land they will also be rebuilding upon?"

"The cookshops were failing," Master Achard said, and Mistress Vo Kaln made a sharp, high noise. "But their contracts hadn't run out yet, nor could they simply be pushed out since they lived within. The evening courtyards was a loss, but Mistress Vo Kaln said they'd make up for it with the expansion into Soren's space. Pillared Circle sees a lot of folk coming in for a bite to eat and some entertainment. Owning the largest evening courtyard in Lityen made a good investment, she said."

"She said this to you, specifically," Captain Talsconis asked.

"No, I did not," Mistress Vo Kaln snapped. "Nor would I!"

"She said it to one of her cousins—young, blonde, has a dot on the cheek—while I was in the room." Master Achard breathed in deeply and shook his head. "It was straightforward enough. And, I thought, it wasn't so bad, was it? I do a lot of these jobs for them."

"You do?" Ladyship asked.

"Kenda Trading," Achard said. "The Vo Kalns like a workforce who can be put to all sorts of tasks."

"I'm sure they do," Talsconis said, and glared across the table so hotly Ibram felt steam rising from the water cups.

"I protest this entire farce of a dinner," Mistress Vo Kaln said. "How can you believe a word this man speaks? Look at him, he's just trying to protect his brother!"

"Of course, I am," Achard called down to her. "I know what your sort will do to him."

"Whereas I know that nothing will happen to Albin Finar at all," Ladyship said. "Because I will ensure it."

"It's a lie," Mistress Vo Kaln insisted.

"The Vo Kalns have relatives in the Sect of the Iron Hand," Achard said loudly. "They've been making money off the destruction of their own property for years! I know where they keep their records!"

The table exploded into shouting, threats and accusations, pleas for quiet and all manner of personal business that Ibram would have found amusing on a normal day. As it was, his chest ached and his feet were congealing into frozen stubs within his boots. Lady Azadiya clapped her hands together sharply; the sound smacked into Ibram's ears as if he'd been boxed like a ten year old. He winced and pushed the side of his head into shoulder.

"Do you recall Captain Talsconis, when I requested a certain jurisdictional latitude from you?" Lady Azadiya asked as everyone recovered quietly.

"I do," Talsconis answered slowly.

"The Vo Kalns, to be sure, have been the victims of so many crimes by fire. It's shocking that no one has taken up their affliction and left rose cake by the temple door." Lady Azadiya turned to Mistress Vo Kaln, and moved her braid over her shoulder. "Who hasn't heard the tragedy of their losses in Kandrilat, during the fire that claimed so many imperial subjects' lives and so very much imperial property?"

Mistress Vo Kaln appeared to be looking beyond her company into the vast and uncomprehending heavens above. Her hands rested limply on the table, covering her serviceware. She swallowed once, convulsively.

"It's my property," she mumbled, almost as if she were speaking to herself. "I can do what I want with it. It's *my* land."

And it had been Philendra Dubidat's life's work, and Albin Finar and Soren Rennab's home. It had been the cookshop owners' only refuge, and the candle dancers' lives and Ealar Ozol's parents. Ibram couldn't say he felt sympathy in that exact moment.

"Pity about the murders, then," Ibram said to her.

"And," Ladyship continued, as if she hadn't heard, "You must know that I give all due deference to you and your work, Captain Talsconis. I fully understand that the captain of the Cohort of Vigilance—strictly speaking—should be responsible for an investigation when imperial liability is at stake."

"But she doesn't accept your invitations," Talsconis reminded her.

There was sharp satisfaction in his rough voice, the anticipation of scoring a hit off of a rival cohort and having the extreme honor of bringing to heel a far reaching and decidedly criminal enterprise. Warder Claes was already up and unbinding Achard Finar from his seat, and her employer had not called her back again. Ibram couldn't say he blamed the good captain.

"Alas," Ladyship said. "I must rely upon your good aid in bringing my assertions to the proper authority."

It did not take long for the party to break up after that. Even though the kitchens had prepared a posset for dessert, none of the guests seemed in the mood for it. Ibram watched as they all trooped off down the living mountain, headed for the relay system which would take them back to their homes and, hopefully, a little respite from what the next day will bring. Dihya and the servants began breaking down the tent and the dining table immediately as it was abandoned. Captain Talsconis took charge of Achard Finar, and Warder Claes took charge of Mistress Vo Kaln. Amota Berac provided a guard to make sure no one wandered off. The Preceptory of Yseult was easy to get lost in, if you didn't know your way.

"I hope the folk in Pillared Circle will be all right," Ahksell said, and sighed. "Fires, arsons! It's all a horrible business."

"And murder," Ibram said. "Even if she didn't order it, she still bears the responsibility. It's their dwelling after all, she only has rights to the building and the land. Not their livelihoods."

"They purchased a great deal of land with the money they earned from destroying what they already owned in Kandrilat and in other places," Lady Azadiya said, as they escorted her up to the tower. "I suppose it made them careless."

Ibram shook his head. "Do you need me to go about and check on the remaining folk?" he asked.

"It will wait until tomorrow," Lady Azadiya said. "Berac's reports will have to be redone. The fire alliances are still a matter of public record, but the Vo Kalns will need a new representative."

"And Master Albin Finar and Master Rennab?" Ibram asked.

"Are well out of it in Master Albin's caffa," Ladyship said. "We shall look in on them from time to time."

"Yes, Ladyship," Ibram said.

"How do you feel now, Ibram?" Lady Azadiya asked.

"He let Achard Finar almost kick him to death," Ahksell said from the other side of her.

"He—I did not!" Ibram protested. He winced, and resolved to breathe a little more carefully in future.

"I am only saying that I could have grabbed him before he ran," Ahksell said, and held his hands up.

"A little healthy exercise is no bad thing," Ladyship said. "Though in future, perhaps you might grab a fugitive with a tiny bit more care, Ib-la. Verena will have a fit tomorrow."

"Ama will understand," Ibram said. "She was an agent too."

"Yes, but she never let anyone kick her in the chest," Ahksell said.

"Not more than once, to be sure," Ladyship said.

She pushed out with her right hand, and the stone doors opened wide. Warm light poured out from the within the tower, spilling an orange glow onto the path. Ladyship sighed and readjusted her fingerless mitts as she walked forward. She entered first, and already Ibram could hear the swell of voices as they greeted her. Ahksell clapped him on the shoulder, and dragged him over the threshold. Ibram just managed to enter as Lady Azadiya flicked her fingers, and caused the door to shut behind them.

THE LANGUAGE OF MERRILIA

Commonly known as Merrilian or 'Western,' the language is primarily spoken amongst the people who live in the western provinces of Artenna, Edetanna, Hervenna, and Merrilia, in the Grand Empire of Vissilia. These provinces form what was once the Empire of Merrilia conquered by Odalis the Great, whose skill at arms circumvented the Emerald Mountains, which were themselves cataclysmically formed from the sacrifice of three great alchemist clans under the command of Alchemist-Emperor Athol three hundred years earlier.

Vocabulary Words
  Ama — "Mother"
  Avaena — "Lady"
  Amota — "Uncle on my mother's side"
  Badosh/Badoshai — "Fool/Fools"
  Amita — "Aunt on my mother's side"
  Cangsa — A vast grey land ruled by the goddess Catha the Grey. Here, the unnamed languish in purgatory until rewarded with a name by Catha in her service
  Riant — "Wonderful"

Merrilian Phrases

Naja shin na'lun — lit. "It could be darker" fig. "It could be worse"

Naja shin na'lun, Avaena, per Di ploune agoreuo mid bai alligantai — "It could be worse, my lady, but I need to speak with both alliances."

Ve leusian bo Ibram...amang bo Evren — "We have lost Ibram...and Evren"

Do Ama na'nu eeteight huskvith di monen — "Your mother never taught you caution, I think."

Ker Ama — "My mother..."

Di na'shin sorela — "I can't remember."

Di eekent zicata — "I know something."

Do selu badosh — "You absolute fool."

AUTHOR'S NOTE

Thank you for reading my novel! I hope you enjoyed reading *The Price of Fire* as much as I enjoyed writing it. I can't believe this is my third book (fourth in the entire series!)

If you've left a review for my work, thank you again! Reviews help others find my books.

THE ALCHEMIST'S AGENT

The Gilty Party

The Elixir of Inheritance

The Price of Fire

RELATED WORKS

Cursebird On A Wire

The Alchemist's Agent Omnibus 1: The Gilty Party/Cursebird On A Wire

ABOUT THE AUTHOR

E. M. Burnham likes fantasies, mysteries, and stories of all shapes and sizes, which is why she's decided to write them all at once. She's been a Jedi, a Fellow of The Ring, a Trekker, and even a Newsie, raised on Agatha Christie with a shot of Dorothy L. Sayers and a chaser of Margery Allingham.

She has lived and worked on three continents (and somehow earned two masters degrees in the midst of all that moving!) but settled down to be near her family in the United States. Check out her other work at emburnham.com

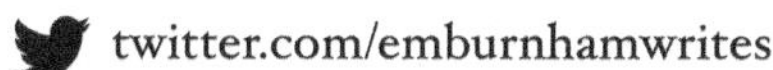 twitter.com/emburnhamwrites